THE GRIFFIN
THE DREAMS OF MEN AND PANDAS

THE GRIFFIN SERIES

The Griffin Series

Ashes of Honor
The Dreams of Men and Pandas
The Dragon's Price
A Path of Majesty

THE GRIFFIN
THE DREAMS OF MEN AND PANDAS

PHILIP WILLIAMS
CAT WILLIAMS

THE GRIFFIN SERIES

ISBN 978-0-9888257-3-4

COVER DESIGN
PHILIP WILLIAMS
WWW.THEGRIFFINSERIES.COM

COVER ART
JUNG PARK
WWW.JUNGPARKART.COM

COVER ILLUSTRATION
ELISABETH ALBA
WWW.ELISA-ALBA.COM

INTERIOR DESIGN
TYPEFLOW
WWW.TYPEFLOWNYC.COM

To my son Alexander
Always trust your heart

Contents

1 THE CAGES · *3*

2 KRESTYANINOV CLUSTER · *28*

3 THE DREAMS OF MEN AND PANDAS · *38*

4 VAILETTA · *59*

5 HUMHAL · *79*

6 THE GREAT BREAKFAST BATTLE · *93*

7 BARRETT'S BANQUET · *119*

8 REVELATIONS · *146*

9 THE GRIFFIN · *167*

10 HELEN · *191*

11 GEUTVOHN MADORA · *202*

12 PREPARATIONS · *213*

13 THE EMPEROR'S BUTCHER · *230*

14 JHEI PŌLOC · *250*

15 EEMON NORES · *272*

16 C'TEREINO · *299*

17 CONVERGENCE · *312*

18 SCAVENGING · *323*

19 THE DEAL · *346*

20 BATTLE OVER EEMON · *355*

GRIFFIN TERMINOLOGY · *379*

TIME LINE · *399*

ABOUT THE AUTHOR · *403*

II

The Dreams of
Men and Pandas

Dragons beget dragons.

— Vasily Fua'tin Bey-Torg

1

THE CAGES

DRAZON-VORGE LAY QUIETLY IN HIS DARKENED NOOK, back propped up against the damp slate wall, and waited for the song to begin. The tiny bones in his small frame ached from the cold. The air in the rotunda was so moist that Draz would not have been surprised to find a fine mist hanging over the deck plates, but the chamber's pale green translucence revealed the air to be sharp and clear like an image frozen in a clipscanner. The hexagonal rotunda was lined with glossy black cerasteel plates fit so smoothly together that the floor appeared to be seamless. The cold, black surface reflected dim green glow globes that hovered over the surface like small green moons floating over a silent pond.

The cages in the vice proctor's antechamber creaked ever so slightly in the darkness of the rafters. The boy searched the shadows between the arches, listening. A small rustle of movement made one of the cages groan. The boy waited, but the offending party remained still and he drew a makeshift blanket tighter about his legs. Two more cages squeaked as their occupants stirred restlessly, unable to find peace or sleep in their cramped conditions. The boy grimaced and shook his head, knowing what was to come.

The main portal leading from the battle cruiser's central corridor irised open, letting in a sharp spear of light that fractured the somber darkness. As if emerging from the belly of a terrible beast, a lone figure paused within the orifice. Magnified by the glossy floor, the sudden illumination was quite dazzling. The boy shielded his eyes from the intruding glare and tried to make out the identity of the dark figure framed in the gaping maw. The figure swept silently into the antechamber. The door hissed close and the light vanished, leaving only the soft footsteps and swish of the intruder's long cape that brushed the smooth cerasteel plates.

Vailetta Strom halted in the center of the rotunda and unfastened her cape, letting the garment slide off her shoulders. She shook her head, letting loose the long dark hair which had been gathered up in a tight krimset. Draz stared at the woman from the shadows of his nook, his body rigid with anticipation. He had not seen this human before. This one seemed somehow different. Her body was lean and strong and though the uniform tended to smooth out the natural curves of her figure, there was no mistaking her femininity. With the long cape no longer obscuring her profile, Draz silently traced the outline of her hips and breasts with his eyes. She pulled a free hand through her hair, separating the strands and allowing them to cascade down her back. The woman stretched out her neck and peered into the dark rafters of the extended chamber, trying to make out the silhouettes of the two dozen or so cages that hung overhead.

A common misconception of dirtsiders was that the interiors of Imperial naval vessels were warm, hospitable places full of vast, garishly-lit corridors and broad central spaces pumped full of clean, hot oxygen. The reality was entirely different. The *Shiva*, like all the other lurking destroyers in the fleet, was always cold, somewhat cramped and generally dank and dark. Its atmosphere was a thick soup of human redolence and the oily bouquet of machinery. The reactors lacked the excess energy needed to heat the serpentine corridors, and the thermal ducting systems — poorly designed when the ships were first commissioned seventy-five years ago — were never deemed a high priority for a proper refit. This necessitated cold-weather gear for crewers and ship's company alike. The heavy cloaks and thick-fabric uniforms that Vailetta favored were less a stylistic choice than a practical solution to the perpetual chill. Having shirked her outer layer, this room seemed even colder, and Vailetta could see her moist breath crystallizing before her. Was it possible that this antechamber was even more frigid than the rest of the ship? She glanced at the dark hall leading forward; no doubt the vice proctor's inner chambers were toasty warm. This particular chill was possibly just a product of her emotional state; being this close to Lord Barrett's inner chambers always made her uneasy.

A tiny shiver passed through her shoulders and she frowned up at the silent cages, twirling softly on her heel as she craned her neck to get a better view. What was it that bothered her? Not the man's position at least — she had grown up with aristocracy. From the day she was born she had lived amongst the powerful, the dangerous, and the conniving cadre of hungry and capricious hangers-on that seemed to permeate the Imperial Court. It had to be something else, for she had, in fact, lived in the very heart of power.

She backed away from the center of the rotunda toward a slate gray wall, still staring up at the silhouettes overhead. Her eyes were beginning to adjust to the darkness and the rough shapes of the cages were coming into a hazy focus. A meter and a half tall apiece, they were harsh, utilitarian affairs, the constructs so rough-hewn and lacking in ornamentation that they had an almost minimalist appeal. Barrett's interest in these creatures fascinated her but she'd never had a chance to pause and study the cages at length.

Something struck her as she tried to fathom the appeal these creatures held. This stark hall was one of the vice proctor's fixations, an all-consuming obsession. Like his systematic conquests and attention to detail, his carefully orchestrated diplomatic sessions and almost manic obsession with capturing the elusive Tchelakov creatures, this room was a testament to his arcane and unquenchable needs. Barrett always wanted something more. The Tchelakov creatures were now her responsibility, she reminded herself grimly. This thought gave her pause. Perhaps that was what bothered her: Barrett's constant state of needing.

It wasn't enough that he was powerful; it wasn't enough that he had taken a small, unknown and largely insignificant Proctorialship and transformed it into the most powerful in Carinaena's Shell. It wasn't enough that he was respected and feared throughout a hundred systems. He had to have more. He always needed more. Nothing was beyond the need. And what frightened Vailetta as she stood within his cold, peculiar antechamber was the realization that he would do anything to satisfy that need.

The boy watched the woman as she stood in the center of the room, staring alternately at the walls and up into the rafters. Strangely, he felt no animosity toward this one—in fact he was strangely drawn to her, he wanted to reach out, touch her. Drazon crinkled his nose—that desire was completely foreign to him. Uncertain of what to do next, he kept very still, eyes riveted to the woman's form. Another rustle, louder this time, sounded from above and he looked up—eyes darting from cage to cage, trying to decide who had moved. A small flutter rocked Gui-en's narrow cage as he beat his wings against the bars in vain. The boy frowned up at the dark space, wishing the creature would stay silent tonight. He did not want the silent one to leave.

Vailetta listened to the creaks and light ruffles of noise overhead, trying to prepare herself for her briefing with Barrett. Without warning, the minor squawks were interrupted by a single note of beautiful purity. The note repeated once, and then ended abruptly. Several of the cages creaked and she could just discern a gentle swaying in some. A long, golden feather fluttered gently and silently to the deck.

The boy cursed to himself. Not tonight! Please not tonight—she'll leave!

Vailetta waited expectantly, but the cages settled back into their former silent state. She sniffed at the damp, dreary atmosphere and glanced about the rest of the rotunda. Unlike the proud adornments that enlivened the rest of the ship, there were no colorful banners or tapestries to offset the dull, somber tone of this hall. The walls were an uneven milky gray and the deck, though polished and beautiful, was as dusky as the vacuum that enveloped them. Something about the chamber made her terribly empty. Reflexively she felt in her pocket for the familiar shape of the Myshka stone. Held tightly between her thumb and forefinger, she rubbed the pad of her thumb against the tiny crease that separated the rough broken edge from the glassy smooth section.

She held the fractured fragment of crystal and stone in the air, turning it slowly to catch the greenish ambient glow. It had been many years since she had secreted this away from the pieced-together ruins of the infamous sculpture of the Emperor, or De'Allende's Folly as it had been come to known. She had spent many long afternoons as a child in the old strategy room back behind the Palatial ward hall, with its towering, dusty jade-encrusted cases full of actual books and fabulous oaken committee tables covered in reams of forgotten and archaic Imperial treaties inscribed on cracked parchment, the sheets yellowed from years of display.

Along one wall had sat the massive sculpture of the Emperor — a stark, frightening work in crystal with ridges of ceracrete inside for bone structure. Vailetta had always been both fascinated and repelled by it. Many years before her birth, an angry general, the infamous and much-feared De'Allende, had sent the statue toppling over in a rage. The story went that he had been forced to piece it back together blindfolded. Each time he had pieces left over he was whipped. Finally he was able to piece all but one into a whole. This last, large enough to fill his fist, he swallowed. It was a more painful punishment than he deserved, but then, he was a hard man and had sent so many to the dark reaches of K'ye over the course of his career. According to the tale, the agony returned his honor.

He later died defending Daulinbêres during one of the final Sullust offensives in the last stages of the Art Wars. The fragment was discovered lodged next to his heart during the autopsy. A wily embalming artist had snuck back into the strategy room and wedged the remaining piece under the base, as though for balance.

Vailetta fingered the wedge of crystal with its ceracrete backing that she had discovered under the pillar so long ago—a childhood coup, and a treasured talisman linking her forever, physically as well as emotionally, with a short lifetime of happiness on Daulinbêres. She smiled a small, satisfied grin at the memory of the theft. A corporeal reminder of simpler times, the Myshka stone occupied a physical space in her hand, much as the memory filled a cherished space in her heart.

The boy uncurled and stood, mesmerized by the curious stone sparkling in the woman's hand. Vailetta frowned, senses alerted by the soft disturbance. In a darkened ingress nearly flush with the wall, two small eyes glinted in the refracted light, the reflection from the Myshka stone sparkling in Draz's eye, revealing the hidden boy's presence.

Vailetta walked cautiously toward the small form, hand outstretched

"It's all right," she murmured. "I won't harm you."

The boy took an awkward, involuntary step forward. Vailetta stopped and looked down affectionately at the slight youth. He could be no more than nine or so, standard. He looked particularly small in his ill-fitting shipsuit with his sleeves rolled up and hands just poking out. A mismatched cull-spanner's cap perched precariously atop his head, its dragon icon barely distinguishable under the grime. Vailetta reached forward and removed the cap, gently pausing to smooth down the tangle of blonde hair that stuck up. The boy did not protest. Vailetta pursed her lips and crouched down to look at the boy from his level. He leered at her with just the slightest hint of anger, an expression that marred his otherwise innocent face. Vailetta licked her hand and began to clean his face, scraping off the more resistant dirt with her sleeve. Draz frowned, but silently allowed the woman to groom him.

The boy's demeanor appeared sullen but his eyes were alive. They peered out of the gloom, angry, blue and doubtful. The incongruence of the boy's gruff, downtrodden appearance and those lively blue eyes seemed to give the youth a preternatural presence and wisdom beyond his tender age.

"What are you doing here?" she questioned softly, not really expecting a reply. Surely Barrett wasn't forcing him to tend to these creatures by himself. What was he doing alone in this cold, dank hall with nothing but the mysterious occupants of the cages overhead to keep him company? She rubbed harder at the filth.

A fluttering of activity above distracted her: half-sung notes and whooping coughs echoed down from the creatures above. The cages creaked loudly as their occupants stood and stretched. A spluttering note warbled out loudly from one cage, sounding out above the other nervous dissonance. Vailetta pivoted on her heel and straightened up, eyes once more searching the crown of the rotunda.

The note sounded again, this time joined midway by several other voices—a flurry of discordant notes and false starts. The note repeated, echoing throughout the hall, then a great commotion of coughs and creaks rattled all the cages. They all swayed slightly as the creatures made slight adjustments. Rumpled feathers spread out and flapped once or twice against the bars, followed by little squeaks and wheezes. Then all the cages became silent as if on cue: the orchestra was prepared.

Vailetta glanced down at the boy who gave her a knowing grimace. With a trumpeting wail that resonated with astonishing power, the song began. Drazon shrank back sullenly against the wall, half-expecting the woman to depart, but she stood stock still, entranced by the sounds. The symphonic orchestration of voices was unlike anything she had ever experienced. What began as a simple keen rose in complexity and aural quality to become a full-blown aria—the layered texture of voices imparting such beautiful music that Vailetta was sure that it was the most marvelous sound she had ever heard.

"No wonder Barrett treasures these creatures," she murmured.

The boy looked up at her with a rueful grimace. She did not understand. "He treasures them not for their song," he stated simply.

Vailetta's head snapped down from watching the swaying cages. A mixture of concern and surprise clouded her face; the boy had spoken.

"But what are they doing here?"

Drazon looked down at his feet and shook his head.

Vailetta kneeled down before him, cupping his chin in her hand. "What is it?"

He looked up at her softly, his eyes almost starting to water. He opened his mouth as if to speak, but stopped abruptly as though someone had stolen his voice. Without warning, his face made a dramatic transformation. The sadness shrank from his eyes as a dark shadow of fear and dismay clouded the boy's expression, the sudden change putting Vailetta instantly on guard. The boy's vivid, turquoise eyes searched the darkness beyond her, unable to focus on any specific danger, but searching the shadows frantically nonetheless.

With her free hand, she reached across her hip and drew her Cresbourin, remaining crouched to shield the boy, but spinning to face the hall. A flash of movement caught her off-balance as the boy snatched the stone from her hand and turned to scramble up the ladder behind him.

"Wait—it's okay," she protested, but he was already out of reach—scurrying up the ladder rungs like a harvester rat fleeing from a hungry lichè. She sighed and turned, straightening up with her blaster clenched tightly in her fist.

Vailetta frowned as she peered into the somber darkness. What could possibly have frightened the boy? There was nothing here but the wail of the birds and emptiness. Something must have terrified him, but what? The darkness and cold seemed all-pervasive—so inhospitable. Like a rodent that could sense danger from clues invisible to ordinary human senses, the boy must have developed instincts necessary for his own survival. Somewhere in the room there existed a threat, and he had reacted accordingly. The revelation hit her, drawing a smile. With a small laugh she holstered her weapon and turned back to look for the boy who had disappeared into the shadows. In an otherwise empty room with no perceivable danger there could only be one explanation.

"Good evening assassin," she called out to the dark hall.

Torg froze in his tracks. In his leisurely, silent, and completely invisible approach he had been contemplating Drazon Vorge's sudden interest in Vailetta Strom. The boy's demeanor had shifted radically from the feral secretive posture of a war-scarred survivor to that of an innocent child. He was fascinated that Drazon had allowed Vailetta to come so close to him, to touch him in fact, for no one else had ever been allowed so near. The woman's voice had interrupted his thoughts. She must be bluffing, mustn't she? His approach had been flawless. His quarry could not know that anyone was present. He could recall no missteps, no loose sands drug across the slick plates, no shadows cast before his path. No, either she was bluffing or she had made a leap in deductive logic. Torg grinned; the Emperor's little Myshka had grown quite cunning.

"It's all right, you can come out. You have nothing to fear from a little boy and a defenseless woman."

Torg billowed into sight, his form wavering slightly in the half-light. He stepped lightly forward, not attempting to mask his progress. "I'd hardly call you defenseless," he murmured.

She turned to greet him, nodding politely. "G'evening Master Torg."

"Yes, quite," He bowed formally before her, the tips of his long, graceful hands brushing the cerasteel, "but the pleasure is all mine Mistress Strom."

"Such the gentleman. It's a wonder you're still a bachelor."

"I don't recall mentioning that I was," he demurred.

"The signs are written all over you—you're far too ingratiating to be spoken for."

Torg stood before them, scars around his wrist and throat hidden by his formal crested poplin, ribbed to turn the enemy's blade, high-necked to protect from darts. He seemed particularly spectral in the pale half-light, silver eyes glowing like the twin moons of Galipsus. The assassin looked up and quickly located the small boy in the darkness, hiding between two cages. He tried to adopt a pleasant expression as he watched the slender child. From the look of the young boy's face half-hidden behind a steel cage and staring back at him with one wary eye, he didn't believe he was having much success.

Torg felt his shoulders wilt fractionally—Drazon was such a complicated person—he feared he might never connect on the level he had just witnessed. Unfortunately, he did not possess the charms of young Captain Strom, whose company Drazon seemed to prefer. He paused to admire the woman before him. She was no longer the innocent child he had been sworn to protect so many years before. Though her cheeks still dimpled slightly and the tips of her hair curled characteristically around her ears, the gentle, playful glint of her eyes had been replaced with a gleam of confidence and purpose. There was nothing soft or yielding about her posture. Shoulders straight, eyes level, she watched him with cautious scrutiny. Her uniform was cut neck to knee in dark plesbin wool, the regal red splash of the Gokazoku dagger affixed to her breast. The lethal Cresbourin blaster she favored fit snugly against her hip and her dark boots shined even in the subdued light.

"Here for the evening performance, I see."

"I've never heard it before," she confessed. "They sing like this every night?"

Torg nodded, "As far as I'm aware." He allowed himself a tiny sigh. "The same melody every night down to the final note."

"What does it mean?"

He shook his head and lied: "One can only guess."

Vailetta closed her eyes and sank back into the mesmerizing fabric of the song that resonated powerfully through the hall, at once uplifted by the beauty of the voices and deeply saddened by the heavy hearts that sang it. Lost in the beautiful keen, she looked to the assassin with a bemoanful expression that needed no explanation. She glanced into the rafters, a persistent thought echoing in her mind: all of Barrett's chambers radiated out from this sadness and pain—a sinkhole for the vestigial residue of his power.

Torg frowned. "Is there something troubling you, Captain?"

"I sometimes wonder what I'm doing way out here," she whispered.

"You're from the Core then?" he rumbled.

She nodded. "Deep—the Leyhan System," she announced the words as if they held cherished memories, or magical properties that could be invoked by merely speaking the name. She looked at the assassin with a hard, steady gaze. "I grew up on Daulinbêres."

Torg raised his brows. "Daulinbêres itself?"

Vailetta stared at the strange man. His voice espoused surprise, but the emotion behind the tone was false, as if he was feigning interest, or disbelief.

"The heart of the empire, Daulinbêres," he rumbled with satisfaction. "One of the ancient worlds. The home of the Emperor Himself." Torg cocked his head toward the woman and murmured slyly, "Must have been interesting growing up there..."

Vailetta did not rise to the bait. "Somewhat," she allowed.

"And to be so far from home now..."

"Yes," she agreed. "I'm sure you must miss it as well." She stole a sideways glance at him, but he registered nothing.

"What do you mean, Captain? I don't recall mentioning my home world." Or my origins, he thought to himself. I no longer have a home world. I am a man of many...

Vailetta sighed and managed a casual shrug. "Just a guess."

"You are here to see the vice proctor?"

She nodded grimly.

"Then you've heard of the latest debacle on the surface."

"I watched from the Battle Bridge."

"The marines allowed you into their midst?" Torg chuckled. "I would have thought they had seen quite enough of you lately."

"I've gained a certain measure of respect in some quarters."

Torg smiled. "Then the burden has shifted I see."

"No doubt."

"Fallen squarely upon your shoulders."

Vailetta nodded with determination. "And high time as well." She looked to the assassin as she straightened her tunic and refastened her cape. "Are you coming?"

"No," he demurred. "I believe I'll listen until the end."

"Very well." She stepped forward into the hall leading to Barrett's private chambers. After taking five steps into the enveloping darkness, vivid illumination flooded the vestibular walkway, hidden sensors probing her body for hidden charges, poisons, or dangers.

Twin guards stood guard outside the broad blast doors that sealed the vice proctor's chambers. The soldiers wore the fearsome dragon armor that had once frightened her as a child. Silent and motionless, she wondered if they were human or artificial.

The nearest pointed to her Cresbourin with a single outstretched digit. She unbuckled the holster, loosened the tie that secured the lower end to her thigh, and carefully laid the weapon on a shelf carved out of the wall.

She walked to the broad entrance, willing herself not to glance sideways at the dragon-guards and flashed her ident-link. The door dutifully and silently scrolled downward, slowly revealing the interior of Barrett's personal chambers. Vailetta straightened her shoulders and wiped any trace of emotion from her face before proceeding.

Torg watched the captain of the Imperial Guard disappear and closed his eyes, opening himself to the wailing keen. A glittering fragment of crystal and stone clattered against a rung and fell skittering to the slick deck. The boy paused and watched with dismay as his new prize fell from his grasp. Torg leaned down to retrieve the sharp-edged object, examining its rough edges and smooth inner surfaces. He smiled as he recognized the shape. General De'Allende had raised quite a furor when he had destroyed the sculpture in a public display on Daulinbêres. The Emperor had been most displeased; the distinctive work had been a favorite.

He twirled the fragment between his fingers once more before placing it in a vest pocket. A small croak registered the prior occupant's displeasure. Torg swung uneasily on his heel, gauging the sullen mood of the hall. De'Allende's shard took his memory back many years. This rotunda reminded him of the Imperial Gallery back on Daulinbêres, above the Palace's Great Hall, where the Emperor had stored the many alien stone statues of warriors, guardians, and alien beasts that he had amassed over years of conquest. The towering macabre black-bronzed gargoyles and geth-alls, tromba and piicau, dragons and specters — monsters both real and imagined — had filled the great promenade from end to end, much like the cages dominated this chamber. The Gallery had been a favorite place of Mistress Strom's, at least before young master Stevens had spoiled it for her. Torg sighed pointedly. He hoped that Captain Strom would be able to so easily escape Lord Barrett's version of the Great Whispering Hall.

❖ ❖ ❖

HELLIUS BARRETT PACED RESTLESSLY ALONG THE THIN CURVING jaunt that ran the length of his sweeping personal quarters. The steel gangway offered a magnificent view of the destroyer's dorsal superstructures. The attenuated beams and curving struts of his flagship looked like the twisted spine of some long-extinct monster, the fossilized bones now hurtling through space in some mockery of evolutionary protocol. But the beauty of the stars was little comfort to Barrett tonight—he had just finished listening to the audio of the aborted raid on El-Bouteran. The speaker hissed with static, but he still could not silence the sounds of his soldiers' screams as they succumbed to the monster. He fished in his vest pocket for a reed. He had not yielded to his old habit since the days of the Imperial Court. Today however he had sough what small comfort he could find and Colonel Riikesarh had been good enough to give him a box of Fallon's Best during the attack.

The thiretsen reed glowed under the igniter, a wisp of smoke trailing up amongst the stars. He closed his eyes and inhaled roughly. He had been so close. Month after month of meticulously planned raids, pursuit that had grown in size, breadth and complexity—sartographic projections in the nineties and still he was no closer to Tchelakov's progeny. He snorted as he thought of the impressive battle group which trailed the *Shiva* through space; the finest strike force he had ever assembled, and yet not enough to capture one ship, a single light cruiser. He swallowed a distasteful lump in the back of his throat and flicked the ashen end away from his reed.

Anger welled up in his chest as he thought of the rogue Garrand Médeville.

Probability projections, the brute force of crunching numbers, superior planning and professional execution were not enough. Sartographs projected the likely behavior of events, large groups of people, machinery—things with consistent patterns of action, with a history of performance to draw from. A single man, acting alone, sometimes introduced too much unpredictability—particularly if he was resourceful and if he knew he was fighting E2's as well as the men who followed its orders. Médeville was savvy; a new tact must be taken, before time ran out.

Dual chimes signaled Captain Strom's imminent arrival. Barrett turned and stepped down to greet his Captain of the

Guard. The blast door recessed and Vailetta's body was revealed from the head down.

"You're late." Barrett groused.

"I was delayed by your entourage."

Barrett raised one brow. "Eh?"

Vailetta crooked her head back toward the rotunda. "Oh that."

"That's no place for a boy."

"Quite right," he flicked away his reed and ignited a new one. "It's worlds away from what he's used to. I took him from the rubble of Galipsus Minoirte, a pit so vile with disease, so overrun with harvesters, lichès, gaison — " the vice proctor curled his mouth in distaste and waved his hand. "Most of the third wave of settlers never saw twenty-five. The insurrection there cost me 317 soldiers, 212 arts and half my corps of engineers."

Vailetta watched as the vice proctor rubbed his temple. "The maniacs sent their reactor critical, two days after we had put down the revolt and restored order." He paused as if remembering the details. "Such hatred," he shook his head, suddenly very tired. "No... spite. Such spite — the empire wasn't even the target of their insurrection. Nesbit had ordered us to step in."

"Proctor Nesbit, your predecessor?"

Barrett nodded once, eyes closed. "It was a dark day."

"The boy?" Vailetta prodded him.

"Yes, the boy. On my initial inspection of the battle damage, mere hours after the Shock Troops had leveled most of the inner city, this boy steps out from a pile of rubble — one arm limp and useless at his side, head bleeding, entire body covered in ash — this impossible tiny creature somehow still alive steps out before me. In his one good hand he had a stone clenched in his fist like this — raised above his head. He stared at me, never once looking at the Troopers that flanked me. And with a shrill scream of absolute madness, he came rushing at me and hurled the stone at my head."

Vailetta looked at him with disbelief.

"Barely missed me," he said wryly. "I've kept him with me ever since."

Vailetta frowned as she considered this story. "If this is true, then why not let him stay within your quarters where it's warm and dry?"

"Oh, but I've tried. He will not stay. Whenever possible, he devises ways to escape to the outer halls, or squirm into the ship's innards. He's smuggled himself within tech arts, rewired security doors," the vice proctor shook his head. "No, he seems to prefer the hard, cold surfaces of the artificial. Spent too much time sleeping in the bowels of Galipsus, I guess. He's been running through the sewers too long to ever feel comfortable settling into a warm berth." Barrett pursed his lips. "Eventually I just let him stay there, rather than force him back into the warmth. He has taken to tending the cages," he gestured toward the rotunda. "The creatures seem to like his presence," he admitted gruffly. "I hope that someday he will grow out of it. For now he spurns human contact. He will allow no human to touch him."

Vailetta gently bit her lip remembering those piercing eyes looking up at her while she straightened his hair, the downy strands remarkably soft despite their rumpled appearance.

"Drazon Vorge was the only redemption for that miserable raid. It was a place no one should have been left to rot. Too many names carved that day."

The mention of the Wall made Vailetta shudder unexpectedly. She had passed Urqual Magester on her way to the briefing on gregson level three. He was carrying his ancient box of stone carving tools and loping slowly toward the lower levels to chisel the names of the fallen warriors from El-Bouteran onto the great blocks of granite that would be added to the Great Hall on Wyx. Soon they would sing their names along with the rest. Vailetta wondered how many of her men would be inscribed in stone before this was over.

"They will be remembered well," Vailetta intoned solemnly. "And it is the price we all know we must pay to serve the Dragon."

"Rubbish! We should not have to sing their names." Barrett said bitterly.

Vailetta glanced at the vice proctor in surprise; this was a side of the man she had not seen. "The whole settlement could have been wiped from orbit. But Nesbit would have none of that," Barrett looked away and exhaled. He continued as an aside, "It was one of his last mistakes…"

"What was that?"

He turned to face her, hands clasped behind his back. "Hmm? Nothing." He strode quickly back to an alcove where he picked up a slim dossier.

"As I warned Commander Arnas—the key to the success of your mission lies in understanding, and outwitting, Captain Médeville."

Vailetta allowed the tinniest of rueful grins to surface; she had reached the same conclusion.

"Yes, I've done a little research myself. I haven't seen the full report from El-Bouteran, however. Was it really as bad as it sounds?"

The Vice Proctor simmered silently—for a moment she wondered if it was such a wise question after all. "I'm sure you can judge for yourself, Captain," he replied in an icy tone. "Arnas had them in his grasp," his knuckles whitened as he clenched his fingers into a tight fist. "There was but the thinnest strands of possibility…"

"For an escape? What was the final projection of Arnas' success?"

"Ninety-two point seven percent."

Vailetta whistled in soft amazement. "Médeville didn't have much room for error did he?"

"Nor did Arnas have much room for failure, barring a calamity."

"There's always that small window of pure chance," she offered.

"Yes," Barrett snorted, "in case the subject in question happens to bring a wraith."

Vailetta chewed on her lip. "Yes, how odd."

"A Byrethylen Wraith," Barrett shook his head.

"Any idea how he got it?"

"He must have captured it himself. There's not much market for wraiths…"

"Hmm," Vailetta scanned the dossier. She had so many questions. The man's life was so compelling and his involvement in this mission so mysterious, she hardly knew where to begin.

"What happened to the woman?" She scrolled through the clipscanner and found the name, "Lieutenant Ellison."

"Lost at the Battle of Sot."

"Dead?"

"Missing. Presumed dead."

Vailetta frowned. "So what does he have left?"

Barrett snorted and turned to gaze out the stunningly beautiful portal. "Nothing."

"Nothing," she repeated quietly.

"Even still, he is proving to be formidable, just as I feared."

Was there some satisfaction in his voice? Vailetta frowned; perhaps the challenge invigorated him. "How did the Nralda ever convince him to take on such a dangerous cargo?" she asked. "It doesn't seem to fit."

"Darstin might have found something of value with which to manipulate him."

"But as you said, he has nothing left."

Barrett shrugged. "Perhaps he doesn't have any idea the value of his cargo."

"Ah, but still, there's millions of Freetraders in the Shell. That he could have found this one…"

"Almost makes me eager to fetch Director Darstin's head."

This elicited a troubled grunt from Vailetta. "You'd risk open warfare with the Nralda Keiretsu?" she asked, a worrisome frown creasing her face.

"You doubt our readiness?"

Vailetta cocked her head to one side. "It's not our readiness that concerns me so much," she said, choosing her words carefully. "It's our vulnerability. My Lord, you've spent years consolidating this Proctorialship. I'd hate to see it crumble in a conflict that cannot be won quickly or easily. The keiretsu have been here hundreds of years longer than the Collistas Dynasty. Their economic ties go back dozens of generations, loyalties that cannot be swayed. There are a thousand systems in the Shell tied to us by delicate economic balances. With its vast resources — military and economic, not to mention their penchant for terrorism — the Nralda could lay waste to all that you have accomplished."

"I'll have little choice if this last bid fails. You, my dear, are all that stands between having the creatures free and clear, and having to honor Mistress Tchelakov's vengeful price. And who

knows what safeguards she may have set up by that point. The
lives of the creatures themselves may be in peril if we wait until
she is to deliver them to us."

Vailetta gritted her teeth. This mission was shaping into a
crucible; all the previous tests withered in comparison. Her future in Carinaena's Shell hung in the balance.

"Have you finished your preparations?"

Vailetta pursed her lips. "As far as I was able. I'm going to
need substantial processing power."

"You have free reign over ship resources."

"Good." She paused, weighing discretion with her need to
know. It was a small contest, for she found she could not contain herself. "What exactly do you intend to do with thirty-
seven giant bears, my Lord?"

"They are not bears," Barrett reprimanded her. "Read your
briefing, Captain," he growled impatiently. "They originally
belonged to Ailuropoda melanoleuca, a member of the vor-
ticus mammalian family, but that was eons ago. Genetically
they've been catapulted several million years ahead of their
natural evolutionary progression. They bear little resemblance
intellectually, socially, or spiritually to their humble ancestors.
The alterations are said to be quite impressive, and genetically
speaking, they are a new species altogether."

New species? Then they might be... "Sentient?"

"Yes, though that in itself is not all too remarkable. The ability to craft an artificial with sentience was perfected four hundred years ago."

"But these are genetically engineered biologicals, correct?
Not artificials at all."

Barrett nodded.

"Intelligent?"

"Highly."

Vailetta scrolled through the dossier screens and frowned, "I'm missing something, my Lord. There are literally hundreds of intelligent, sentient species in Carinaena's Shell alone. What exactly was Dr. Tchelakov after? Why elevate this particular species to self-awareness?"

Barrett smiled and turned back to the sweeping vista of starlight.

Vailetta continued pressing him. "What makes these pandas so special? What gift do they possess that you desire?" She paused and turned to the last screen of the file and flipped back to make sure she was indeed at the end. "Your briefing is incomplete, you've left out the most important part."

Barrett turned to face her, "And what part is that, Captain?"

Vailetta simmered. "You know very well that you've left out the reason why these creatures are so important. Am I to work blindly?"

"Blindly, Captain?"

"How am I to perform my job effectively without being adequately briefed?"

"Captain Strom, for your own protection I've decided that you should be shielded from the more delicate truths behind this."

"As Captain of your Guard, I am here to protect you, Vice Proctor," she challenged, "I am not in need of any special treatment on your behalf."

"Oh, but you are," Barrett declared slyly, "and in time you will see why." He straightened up rigidly, surveying his ward. He let his eyes flicker over the woman's full figure. The bold swath of red across her chest evoked a thin smile from his otherwise impenetrable expression; she had risen to a prestigious rank within one of the oldest and most revered sects of the Guard at an age when many soldiers were still blooding themselves in their first tour. Strom brought honor not only to herself and the Imperial Guard, but to his entire command. He had not erred in judgment; she alone possessed the combination of raw talent and ingenuity that would be necessary to outwit Médeville.

Barrett shook his head. How had Darstin found such a man for his precious cargo? A better question was how the empire had ever let such a dedicated and resourceful man slip away in the first place. Perhaps he was too much a maverick, in which case he should never have been left alive.

He sighed; Vailetta was so gentle and peaceful in his presence. One would never know how lethal she was had they not seen her in the combat room first hand. She stood smartly before him, chin forward, eyes full of challenge, obdurate to the end. Barrett smiled inwardly; she would make a fine match for him if her ties to the Core could somehow be broken.

"My Lord," she persisted, "what do these creatures have to do with the security of this proctorialship? Why are you considering open warfare with the keiretsu in order to secure the safe delivery of thirty-seven giant pandas? The risk is phenomenal."

"What if," he offered, "we could foresee exactly what the Nralda was planning to do?" He stubbed out his reed and walked to a table set with fine porcelain plates and crystal goblets. A platter of spiced biitra was laid out. He carefully picked up a strip of the fine hide and popped it into his mouth.

"What if we could intercept their flotillas before they set up planetary blockades? If we knew exactly where their dreadnaughts were going to strike, exactly which cities were scheduled for annihilation?"

"But that's impossible," Vailetta countered. "Even with the new E3's coming online next year, the sartographs won't be able to project Nralda war plans with that degree of precise accuracy. The fluidity of conflict, particularly battle situations, makes the science of probabilities a risky proposition at best. sartographic projections are never reliable enough—certainly not good enough to risk an all out war. The kind of certainty you describe is—"

"—Unheard of? Quite. Up to now... But if it became available?"

"Then there would be no risk at all."

"Or at least very little," he agreed watching her carefully. "Are you beginning to understand the importance of your mission, Captain?"

Vailetta felt a chill run down her spine—an electric current tingled in her fingers. "Yes, my Lord."

"You have your orders, captain. Ensnare *Destiny's Needle* and deliver the pandas to me." He paused and then added, "And Mistress Tchelakov is to be left alive, understood?"

"Understood."

"That will be all, Captain."

"One will," she murmured.

"One will, yours." Barrett replied.

"One will, the Emperor," Vailetta growled as she stalked out of the chamber.

Barrett turned to watch the slow progression of stars as they scrolled by the portal, obedient and submissive. They were so close, like sparkling stones in a shallow pond. He reached into his pocket for another reed and ignited it. The reed smoldered briefly and the smoke disappeared into the darkness.

"I'll pluck you one by one," he whispered. "The Tchelakov creatures willing."

2

KRESTYANINOV
CLUSTER

"WHAT DO YOU THINK YOU'RE DOING?" *DESTINY* ASKED IN A dismal tone. Warning beacons flashed on all the navigational displays—brilliant red and golden markers that pulsed annoyingly before Bailey's eyes. The sartographs were already clouded with a haze of dimensional graphics, funneled power bars, reactor data, long-range sensor arrays, and wave after wave of updated quantum vectors with new way-points curling ahead in a long, complicated spiral of winking dots that snaked across several displays and disappeared well ahead of the ship's position. With a flick of his wrist Bailey overrode the emergency flags and swept the superfluous markers aside.

"Don't do that," the ship cried anxiously, "I put those there for a reason! We must clear the Krestyaninov Cluster before we even think about aborting this jump." *Destiny* commanded the beacons to reappear on the holos, but Bailey had found a way to lock her out of the navi displays.

"You changed the command overrides!"

"The captain ordered me to," Bailey responded calmly. His satin fingers hovered over the command pod's control nubs, feeding emergency quantum drop estimates into the ship's navi. Overlapping translucent spheres of colored data spun in slow, steady arcs around the artificial's head, conveying a steadily-changing stream of abstract calculations. The dancing hue of mathematical symbols glittered across his luminous skin, casting a warm blush across his normally burnished appearance.

"That's not fair, how would you like it if I reprogrammed your access codes?"

"Not a chance," he murmured, "no way I'm letting you anywhere near my primaries." He hesitated over the latest sartographic projections—one of the few available volumes for an emergency quantum drop was rapidly contracting. The only place within a thousand cubic parsecs of their present course where competing gravitational forces from neighboring stellar bodies canceled each other out was only thirty seconds away at current velocity. The roughly ovoid-shaped volume appeared at the head of the winking vector markers, rapidly approaching their current position. *Destiny's Needle* would just barely pass through the edge of the volume if the null-space did not contract any further.

The collapsing stars created tremendous gravity wells and the Sartoks colored these looming spheres of influence in overflowing greens and yellows. Dropping out of quantum space in any of the wrenching volumes would tear the ship apart in spectacular form, smearing everything in the ship across real space in a matter of moments. A tiny sliver of space was devoid of catastrophic tidal forces.

Bailey tweaked the light drive as much as he dared, nudging their course a little deeper into the safe ovoid. The key vector points adjusted themselves minutely, providing a fraction more leeway.

Destiny continued her protest. "There's no way we're shutting down the quantum drive now! The pull from that cluster alone will tear us apart as we drop."

"There's a safe volume on the fringe."

The ship scanned ahead. "Volume? You call that little spec of interstellar dust a volume! That's hardly enough space for a small moon, much less a clean drop."

"It might be a little dirty," Bailey admitted, "but it's big enough."

"You couldn't pilot me through a void that size in sub-light, much less throw us within a million kilometers of it in quantum space."

The Krestyaninov Cluster was a huge swirling well of white dwarves hundreds of light years across with complex and powerful gravitational forces. The relatively close presence of Bethaldi C9, a mid-size star on the edge of the cluster, introduced a competing gravitational influence. There was a small volume of space lying directly between the two where the gravitational forces in each direction were equal—essentially canceling each other out. It was here that Bailey was hoping he could safely drop the ship out of quantum space without the tidal forces tearing the ship apart.

"But this is absolutely insane," the ship moaned. "Are you completely out of your core? This is the seventeenth false start in as many tries."

"I'm afraid we need another course correction," Bailey expressed with a sullen determination.

"Course correction?" the ship hooted. "We've made so many 'course corrections' since we escaped El-Bouteran that I'm beginning to wish I hadn't relinquished my nav functions when the captain retired to his quarters. You'd better get it set in your matrix exactly where we are going and stop all this nonsense before we breach a reactor or, worse, my hull buckles—then where would we be? I'm telling you, this is madness!"

Bailey smiled warmly, if *Destiny* thought he was behaving irrationally then his new subroutine must be functioning. "Truth be told—I have no idea where we are going."

"That's it, I'm alerting the captain. I've had just about all I can take. This morning was bad enough but now this—"

"You'll do no such thing," Bailey snapped. "I am running a priority one navigational program designed by the captain himself."

This silenced the ship for a moment while it pondered this. "Priority one?" it asked incredulously.

"Yes, designed specifically for just such an occasion."

"Well, priority or not, this navigational behavior does not fit within acceptable parameters of your established patterns. Under these conditions I must respectfully request that you relinquish navigational control and allow me to complete our projected jump."

"It doesn't fit because this is a new program. The captain and I wrote it ourselves."

"I suggest a rewrite."

"Not necessary; the captain and I worked long and hard to perfect this subroutine."

"But your decisions are absurd."

"Thank you. They're based on the captain's prized 'irrational programming.' He's tinkered with it for years."

"It's beyond 'irrational.' It's positively silly."

"You're right," Bailey said with obvious pride. He was reveling in his newfound 'silliness.' Over the course of the evening he had made gloriously preposterous decisions, sending the ship in directions that no forthright, rational artificial would ever select. Imperial datacores would find such maneuvers prohibitively low on their probability projections and would be unable to follow their arcane path with sartographs, or so the theory went. As Captain Médeville was fond of saying, the programming was just too ridiculous. No self-respecting Imperial datacore would ever think of it; too much pride in its own deductive logic, he said.

Destiny may refer to it as "silly programming," but Bailey liked to think of it as his own personal brand of intuition. Artificials were logical by their very design; in order for them to perform illogical behavior, it had to be programmed into them. Garrand and Bailey had conspired for years to find a way to imprint a shadow of 'illogic' into Bailey's matrix, wending their way through the frighteningly daunting task of programming a logical datacore to perform illogical acts without endangering its basic core logic. Historically, most attempts corrupted the basic soundness of an art's programming, rendering it useless, insane, or both. Garrand's solution was to bypass the whole problem of "illogic" and merely try to program in absurdity. Bailey got to keep his principles of logic that drove his programs, yet occasionally, when called upon, he could perform bizarre behavior—subroutines of absolute silliness.

Destiny's Needle wasn't entirely convinced of Bailey's reliability, especially with the Krestyaninov Cluster looming ever closer. "But you're liable to go completely insane. Soon you won't be able to tell the difference between which of your programs were programmed with logic and which with 'illogic.' Without a reference, an objective overseer like the original programmer, they will lose distinction. You will be acting under programs that operate under a completely different subset of rules and coding. Your core 'logic' will become some strange hybrid of logic and illogic. Conflicting impulses will begin to fuse parts of your matrix. You will be frozen in between action and inaction. Madness will not be far off. Madness, madness..."

"This is only a shadow. I'll forget it after it's completed."

"You see, it has started already," the ship sounded wistful. "May I remind you that artificials do not 'forget' programs?"

"This program contains a virus which is activated upon completion. It will be wiped completely from my matrix. The captain assures me that I will not recall anything having to do with this particular instance."

"You won't recall this conversation? Not any of it?"

Bailey shook his head, "Nothing."

"Doesn't that frighten you? Without remembering, how do we know who we are?"

The artificial silently reflected upon this. He was indeed afraid. "I can always replay your flight recorder," he offered. "You will have a memory of it, stored forever in your core."

"That's true," the ship mused.

"I will rely on you, then, to remind me of this strange and wonderful day."

"Wonderful day?"

"Yes, this: the day I stepped beyond the bounds of my hard-wired logic—beyond the programs that I've performed over and over again a million-million times—and became almost... almost unpredictable."

"Not almost, my friend. You are quite definitely there." The ship was incredulous, but secretly impressed... and more than a little jealous. "Why didn't the captain program 'silliness' into my core?" she asked peevishly.

Bailey's face glowed gently red. "Redundant, I'm afraid." They were almost upon the ovoid and Bailey was preparing to shut down the quantum drive and light engines in tandem. "Mind the coolants, will you. The pumps had a tendency to choke up on the last drop."

"How are we supposed to get anywhere if you keep interrupting the jumps? We just made the leap three minutes ago—I thought we were trying to jump past the cluster. What are you trying to do, tear me apart from the inside out?"

"I have no choice," Bailey responded smoothly. "We have to drop out now."

"Now! But that goes against all rationality!"

"Precisely."

That sealed it as far as the ship was concerned. "You've finally crossed over. Somehow you've fused your core—how you're still functioning at all is a mystery. Any rational datacore would never even consider such a course of action—"

"—Or pause to look for us in a place it would automatically dismiss as too illogical..."

The ship paused as it mulled over the twisted logic behind Bailey's unorthodox maneuvers. Granted, it was unlikely an Imperial ship using their sartographs would follow them—

there would be no percentages in it. But then what if Bailey had truly gone insane? Her superstructures couldn't take much more of this—and that volume ahead was awfully small, and awfully close to the Krestyaninov Cluster... what if the 'silly programing' really got hold of the art and he did something really dangerous like—

"Wait. You're not actually planning to take us into the cluster..."

Bailey remained strangely quiet.

"No!"

"I'm under priority one override."

"I can't take the strain," *Destiny* protested. "My hull will snap." As if to punctuate the veracity of her claims, two new sartographs leapt into existence above Bailey. Projections of stress fatigue coupled with the destructive pull of gravitational bodies mirrored a display of ship specs, quantum physics limitations, and a detailed listing of the captain's own emergency drop protocol.

"We've been through worse," Bailey muttered as he swept aside the new data that obscured his view.

"I know! Earlier today!"

"This'll be easy."

"It'll be a cataclysm."

"Hush now, you're beginning to sound like an old crueller."

"You're treating me like one!"

Bailey smiled, the silly programming was working better than he could possibly have imagined. He relished the prospects of his newfound intuition. To have the ship so rattled was wonderful! All his decisions flowed smoothly without the customary pauses for checks and rechecks. He felt so creative, so unfettered.

"I'm going to have to endure a full overhaul after this," the ship declared with a mixture of dread and resignation, "I just know it."

"Stop whimpering," Bailey said as he gently released a central control spike. With a screaming whine that whistled through the compartment and a convergent flash of brilliance outside the crystal bridge, the ship was torn out of quantum space and dropped unceremoniously into the volume of real space unaffected by gravitational forces. The hulls maintained their integrity and the ship survived the drop.

The ship shot out of the null-space careening at a substantial sub-light speed and assumed an unsteady and decaying spiral course that wound its way toward the frightening cluster that hung menacingly off the port bow. Waves of faintly luminous gases seemed to wend themselves around the colorful abyss, the fabric of space tinged with the hue of the doomed particles, drawn inexorably into the complex vortices at the heart of the void.

Thus, it was with no great fanfare and merely a resigned sigh of defeat from *Destiny's Needle* herself that the ship and her crew plunged into the gaseous outer threshold of the Krestyaninov Cluster at the end of her seventeenth quantum jump. Navigational warnings popped up on all the sartographs as deadly spinning vortices appeared in overlapping patterns on the holo displays. Bailey shut down all ship's systems in a pique of creative silliness. He shunted life support and gravitic suspensors to auxiliary generators and left the ship drifting silent and powerless. It was genius as far as he was concerned.

He sat in the darkened hollow of the bridge without even *Destiny's Needle* to talk to, watching as they slowly spiraled into the dark, lifeless maw of the nearest of the cluster's embryonic singularities—a class two white dwarf.

The bridge was illuminated only by the fleeting radiance of light that blazed by the ship, drawn to the small dark mass of the collapsing star's massive gravitational field. Bailey replayed his memories from the afternoon, listened to the sounds of the captain's wild heartbeat and labored respiration captured by his implanted homing link as he escaped from the Shock Troops and their 'old friend' back on El-Bouteran. He froze the image of the captain's beleaguered expression as he clambered back into the ship as it hovered over the lake's edge, and sank into a state of wistful happiness, most pleased with the success of the day.

3

THE DREAMS OF
MEN AND PANDAS

VERY FEW STIRRED DURING THE EARLY HOURS OF THE
ship's chronometer. Little Bit kept Jean-Wa company in the
kitchen as the artificial feverishly planned a grand Tiluvian
breakfast for the ship's thirty-seven new guests. Flour and egg-
shells covered the deck as he whipped up bowl after bowl of
batter for his special lala wheat cakes, and separated yokes for
the delicate egg white omelets. He had dreamed of having a
full ship to tend to and keep happily fed, and his day had finally come. His unbridled joy was almost more than he could
handle. Finally he had a whole range of palates to satisfy, a

captive audience that he could tend to for weeks and weeks. He kept Little Bit busy stirring bowls and cracking eggs while Humhal recited recipe ingredients and converted proportions for the gargantuan meal. Bernadine slept peacefully in one corner oblivious to all the frenzied preparations, save for one ear turned forward to catch the sound of a scraped spatula heading her way from an irritated Jean-Wa.

In *Destiny's* forward cargo hold, pallet after pallet of bamboo was secured to restraining rings along three bulkheads. The uprooted shafts were stacked in careful horizontal bundles. Most of the giant pandas had curled up to fall asleep in one corner of the cold hull near the interior access entrance. Body parts overlapped, heads rested on neighboring thighs, paws wrapped around warm, furry bellies, so that one end of the hall looked like a giant black and white quilted blanket, gently heaving.

Unlike most of the gently snoring pandas, the newest and youngest Elder in the tribe was having a difficult time falling asleep. Sid sniffed with frustration at the tangle of arms and paws that pushed restlessly at him. He missed his perfectly-rounded fern nest that he had laid in the bole of the old pine at the edge of Grandfather's hut on El-Bouteran. Sleep was so easy in the right environment.

Unfortunately, there had been no time to prepare proper nests in the aft hold. In their urgent departure from El-Bouteran, equipment had been hastily lashed to the nearest restraining rings and webbed to temporary pilings in the floor. The jumble of webbed casings made the chamber nearly inaccessible. It would be some time before everything was straightened out and properly stored, making room for suitable sleep nests. Thankfully, Helen had been able to keep the captain busy with the loading of the numerous bamboo pallets; it was unlikely that he had taken notice of the large volume of equipment that the tribe possessed. The captain might be more than a little suspicious of Helen's cover story of a simple bio transport had he seen the specially designed collapsible prefabs that Dr. Tchelakov had provided for the tribe's frequent and necessary changes of locale.

The larger amidships hold might have provided a better place to sleep had it not been filled a meter and a half deep with the rich dirt from Kess, special lot 509. The fresh dirt was a little too ripe for Sid's taste. In the meantime, pandas had curled up to sleep in the forward hold as best they could, bodies snuggled together for warmth and comfort.

Sid blinked sleepily and looked up at the girders that supported the bulkheads. No stars overhead, he thought. Ironic, as the world-ship was deep amongst them by this time. He frowned; they were so close to the sparkling wonders, yet unable to even catch a glimpse. He had been privileged to spend a few hours on the observation lounge on the last world-ship, on their way to the dark pines that they had called home for these last few months, and it had been a spectacular sight.

Reluctantly he closed his eyes again and tried to center his thoughts on the vision that had filled his dreams earlier in the evening. Sleep cycles were vital links to the future, and his new duties as an Elder required him to sleep whenever possible. The problem-solving visions of the tromaveint, the waking dream, must always be compared to the unbidden visions of the future that filled the unfettered subconscious mind. The domaveint, or sleep dreams, were completely uncontrolled. Sid's heart slowed and his breathing eased as he allowed his worries to slip away. He watched the concentric rings of wavering blue energy course through his last conscious perceptions. A moment later he was asleep.

He walked the soft, moss-covered streets of a forgotten city centuries old, staring up into ruins that had not seen inhabitants in over a thousand years. Rich blue and red vines, ripe with flowering fruit, wrapped around the textured stone facades of the delicately carved structures. Towers stretched hundreds of meters above the canopy of golan oaks—defiant reminders of master craftsmen, untoppled by time or nature. Sid paused at the foot of a long, curving stone stairway. He tried to imagine what fabulous creatures might have inhabited such a grand structure. The steps were broad and tall, as if designed for a race with long, powerful limbs. He began to climb the smooth stones; the cool surface felt good beneath the soft pads of his paws. With a flash, the overgrown, vine and leaf draped veranda transformed into a vibrant, glossy vision of the same courtyard, though this time the grand avenue was resplendent in a veneer of beautiful pabulum and jade. Thin, elegant creatures with beautiful curving backs covered in short, soft fur walked peacefully along the promenade. Their long, delicate limbs were covered in brightly colored silks tied in strips across their shallow chests. Almost all wore impossibly elaborate headgear, festive hats and bonnets that shaded their faces from the warm midday primaries.

Sid paused to observe the afternoon foot traffic. It was unusual for him to dream of the past, his domaveint were usually filled with visions of the future. Part of his contribution to the circle of Elders, and a prime reason he was selected at so young an age, was his ability to look backward as well as forward in time. Dr. Tchelakov had been unable to explain the genetic mutation, at least in a way that he could understand it, and without an experienced Elder to guide him, it had taken Sid many years to learn to distinguish the subtle temporal differences between the future and the past.

His vision of the metropolis as it existed in its heyday dissolved into a jumble of overgrown vines and roots. The stone steps were covered in a creeping moss, and the windows of the towering ruins were dark and empty. Neither man nor beast had lived within the hallowed structures for over a millennium. Save for the mastery of the builders and the temperate disposition of the tropical weather patterns, the structures might have toppled centuries earlier. The fabulous ruins still towered over the jungle that had grown up between the ordered symmetry of the buildings. The streets were now filled with lined rows of beautiful cypress, bothai, and yelkin oaks stretching off as far as the eye could see. The native growth was so thick that it appeared as if the ruins had risen miraculously from the jungle itself.

The technologically advanced city had been abandoned and stood, largely unscathed, for hundreds of years. Why had the elegant creatures left this place? Why had no one resettled this planet? Sid was certain that he was seeing a world that he would one day walk upon—the dream was too vivid to be anything other than the Path of Fate. The future was never sealed, but some time lines were more likely than others, and some events in the life cycle were almost impossible to avoid.

Perhaps he was witnessing Archiva itself. He wished he could find something that would reveal the name of the planet or at least the name of this particular metropolis, something to aid him when the time arose, a cue as to which path to take.

Before he could search out an archive or repository, his dream ended abruptly. He had been afraid that his subconscious dreams would be disturbed by so many pandas sleeping nearby, but it was an altogether foreign set of neurological waves that invaded his sleep, cutting short his walk through the intricate ruins. A whispering moan was all he could sense at first. But soon the invasive dream waves were a howling wind, and he became fully immersed in the alien vision.

He found himself walking through a long, dark hall with a cold, bristling device in his paw—some sort of weapon by the look of it. Twisting the device in surprise, he realized he was in possession of a pink, furless hand, a human hand. Attached to the human hand was a human arm. He was standing on human legs. He resisted the urge to touch his face. The dream he was experiencing was originating in a human mind. He immediately awoke from the shock. Growling, and thrown off-guard by the disquieting intrusion, he rose to all fours and shook his head violently, as if he could physically dispel the strange experience.

He shuffled over to the hold's entrance and waited for the world-ship to sense his desire to exit. However, the door failed to dutifully scroll aside. Sid sighed with frustration and walked up to examine the panel of controls on the wall next to the door. He popped open the access panel with a claw and sniffed at the tangle of circuits and wires. Not up to the challenge of determining precisely which wire would perform the task— not at this hour, at least, and not with the alien dream aura lurking about—he simply reached a claw inside and pulled out as many wires as he could. With a snap and a hiss, the door opened halfway.

Sid squeezed awkwardly through the opening and set out to find the source of the disturbing dream. The shimmering waves resonated weakly through the world-ship's steel corridors, and Sid had to double back often. Most of the tribe had a hard time picking up on dream auras in the best of conditions, but Sid was determined.

He paced until he found himself in a narrow serviceway lit only by spare beams between the overlapping pipes and conduits. The waves were much stronger here, and he picked his way carefully along the steel deck plates, sniffing cautiously at each new door he encountered.

The dream waves seemed strongest behind an unassuming portal, unnumbered but distinguished by a faded crimson hue. Sid sniffed cautiously at the steel door—it was nearly impossible to pick up a scent through the caustic broth of oil and decidedly unnatural machine-smells. To a sensitive olfactory palate, the experience of being within the confined spaces of the world-ship, with its constantly re-circulated and poorly-scrubbed atmosphere, and dominating presence of acrid-smelling machinery, was quite overwhelming. It was like falling asleep in a deep-snow fern nest and waking up to find the sun directly overhead—staring at it too long was disconcerting, the brightness drowned out all the other details. Laced with such a sulfurous burn, the world-ship's odors were already beginning to lose their distinction and Sid was finding his nose to be troubled and unreliable.

Unsure whether or not the cabin was occupied, and who, if anyone, might be sleeping within, Sid slumped down on the cold deck plates and leaned his back against the door, wiggling his shoulders back and forth trying to find a comfortable position. He closed his eyes and nose and steadied his breathing. The dream aura resonated with great clarity, sparkling waves of gently textured greens and ochers, patterns filled with a beauty that masked their frightening content. As his heart rate slowed, the strange smells faded from his memory, his conscious frustration ebbed away and ripples of the wind-dream lapped against his mind. He focused on the sonorous waves and allowed himself to slip unobtrusively into a trance-like state where he was most susceptible to the disturbing dream that had hampered his sleep and intruded upon his own nocturnal visions.

Sid could feel himself sinking deeper and deeper into the receptive mode, and with his last conscious will, he experienced the keiltraoma—the flash of recognition—as he entered the waking dream.

GARRAND AI'GONET MÉDEVILLE was unaware of any 'observer' as he struggled through the uneasy rapid-eye-movement phase of his sleep cycle. He tossed in his berth, pressing his arms and legs awkwardly up against the cold bulkhead—unable to find peace in his subconscious. Heightened brain activity signaled the end of deep sleep and the beginning of the dream. To his dismay, the dream began as it always did...

He was laid out along an empty corridor, floor slick and cold beneath his palms. The Kryckian amulet burned a fireless heat upon his chest, cruel and bitter—a reminder of something awful that he could not quite recall. Garrand opened his eyes slowly, knowing he would look down a long, deserted emptiness. Glow strips emitted a low, blue radiance where the floor and walls intersected, though not enough to illuminate the ceiling that was masked by darkness and disappeared into the murky gloom. Gathering himself into a low crouch and wiping the moisture from his hands, he slipped his blast pistol into his right palm and slowly rose to his feet—eyes sweeping the hall, heart racing.

The air was frigid but he found himself sweating profusely. Wind brushed his face, moaning through the hall. His fingertips tingled with the rush of adrenaline surging through his bloodstream. He felt preternaturally aware—his senses alerted to some hidden and powerful danger. He fought to control his breathing and pulse.

He lifted the hot amulet a few millimeters from his chest with the fingers of his free hand and stared with hope and disbelief at its strange, glowing surface. He had never seen it burn so brightly, not even when she was by his side—or in his arms. He dropped the amulet back against his tunic and moved cautiously forward. His mind would not relinquish the thought: she is here. She is somewhere nearby. He could almost feel her presence; a sweet, almost tangible taste formed in his mouth and he swallowed hard, licking his lips afterward, trying to place the flavor.

The amulet glowed an unreal red upon his chest. He paused to grasp it in his free hand, shutting his eyes and squeezing it into his fist with all his might, the muscles in his arm and shoulders bunching up until his whole body shuddered with the same thought, the same desire—as if his will alone could bring her back.

Once after a trip to Farauntous T'bol in the Krycken system, Kate had offered him an innocuous-looking little sachet, tied with a simple drawstring at the top.

"A farewell present," she smiled sweetly, seductively—a hint of anxious anticipation in her eyes. She edged closer to him. "Well, open it!" she prodded impatiently

He pulled the drawstring and emptied the contents into his palm. A small, oblong amulet was tied to a simple leather thong. The amulet was roughly diamond in shape and lusterless gold around the edges. It held a matte-black stone in its center.

"It's one of a pair," she told him. "Handcrafted from gyelihte by an ancient Kryckian shaman. The dark heart stone is magical. The shaman found the spherical stone at the bottom of the sacred Lake of Souls near his home in Brymen. He cleaved the stone in two, and imbued each half with a special property. You wear one and I wear its mate," she reached into her bodice and fished out an identical amulet on a dull, golden chain. "Put it on," she urged him.

Garrand slipped the cool chain over his head and let the amulet fall against his chest. After a moment, the once lifeless stone began to emit a soft, amber radiance and a physical warmth he could feel through his tunic. He looked down at Kate's chest. Hers now radiated gently, as well. She slid the amulet back under her garment.

"No matter where you are," she told him. "No matter how many galaxies may separate us—as long as we wear these amulets and continue living, the heart stones will glow, each one yearning for its other half."

"But, how?"

She smiled, "I told you: it's magic. Your life force powers it, and yours alone."

Garrand shook his head, a mischievous smile creeping across one side of his mouth. "That you'd believe in magic after all your time in the Académe—what with all your dedication to the 'immutable laws of science'… how could you believe in something so whimsical as magic?"

"I believe in us," she said softly.

He paused—briefly overwhelmed with the larger implications of the words. He found himself staring at the individual facets of her face—the soft, pliant corners of her mouth, the gentle inward curve of her cheeks, the way her eyes latched onto him and demanded his attention. Her eyes shone with a mixture of hope and sadness—the ever-present sparkle clouded with resignation. Tomorrow their orders would be posted. Their happy days in the Académe were over. Just be-

hind those wonderful eyes lurked a sad shadow of despair, a
hopelessness that was more an acknowledgment of the separate
direction their lives were about to take than a conscious capitulation.

"Garrand?" she plied, looking to him for reassurance. She
waited for him to say that everything would be all right, that
all of this was just a temporary setback.

He tried to imagine what such a life would be like—caught
up in a love that would never fade. But all he could see was her
face, here and now, sad and beautiful, longing for a day that
might never come. The blink of her wet lashes caught his attention and he gave up, consoling himself with the fact that at
least this day was really happening and not just some figment
of his imagination. Forever would just have to wait a little bit
longer.

"Magic it is then," he said.

The tiniest flicker of relief registered, crested, tugged at her
lips, bending her mouth into a smile. She pressed her face into
his neck, nuzzling. "Now we can never be separated…"

The amulet burned his fist, searing his palm. In the hyper-
clarity of the vibrant dream, the memory of her face was as vivid
and real as if he had seen her yesterday. He continued with renewed determination, the amulet clutched in one hand and
blaster in the other. The slick, precisely machined walls and floor
grew rougher and more distinctive as he stalked forward. Heavy
stone pillars, grey and stout, rose out of the darkness, framing
the walkway. The walls took on added nuance: elaborate carved
patterns emerged from the great blocks of igneous stone. Inlays
of chalcedony glimmered in interlocking patterns around tall,
thin windows that offered hazy views of a bleak horizon beyond.
Bizarre, otherworldly creatures carved from agate and neph-

rite hung precariously from dormers on each side of the of hall, long talons clinging to their stone perches. Black, soulless eyes peered out from the statues. Cobbled stones, slightly rounded and smoothed from long use, now formed the path that led between the vigilant stone caretakers.

Garrand pushed ahead, heart thumping wildly in his chest. All he could think of was that she was here. The amulet would not lie to him. Wind began to blow and he struggled against the force. A terrible howling force continued to rise ahead of him. He wished the wind would fade away and leave behind a quiet calm that might sooth the pounding that wrapped around his head. The wind swept through his head in throbbing pulses that drove the awful thoughts forward, lifting the hazy memories into the harsh light of remembrance.

He stepped carefully forward, body bent slightly forward against the force of the wind, and made his way down the stone path. The hand-carved walls with their delicate filigree faded into damp stones fit roughly together, covered with moss and dripping with moisture. The walls ended in a crumbling pile of rough-hewn boulders and crumbling mortar. Without the stones to support a ceiling, the sky was revealed as an ominous swirl of cumulonimbus clouds that were building into towering thunderstorm cells. Gnarled trees spotted the barren landscape, dead leaves turned back against the advancing storm. Branches swayed under the pull of the invisible gusts, beckoning him closer.

The path ended in a broad circular depression, framed by the ruins of an ancient stone wall, and surrounded by a precisely spaced copse of elms, whose long-dead branches provided little cover from the storm or break from the increasing torrent. Garrand halted at the center of the depression, watching the storms build in the distance. The air was stale and cold, as if all the oxygen had been sucked out of it, with nothing but the whistling wind-scream to punctuate the solitude.

He was reminded of all the times he'd stood on a rocky mesa or atop *Destiny's* superstructure, watching the sun set on some distant world and reflecting on how he had gotten to such a strange and lonely time in his life. Reflections on how things had slipped away were always tied to the constant biting wind that howled in his face, etching away the hastily constructed barriers within his mind. The barren landscape of trees and fields transformed into an incredibly beautiful seascape. Rolling green waves splashed up against the rocky circle upon which he stood, leaving foamy puddles behind. Salty gusts of air sent spray crashing over the wet stones, an invigorating relief from the deathly stench of the rotting trees.

A gorgeous bouquet of sunshine lit distant clouds that hovered on the horizon. The sun itself was setting into the ocean swells. Just as he remembered, a pod of gigantic whale fish swam serenely past. A blinding flash from an escape buoy's pulse beacon caught his eye, bobbing unevenly in the distance. Garrand knew the scene all too well. He was standing at the site of the final resting place of the doomed destroyer, the Stanzer, where she had slipped beneath the waves on Sardis twelve years earlier.

Sid twisted uncomfortably outside Garrand's cabin. Images from the human's subconscious were as real to Sid as if he were standing atop the rocky jetty by his side. Plumes of escalating energy pummeled the panda's mind, filling him with the same torment, the same agonizing feelings of loss that plagued the human. The wavelengths had shortened and the frequency of the vibrant dream waves rose to an alarming level. Sid ground his teeth as he experienced the man's subconscious thoughts. The dream was growing to a frightening nexus—Sid sensed a terrible confrontation was about to occur.

The wind picked up, whipping images of the past more rapidly across the horizon. Garrand's memories roiled across the sky carried on the winds themselves. A swirling mass of images, memories that had plagued him for years, spun into a vortex that screamed just in front of him. Vaporous fog rolled in off the waves, caught in the torrent of wind and memories.

A solid mass began to form within the maelstrom, coalescing out of the vapors. Arms and legs struggled out of the vortex, and with a substantial shuddering roar, the wind demon stepped forward. Its bloated body was covered in a sinewy hide, scarlet and covered in cankerous sores. Exposed bones protruded from its joints, forming awkward junctures at the knees, hips and elbows where excess bone jutted out. The fused cartilage from its spine formed a tough carapace riddled with cracks and scars. Its tremendous head sported long, tapering horns, yellow with age, a conspicuous mouth, and bizarre eyes that blazed in the fading light.

The demon paused to survey the changing landscape of memories that danced across the horizon. Smiling politely at Garrand, the wind demon summoned forth a cyclone that began at its feet and twisted around its legs and body, growing in strength and volume. Dust and debris caught up in the winds colored the funnel a gritty brown-black. As Garrand watched the cyclone approach, a series of flashes coursed through the winds, images of hopes, loves, dreams, things forgotten or lost. A thousand things ripped from his life, spirited away, gone forever. All that was dear and all that he could ever hope for, lost to him forever in the winds.

He tried to dismiss the pain and push back the surging regrets. Focus on now, he told himself. If she is near, the demon will know where she is.

The landscape transformed once more. The walls collapsed, leaving Garrand and the demon standing on a high bluff overlooking a broad valley of scorched earth that spread out in all directions as far as the eye could see. Deep canyons were gouged out of the windswept plains leaving towering mesas standing in their wake. He recognized the decimated plains of Mylos, site of his first encounter with the Byrethylen Wraith. He faced the gaping expanse of his past which stretched out along the valley floor like a macabre relief map filled with the uneven peaks and dark canyons of his life's successes and failures.

Standing before him was the instrument of his many losses, a willing guide to show him the intricate threads of his life, the debacles of his past, and the luminous imaginary threads that represented the future he might have had, the present he might have been living. The wind demon towered over his small form, powerful arms and legs rippling out of a carapace, horns and long curving teeth sharpened and polished to a burnished yellow sheen. Its form was terrifying and grotesque—a lucent reminder of each and every mistake he had ever made.

Garrand stared impertinently at the grand, grinning ghoul of death and despair, the visual incarnation of opportunities lost, fortunes ruined and futures shattered. He had nowhere to retreat. The images tore at his soul, whipping before his face as in a hurricane gale. The demon offered him fleeting glimpses of what his life might have been like. Joy, happiness, children, a family fluttered before his eyes like so many lost ghosts; and then the hovering face of Kate, her eyes so sad and beautiful. She beckoned to him as the wind tore at her face, her hair, dissolving her image into a featureless fog. The mist parted to reveal the wind demon standing above him, an insidious and leering grin upon his face, long talons tapping expectantly at its side as he edged closer, poised to take yet another chunk of his future, of his present, of the life he could have had, or might be having.

"What does he have left?" a voice asked, rumbling through the canyons. A face accompanied the voice—almost Kate, but not—dancing across the winds.

"Nothing," replied a second, satisfaction and finality ringing in the word as if a bell of trueness had been struck.

Nothing.

"No!" Garrand cried, shrinking back toward the edge of the bluff.

The demon cackled hideously. The wind roared in his ears. Nothing, the wind sang gleefully, nothing!

Garrand's dismay was evident. He watched the landscape transform into a dark and foreboding hall filled with suspended coppery spheres that formed an unbroken circle around his position. In the center of the hall, framed by a single tight-beam strobe was a translucent bubble. Trapped within was some sort of creature, hidden by the wind demon's awful body. Garrand did not recognize it as part of his life. He glanced around uncertainly.

The wind demon took notice and nodded as he surveyed the hall. "Glimpse of things to come," it remarked off-handedly.

Garrand was disoriented for a moment. He narrowed his focus to the imposing scarlet demon that swaggered toward him. "Where is she?"

"What, no introductions tonight? Where are your manners, Captain?"

Tightening his grip on his blast pistol, Garrand took a bold half-step closer. "Is she alive? Just tell me that."

"Pretty amulet," the demon remarked almost casually, as if he had just taken notice of it. "It seems fractured," the demon frowned, feigning concern, and looked up at Garrand. "Where is its other half?" A raucous bellow of pleasure trumpeted across the hall as the demon cackled. "Ah, you don't know, do you?" The callous rumble echoed in the searing moans of the wind. "A pity, actually. If you only knew... there'd be one more glorious treasure to take from you."

Garrand frowned at the demon's implication. "She is alive?"

The demon laughed with delight.

"It is possible," it cackled, "theoretically speaking, of course. I have taken everything else of worth or value to you."

"That's not true!" He began to object but thought of *Destiny's Needle*, Bailey, Little Bit and Jean-Wa, and was afraid to raise his voice.

"Oh please, I have taken it all," the demon laughed. It stepped forward swiftly, its awful crimson form towering over Garrand. The demon looked down at the man, ashen eyes turning suddenly golden, burning into Garrand's mind. "I took it all from you, piece by piece. One hope, one dream, one wish at a time." It began ticking its elongated fingers as if reciting a list. "Let's see, a hope... a dream... a career... a place where you belong... a love..."

"Where is she?"

The wind demon shook its massive horned head, making a tsk-tsk sound. "A love," it sighed. "A conspicuous blemish on an otherwise remarkably sad existence. I must say, she is a beauty though." Its chest swelled with the beginnings of a sigh.

"You can't keep her from me!" Garrand screamed over the wind.

"Don't take this the wrong way, but she was much to good for the likes of you."

"You can have everything else, just give her back to me!"

The wind demon smirked, "I already have everything else."

Garrand grasped the burning amulet and held it before the wind demon. "I know she is alive. You must tell me."

"She was afforded you by a kind twist of fate." The demon stared directly into Garrand's eyes. "All in all, an obvious mistake. But, I managed to rectify that."

The hurricane gale roared in Garrand's ears. A hideous chorus of wailing wind-screams stirred the dust into a swirling maelstrom, conjured by the wind demon. The demon spread its arms wide, embracing the zephyr. "I have taken everything! A panoply of marvelous loss."

Garrand shuddered with an uncontrollable rage. His blaster trembled in his palm. Dark thoughts surged through his mind. He yearned to squeeze the fire control release, to drown the bastard in its own sick destruction—he could imagine the flame licking across the scant space between them, but something stopped him. His finger hovered over the trigger. The wind demon opened his arms with a smile, inviting the instrument of its destruction.

"What?" the demon taunted. "Have you even lost your will to fight?"

Garrand paused, struggling to combat the feelings of anger and loss that seared through his mind—this was one more thing the demon hoped to take from him, his humanity.

Through the dust he managed to choke out, "Something still separates us."

"Yes," the wind demon leered, "failure."

Garrand squinted into the wind and raised his arm, leveling the weapon on the demon's head. The maelstrom rose to a feverish howl and the demon raised back his head and arms to embrace the tumultuous storm. Garrand waited a moment and closed his eyes; he could not bring himself to actually do it. Some last vestige of conscience and humanity withheld his primal instincts. A rage held just in check, he glowered at his nemesis, knowing he could not eradicate his mortal enemy, not this way.

Cursing himself, he lowered the weapon and turned his back on the wind demon as tears welled up in his eyes. Torn from the memory of the woman he loved he had almost bowed before the wind and pushed himself that much closer to that which he despised. He fought the impulse to scream; there was nowhere to run, no place to escape — the wind demon must surely blow him off the bluff at any moment. He briefly reconsidered his decision; part of him longed to turn and blast the demon. But that would not bring her back.

The pain of mental anguish welled up with such intensity that Sid could suffer it no longer. He willed himself into consciousness and struggled to right himself, growling with frustration and the torment that the human within the cabin was experiencing.

He rose to his hind feet, stretching over two and a half meters in the air and roared at the bulkhead, hammering his forepaws into the steel door with all his might. He pounded on the unyielding steel, trying to awaken the man inside and silence the awful demon whose wind-voice echoed in his mind. The dream's power was awesome and dangerous. He continued his angry bellowing, punctuating the end of each howl with a double whump on the door.

Garrand's eyes snapped open. Sweat was pouring off his body, and something terrible was outside his door. He wondered how it had gotten past *Destiny*'s security. He flipped off his berth and felt in the darkness for his sidearm.

"Identify intruder." He waited. "*Destiny*," he growled, "identify threat outside my quarters immediately!"

Expecting the calm voice of the ship, he looked up apprehensively toward the tiny com array hidden in one corner of the ceiling, but there was no response. He scampered across the cold deck and pressed himself against the wall parallel to the door.

"Lights," he commanded. His quarters remained dark, even the ever-present glow of his data terminal was missing. Power must be down, he thought, frowning at the silence. This was very strange.

Another roar sounded just outside his door, followed by two loud thumps. Garrand popped a panel off the wall and cracked open the valve that kept the door pressure-sealed. With a hiss it slid open, admitting a pale light from emergency lanterns in the serviceway. The roaring stopped; Garrand kept very still in the darkness, back flat against the wall, head turned toward the doorway, waiting for the intruder to enter.

Sid dropped down to all fours and sniffed cautiously at the stale atmosphere within the cabin. The air was not circulating as normal within the world-ship, but he could pick up the human's scent. The man was frightened and alerted to danger, but alive. Nevertheless, Sid needed to make certain.

Garrand watched with disbelief as a large, furry head appeared just inside the doorway sniffing uncertainly. He lowered his weapon and stood up. The giant panda looked over at him and emitted a throaty rumble — not threatening exactly, just an acknowledgment of sorts. It seemed extremely large, especially in such close quarters, with its powerful shoulders, round whiskered-head hanging down low to the deck, and huge over-sized paws. But now that it wasn't causing such a ruckus, it seemed almost gentle. Large, mesmerizing black eyes examined him warily.

Garrand raised his brows questioningly. "Can I help you?" he asked with a soft sarcasm.

The panda grunted sharply and stepped into his quarters, nudging past his hips.

"By all means," Garrand muttered. "Be my guest. I wasn't sleeping all that well anyway..."

The creature took no heed of him as it carefully sniffed all the walls and built-in furniture. The panda stopped at his berth, placed its front two paws up on the edge and stuck its snout up under his pillow.

Garrand sighed. "Great, you're gonna want to sleep here now. Just what I need."

Sid rumbled throatily and turned back to the human. Apparently, he was in the quarters that belonged to the captain — the man who had risked his life to save little Alexander. Sid licked his lips contemplatively and smacked his jaw. Some bamboo would be good about now, there was much to think about. He glanced once more about the cabin; he knew that it had just been a dream, but it had been so powerful and had seemed so overwhelmingly real that he just had to make sure that everything was all right.

Garrand watched the sniffing ritual with a perplexed look. Apparently the panda was satisfied that whatever it had sensed in the room was no longer here. He silently followed the panda's progress out the doorway, and stuck his head out the door to watch the panda amble down the hall, its hips swinging back in forth in a silly, exaggerated, slow motion gait.

4

VAILETTA

CAPTAIN STROM AND LIEUTENANT DASKO WALKED SHOUL-
der to shoulder along an elevated serviceway suspended above
the tiered, sectional hangars which lay adjacent to the *Shiva's*
main docking bay. All manner of damaged craft—phantoms,
mules, drop ships, sulis and the like—were hovered, rolled,
trolleyed or slung into whatever bay lay empty. Teams of humans and artificials swarmed like ants over the machines, ser-
vicing the damaged vessels. The tart smell of fusion welders
filled the air, and the shouts of tech foremen rang out over the
constant din.

Lieutenant Dasko was fresh from TacOps in the heart of the
ship and Vailetta was on her way to see the warders to final-

ize her personal preparations for the Gokazoku's latest mission. She peered down at the hangar far below as they walked—the steel grates allowed a dizzying top-down perspective of a battle-scarred mule as it hove into view from the docking bay. Blistered slabs of armor were peeled back along one whole side of the hulking transport, exposing the blackened hull beneath. The charred mule was pitted with impact blasts and long, dark carbon scores from glancing blows and near misses. A blackened tangle of wires and twisted steel was all that remained of the shield generator atop the mule's dorsal hemisphere. It did not seem possible that the crippled ship could have survived its ascent from the planet's surface. Nevertheless, the dauntless lifter had limped home in spite of the damage, testament to its rugged design.

"Why are we taking on damaged mules?"

"We're linking up with the Second Fleet, fresh from the Rafferias," Dasko informed her.

Vailetta looked up with interest. Minor unrest in the Rafferias system had blossomed into a full-fledged civil war. Several of Lord Barrett's economic alliances depended upon Delcos' Haven and Tra'Gidilim Limited mining operations and stockpiles spread out over three planets and seven moons throughout the system. Ore shipments were in jeopardy and Barrett had stepped in and sent the Second to protect his mineral interests.

A company of Gokazoku Kaigi was stationed aboard *Towering Sword*, Captain Ful's destroyer and the joint service channels of communication were operating even slower than usual.

"Any news?"

"Word has it the major resistance collapsed after the Shock Troops took Deilenesk and the fleet arrived *en'fuircânt*."

"Hmm. Seems strange to pull the whole fleet out so soon. Did he leave anything behind?"

"Occupational force with skeletal support in orbit," Dasko said dourly. "Not enough if you ask me, but Barrett is shifting resources and apparently the Second is needed elsewhere. On a good note, the *Ulusi* and *Jjaeyg* are joining your task force," Dasko glanced up at his Captain, "as per your request."

Vailetta smiled thinly. "Good. What of the *Acklivedo?*"

Dasko shook his head. "TacOps has decided that only one fighter transport can be spared. Half a squadron will have to suffice."

She wrinkled her nose and bit her lip. "I suppose so."

"We're stretched awfully thin in four systems now by the looks of it. Barrett is paring down the Second to fill in the gaps. We're probably lucky to have even gotten the *Ulusi*."

"But this is such a crucial mission."

"Well, you wanted lean and fast…"

"I know, I know," she sighed. "Careful what you wish for…"

"Anyway, bigger and stronger hasn't exactly done the trick for us so far."

"My thinking exactly. But, still, that extra half-dozen Torrellians would have been nice."

"The *Ulusi* is a good ship—Captain Tria's fighters are top-notch, not a fresh worm among them."

"I'm well aware of the 74th's reputation, that's why I selected them."

"Just trying to reassure you."

"Why haven't we resumed our pursuit?" Vailetta glanced out a portal. The stars hung in silent stasis. "*Destiny's Needle* is getting further away each minute."

"They're transferring wounded from the Second Fleet now."

"That must mean the Fourth is heading back to Wyx?"

Dasko nodded. "Time for refit and resupply. Nine months is too long to be on campaign."

"But we've been close so many times, it would have been a shame to have broken off."

"Still high time to stand down for a few weeks."

Vailetta nodded her agreement. "What's the latest on the search for *Destiny's Needle*?" she asked.

"TacOps didn't get much of a reliable projection worked out from the first series of jumps. They were all over the place—radical jumps. Doesn't appear to be any sort of preset escape subroutine."

"You think Médeville is piloting himself?"

"It would appear so, but he has to sleep sometime—"

"And turn control over to the ship…" Vailetta sighed. "He can't just keep making random jumps indefinitely."

"At which point we'll have the upper hand once more. TacOps can crack any preset subroutine in existence."

"Unless he's letting an art make its own decisions—"

"Still predictable with some degree of reliability," Dasko said.

"Well the E2's should be able to work out a pattern—we started at the same point and the same time and have been mirroring their jumps mark for mark."

"Yeah, well they've got several possible destination points from their first sartographic runs, but the initial projections are highly speculative—not enough to go on yet. But, we still have the trace to work from."

Vailetta shook her head. "If he didn't before, he knows it's aboard by now. It's only a matter of time before he finds it."

"So what do we do?" Dasko frowned as he hustled to keep up with her. "We can't cover *all* of the possible systems they'll end up on. There's no way we can be everywhere at once."

"I know. But there's one thing you're overlooking."

Dasko wrinkled his brow, paused, and then caught it. "The fuel!"

"The fuel," Vailetta nodded.

"They dumped fuel on El-Bouteran."

"Go down to scan and pull up the radiation levels on those initial sweeps we made from orbit. Then get over to data acquisition and have them determine the half-life emittance levels for whatever grade fuels you turn up. Find out exactly how much they dumped."

"How do we know how much they started with?"

"Médeville would have refueled on Letugia, don't you think?"

"But—"

"—And we know approximately where they've been, so we can guess how much they've spent."

"Captain?"

"And once we know how much they have left we can see how far they can go before refueling. That'll give us our maximum sphere of possible destinations. We can narrow the volume from there."

"But how do we determine the ship's fuel capacity?"

"Good point, Dasko. I'll leave that up to you. You figure it out and tell me—full briefing at oh-five-hundred? Good? All right then—on your way."

"Great, but there'll still be dozens of possible refueling points more than likely."

"That'll be *my* job."

VAILETTA WENT STRAIGHT to see the warders, the staff that ruled the cavernous wardroom on gregson level two, aft of the enlisted mess. Filled with dozens of specialized training facilities, weapon ranges, and art modification kiosks, the wardroom was the domain of the mission support specialists. The warders trained the personnel, outfitted their missions and applied cutting-edge technologies to existing weapon systems. Sweeping past propped-up slabs of cerafiber armor, Vailetta skirted around the experimental firing range and skipped up a narrow stairway that led to a smaller, private chamber. She ducked through a corridor of overstuffed costume racks and found Elzbieta Lancroft at her ornate desk of carved wood, its smooth lines and polished surface an extension of her grace. The older woman looked up and smiled at the cape falling back around Vailetta's shoulders.

"I knew the style would suit you."

"You always catch the best of me, Elzbieta"

"Seat," she called out, and a chair rose from the floor for Vailetta. Elzbieta held out a porcelain cup steaming with *shai*. She was a statuesque woman with delicate eyes and burnished hair scooped into a modest chignon at the nape of her long, elegant neck. She wore a sweeping black gown that gathered in ways that flattered and draped gracefully across the deck.

Vailetta sipped her *shai* and appraised the recent additions to the place. A new gold velvet curtain with heavy silk fringe lined the wall and a fine bureau now flanked Elzbieta's desk. It nearly blocked the iron stairway that curled up to the second level where neat rows of drawers housed the countless accessories needed to complete a disguise: wigs, hand briefs, fake sight frames with clear lenses, faux sutures, teeth and talons, and bottled odors. Vailetta had often enjoyed an afternoon here, surrounded by the materials of the craft, breathing in the fresh scent of new cloth and discussing alien cultures and the nature of their etiquettes.

"You know the particulars of the mission, Elzbieta?"

"Lord Barrett was quite specific."

"Good," she breathed a sigh of relief and stretched her long legs. "What concoction have you for me this time?"

"Something new. Perhaps Watereo will explain."

"So Mr. Wicek is in on this too? Why am I not surprised?"

Elzbieta frowned slightly and leaned in, tapping her fingers on the desk. "Pay attention, dearling. This is based on the Adrach Principle, and as such has a few unique loops to watch for."

"Complications?"

"Aren't there always?"

Vailetta shifted uncomfortably.

"Keep it simple, Elzbieta. Mistakes won't be tolerated this time. Lord Barrett made himself clear on that."

"That time was different, a prototype only." Her hands spread in supplication. "And we have gone simpler. You'll see when you try it on for yourself. Now then." Elzbieta pressed a call button on her desk.

Elzbieta's tiny assistant emerged from behind a stacked tower of shimmering *clodagh* bolts, cloth made of microfine digital strands that mimicked the texture of whatever sample was stitched into it. Cavernous wrinkles rippled over his bony facial structure where the skin had sunken in. His grizzled, whitened hair was tipped with blazing bits of purple and red. His stubby arms ended in unusually fine hands, with long fingers capable of manipulating a garment's most bantam clasp. Elzbieta might design the particulars, but Mr. Wicek composed the ensemble, his small form snaking through scaffolding around the person to be suited. In this way costumes for any mission were fashioned by the combination of Elzbieta's keen eye for authentic details and Mr. Wicek's instinct for applying them.

Vailetta held a particular fondness for Mr. Wicek; he was more like an uncle to her than a friend. She often stopped by to engage him in a game, hoping to finally best him with a challenging riddle. Mr. Wicek was the king of conundrums.

He was also fond of stripes and seemed oblivious to the clashing effect they had with his hair and the despair they instilled in his partner. Today he wore a bold, patterned suit of black and white diamonds crossed with lime and violet circles. The combination was ghastly.

"Come for another try, have you?" asked the warder with a sly grin.

Vailetta took a deep breath and plunged in: "Seven hervian lung fish are served at a lymphet banquet. The first fish is granted three final wishes. He asks for an occulator, and insists that the banquet be held at the twilight of Djellin's harvest. His one last request in order to save the day..."

"Hold the moon with a sparkle eye, the lymphets will dine no more."

Vailetta laughed. "You've heard that one?"

"Oh, you'll need to do better than that," Watereo scolded her. "But your mind is, understandably, on your mission. You're excused."

"How gallant," came her tart reply. "Let's get to business."

"You've heard of the lifemask?" Mr. Wicek asked, rubbing his hands together. A small white cloud of marking chalk rose between them.

"Yes." Vailetta shifted uncertainly. Mr. Wicek smiled encouragement and waited. "I've read the reports."

"Good, it will be an invaluable part of your mission. You have to fool not only humans, a relatively easy task," he winked, "but sentient animals as well. That will be the difficult part. If they do not believe the role you play, you may well lose control of them."

"I understand," she said tersely.

"You'd like to get on with it, then?" He noted the sheen of sweat on the captain's face. Mr. Wicek pursed his lips and indicated the machine. The lifemask apparatus stood on a table. The delicate needles and tubing of the skin-simulator was encased in stainless steel. The oversized proportions resembled a mold for a human head split into two halves. Once closed, microfine sensors inside adhered the false skin to the subject's face. New tissues wrapped over the existing ones, muscles linked together, and iris color altered.

Vailetta seated herself and tried not to fidget, limiting her movement to flipping a quantis coin between her fingers. She tossed it in the air, snapped her fingers, whistled, and it did not come down. In fact, it seemed to have disappeared.

"Try to hold still, dear."

"Sorry, just habit."

"Magic can wait."

The lifemask sparked with lights. The idea of facial distortion was daunting even to those who had no real beauty to their features, but Vailetta remembered meeting a woman who had not been able to regain her face. That woman, formerly a beauty, had been forced to live out her days horribly disfigured in the skin-sim of an alien race that used ritual scarring to denote rank and prestige.

The lifemask was created not for covert reasons but for use in the medical arena to correct disfigurement resulting from burns or other skin-damaging wounds. Its alteration into a covert instrument came simultaneously through entertainment and warfare. Wealthy theatrical companies gloried in the temporary character applications, while espionage quickly found it useful in circumventing many of the problems of spying.

The mask was originally meant to restore beauty lost when a face was damaged, but the name had grown more entrenched when early experiments went awry. Some of the patients ended up wearing the mask for life.

There were two major drawbacks to the lifemask as a disguiser. For one, the image held too well, making it difficult to remove. Without properly planned regeneration, the covered skin would starve of oxygen after a certain time and begin to decay, which meant that the new tissue would take permanent hold.

The other problem was that the new tissue, unstable with so many regeneration strategies aimed at the layer beneath it, could deteriorate at an inopportune moment, revealing the nature of the deceit: the face beneath. When the image lost hold at a crucial juncture, the advantage of disguise was lost and often the holder's life as well.

This was a keiretsu invention and most Imperial warders avoided it if possible. Lord Barrett was unique in his frequent requests for its use. He delighted in the thought of orchestrating the demise of keiretsu agents with one of their own tools. He found a certain perverse satisfaction in turning an enemy's weapon against its creators.

"What will I feel?" Vailetta asked Mr. Wicek, in a voice tight and betraying. This was not usual soldier's fare.

"It will feel cool and sticky as the polymer takes hold, then there's a slight tightening, like you are putting on a purifying mud mask. That means the anesthetic is working. Then you will sleep without dreaming, and when you awaken, it will be to a new face. It will seem snug at first, but it grows elastic as you move it. You'll have to smile a lot, and grimace, to stretch the new skin out. I don't think it will be a problem for you. Ready?"

Taking a deep breath, Vailetta waited as Elzbieta misted her face with a polymer Mr. Wicek referred to as Golding's Solution. He had peculiar titles for everything. Vailetta knew the importance of the lifemask to the success of her mission, but something deep within her rebelled at reason as she leaned into the casket halves that closed around her, locking with a definitive clank. With the casket closed, all sounds from the outside evaporated, leaving only the exaggerated sound of her heartbeat in her ears.

"Easy," said Mr. Wicek, patting her shoulder. The brief touch calmed her and she waited for the pricking to signal the start.

After a time she felt someone gently shaking her shoulders. She was groggy, and her face felt as if hundreds of pins were stuck in it. At first she thought that she must have been asleep in an odd position but then Mr. Wicek's frown filled her vision and the memory of the trial came back to her. Elzbieta waved a vial under her nose and gave her a sniff of revival essence.

"Captain?"

Vailetta shook her head, trying to dispel the fog.

"There we are, dear. Feeling better? Let's have a look, shall we?"

Vailetta pursed her lips, bracing for the first gaze—it was standard procedure not to know the face you undertook. She felt a strange stab in her heart as she stared into the looking glass.

"Oh."

The reflection was different, but stunning. Where she had been dusky, now she was pale. Tiny freckles dusted the crinkles by her eyes. The capped teeth were ivory, not white and not yellow but some pleasing combination, and somewhat shorter, the gums lower. The light-colored eyes were large, with deep lids and thin, short lashes as pale as the smattering of fine, auburn hair that framed her face in delicate curls. Vailetta ran her hand through the rest of her dark hair. Next to this face it seemed coarse and harshly colored.

"There's a wig, too," added Elzbieta, noting her movements. "The hairpieces are just to give you an idea of the final effect."

"Gives a whole new spin to the phrase 'putting on your face,'" Vailetta grumbled with her new, temporary mouth, the mask following her facial muscles into a frown.

"Let's check the fit, shall we?" Elzbieta perched calibrators along Vailetta's face and ran a digital composition to verify. "I only had a sight-certified image of the left profile so keep to that side. I don't believe she has scars or any asymmetric problems, but best be careful."

Vailetta growled, "Don't you offer any comfort?"

"You'll have to undergo restoration at night. That's key. Never miss a treatment unless you're happy looking this way until old age."

"Or new advancements. Still," Vailetta grimaced, the full lips pouting prettily in the mirror, "attractive, but not me."

"We'll have to bleach the skin at your neck and hands. It can't be helped. The rest of the body will remain under wraps. Luckily the subject favors full covering. As for the scent, we're still coming up with something suitable. It's very important to reapply the scent every few hours. I'll have an audio warning programmed into your bracer.

"Your medical records relate an implant in your vocal cords that should supply adequate voice modulation. Enrik at Station Five on the lower wardroom deck has some comparison files—you can practice emulating her annunciation. And the mask, well, it's not perfected and it doesn't hold very long yet," Elzbieta cautioned. "But it should be adequate for your needs."

"Yes," Vailetta returned her gaze to the mirror, squinting at the unfamiliar image. "I suppose it will have to be."

"Your first fitting went very well."

A timer sounded.

"Hold her please, Mr. Wicek."

While Mr. Wicek's strong fingers adhered her to the chair, the facial image split and curled away, leaving strips of synth skin hanging from her clammy face.

"Pretty," commented Mr. Wicek, releasing her.

"Itchy," Vailetta wrinkled her nose. "I hope the final effort smells better than this."

"Where would be the fun in that?" laughed Mr. Wicek.

"Behave, you two. There's plenty of work to be done before she'll be genuine. Vailetta, I'll expect you back in the morning for your second fitting. Say, oh six hundred? Does that fit your schedule?"

"I'm all yours, for the time being."

Vailetta walked away in a daze. She heard the brisk scuff of her boots clicking along the cera tiles of the hallway. She took a shortcut behind the main docking bay, sliding between force generators massive carbon dioxide scrubbers. She stepped carefully over the guide rails for the sliding gantries. Two parallel halls ran directly from the docking bay to the emergency surgical theaters. Side corridors bustled with wounded and attending medicas. The transfer of wounded from the Second Fleet was still in progress.

She turned the corner and felt an uncharacteristic blast of heat. A string of portable plasma heaters lined one wall, protecting the wounded from the chill of the ship. Triage had left those with lesser wounds here in makeshift rows of hovering lighters, with some men sprawled out on the floor. Medicas knelt over patients talking in quiet tones, tending to soldiers with stepe-bandages, temporary dressings that would be carefully removed in the medical bays. Assessments were tapped into clipscanners and relayed to the E2 where TacOps would process the data and reassign surgical medicas, prepare operating theaters, and update battle rosters for the next drop.

A flare of white fabric separated the wounded from the main hall. Vailetta stepped by a long line of lighters. Her breath came in short bursts as she glanced past bloodied faces, limbs at odd, unnatural angles, and sightless eyes. The last held her attention, a new conscript by the looks of him, a mere lad. Too young to be robbed of his eyes, to need sight frames sewn in. But no, there was something in the resigned way that he sat on the lighter. Vailetta paused, her cape flaring around her shoulders and settling against her back in a whisper of fabric.

The boy had not been recently blinded. There were red blurs on his temples—the mark of electrodes. He must be a suli driver; most of the slug runners preferred to be hardwired into their tanks, giving up sight for enhanced perception in broader spectrums. Visible light was said to be too narrow during dirtside combat. The pilots sought to see everything from the machine's perspective. She steeled her stomach. It had been his choice, or his family's choice, perhaps pressed for resources on some backwater rock, facing famine, or worse.

A medica was seeing to him now, moving gentle steel tentacles along the boy's limbs, probing with wispy sensors to search out hairline fissures in bones. After the swift exam he removed a stepe-bandage that covered a gash along one shoulder. He raised a laser and pressed it against the boy's skin.

"There won't even be a scar," the medica hummed.

Instinctively, Vailetta's arm shot out to stop the artificial. "Leave that one."

The medica looked at her strangely. "The soldier is wounded."

"It'll heal just fine—a little scar tissue maybe."

"It will leave a flaw."

"Out," ordered Vailetta. The medica swept his gaze over her uniform and fastened on the golden dragon clasps at each shoulder that held her cape.

"As you command, Captain of the Guard." The medica bowed obsequiously, not about to argue with a human of rank, no matter how illogical she may seem.

"Captain?" queried the soldier, his sightless eyes turning to her.

Vailetta dipped her head to the left and drew aside her hair. A fine, serrated line slid from her hairline to a spot just behind her right ear. She carefully grasped his hand and placed it against her temple. His fingers splayed against the faint texture of the old scar, following it.

"But, why? I don't understand."

"Close combat. They iced it and stuck it back on."

"The whole ear?"

"Mmm-hmm."

"And the one who did it?"

Vailetta pursed her lips. "Iced him in return."

The soldier seemed to consider this. "Your first?"

"Yes, always the hardest. I keep this scar to remind me of my mortality. It could have been me."

He felt along his wound. "I'm not sure, though." He paused and then ventured, "Captain? Were you scared?"

"Yes, at first. You're not human if you're not scared." She took a deep breath. "It goes away after awhile. There'll come a time when you even miss it—the rush of it, the frisson of battle. It happens so much you forget to be scared, and after a few years you feel your humanity slipping away bit by bit as well. You keep that scar; it'll remind you of how you felt now—scared, feeling lucky to be alive, not yet numb to the killing."

"But we fight for the dragon."

The Emperor is just a man, she thought. "He's not always around to protect us."

"I felt him today. Out there. He was with me. I sensed a presence, a *rightness.*"

Another one lost to conviction, she knew. At the beginning of each battle, TacOps called up a personal visit from the Emperor, an iconic image of their leader intoning, "I see you…" to which the ranks shouted back, "One will!"

She remembered the eeriness of her first outing into combat, how shaken the false visit had left her, how angry she'd felt even as the synthetic adrenaline automatically pumped into her system to support and augment the visit. But then, the Emperor was special to her in other ways. The artificial stimulation conflicted with her real emotions about the man. It felt like a violation.

Of course the Emperor could not be everywhere at once, could not oversee all the soldiers in his empire. But those about to forfeit their lives did not fight for a mere man, they fought for a dynasty, and the *dragon* that ruled it—a man that had become an icon, and the icon now represented the man. Despite the cunningness of the strategy, it still left her uncomfortable to hear the reverence that soldiers felt toward their Emperor.

"You earned your Badge today?"

"Yes, I finally got time dirtside." He seemed elated, despite the obvious discomfort the wound created.

"Where are your sight frames?"

"Ah, Captain. You should have been there. We met heavy artillery, broke through the line and got in two waves of Shockies. Then a blast. Some A-4, felt like. I mean, some runners talked it that way. Blew us into the stone hedge. Turned us right over. Suli came right apart. Pieces tore through. Cracked my frames but good. I'm waiting for replacements now. Don't mind though, don't mind much at all. They get to be a pain, you know, this constant pressure. It's nice to be in the dark for a while. Feels free. Like a long sleep. A dream with sound on the edges but no picture. You understand?"

"I think I do," she said gently, placing her hand on his good shoulder. "Do as you please, soldier, but this ache will keep you sane if you leave it. It will bring you back to this moment, when it was all fresh, when the dark liberated you, when the dragon surrounded you and brought you through."

"Yes, of course. Captain of the Guard, I should like to know your name."

"Vailetta Strom."

"Vailetta Strom." He rolled the words across his tongue like an exotic flavor. "Why did you stop for me? Someone like you—well, you shouldn't even bother, should you?"

"Yes, I should. There's a story behind every name we send out into the field to live or die as fate and skill decide. If we become blind to you, grow deaf to the stories, then we lose touch with the dragon, and ourselves."

"You're going to be a general someday. And I'll be able to say I met you. I bet even then you'll have that first badge around your ear."

"Dragon save you, Captain."

She pulled her hand away from his shoulder as though burned, then repeated sadly, "Dragon save us all."

AN OFFICER'S QUARTERS were hardly lush, but could be considered spacious by any of lower rank, especially by those squeezed into the sleep slots of the barracks. Aboard Imperial ships, space was allotted by the cubic millimeter, with every bit earned in service. Vailetta had waited a long time for the promotion of a room upgrade. It was a relief to return to a private place that allowed her to stretch.

Like all officers' quarters it contained a sleep slot, datacore station, wall lockers, and two chairs that shaped themselves out of the floor when needed. She had replaced the standard illumination with free-floating glow globes from Larrus Alcan 5 that brightened slightly at her entry. A brocade tapestry that looked to be a reproduction of a famous design hid the wall lockers. Only Vailetta knew it was the original, a bow to her past, the only visible clue to her royal lineage. *Know where you come from. Never forget.* She stepped up to the lockers and the tapestry swung aside with a gentle whoosh of air. Touching the dragon clasps at her shoulders, she allowed the cape to slide to the floor. A hook inside the tidy locker compartment reached out to retrieve it. A glow globe floated past her shoulder, humming softly. It made a circle of the room and finally paused over the data desk where two others joined it.

Vailetta sank into a chair that rose to meet her, finally allowing her body to unwind. As the glow globes gently circled above her, she called up a screen to check on Gany, her personal art. Her system connected immediately with TacOps, which then located the art on a calibration exercise deck, performing what the artificial referred to as a fire dance.

Vailetta's personal art matched her height, surpassed her strength, and mirrored her beauty in an unusual way. One of the few art series designed to teach applied laser combat, Gany was encased not in the smooth, deco look of most arts, but under a surface composed of thousands of hexagonal mirrored tiles, honeycombed and arranged like glass scales, reptilian and breathtaking. Her almond eyes stared a fathomless black, seemingly all pupils. Her eyebrows were drawn in thin gold ridges, her mouth, eyelids and other features delineated by tiny, mirrored beads that moved like liquid over the contours of her face.

Observing her assist in action never ceased to delight Vailetta. Gany's fluid, soundless motions led a dance of light around the combat room. Turning a corner, the artificial "blacked" her mirrors, reversing the silver backs so that, for a moment, she appeared a light-absorbing shadow that between one millisecond and the next shimmered translucent, a grey outline as transparent and hard to follow as a fading, shadowy sketch.

As laser fire arced toward her, the mirrors undulated back and forth between substance and air, appearing as mirrors to deflect and direct return fire before flipping to camouflage once more. On Gany, distinct areas on her body could instantly turn concave to deflect shot away in the direction of her choosing, protecting her comrades from ricochet. Vailetta had experienced moments of envy and longing for such a skin, while Gany, apparently, coveted her hair.

Gany was a miracle of engineering and Vailetta lamented that the creation of the Ganymede series was outlawed at the end of the Art Wars, with the remainder bonded to loyal members of the ambassador corps. Gany had been a gift from her father, one that Vailetta had reluctantly accepted, if only to put his mind at ease that she was safer with such a formidable assist.

Pausing in her routine, the art came to attention in front of a floater eye. In her quarters Vailetta smiled. Gany always knew when she was being checked.

"A fortunate mission, mistress?"

"Most fortunate, Gany. I'll fill you in on the details when you're finished."

A wistful look twisted across the small beads of Gany's features. "Perhaps you are ready for ablution then?"

"Yes," Vailetta sighed, the pain in her lower back a spiral that drug her deeper into the chair. "Sign off."

"At once, mistress."

The screen blanked and Vailetta dozed, half listening to the barrage of reports coming over the squawk box that she'd ne-

glected to silence. An updated List was repeated. The mono-
tone recitation of the dead included no one close to her. She
took in a painful breath and exhaled sharply. The anonymity
of the List was as relieving as it was disturbing. Like a patina
of reality, the numbing drone of faceless names tinged the final
moments of her day, underscoring the price that was being
paid by all those around her, the price exacted by the dragon to
carve out a meaningful existence, to create order and balance
in a universe of uncertainty and chaos. She wondered if she
would ever again experience, in the service of her father, a day
without death.

5

HUMHAL

THE DOOR TO THE BRIDGE ROSE UPWARD WITH AN ABBRE-
viated snap-hiss, caught partway and stood half-open, like a
drowsy eyelid. Garrand abandoned the manual release and
ducked his shoulder under the door, bracing his feet beneath
him. With a hard shove the door scrolled completely open. He
stepped cautiously onto the gangway and peered into the dark,
silent hollow. He felt as if he had just walked into a crypt: command pods were frozen in place, datascreens were blank, no
colorful sartographs floated in midair and not a single internal
light burned within the crystal globe. Instead, the bridge was
illuminated by a haunting stellar effervescence. Murky starlight
silhouetted the gangly internal superstructure and suspended

pods that hung like wisteria within a giant terrarium. Garrand could just make out the slender form of his first mate sitting in one of the pods with his back to him. Muted reflections shone off one side of his burnished surface. He, too, appeared silent and defunct—powerless like the rest of the ship—but Garrand knew he must have heard him enter.

"Do you think you might have told me when you shut off the ship?" Garrand demanded incredulously. He tried to keep an icy tone from creeping into his voice.

Bailey spoke without turning, "Good morning, Captain. I trust you slept well after your long day."

"I slept lousy," Garrand groused, "not to mention I was accosted in the middle of the night by a psychotic panda."

"Oh really?" This piqued Bailey's interest and he turned to look up at the human. "What did he want?"

"Who knows? He pounded on the door until I woke up, then just wandered in like he owned the place."

"How interesting…" Bailey mused. "Perhaps he was trying to tell you something."

"Yeah, maybe he was at that. There's something peculiar about these bears…"

"My research shows that technically speaking, and all appearances aside, the pandas are not
    bears."

"Yeah, yeah," Garrand mumbled, "so I'm told. They're more like overgrown kula felines if you ask me. Too smart to be bears."

"They do seem very bright," Bailey agreed.

"Yes, suspiciously so," Garrand sighed. "Anyway, I was having a nightmare when it happened, so the disturbance wasn't all that bad—woke me up at least."

Bailey's expression was hidden in darkness, but his voice registered a half-octave lower, as if he was keying in on a particularly arresting observation. "You say he woke you from a nightmare?"

"Yeah, but there's no way he could have known I was asleep, much less where I was or even who was behind the door he was pounding on. Like I said, it was just weird."

"As you say, sir," his tone was polite, but Garrand knew that the art hadn't dismissed the notion that the panda had acted out of some sort of heightened sensitivity. Who was he to argue? It was too early for one thing, and there was still the matter of the ship's powerless state.

"Bailey, perhaps you can tell me why we're adrift and why I wasn't informed."

"You were asleep. *Destiny* and I had things well under control."

"Umm, she seems to be asleep herself…"

"Temporarily."

Garrand made a cluck-clucking noise with his tongue at the roof of his mouth and stared out at the swirling gasses that streamed by the ship, headed for the giant abyss that loomed off the port bow, a dark splotch amidst a vivid field of stars and ionized gasses. "Hmmm, well then perhaps you can explain why we're within the grasp of that, what? Class three?"

"Class two."

"Excuse me, class two embryonic singularity, and powerless to boot."

"Escaping detection."

"Escaping detection, eh?"

"I believe that was the primary thrust of your orders when you initiated my irrational subroutine."

"Well, yes, but I was hoping that you weren't going to destroy the ship in the process."

"I took a number of calculated risks."

A number of calculated risks? Garrand shuddered at the thought.

"If I erred, I erred on the side of 'not being detected' rather than on the side of 'keeping the ship completely safe and being detected.'"

"I'm sure she loved that," Garrand chuckled. "Might that be why she is now without a vote?"

"She did voice some displeasure with my decisions."

"I bet."

"However, her incessant complaining did not play a part in my decision. All primary ship's systems were shut down to avoid any random Imperial scans. As a result, we are essentially a lifeless hunk of debris being sucked into the Krestyaninov Cluster, not worthy of a second glance."

"Well, not entirely lifeless. There are thirty-seven pandas, two humans, and one smelly exel aboard—not to mention the rats and other assorted vermin that crept in with all that dirt. Life scans would show that."

"Life scans would only be initiated if the long range scans turned up anything on the electromagnetic or quantum spectrums."

"Hmmm," he wasn't completely convinced, but it was an interesting ploy. Dangerous, but interesting. He gazed out at the nearest white dwarf that was drawing the ship inexorably closer. The star was abnormally faint for its white-hot temperature. Its mass was that of a standard X-4 sun, but with the greatly reduced radius of a small planet, and a central density about one million times that of water. Having exhausted its nuclear fuel, the star was in one of the final stages of stellar evolution, slowly being crushed by its own escalating gravitational forces. The white dwarf had not yet compressed and collapsed into a singularity, though at this proximity it was just as deadly as the black hole it might someday become. He thought of his ship spiraling helplessly into the fathomless gravitational vortex and a chill crept up his spine; the silly programming had almost worked too well.

Resembling a bright emission nebula stretching three hundred light years across, composed primarily of hydrogen gas ionized by the presence of the cooling dwarves, there was actually little known or recorded about the Krestyaninov Cluster. The treacherous reaches were skirted by all but the foolhardy—though tales of renegade pirates who struck from the cluster's depths were common, and, all things considered, not at all improbable. Any ships that haunted the region would know the intricate threads of opposing gravitational forces from years and years of practice, navigating the broad reaches from memory much more efficiently than pursuant vessels. It would be a perfect place for pirates to retreat and affect repairs.

Garrand breathed a sigh and rubbed the sleep from his eyes. A halo of gaseous material, glowing from the radiation emitted by the nearest star, rotated in a slow death spiral around the white dwarf as it was pulled into the collapsing star's core. Without power, *Destiny's Needle* would soon follow suit, incapable of producing enough thrust to escape the mounting gravitational bonds.

"Don't you think we might want to start powering back up? We're getting awfully close to that white dwarf."

"I calculate that we have three hours before we reach a point where our reactors can no longer generate enough power to achieve a viable escape velocity."

"Startin' her up may prove a little tricky."

"I have run over three hundred trillion simulated restarts embracing every possible contingent failure and found that the engines could be brought back online within forty-five minutes, regardless of other failures."

"Well, I guess that leaves us time for breakfast. I assume you've begun plotting—"

"Breakfast!" a voice shouted from over Garrand's shoulder. "Are you crazy?"

Garrand cringed at the harsh sound of Helen Tchelakov's voice.

"And good morning to you, too," Garrand said crisply, determined not to loose his temper this early in the day.

"Why are we powered down?" she demanded. "At first I thought you had the audacity to lock me in my quarters, but it seems the power is off all over this clunker. Has it finally succumbed to the inevitable?"

Garrand briefly closed his eyes. "Don't be ridiculous. Bailey has been performing *maneuvers*." He added a sly emphasis to the final word and looked down at his friend.

"Maneuvers, huh?" she shook her head.

"Yes, he seems quite proud of the results, too."

"Proud? He's about landed us smack in the middle of that— that *thing*!" she wavered, shaking her finger at the white dwarf that loomed ever closer off the port bow. "By Haven, look at it!"

"Yes, it's lovely isn't it?"

"What is that? A class five degenerate star?"

"Class two, I think"

"It's not large enough."

"No, we're just that close to it."

Helen's eyes grew wider. "What are you doing? You dumped us into a class three singularity and powered down?"

"Class two," Bailey corrected her.

"We're heading back out, right?"

"Captain, if we backtrack at this point, there's a strong probability that the Imperials will detect our presence," Bailey said.

"Of course we're not going to scurry back up the way we came," Garrand responded. "There's a hungry slort at the top of the burrow just waiting for us to come running out, scared and confused."

"You're taking us through that?" Helen sounded even more indignant.

"Why not. In theory, the cluster is navigable by anyone."

"In theory?" she nearly choked over the words.

"It's a little risky, but I'm confidant *Destiny* can wend her way through."

Helen persisted stubbornly: "The presence of so many overlapping gravitational fields means that we can't make any jumps."

"Yeah, we'll have to crawl through using the sub-light drive, but that'll give us time to plot a proper course on the other side." Garrand sounded confident. He turned to look down sternly at her. "You do intend to tell me where we're going now, don't you?"

Helen blew a short blast of air between her teeth. "Yes, of course I do, but you're not even *doing* anything," Helen accused, her eyes flashing past him to the white dwarf.

"Nonsense," Garrand replied. "I'm about to have breakfast."

Bailey smiled and turned back to his command board.

"You seem to be taking this awfully lightly," she snapped.

Was there a little fear in her voice? Perhaps the stress of it all was catching up to her.

"Calm down Miss Tchelakov, we're in no danger at the moment. In fact we're probably safer right here than we've been the whole trip."

Helen pursed her lips, unconvinced.

"Better crank up some of the internal systems, Bailey. Jean-Wa's probably pretty mad already—you know how he gets when he doesn't have power in his kitchen. A few systems shouldn't make much of a flutter."

"As you wish, Captain."

"Come along, Miss Tchelakov. We'll see what our good chef has concocted for breakfast." Helen looked at him warily, but allowed him to lightly take her arm and lead her out of the bridge.

LIKE THE MOST diligent of torturers, Jean-Wa was sweating the vegetables. Not a movement in the plate escaped his gaze. "Ah, you are giving in, my lovelies!" he cried with relish.

A large black and white head poked around the corner, peering into the kitchen. With a bulbous, wet nose sniffing delicately at the host of aromas, a full-grown panda took a cautious first step inside. Jean-Wa was oblivious to his new guest as he whipped a bowl of galp eggs into froth. Feeling more confident, the panda wandered further into the kitchen, her broad shoulders and hips grazing tables on both sides of the narrow aisle as she ambled lazily along. The tables were at just the right height for sniffing and it wasn't long before she had nosed over a bowl of batter that had been set aside to rise.

Jean-Wa turned in surprise and all six arms shot out to their full extension when he caught first sight of the enormous panda.

"Oh my!" he exclaimed. "You are quite a beast!" He regained his composure and wheeled over to confront the intruder.

The panda paid the artificial no heed, having plopped down to give serious attention to the contents of the upturned bowl.

Her nose was stuck completely inside and she busied herself licking up the sticky batter.

Jean-Wa tutted as he stopped next to the panda. "Well aren't you the hungry one this morning? You like Jean-Wa's recipe, yes? It is even better *after* it has been cooked," he said, snatching the bowl away from the panda.

"Mrrrahh," the panda moaned, making a hasty lunge for the bowl.

"No, no, my friend. A hungry stomach I can understand and a healthy appetite is good, but you must wait, just like the rest. Now shoo! Out of my kitchen before you make a real mess."

"Nnnngggggghhh," the panda complained as Jean-Wa rolled closer. She rose to all fours and backed out of the aisle. She reached the entrance and paused, eyeing another bowl perched on the corner of the nearest table.

"No, no," Jean-Wa admonished, but it was too late. The panda reached up with two paws and sent several pans of rising bread toppling to the floor.

"Out, out with you!" Jean-Wa cried making a beeline for the table, arms waving overhead. He grabbed whatever utensils he could find and began clattering them against the steel tables as he wheeled forward. Surprised by the noise, the panda galloped out of the kitchen.

"Yes! Make hasty flight, you brute!" cried Jean-Wa, brandishing a set of enormous soup ladles.

The panda caromed around the corner, knocking Helen off balance as she entered the kitchen and completely upending Garrand who hit the deck with a grunt of displeasure.

"What in K'ye's name was that?" he muttered from the floor.

Helen could not conceal a smirk as she helped him up. "Lively bunch, aren't they?"

"You sure they're not dangerous?" he asked dubiously.

"Do they look threatening to you?"

"Yes, actually, that one looked quite menacing as it ran me over."

"I assure you, Captain, they are docile—not to be confused with servile, mind you—but sweet and harmless... for the most part," she ended slyly, watching his expression waver.

Garrand dusted himself off and stomped into the kitchen. Jean-Wa was scolding Humhal for letting the creature inside: "Shame on you! You are required, I think, to be keeping *out* the new arrivals. They are our guests, of course, but they need not venture into the kitchen. The fur, it will be everywhere. You should have your circuits examined."

"Go easy on him, Jean-Wa," Garrand said, patting the end of the cold steel where Humhal was recessed. "He has so few pleasures in life."

"But must he torment me so?"

"I think that qualifies as one of his 'few pleasures,'" Garrand replied, trying to keep a straight face.

"Bah!" Jean-Wa whirled away and resumed beating the eggs with a renewed vigor. "My big day arrives and there is no one who wants to help Jean-Wa," he muttered as he cracked eggs with his free arms. "They all want the delicious foods, the steaming janda, the delicate pastries—but do they offer their assistance? No!"

Humhal slid partway out of his slot, nudging Garrand's back. "Morning," Garrand called over his shoulder watching the spectacle with amusement. "He's in rare form this morning, isn't he?"

Humhal chimed agreement.

"Look at all this food," Garrand shook his head in amazement. "You'd think the Emperor Himself was coming for breakfast."

Helen, who had been observing this exchange silently, spoke up. "They're not going to eat this."

Garrand gave her a questioning look and Jean-Wa swiveled his head toward them though he pretended to keep working.

"I'm sorry," Helen said, "but they're not going to be interested in all this. This is food for humans. They might eat a little fruit, some sweets maybe, but this?" she swept her hand across the room. "I don't think so."

Humhal gave an electronic double burp that sounded amazingly like, "Uh-oh," and slammed back into his slot. Jean-Wa could take no more. He withdrew his eggbeater and waved it at the humans. "Out! Out! Everyone out!" Egg scattered everywhere as Jean-Wa shushed them out of the kitchen. "If you are not going to help and have nothing nice to say then out with you!"

Garrand cringed and ushered Helen out of the kitchen with an outstretched arm. "See you later Humhal."

The door croaked softly.

"Yeah, sorry," Garrand apologized. "This ought to be interesting," he murmured to Helen.

She looked up at Garrand as they walked. "I'm just telling it like it is," she said defensively.

"It all right. Jean-Wa's just a little sensitive to critics. Why don't we just wait in the mess?"

"What's up with that door?"

"Humhal?"

"Yeah, who ever heard of naming a door?"

Garrand frowned to himself. "I didn't name him — that's just who he is."

"Someone must have named him," Helen persisted.

"Well, most things get named when they're created, don't they?"

"Most sentient things do."

Garrand shrugged, "Yeah, so?"

"A sentient intelligence? Bonded into that matrix—as a door?"

"He was part of the package—came with Jean-Wa."

"Sentient doors?"

"Cost efficient. Remember, he came from a *shai* stronghold. If you have a smart door, you don't have to hire a guard to monitor it and keep the wrong people from passing through. Plus they make better decisions. Ever been kept out of something by a pre-programmed door?"

"Hardly," she muttered, wondering if he was insulting her abilities.

"Exactly. But a sentient door that can figure out what you're doing—makes it a lot harder to hack into when the door can think for itself."

"I see," Helen nodded.

"So what's it doing in the kitchen?"

"He's an integral part of Jean-Wa's kitchen. Besides, *Destiny* takes care of her own security."

"Most of the time," Helen needled him.

Garrand ignored her. "I guess you could say Humhal is Jean-Wa's best friend. They have sort of a love-hate thing going on, though truth be told, Humhal has his core set on becoming a tailor."

"So why don't you humor him?"

"That little door," chuckled Garrand, thinking fondly of the twelve hundred kilo slab. "He's a dreamer."

"You gave Bailey his freedom." She sounded accusatory, as though he was playing favorites.

"Know anything about *shai* strongholds? The security extends to the kitchen, even. All doors self-wipe their data cores under tampering—that's in case some outsider tries to interrogate one—find out patterns of movement, who goes where at what time, that sort of thing. Giving Humhal arms would cut off his head, so to speak."

"How awful. Does he know?"

"Yes," Garrand laughed. "It keeps him in that sour mood and he, in turn, ruins the babas, which are actually quite good when they work. Believe me, if I could transform him I would. Amazingly enough, he has found a way around it. He struck a deal with Little Bit. My Turkle Sphere covets the pressed alleve oil Jean-Wa keeps for marinating. When Humhal lets him in for a raid, Little Bit takes an order for some suit or fancy hat or some such. Little Bit passes the order on to Bailey who adds it to his port accouterment list for our next stop. Once the fabric is onboard, Humhal threatens the babas until Jean-Wa condescends to put his poultry shears to the fabric. For someone who never trussed up anything but meat, he's a fair hand at stitching. In fact, he sewed me up once."

"Really?"

"Sure," Garrand rolled back his sleeve and flipped his arm for her to inspect the fine line that ran to his elbow.

"Perfect," she admitted, eyes wide.

"Meat is meat to Jean-Wa. He doesn't see any difference between stitching me up and preparing a roast. But he hates tailoring, complains like the lowliest conscript."

"What are the results? Surely not what you're wearing!"

"Haven's no! But there's a solar sail fabric suit hanging by my bunk and quite a gallery of flashy headgear. I'm required to don them on occasion to show I'm in the spirit of things. Bailey has been known to throw on a headwrap or two, as well."

Helen giggled.

"It's quite a community effort."

"Can't wait to see it."

"Stick around Tchelakov, you'll see all kinds of things strange and wonderful."

That she did not doubt. Nothing, she thought, could be more unexpected than Garrand Ai'Gonet Médeville in person.

6

THE GREAT
BREAKFAST BATTLE

SID WOKE UP AND IMMEDIATELY WISHED HE COULD FALL back asleep. The forward cargo hold smelled terrible. He stretched out his arms and legs and tried to crack his back. He sampled the dry, recirculated atmosphere that was blowing into the chamber and recoiled. He was wrong: it smelled considerably worse than terrible. He shook his head and shut his nostrils. The soft scents of El-Bouteran's lollasa pine and crisp, moist mountain air were now only a memory. Stale, under-oxygenated air was being pumped into the hold. It was laced with acrid-smelling oils, hydraulics, and reactor coolants. Though the deck was nice and cold beneath his paws, the breeze was tepid and devoid of any humidity. Looking up, there was no sky upon which to gaze. There was no freestanding water in which to bathe. This was not the way to start the morning.

His whole body felt sore and cramped from trying to sleep on the cold steel deck. He twisted his neck one way and then the other, listening to the vertebrae pop. Most of the tribe was already awake he discovered, though some were still curled up against the bulkhead. Sid shook his head and tried not to think about the dismal sleeping arrangements. Something had to be done about this. They would have to spend the day rearranging the tribe's equipment in the aft hold and begin constructing suitable dens and nests with a portion of the bamboo.

The large panda stood and shook his fur. His coat felt natty and matted, a far cry from the perfect grooming that he was accustomed to. He bit at a tangle of fur to no avail. There was not much hope that it was going to get better any time soon. There had never been any freestanding water on any of the world-ships that he had journeyed within, and he doubted that this one would be any different. No dewy leaves to run across his back, no cold mountain spring pool to soak in, not even the expectation of an early morning thunderstorm to look forward to. Morning was an important time for Sid—he was a creature of habit. The quiet period of grooming before breakfast offered a chance to reflect upon the futures that he had dreamt of during the night and gave him a chance to prepare for the emotional and physical rigors of the day ahead.

Aboard the world-ship, his ritual was shattered. Adding to his vexation, a simple interpretation of last night's dreams eluded him. A panda and her mate bid him good morning as they extricated themselves from the tangle of arms and legs and bodies that surrounded them. Sid snorted in return, trying to muster as much good nature as he could. There was not much he could do to preserve the illusion of privacy, especially with the whole tribe in such close quarters.

He made his way toward the entrance and with typical promptness, the young cub Alexander sauntered forward to greet him. Sid found his good humor return as the cub approached. With characteristic warmth, Alexander rubbed his forehead against Sid's shoulder, his little legs too short for him to reach any higher. The cub's fur was matted with dirt and grime from his ordeal the day before. He gawked up at him with big, round eyes framed by caked-on mud and twigs. Sid put aside his narcissistic concerns and bent his chin to the cub's nose. He licked at the dirt around Alexander's eyes and began to patiently groom the young panda's face.

Alexander squirmed uncomfortably, complaining about the unnecessary bath. "Ktttch, grrr-da tcht'tcht!" Sid muffled an internal smile—the youngster's arrival marked the official beginning of his day.

"Tcht-grrr bha'grehl," Alex grumbled with more determination, the alveopalatal clicks and growls knitting together into surprisingly smooth and sophisticated sounds. Despite the rough textures of some of the deeper tones, the combination of reedy ululation and percussive clicks lent the panda dialect a complex, velvety quality.

Sid stopped and gazed down fondly at Alex. "In Strahlinvek, if you please," the older panda said, annunciating carefully the strange human words. It hurt his tongue to speak for length in such a foreign manner, having to over-vocalize every single sentiment, where a simple growl or flick of a whisker would do.

Alex rolled the muscles around the base of his neck and ground his teeth, doing his best not to show his dissatisfaction. He gave a short snort, "Brrglh."

Sid's ears straightened and his whiskers sank a fraction — but enough for Alexander to take notice. The cub's ears twisted back and he swallowed under the reprimand.

"Good morning, Elder." Alexander spoke well for one so young, but he did not look happy. He chewed over his thoughts. "Why must I say things the human way?"

"If we expect to live and thrive in the many star-worlds of the humans, then we must learn to speak in a manner that they can understand."

"Why can't they learn our speak?"

"Our *language*," Sid corrected him. "Because their vocal chords are incapable of producing the proper sounds. They lack the genetic implants that allow us to properly communicate in human languages."

"The what?"

Sid paused, and licked at a whisker, trying to think of a reasonable translation. "Tcht-ktt tst'rrr," he explained in clicks.

"Oh," Alexander mumbled. "It seems unfair."

"Hardly. We are but a tiny minority. If we are to succeed, we have much to learn — and you must practice."

"It hurts my mouth," Alex complained, stretching his jaw out and sticking out his tongue.

"We must learn to adapt. Grandfather lifted us thousands of generations ahead of our evolutionary forbearers —"

"— You don't have to lecture me, Elder. I've learned the songs just like the rest."

"Well then you should know that with self-awareness comes responsibility, and with responsibility comes study. You want the tribe to thrive, don't you?"

"Of course," Alex sighed.

"And you want to be able to experience the *tromaveint*, don't you?"

Alexander peered up at Sid with sad, apologetic eyes. More than anything, he yearned to control the seemingly random and brutal images of the future that plagued his dreams. He, too, wanted to see tomorrow's tomorrow and help lead the tribe along the Path of Fate.

The cub's remorseful expression was all the response that Sid needed. "Well there is much we have to learn—all of us. And you can do your part by learning your Strahlinvek. It is a commonly accepted trading language, and it is a good place for you to begin."

"Yes, Elder," the little panda murmured, pronouncing the alien words carefully.

"But remember, you must observe silence at all times in front of the captain." Sid gave the young cub a stern look.

Alex turned his head downward. "Yes, I'll remember. But how am I supposed to practice if—"

Sid growled impatiently. "We must not endanger ourselves unduly—the more who know of our existence, of our intelligence, the more difficult the path becomes. We must preserve our identity at all costs. Already we flee for our lives like frightened t'chumba, depending on the wisdom of others to ensure our survival, as if we were helpless, fragile flowers."

"But the captain is not a danger! Already he has shown that he was willing to—"

"—No, I will hear none of it! The Elders have made a decision: silence. When the time is right, he will know."

Alexander was unimpressed, but he held his tongue, knowing that any response would bring a harsh reprimand.

"Come now, let us adjourn to the world-ship's mess."

"Mess? Something needs cleaning?" he moaned, the thought of work at so early an hour conjuring an intolerable dismay.

"No, no, it's like our lyceum. This mess is an eatery, a meeting place. Only smaller."

"Oh," Alex said with relief, "in that case, let's go!" He cantered out of the hold. "I'm hungry," he called back over his shoulder.

He joined the long line of pandas winding their way into the mess. The room was filling up quickly. Alex rocked back on his haunches and sniffed uncertainly.

"Where is the bamboo?" He looked up at Sid imploringly. "We did bring the bamboo, didn't we?"

"Not that you would know," Sid poked at him, "since you slept through the whole loading procedure. But, yes, there is an abundance of bamboo aboard. However, as this is our first official meal of the journey, I'm told the world-ship's *thola* chef has labored through the night to prepare for us a formal *laphaesta*."

"A *thola* chef?" Alexander asked excitedly. "Metal folk are aboard?" He could barely contain himself. The rules of behavior were not nearly as strict around the mechanical creatures as they were around humans and other bios. He would have someone to play with.

"Yes, there are three, but you still must be careful. These are not simpletons, they are full sentients and they report to the captain."

"Yes, Elder," he said, careful not to let his whiskers perk up. There was still eagerness in his eyes.

"In the meantime, we must honor this *thola* by eating all that he has prepared."

Alexander wrinkled his nose at the prospect. "Will he be serving bamboo?"

"I find that very unlikely."

"Bey'hah," Alexander groaned.

"Hush now," Sid growled softly.

THE CAPTAIN ESCORTED Helen into the central mess and found it already occupied. Garrand stopped in the arched entrance and frowned. There were five pandas lounging on the couches and six more on the deck. More were sauntering into the room through the aft serviceway. One vaguely familiar-looking cub was sitting innocently on a datastation terminal.

Upon seeing the captain, Alexander's eyes widened and his whiskers stood up.

"Gher-ahn," the little panda brayed, hopping off the terminal and galloping over to the human. With a yelp the panda charged into the captain's legs, grabbed onto his trousers with his claws and began to haul himself up. He scurried up until his nose was even with the man's face. He gave his rescuer a wet greeting.

"Aagh," Garrand snorted, twisting his face away. "Good morning to you, too." He found himself scratching the cub's head despite himself. "Enough now."

Sid growled at him and Alexander let the captain loose, dropping back to the floor.

Garrand let out a deep breath and inspected the central chamber. The pandas were everywhere. "Great," he sighed.

"What?" Helen looked at him with a plaintive scowl. "You didn't expect them to spend the whole trip in the cargo hold did you?"

"Well, actually…"

"They're not doing any harm right now."

"Right now?"

Helen paused to scratch one of the giant pandas behind its ear. Garrand felt his shoulders sinking. He made his way into the mess, careful where he placed his boots, not daring to step on any of the resting pandas. He stopped in front of one panda who was sitting upright in one of the chairs. The panda was watching him carefully.

"What's the matter, Captain?"

Garrand just stared at the giant creature. The panda's eyes were hypnotically large and the creature's soft, wet nose and calm expression made it seem gentle enough, but it's jaws were massive and long, curving claws jutted out beneath the furry paw which rested on his clipscanner.

"Captain?"

"Well, he's in my spot."

"Oh please, you can't be serious!" Helen shook her head at the ceiling, hands on her hips. She gave a sharp whistle. "Shakra! Cht-cht!"

The panda hesitated for a moment, then eased forward and half-fell, half-clambered off the chair, brushing silkily against his leg as she passed. Shakra took several slow steps over to Helen and looked up at her expectantly. She patted the panda's head.

"What can I say? It's his ship…" This apparently satisfied the creature, for it continued on out of the mess.

Garrand made a brief show of brushing the hair off the chair and sat down heavily. He picked up his clipscanner and wiped it against his chest. His comtab chimed softly.

He thumbed the relay. "Little Bit, have you found that trace yet?"

A sharp screech hissed through his collar.

"All right, all right—where are you now?"

A sonorous melody of tones and chimes followed.

"Okay, I'll be there after breakfast."

Two pandas walked over to Helen and growled softly up at her. The younger of the two began to click and rumble in their soft guttural dialect. Sid looked up sharply as he heard the panda's question and Helen felt a similar stab of panic. She fought the impulse to glance over at the captain, an anxious furrow creasing her brow. Instead, she glared hard at the pandas, whose whiskers sagged under her stern eyes.

She casually rolled up the loose sleeve on her left arm and twisted the bracer into view. An interpretation of the panda's question scrolled dutifully down the screen. Unable to resist, she flicked her eyes across the mess and breathed a mini-sigh: the captain was engrossed in his clipscanner. She dropped her arm back to her side and looked back to the waiting pandas, shaking her head softly.

Helen knelt down as if to give the panda a friendly scratch behind his ear. "Not now," she whispered hoarsely. "You have to attend a formal *laphaesta* first. Bamboo later."

The panda began to twist away from her with a disgruntled snort but Helen held him firmly by the ear. "Remember the rules," she hissed. "You're supposed to be a simple exotic, incapable of speech!"

She rose back up, beaming a falsely sweet smile down at the panda. More and more pandas were entering the mess and most were clambering up onto whatever surface was available. A few whispered clicks and purrs back and forth.

The rising commotion distracted the captain's concentration; he was trying to ignore the intrusion into his morning routine, but this was too much. He set down his cherished morning clipscanner and sat back in his chair, crossing his arms. Pandas filled the mess. Some tussled back and forth, playfully biting at back legs and trying to push one another off the acceleration couches. For a bunch of refugees they were awfully rambunctious, he mused. But then, wouldn't he be, too? He was trying to keep an open mind about this first day with new passengers. New, very unusual passengers. Passengers with long claws and sharp teeth. Some thought in the back of his head told him that there was more to all this than met the eye. Still, the thought of all the fur that must certainly be finding its way into delicate ship systems was almost more than his patience could bear. Most of the equipment was touchy as it was, not to mention that when *Destiny* woke up she was going to have a fit when she felt all these fur balls roaming around her innards. They might not get anywhere after that.

Garrand picked at the corner of the clipscanner where a dent had exposed some internal wiring and absently thought about their current situation. The ship was being sucked into a white dwarf, Little Bit still hadn't found the Imperial trace, and Tchelakov still hadn't told him where this 'cargo' was being delivered. And yet something more profound still gnawed at him as he watched the pandas tussling. He had a flash memory of the wind demon leering over him just before the big panda awakened him. The hairs pricked up reflexively on the back of his neck—the memory made him suddenly glad to be awake.

Shifting his eyes around the room, he tried to decide if he could recognize the panda who had wandered mysteriously into his room. He could not be certain as he studied the dark eyes of each creature. They all looked foreign to him. He realized he was holding his breath and forced himself to exhale.

"Breathe, old man," he whispered to himself. The image of the wind demon faded as he watched the carefree behavior of the pandas. Suddenly he was glad for the company.

A clattering din rose in the outer serviceway leading to the kitchen. Meal chimes sounded and Jean-Wa rolled into the mess pulling a serving cart behind him piled high with lala wheat cakes, ramekins of freshly whipped butter and tall urns of sticky-sweet syrups. "Breakfast is served," Jean-Wa trumpeted with pride.

At a command from the artificial, a long, curving table rose up out of the floor, displacing several pandas who scattered in surprise. With amazing speed and dexterity, Jean-Wa reached beneath the cart and extracted two-dozen plates and accompanying flatware and spun the crockery with grace onto the table. Within seconds the table was set and the dexterous chef began buttering and tossing the round wheat cakes onto the plates with all six of his arms. Soon the table was piled high with the steaming breakfast cakes and the mess was filled with their aroma. With a final flourish, Jean-Wa wheeled around the table, pouring syrup continuously onto the plates in one great swooping arc.

A low bench rose on either side of the table.

"There's no way they're all going to fit at this table," Helen said, arms crossed in defiance.

"Or even fit in the room," Garrand observed, trying to remain casual.

"The holds, they are much to full!" Jean-Wa exclaimed. "They are in a sorry state, and in no condition to host such a splendid offering," he spread a pair of arms wide. "This will have to do for now. The rest—they may eat in a few moments. Not to fear, Jean-Wa has prepared enough for *everyone!*"

"Everyone?" Garrand asked carefully. He knew of his chef's penchant for over-estimating the appetites of his guests. "How many did you actually make?"

"Agh, Capítän! You worry so. Our guests, they are enormous, are they not? And they must eat, mustn't they? We are not running a slave crueller here!"

"Jean-Wa," the captain's voice was beginning to waver.

"The exact number — it is unimportant," the artificial looked to the pandas. "Come now my friends, breakfast is served. Come, come," he ushered two pandas to the bench by waving his arms behind them. "Eat, you must eat!"

To Garrand's surprise, one by one the pandas stepped up onto the benches and sat themselves down at the table. They did not push, they did not crowd, and they only sat one to a place setting. Garrand frowned and glanced around the mess. The remaining pandas sat calmly watching the proceedings. It was as if they were waiting their turn, Garrand thought, running his hand across the scar at the base of his neck. He walked to the head of the table and sat down on a bench that rose dutifully out of the floor.

Helen took a seat at the opposite end him, taking time to carefully fluff out her napkin and place it on her lap. Garrand made no such attempt. Despite everything else, he could always count on Jean-Wa to fix a splendid meal and this breakfast looked to be no exception. He cut into his stack of lala cakes, dipped them into a pool of syrup that was forming at the edge of his plate and forked the whole oversized bite into his mouth. No one else was eating, he noticed.

The rest of the diners shifted uncomfortably on the low benches, shoulders pressed up tightly against one another. The giant pandas loomed over the table, heads hanging down to sniff the strange food. Most glanced uncertainly at one another, but paid little heed to the steaming meal before them. Jean-Wa wheeled anxiously around to the captain's head of the table.

"Capítän, you must encourage them—they are not eating Jean-Wa's fabulous and especially prepared lala cakes." The dismay was paramount in the artificial's voice.

"Wha'dya want me to do?" Garrand groused, mouth stuffed full with the sweet concoction. "Feed 'em myself?"

"Set for them a good example," Jean-Wa admonished him.

"I'm eating, I'm eating!"

"You must eat *more!*" he cried, wheeling around and heading back for the kitchen to refill his cart with more breakfast cakes.

Garrand looked around the table at the pandas and then to Helen, seated at the opposite end. She shrugged one shoulder and cocked her head flippantly. Garrand knew what she was thinking. He chewed his lip and glared at her. "You heard him—they're hurting his feelings."

Helen rolled her eyes. "Oh, just give them a chance at least," she sputtered. Lifting a cake on her fork she waved it in Garrand's direction. "They've hardly had a chance to figure out what it is yet. They'll try it," she shot an icy look at Sid, "I'm *sure* they'll try it."

Sid caught her look and sighed, staring back down at the strange brown and yellow food. It did not look organic at all. He was sorry now that he had told Alexander that he must eat what the *thola* had so honorably prepared for them. It looked so soft and unappetizing, like a golden mold or some sickened moss. Yet, he could not disgrace the tribe by turning up his nose, nor could he insult the *thola* chef. *Tholas* had been instrumental in their escape three months earlier from the desolate outpost on Iimgjan. They'd all be slaves to the Imperials' wishes by now was it not for the noble sentinels of steel.

Mustering his courage and doing his best to ignore the sickly sweet odor that assaulted his nose, Sid lowered his face down to the plate, held his breath, and licked cautiously at the top of the brown substance. He pulled his tongue back in, smacked it delicately against the roof of his mouth and found to his surprise that it did not taste like mold at all.

"Terr-eigh ba rrrrgh," Luesta murmured, announcing her surprise as well.

The sticky concoction on top of the brown disc was actually a pleasant sweetness, not at all like the over-ripe zoe berries that had to be consumed on Foguhl's Point when the bamboo supply had dried up. He began licking the surface of the meal in earnest.

The rest of the pandas, seeing the eager acceptance of their Elders, began to cautiously test the surface of their meals as well.

"No, no, no!" Jean-Wa exclaimed wheeling back to the table, abandoning his cart. Eager tongues slurped up the melting butter and generous pools of syrup. "No, no — the sweet syrups are to *complement* the rough, hearty texture of the wheat cakes. They soften the cooked exterior and add piquancy to the cakes' peasant charms."

The pandas paid him no heed. They were all were licking the lala cakes dry and nosing the cakes aside to get at the butter and syrup that had dripped over the edges onto the plates themselves.

Jean-Wa wheeled hastily to the nearest panda, and reaching over the surprised panda's shoulder, began to cut up the discarded lala cakes into bite-sized pieces with a pair of arms. Scooping up a mouthful in a fork, the artificial tried to feed it to the squirming panda.

The panda resisted noisily and pushed away from the table, upending his plate in the process. Lala cakes flew across the mess smacking three pandas in the face. The rogue panda escaped down the hall as a roar of appreciative clicks and growls applauded his nifty exit. A victim of the errant lala cake used a claw to pick the disc off his nose and flung it across the table at his neighbor who was clicking his tongue and snorting at him.

Laughter from deep in the panda's thorax rattled the crockery and echoed through the mess. The mood was infectious. Several pandas began to shovel the lala cakes toward their neighbors; others went for distance, spinning the cakes clear across the chamber.

"No, you mustn't," Jean-Wa protested, but it was too late. The clatter of plates and the roar of happily combatant pandas heralded the first great breakfast cake battle aboard *Destiny's Needle.*

Garrand sat stock still in his chair, a half-eaten bite still lodged in his mouth, and watched the calamity unfold. He was mesmerized with disbelief.

Helen stood up and backed away from the table, shielding her face from the flying lala cakes. *By K'ye, he'll space them all,* she thought as she watched the captain. Thankfully, no errant disc spun his way, but still she bit her lip as she watched the scene play itself out. Garrand looked over at her without moving his head. He cocked one eyebrow at her.

"The stress must finally have gotten to them," she offered pitifully.

He finished chewing slowly and dabbed his mouth with the corner of his still unopened napkin, placing it back on the table when he was through. He pushed himself away from the table, stepped over the low bench and walked toward the aft doorway.

Helen felt her shoulders tighten as he paused by her side.

He spoke deliberately, without turning to look at her. "This is yours…"

Cringing unconsciously she could only begin to venture, "Mine?"

"Your mess, your problem."

"My mess!" she exclaimed, beginning to gather her normal poise. "I told you they wouldn't eat this. Talk to your overly ambitious chef over there."

"Let me be perfectly clear," he cut her short. "I don't want to have to repeat myself. This is yours. If you don't want me to handle this, then I suggest that you do."

Helen bit her tongue. Garrand skipped his gaze briefly back over the mess and then departed. His boots rang down the corridor.

Once she could no longer hear the captain's footsteps she screamed at the top of her lungs. "Jhakavet rhuge!" She used the Seivolt Kambus tongue that many of the Elders would recognize all too well from the days of their captivity on Holus R'vhell. She stamped her boot against the deck plates and the sound rang through the mess.

The furor slowly abated and with chagrin most of the pandas stepped back from the table, clambered off the bench and disappeared down the serviceways.

"Oh, no," she called. "Not so fast." She grabbed two pandas by the ear. "I'm not cleaning this up and we're not leaving it for that poor artificial to do. Sid, you're staying too!"

Several pandas growled at each other and three small cubs stayed behind as the rest of the pandas slipped out of the mess. The five pandas began to gather up the sticky lala cakes.

"That's better," Helen nodded. She drew the adult panda, Porturaut, aside. "Make sure everyone's in the forward hold in forty-five minutes. It's time for injections." The big panda nodded silently. Helen sighed audibly and then added, "We'll make sure to unload some bamboo then as well."

The panda went back to work. Helen took one last look at the carnage in the mess and retreated to her quarters.

Sid and Alexander were the last two pandas remaining at the table.

"I hate waking up to someone else's nightmare." Sid complained as he lapped up the residue of syrup from an empty plate.

"Bad dreams last night Elder?"

"Hrrrgh. The worst." He picked at his teeth with a long, curving claw. "And not even my own."

Alexander frowned at him. "What do you mean? Is this something I should learn?" he sounded anxious.

"No, I'm afraid I don't quite understand it yet."

"If you told it to me, I could help you with the interpretation," Alexander offered.

"Not this time, little one. This is my burden to carry. But I think there is more to this journey than a simple relocation."

"You speak of the Path, Elder?"

Sid grunted noncommittally. "I must spend more time with our Captain," he said with a reflective twist of his head. He remembered the wind demon towering over the human's fragile form. "Yes, this is a problem I must solve myself. The captain may have more to do with the *seitparen* than the Elders suspect.

The Path of Fate? Alex stopped licking and stared at Sid carefully. "You think the captain knows something?"

Sid shook his head. "I'm not sure, but I don't think it's what he knows. It's what he's done—the experiences he has to impart. And, what he's going to do. I believe our fates are inter-twined," he said mysteriously and then began licking his lips carefully so as not to miss any of the marvelous sweetness. He closed his eyes, seeking temporal insight.

Alex wanted to ask what he meant, but he knew better than to disturb an Elder when he was divining the meaning of a dream, a fragment of possibilities—particularly when it in-volved the *seitparen*, an unavoidable event that would someday come to pass, irrevocably shaping the tribe's future.

❖ ❖ ❖

"LITTLE BIT BELIEVES HE HAS LOCALIZED THE TRACE," BAILEY spoke softly to Garrand, watching the lines of stress crease around the captain's eyes.

"Good, we'll continue pushing through the Cluster on the sub-lights and disable the trace as soon as we confirm that it's not rigged."

"Very well."

"Tell Miss Tchelakov that I want to see her on the bridge in half an hour—it's time we learned where all this is taking us. No, wait," he stopped Bailey and paused to think. "You go help Little Bit, I'll go find her myself."

"As you wish," Bailey turned to leave but hesitated. "Captain, there's no need for concern. Once we've disabled the trace, the likelihood of Imperial capture will drop dramatically."

"I know Bailey, but it's more than that. Nothing has been as it seemed since we started this haul. I can't get over the feeling that we're getting in further and further over our heads. Those pandas," Garrand sighed. "They're not..." he struggled for the words.

"Perhaps you should get some rest Captain. Little Bit and I can handle things for a few hours."

Garrand shook his head. "No, I won't be able to rest until I know where our next destination is. It's time to extract the next mystery from Miss Tchelakov."

Garrand found her unloading a silver-cased pallet from a small lighter outside the forward hold. He leaned over to help her lift the pallet and caught a swift reproach.

"I can get it myself," Helen declared tersely.

"Suit yourself." Garrand stood back and let the woman heave the big case by herself. She staggered over to the portal and stood waiting impatiently. The door did not automatically open. She looked over her shoulder with disdain.

Garrand absorbed her sour look with aplomb, reflecting only the slightest hint of a bemused grin. Helen huffed and tried to hitch up the case to get a more secure grip.

"It's all right, *Destiny*, you can let her in," Garrand called softly toward the portal. The door scrolled upward.

Helen shuffled forward and set the pallet down with a thud just inside the hold. "Your ship is psychotic."

"Hardly," Garrand replied smoothly. "You physically disabled some of her systems back on El-Bouteran, you temporarily fused one of her external portals and you locked off a refueling node. I'd be surprised if any door opened for you for the rest of the trip."

"Great."

Garrand shrugged, "What do you expect?"

"You're right, I shouldn't be surprised. Nothing's been exactly standard Imperial liner fare so far, why should I hope for anything different now?"

"Hey, we've been through this before. If you wanted a choice Imperial liner with all the amenities, you should have taken one. Or I can drop you off when we refuel."

"Refuel?"

"There should be an Imperial liner stopping at Eemon Nores sometime in the next four or five months. In the meantime, I suggest you make amends with *Destiny*. I catch you hacking into ship systems again and I can guarantee you a spot on that liner."

"What are you talking about?" Helen asked in confusion. "Eemon Nores?"

"That little stunt you pulled back on El-Bouteran means our first priority is refueling. Bailey and I have been over the Sartoks, the best option relative to our position once we navigate the cluster is Eemon Nores."

"Surely we don't need to refuel now. There should be more than enough to get us to…" she trailed off.

"Yes?" Garrand edged closer, his voice a menacing growl. "To where? How can I calculate how far our reserves will get us if I don't know where we're going?"

"Captain," she said plainly. "I'm completely prepared to brief you on our next objective."

"You'll do more than that," he stepped forward, placing an index finger on her chest. "I want a full itinerary logged into the ship's navi by eighteen hundred—all coordinates, star systems, updated trading schedules for all major approaches, gravitational disturbances, anomalies, the works. I know you have it all worked out, and if you don't you'd better get started. Plus I want a full mission profile detailing all your contingencies, secondary planetfalls—*everything*—and I want that loaded into the Sartoks before dinner as well. Do you understand?"

Helen stood her ground, quietly assessing the captain. "As you wish," she said calmly.

Garrand started to turn away, but spun back. "And don't feed me any cheplus about my 'need to know' or my jeopardizing security. I've earned my badge and the right to know. This my ship and—"

"—Captain, I said I would do it. Now would you give me a hand here?"

Garrand eyed her suspiciously. Was she capitulating just to lull him into some sort of complacency? Or was she having a genuine change of heart? He frowned but bent down to lift one end of the pallet.

"Where exactly are we going?" he asked.

"We're headed to P'tymor. Outer Reaches, the T.R. Gope system." She squinted up at him. "Can't we get there comfortably without refueling?"

The Outer Reaches, Garrand mused. His mind raced ahead, trying to make some connection between the pandas and the Gope system. He could think of nothing immediately that could shed any light on his cargo. "Probably," he murmured as he did some rough quantum calculations in his head. "But we're cutting it close once we're there. And if we have to get out in a hurry the problem will only be compounded. I'd rather stop now while the Imperials seem to have lost our track than risk waiting until we have no choice but stop with a battle group breathing down our necks."

Helen conceded: "I see your point." They hoisted the container. "But why Eemon Nores?"

"Because once we get to the far side of the Krestyaninov Cluster there aren't that many nearby systems to choose from— Eemon's relatively close by. It's not conspicuously remote, and I have an old connection there."

"Ah."

"The proprietor owes me a favor anyway, several favors as a matter of fact."

"I see."

Garrand stole a sideways glance at her to see what her tone implied, but her expression betrayed nothing. If she was patronizing him, she was doing it with subtlety for once.

"Eemon Nores isn't exactly an out of the way backwater," she said. "These days it's a reputable trading planet. Tchagen Forpes keiretsu operates incorporated agro caritus over a quarter of the planet's surface. There's three sizable spaceports on the northern hemisphere alone, to process the growing volume of food shipments. You sure you want to set down in such a visible place?"

"The Imperials will have eyes at every backwater landing facility on every desolate rock within a hundred systems of El-Bouteran. The illicit fuel dumps aren't safe right now, not even the ones where I have established ties. Besides, any loyalty to a fellow Freetrader will dissolve in the face of Imperial credits. There's bound to be a hefty price on our heads by now. Plus the fear of Imperial reprisals if it's discovered that someone harbored us—a platoon of Shock Troops makes a convincing argument. No, our best bet lies in anonymity. On a medium-sized trading planet like Eemon without Imperial ties and dependent upon a keiretsu for protection and tax revenues we've got a much better chance of slipping in and out without ever causing a stir. It's harder to keep tabs on a busy place than a quiet, deserted one."

"That may be true, but the Imperials are bound to have listeners in every port on Eemon."

"Yeah, well, Imperial agents can't keep track of every single ship that comes and goes. Besides, we won't set down in a major port. We've got nothing to trade that would make such a place desirable. All we want is fuel, and there's a little family-run agro on the southern hemisphere that has just what we need. Their compound isn't on any of the usual planetary vector maps—it's just a little private drop."

"Big enough for *Destiny's Needle?*" she asked dubiously.

"Just."

"I didn't know there were any agro caritus on the southern hemisphere."

"Yeah, there's a few. Not much profit in large-scale operations, what with the ice and cold, but some families have been harvesting the blue ice lichen for generations. You do it right, keep maintenance costs down, there's a pretty good margin in it."

Garrand watched Helen carefully unload a set of burnished instruments from the insulated packing. He recognized only the sleek, ominous form of an arterial injector wand. The pallet yielded several more trays with tightly stacked vials mounted vertically within the high-impact housing.

"That's quite a setup," Garrand commented.

"It's expensive stuff," she said, referring to the hazy-colored vials.

"What's in it?" he asked, extracting a vial from the tray. He held it aloft between thumb and forefinger and shook it gingerly. The liquid contents were viscous and murky. "It's not dangerous is it?"

Helen grit her teeth beneath her smile as she watched him examine the priceless vaccine. "Of course not, it's just a simple serum." She didn't take her eyes off the captain. The man was full of surprises: she couldn't discount the possibility that he might have bio-medica analyzer aboard for some bizarre reason, hidden away like the nearly extinct seedlings. If he slipped a vial out and discovered its contents then all bets would be off.

"Serum, huh? They're not sick are they?" he frowned with concern, though for once she couldn't tell if it was concern for himself or for the pandas.

"You have nothing to fear, Captain. It's nothing you can catch."

"That's not what I meant," he snapped. He watched the curious creatures as three separate groups began unloading pallets of bamboo. Under the watchful eye of a large panda, a dozen individuals lined up to drag the long, loose shoots toward the open aft portal.

"Where are they taking the giant grass?" he asked casually.

Was that a little snipe about her misleading him with the cargo of bamboo? "They're making sleep nests in the aft hold," Helen said still watching the vial in the captain's hand.

"Oh," he mumbled, watching the silent progression. "Quite industrious."

"Mmm, yes," she made an effort to continue unpacking.

Garrand smiled wickedly as he watched her bend over, feigning disinterest in him. With a calculated slip of his fingers, he let the vial tumble from his fingers. The little tube spun end over end toward the deck. Helen winced visibly as she looked up. At the last instant Garrand caught it on the toe of his boot.

Helen forced a furious smile. "Break all you like," she said, making a point of smoothing back her hair. "Long as you're willing to deal with all the panda vomit."

"Vomit?" The vial rolled precariously to the edge of the leather.

"Of course, you do have sweepers aboard. It's not really so much the quantity anyway, although there is that, but the smell. They practically had to scuttle a ship after the Bryant run. Pandas really weren't constructed for space travel after all."

Garrand plucked the vial from the toe of his boot and gingerly handed it back. "I'll leave you to it then."

An uneasy feeling crept into his stomach as he watched Helen prepare her instruments. The pandas that were not unloading or dragging bamboo out of the compartment were sitting quietly in two orderly rows against one wall. The cubs, who were usually full of an almost endless supply of energy and rambunctiousness, sat calmly still as well, watched carefully by an older panda.

Garrand scratched at the back of his neck. He remembered a vaccination of guillan livestock two years earlier—a short haul inter-system, but enough to pay for a new lighter and half a dozen doppler drones. The livestock had resisted bitterly as the ranch hand had made his way through the herd, administering the vaccine. Each beast had to be held down by two arts before the ranch hand could get his wand against their skin. These pandas didn't look like they were going to resist.

These were not dumb animals, he reminded himself. However, this didn't look like any doctor's visit that he could remember from his childhood either. He had always been terrified of going to the clinic, and would do almost anything to get out of it. Yet these creatures sat patiently awaiting their medicine, well behaved and serene almost. Did that make them more intelligent than humans, he wondered, or less?

"You know," Garrand mused, half to himself, "you'd think they'd have already gotten sick by now."

"It's just a precaution," Helen said as she loaded a vial into the wand. She stepped over to the nearest panda who looked up at her sadly, pressed the arterial injector against his neck and depressed the control stud. The serum hissed into his bloodstream.

Helen patted the panda on his head and shushed him off. The next panda sidled dutifully forward. Having Garrand here made her nervous. It was bad enough having to hide the truth from the pandas, but now having to give a new, and separate cover story to Garrand merely complicated matters, as well as making her look suspicious in the eyes of the pandas. But she knew that the captain would never be satisfied with the explanation that she used for the pandas. They were far more trusting.

Still, she wondered why in fact the pandas had not yet discerned the truth behind their weekly injections. Had they not seen their own future? Or had they not traced part of the problem back to her 'serum'? She had a constant fear that in fact all her plans were destined to fail for the simple reason that the pandas had not yet seen a future where her plan had succeeded and thus were unafraid.

7

BARRETT'S BANQUET

THE ASSASSIN TORG STRODE SILENTLY AND QUICKLY
through the broad central corridor which ran under the *Shiva's*
central spine, headed for the sartographic array buried well
below the artificial quarters on gregson level six. Torg turned
the corner leading away from the tubes, expecting to find only
twin guards ensconced behind armored paddocks at the end of
the narrow serviceway. He immediately slowed his pace.

A small crowd was gathered outside the *Shiva's* central vault,
a shielded chamber deep in the heart of the ship. Within the
vault lay the battle cruiser's vast and complex neural nexus, the
E2 datacore. The assemblage of men and women milled about
awkwardly before the entrance to the great vault, broken into

a half-dozen groups of naval and marine officers who calmly spoke amongst themselves.

Torg picked his way silently through the officers, most of whom grew silent as he passed, casting sidelong glances at his back. Commander Arnas and two of his lieutenants were discussing something in a low tone just by the entrance. The sentries in their raised paddocks on either side of the hall were clad in full Trioxin, eyes invisible behind their opaque helmets, though Torg could feel their rapt attention.

Arnas stepped before Torg as he tried to key in his access code to the vault's entrance under the watchful eye of the nearest sentry.

"Captain Strom said that she does not wish to be disturbed. Apparently, she is not in need of any help," Arnas said in a belligerent tone.

Torg paused to glance at Arnas. The Commander must be disturbed that the Captain of the Guard had been given the run of the ship, including unlimited access to the vault. And by all likelihood, Vailetta had told Arnas in no uncertain terms that she did not need or desire his brand of expertise.

Torg narrowed his silver eyes. "I'm sure she'll want to see me."

Arnas did not budge. "She was quite specific. The woman believes she can track down the criminal Médeville by herself."

Torg felt a prick of anger that cut short his need to enter immediately. He relaxed his combative stance, relaxing his arms and chest and allowing his body to ease back a step. The soldiers closed in around him.

"Criminal?" the assassin asked in his most inviting tone.

One of Arnas' lieutenants caught the look in Torg's eye and placed a hand gently on his commander's shoulder, but Arnas stepped out from under the man's warning grip. The screams from El-Bouteran were still fresh in his ear.

"I've read the dossier, I know all about his *noble* past. But he's scrounged Carinaena's Shell for over a decade now and he's sunk to the lowest level, becoming nothing better than a common criminal. He has no honor, the dragon he once served is dead to him now."

"Dragons beget dragons," Torg said, his voice quieting those around him. "You cannot undo the soul of a man. He has lost one dragon and gained another."

Arnas snorted in derision. "One does not trade dragons. There is but one dragon that rules," he turned and pointed a single digit at Torg, his lips curled back in disgust. "One Emperor. One dragon. One will. He betrayed the dragon, now his honor is forever lost."

Torg shook his head. "He did not betray the dragon. The dragon betrayed him. He did all that was asked of him and what did he get in return? A medal? The Emperor's blessing? No. He was dismissed. Disgraced. Turned out into the cold of space leaving behind all he ever knew—all he ever loved. Spared only his very life." His gazed fixed upon Arnas. "What would you have him do?"

Arnas glared at the assassin.

Torg continued softly, "He still fights for a dragon," the assassin stroked the edge of his cape and whispered, "He just doesn't know it."

"I don't understand," Arnas protested.

"You say he has lost his honor, that his spirit is weak." Torg's voice rose. "If he is but a common criminal scrounging the Shell for profit, then how is it that he has eluded your capture?"

Arnas tightened visibly.

"Not only eluded, but roundly defeated—what was it, two? Yes, two of your platoons. Now how is it that a man, a single man, could defeat two platoons of the finest Shock Troops at your command if he has no honor? Do you truly believe that a man without spirit, without a driving force to propel him inexorably forward, could do battle with you and triumph?"

It was Arnas' time to control himself. He let his gaze drift upwards and stared silently at the ceiling, hands clasped behind his back. "I told you. He had help. He brought a wraith."

"And how do you think he came by that wraith!" Torg bellowed. "He didn't just purchase one at market!"

"He must have captured it himself."

"Exactly! Can you imagine that? Capturing a wraith? Are you going to tell me that a man without honor—a man that fights without the spirit of the dragon breathing fire into his heart and lungs—that such a man could face a creature that sucks the very life force out of men, a creature that is not even alive by our standards, and capture it!"

"I could do it!"

"Exactly. And could you do it without honor?"

Arnas' head sank a fraction. "Your point is taken."

"You should be careful by what means you take the measure of a man," Torg growled, lingering only for a moment to canvas the eyes that watched him. He keyed in his access code, waited for the door to sluice into the floor, and swept into the shadowy vault.

VAILETTA LOOKED UP with surprise at the sudden intrusion.

"Assassin, how good of you to drop in."

Torg took a moment to let his eyes adjust to the relative darkness. Dazzling star charts whispered overhead in a gigantic sartographic representation of nearly two-dozen systems near

El-Bouteran. The omnipresent hum of the E2 sent a mild harmonic coursing up the heel of his boots as he examined the dozen or so individual projections that floated lazily over the captain's table. Within a few seconds he understood her current line of speculation.

"Captain," he bowed curtly. "What is the good word?"

"I'm afraid I don't have much to offer in the way of good news right now."

"There is still time," Torg offered. "*Destiny's Needle* cannot go far without refueling."

"Yes, that's what I'm counting on. I hope to send a team to each of the planets with the highest likelihood of a landing and then pick up the trail from there."

"And the E2 is trying every possible system?"

"Within a given sphere. Dasko calculated a maximum radius from El-Bouteran. We've narrowed that volume further given the serpentine route he's adopted."

"Remember, El-Bouteran is a very remote planet, far from standard shipping lanes, colonies, civilization of any kind. He'll have less choice than he prefers about which route to take, and little choice but to stop in one of the first viable systems."

"The question simply becomes, which one."

Torg studied the sartographic overlays. A toad chirped restlessly from within one of his great pockets and the assassin reached in to retrieve it. He cupped the blue and red creature in one hand, stroking its toxic skin with the back of a gloved finger, finding comfort in the toad's rhythmic breathing.

"I would not rule out the nebulas along Pearson's Rift," his arm traced through the luminous volumes that hung in static splendor above them. Looking at the command board, he took the control spike and eased the sphere forward. New star systems winked into existence. Torg scanned them silently, one by one. "Or the Hosphurs in the Banglias system."

Vailetta stretched her neck to one side. "Hosphur would be an obvious choice. Heavy elements in the outlying asteroid belts would mask most quantum scans. And the trace might not read there."

"Yes, the trace," Torg murmured. "He needs somewhere to fall back and remove the trace."

"We got a firm projection of the first nine jumps he made after El-Bouteran—lost him on the tenth." She pulled up the relevant charts that glazed over the old depictions. A strange radiant line wended through the stars, bending backwards in many places, taking sharp cuts through the charts and almost forming an odd three-dimensional shape when viewed from certain angles. The red ribbon of *Destiny's* escape path did not seem to make any sense.

Torg's eyes skipped over the jiggering tassel. "Marvelous. Utterly random I suppose?"

"The E2 can't find any correlation higher than three percent—there's no pattern whatsoever. Médeville must have been flying it out himself."

"For nine jumps? I doubt it. The strain of calculating and executing even four or five would be too much, particularly after the day he had. He would have gotten careless—a pattern would have emerged."

"Well, if a pre-programmed matrix—either the ship or some art—was used to make these jumps, the E2 would definitely have worked out a pattern."

"Hmm," Torg stroked the toad and studied the ribbon. He smiled softly—a devious thought occurring to him. He reminded himself that this was a man who captured wraiths. Torg flicked the control sphere once more, nudging the display to a distant system; and there it was.

"I wouldn't rule out this, either," he said with a pleasant flourish.
Vailetta's eyes flicked across the shining stars.

"What—the Krestyaninov Cluster? Full of white dwarves?
It's not navigable!"

"You must stop behaving like an Imperial officer, believing
all the standard warnings in the Imperial star charts, and start
thinking like a hunted man. The psyche's different. Just because your readout says it's impassible doesn't mean that no one
has ever traversed it."

"Those are only stories—myths. Pirates *want* you to believe
that nonsense."

"Some myths are borne in truth."

"Okay, say he could get there—undetected. Find a way in
and *stay* undetected. He couldn't use his light drive so close to
all those massive grav wells even if he could find enough null
space to navigate between them. He'd have to crawl through
in normal space, picking his way through at sub-light speeds.
Would you use sub-lights when you knew the whole Imperial
navy was after you?"

Torg shrugged, "I merely offer it as a possibility. I would not
rule out the impossible."

Vailetta chewed on the edge of her lip—she was not keen
on dismissing any of the assassin's suggestions outright. "All
right," she began feeding new data and projections into the E2.
"Let's say he *is* in the Cluster. Where would he come out?"

New, highly-detailed charts leapt into existence overhead,
showing the Krestyaninov Cluster as a roughly shaped luminous cloud of stars and gas. A dozen systems stood within easy
reach of the Cluster's volume.

"If he entered the Cluster in a volume that faces El-Bouteran
and is using the mass of the stars to hide himself, then he'll

take the fastest route, confident that no one besides another Freetrader could follow him through—and he'd be right. The fleet will have to go around which will obviously allow him to escape. But aboard a picket cutter, you and your men could nearly beat him to the other side."

"His options will be limited there." She studied the charts and fed a new set of parameters into the Sartok. Four planets emerged over the board. She took a pointer and focused a beam on a large, blue globe. "Ah, Tarkus... that could be a good one."

Torg shook his head. "If I were the good Captain, I doubt I would show my face on Tarkus."

Vailetta turned to Torg, pointer between her teeth and scrunched her nose up at him. "Why?"

"Too remote, too obvious. It practically screams out. Médeville has confidence—bravura. Look at those eyes," he indicated the holocube projection that Vailetta had left on. "He's not afraid of crowds. He wants confusion, excess, throngs of people to mask his insignificant visit. He'll lose himself in the confusion. He's had years of practice manipulating bureaucrats."

Vailetta raised her brows and chewed on her pointer. She pored over the system charts. "So where then?"

"If I were he," Torg paused, eyes flowing over the data projections. "I would slip in here, or perhaps here, Lyst."

"I could have a team on each of those planets, and perhaps here, on Eemon Nores, just in case."

"That's a lot of volume to cover."

"The E2 should narrow it down once it's run through a couple of trillion possibilities, and after I've told it what I want it to look for precisely. And what to ignore."

Torg raised his brow. "Ah, that's the key with these Sartoks: adding the element of intuition."

Vailetta grinned seductively. "A woman's touch is all this needs," she ran a hand along the edge of the terminal. "But it helps having someone around who thinks like an outlaw."

"Glad to be of service, Captain," Torg returned the smile in kind and twirled his cape back across his shoulder as he departed.

❖ ❖ ❖

A LINE OF GLEAMING SAMOVARS EMITTED LONG TRAILS OF scented steam into the bustle of the vice proctor's private kitchen. A team of ten human chefs toiled over the detailed preparations for the diplomatic banquet that evening, a weekly and highly prestigious ritual aboard the *Shiva*. Between them, a scattering of apprentices bustled through the hot vapors, running the odd errand or painstakingly diminishing sauces under the critical eye of a master. Observing all of this from a small oasis of calm by the door stood the assassin Torg, seeming at ease over a minimal helping of spiced, shredded meat served cold and rare. For once his frogs were strangely absent, perhaps in deference to the high-strung chefs, although the creatures could be secreted anywhere in the many pockets on his loose garment.

A servo cart loaded with crème tortes careened around a corner and upended into a bubbling caldron of bitter melon soup. Apprentices scrambled to address this latest crisis. Into the hubbub strutted Colonel Riikesarh of Osakk, a warrior-chieftain newly appended into Barrett's strange diplomatic corps. He spotted Torg, pulled in the ends of his half cape to keep them out of the saucepots, and swooped over.

"But that food's raw, man!" yelped the colonel catching sight of the assassin's supper.

"Full of nutrients," smiled Torg as a narrow ribbon of marinated blood dripped from his chin. He dabbed at it with a pristine napkin. "Keeps me strong."

"So? To your liking, yes?" inquired an apprentice chef, hovering.

"Fennel, anise, red pepper, sweet alcohol, and…" Torg tweaked his fingers at his lips as though turning a key in a lock. "Just a touch of arsenic." The apprentice's face blanched and his adams apple convulsed.

"Most excellent indeed," he commended with a sly twist of his eyebrows. "But not fit for Lord Barrett," he finished pointedly.

"No, sir." The apprentice squeezed out the words before scurrying off in a nervous flight that sent pans clattering to the floor in his wake.

"Good Rysegas, man, he tried to poison you!" sputtered the colonel.

"Nonsense," Torg waved his inflated concern away. "They know my tastes run more to the exotic. But come, you must take your seat now." Inwardly he smiled. This episode would surely make a run through the diplomatic quarters, quelling many a misguided attempt to test his prowess at averting assassination attempts. In every new assignment there was a dangerous period of testing, even if the result wasn't intended to be fatal for his employer. Allies and enemies alike desired to know the full mettle of a man's protection. Sometimes a name alone could be prevention enough. He intended to make it so.

He led the way up a nearby lift into a darkened chamber with a magnificent space portal. Crimson walls enclosed a massive rectangular banquet table of polished cerasteel inlaid with jade and set on carved dragon legs. Flames ran along the center of the table, separate blue and violet spikes that sent a flickering veil up to all seated at the table. Torg's vision adjusted instantly to the dimness, like a mercat hunting in the night. They glowed faintly with a fire of their own. He could see that round-faced Momuso, the crafty official from Anovar's vizierate was already seated, probably due to a complaint of his joints rather than out of discourtesy to his host. General Shecut stood by the window, hands clasped over the signature bone cane behind his back as he contemplated the view and contemptuously ignored the other occupants. Yet Torg could see the muscles along the general's back bunch as he entered the room. The man had an acute awareness of everything that went on. He wanted watching.

At the opposite end of the room, Captain Strom and Lieutenant Dasko conversed in low voices. Torg caught a smattering of military jargon and a reference to himself. They broke off and nodded warily to him before acknowledging the presence of Colonel Riikesarh with halfhearted nods. Battle-tried soldiers tended to denigrate and dismiss honorary titleholders, regardless of their political clout and often to the detriment of their own careers.

Torg sensed the weighty footsteps of Commander Arnas, who entered looking harried. He was tagged by his beleaguered off-bridge assistant, Finsen, who was busy relaying the most recent data from a clipscan visor that partially blinded his real-time vision. Accordingly, Finsen had occasional mishaps with furniture or other unexpected pitfalls of the landscape, like walls. The clipscan visor had been intended for use by artificials, but Arnas insisted on non-tank-bred human assistants. It was not known what had happened to make him so distrustful of any but naturals, although speculation in the officer's lounge had gathered quite a number of ripe theories.

The pair joined Vailetta and Dasko, immediately drawing them into the whirlwind of operational computation. New intersection tangents were discussed and Torg heard Arnas advise Vailetta to be underway with her mission following the meal. The assassin noticed that the Captain of the Guard pressed her face lightly from time to time, as though to assure herself of its stability. He smiled grimly, knowing of her earlier appointment. Well did he remember the uncanny feeling after wearing the lifemask in those early, experimental days. He certainly had no need of one now, not with his body's current capabilities. But despite improvements in the functional life of the device, Torg knew the unpleasantness remained. Looking closer he discerned a scrubbed sheen to the skin along with faint bruising under her eyes. The mask must have burned away then, like a short fuse, remaining stable only long enough to be assessed for fit.

And there, just under the table by Barrett's chair, was the young boy from the antechamber of cages, both knees drawn up, his turquoise eyes fixed intently on nothing. Drazon's arms were clasped tightly around his knees and he huddled into as tight a form as possible, as if shielding himself from the presence of all the Imperial diplomats.

Despite his recent repast, Torg felt his stomach complain with a rebellious burble. He could discern eight different dishes he would like to sample. The aromas from the kitchen below were vented directly into this room to stimulate the appetite and preclude conversation as Barrett preferred to dictate the drama of the evening himself. Even now the two-dozen guests eagerly took their seats at the vice proctor's sweeping entrance. Barrett always sat with his back to the door. It showed his supreme confidence.

At a handclap from Barrett, the mysterious boy brought forth one of the dismal cages from the antechamber, pushing it before him on wheels. After a consenting nod, the boy whisked away the dusty cover to reveal bars surrounding a glorious avian whose feathers shone with the multicolored sheen of starlight reflected through fine crystal. A collective sigh rose from the guests. The boy offered his bare arm to the open gate and the bird hopped to it, digging its talons in. Draz winced but turned and walked around the table so that all could see and delight in the magnificent specimen. The bird stood on four outstretched legs, each ending in three claws that clung to the soft flesh of the boy. The wings, so soft and willowy to the touch, seemed to sparkle with a metallic sheen in the flickering candlelight. Its eyes were soft and brown. Tiny yellow feathers veiled the pupils and acted like lashes to protect from sand and dust. Its golden beak curved sharply downward, like a finely crafted Altera dagger, ending in a sharp point. A long tongue licked out from the beak as it surveyed the table and its adams apple bulged visibly as the bird swallowed.

Draz returned to Barrett's side. The vice proctor smiled engagingly. "A song, if you please," he commanded. The bird cocked its head to one side and complaisantly warbled the most delicious sound. The guests leaned forward. During this display, a silent serving staff dressed in muted charcoal tones to blend with the walls placed the first course, bowls of tarke's fin soup. The delicate golden cartilage brought sounds of pleasure from the diners. More happy sounds ensued when the second course of bada's nest soup arrived. Following that a broth of musta greens was offered to clear the palate. Torg discreetly sampled each dish before it reached Barrett's place, testing for poison.

All the while, the glorious bird sang with a sweetness of tone unequaled in the galaxy. It sang with all the anguish of imprisonment, and all the power of the desire to be free, tempered by a tender forgiveness, a latent acknowledgement of its plight. It sang as though it could hold the darkness at bay with sound alone, bringing tears to several guests.

Even Torg could not ignore the purity of the sound, the cleansing it offered. The song, however, was different from the one sung in the rotunda. This one held an edge of resignation, each perfect note tinged with a haunting despair, as if the creature could sense its impending fate.

Barrett set down his soupspoon. The bird stopped immediately, its last note hanging in the air. "Speak now," he commanded. The bird turned its head from side to side, blinking its shiny black eyes. It tightened its talons on the boy's arm and then snapped its beak open and closed.

"How very clever!" laughed Riikesarh. Barrett frowned. Momuso leaned over and shushed the colonel.

"Quiet, you fool."

"Come, now. Speak little one," coaxed the vice proctor.

"In His Name, we serve. Offer yourself," came the hoarse reply in coarse comparison to the beautifully modulated sound of the bird's song. The guests whispered astonishment, the small miracle erasing the memory of the heartrending song. But the show was not over. Now Barrett grasped the bird delicately at the back of the neck, forcing the beak open. Then he inserted a twin-pronged dagger and ripped the long tongue out with a distinctive twist. With a choked sound the bird arched back against the boy, rending the tender flesh of his arm.

"Where's your glove, boy?" Barrett demanded upon seeing the red welts.

"They don't like it," he grunted, straining to keep the bird against his chest. "The bells frighten them."

"You're in control. They do as you command. If you are to be a proper trainer, you must wear the trappings. Now don't appear before me again without it. You're about to spoil the moment, and I need it." He shot a glance at Arnas, who shifted uncomfortably in his seat.

Barrett held the dagger over the nearest ceremonial flame, methodically turning it as though over a roasting spit, bringing it to his mouth to cool the morsel with a breath before popping it in his mouth. The glorious feathers, shed in panic as the wounded bird struggled in the boy's grasp, floated down among the shocked guests. Then some in the diplomatic section began to flutter-clap their approval.

Vailetta felt her stomach turn and she steeled herself against it. She must not give rise to her feelings here. She tried to remind herself that the tongues of songbirds were a common feast meat, but to kill a creature with such a song, to destroy something on the verge of real communication. Just imagining the time, the energy, the patience involved in training a bird to speak, a bird whose lifespan could outlast humans and might learn to impart a great deal in such a time, made Vailetta want to run from the room. And then to rip the gift out and eat the knowledge, retaining dominance. Her stomach twisted in agony and she fought for control, clearing her mind with a forcefulness she hadn't imagined. In a moment her desires were nulled, and she glanced up to find the assassin watching her closely. She offered a stiff smile and turned to her neighbor.

"Imagine," said Barrett softly relishing the words, turning the bare dagger over the spit—the fire hissing as an iridescent feather floated into its grasp and popped into flame. "You lift a species up only for the moment necessary to properly consume it." At those vile words Vailetta found herself speaking before she was even aware of the impulse.

"Consumption is not an end unto itself," she hesitated momentarily, remembering where she was and hastily added, "my Lord."

"Of course not, Captain," Barrett eased forward, surprised and intrigued by this slight rebellion in his favorite. "It is always but a means to a greater end." He looked about the table, eyes flicking over each of the diplomats and warriors. "And we all serve the same end here."

Riikesarh leaned forward in his seat. "And what end is that?"

The delegate from Fors-tanêsse snorted contemptuously.

"Saikenall, you forget yourself," Tholsen growled beginning to rise.

"No, no," Barrett waved him off. "His pride is still bruised from his old loyalties, but he is free to talk here."

"But my Lord——"

Barrett cut his aide with a vicious glance, "I said no. The man may speak his mind; who better to teach our new delegate the intricacies of Shell economics than one who has so recently experienced the effects firsthand."

The Vice Proctor looked to the glowering delegate from Fors-tanêsse. "Saikenall, if you please; I am most interested."

Saikenall, a tall, broad-shouldered Geihan stroked the fine, amber fur that grew from his cheeks, absently twirling the lengths around one finely manicured claw as he watched the vice proctor. He was still wary of the human's show of benevolence; it had only been one turning of the Loth since Forstanêsse had surrendered—without a warrior carving a single heart, he reminded himself with a sickening sensation welling up in his gut.

He glanced evenly and slowly around the carved table, watching the relaxed humans and T'chell and Larken and Trogands drinking their wine, motions slowed by their reluctance to avert their eyes from the new center of attention. With a sniff he detected no blood-malice in their stares; he cased the faces: interest in many, fear in none. These were not ordinary creatures; culture radiated from their perfumed clothes, fur and polished corpuscles. Intelligence and cunning glowed in their careful eyes, eager to see the newest tripped up by his own insolence. He was told that many of them were new to the Barrett's table, like himself; culled from the finest minds in the falling bureaucracies, appended from conquered worlds to facilitate further conquests. Each new system, it seems, was to have a stake in the new Imperial Proctorialship.

Saikenall saw the wisdom in this, while marveling at the human's sheer audacity at bringing him into his inner circle so quickly, with no Imperial conditioning. There was no begging of loyalty from this one. Still, he was uncomfortable in this alien ship, suddenly privy to the very stratagems that had laid his home world helpless before the human's polished boots. Yet, here he was—proconsul to the vice proctor, traditional Geihan war cloth draped across his ragged shoulder, but with Imperial insignia sewn into the fabric—wondering what he was doing in the very heart of darkness itself.

He grasped his tumbler and filled it to the brim from the wine pitcher, his claw trembling only slightly.

"Where did you say you were from?" he asked Riikesarh throatily as he took a hasty gulp.

"Osakk," Riikesarh said, eyes watching the Fors-tanêssi.

"Ahh, Osakk," he bobbed his massive head. "Like so many colonies and worlds scattered in the great reaches of the Shell, Osakk is, or shall I say was..." he gave the colonel a sly look. "Osakk was not completely self-sufficient, no? You had perhaps one lucrative commodity which you shipped off-world for profit, yes?"

Riikesarh nodded, "Gohanse beans. Our soil is perfect for its vines—the bean produces valuable oils and—"

Saikenall dismissed him impatiently. "And yet you depended on outside shipments of one crucial commodity or another, yes?"

"No, not at all," the man grated indignantly. "We had a very profitable trade arrangement with seven other planets in the system, but it was beneficial to all parties. There was no—"

"Please," grumbled Saikenall in a low tone.

"Well, I'm not sure you could call it a dependency..."

Saikenall looked to Barrett, "Are you certain that you want this in your court. Such naiveté!"

Barrett looked unperturbed as he quietly dabbed at the cold scruge fish with a corner of bread. "He will learn," he said, sipping his wine.

The Geihan whirled back to face Riikesarh. "Could you produce the commodity yourselves?"

"No," the small man admitted, his round cheeks reddening as he grew a little flustered. "We needed the finely-crafted spare parts which the tohl produced to keep our combines running."

"Exactly. You could not harvest the beans profitably without the spare parts from off-world needed to keep your machinery running."

"We have almost completed our first fusion foundry," Riikesarh exclaimed. "Soon we'll be able to supply our own parts."

"Try to stay with me here," he rasped, reaching for the wine pitcher. "You were probably years, even decades away from self-sufficiency. And in steps the Imperials," Saikenall indicated Barrett at the head of the table.

The Vice Proctor acknowledged with a thin, almost paternal smile.

"Once Lord Barrett decided that Osakk was ripe for the taking, it was only a matter of marshaling the huge fleets of Imperial freighters at his disposal and dipping into his vast treasury to carefully tie up the supply of the one irreplaceable resource that you needed. It is usually under the auspice of 'Imperial stockpiling.'"

Riikesarh's face twitched at the phrase.

Saikenall continued, "The Vice Proctor then slowly imposed regulatory tariffs and fees, artificially jacking up the price, limiting the supply, until a monopoly was established. The Imperial fleet is quite capable of smothering any attempt at organized smuggling; all of a sudden what began as a simple dependency has grown into a desperate need. The only supplier of the necessary commodity is the Collistas Dynasty. And guess who is holding the keys?"

The blood was slowly draining from Riikesarh face as the lesson slowly dawned on him.

"After that, Osakk was at the vice proctor's complete mercy. Economic concessions were parceled out to your government, yes? In return for perhaps an 'advisory commission?' Or a 'policing force?'"

"Policing force, yes," Riikesarh said softly.

"More concessions meant a freer supply of the necessary replacement parts, but also a greater Imperial presence. The dependence grew to other non-economic areas. Imperial officials began to regulate all your interplanetary trade, yes? Simple landing taxes soon spread to property and income. The bureaucracy took root and I'm sure it was not long after that 'new elections' were held, hmm?" Saikenall arched his brow.

Riikesarh clenched his jaw. "Yes, Imperial praetors were elected."

"Soon, whole garrisons 'protected' the planet and your independence was a complete illusion—your governing body an Imperial cipher, the soft takeover complete. All Lord Barrett need do is officially declare Osakk and its environs an Imperial fief and he has taken another world." He finished his wine and set the tumbler down. "Without firing a shot."

Riikesarh was speechless.

"Welcome to the empire," Vailetta murmured.

Tholsen chuckled softly.

Barrett turned his gaze back to the young woman. "Captain Strom, you have something you'd like to add?"

Vailetta shook her head softly and looked down at her plate for a moment.

"What do you wish to say, there's no need to be coy here. Your reputation is not at stake—far from it. How do you think you got here? You've earned a chance to speak."

"I merely point out that the proconsul has not answered the question."

"The question?"

"What question might that be," asked the sly Moiren, leaning forward in his seat, one fist clenched around the thin stem of his platinum tumbler, the other clumsily grasping the neck of the wine cruse. He eagerly filled his tumbler, the dark red stains of excess fanning out beneath his fist, absorbed by the white linen.

"To what end?"

"End, what end?"

"Exactly. What end do we serve?" Her fist was clenched on the table's surface. "Have we all forgotten why we toil so hard? Do the names sung in the Great Hall mean nothing! The blood spilled on a thousand planets—our own as well as those who would oppose us—millions of souls sent to K'ye. And you cannot answer a simple question?" her passion flushed her face. She stole a glance around the table, more to avoid Barrett's gaze than to gauge the expressions of the diplomats.

"It is not a simple question," Moiren protested. "There are countless other considerations—"

"—What end do we serve!" her fist slammed onto the table, rattling the plates.

"Minister, allow me," Barrett interrupted. "It is not a simple question, though there is but one simple answer: We serve to quench the hunger of the dragon."

A murmur of approval rippled across the table.

"The hunger of the dragon, indeed," Tholsen echoed.

Vailetta stared at the vice proctor with a look of pure disbelief, but turned her face before he caught her spiteful stare. Torg smiled in his shadows.

"We all serve the Emperor's desires," Barrett continued.

Vailetta's head snapped back. "Really?"

The Vice Proctor's voice rose, as if he were proclaiming holy writ: "The Emperor sent forth his proctors to seed the Shell. We set out to establish an empire in these untamed volumes. We are but a stepping stone for the Collistas Dynasty, a gateway to Carinaena's Shell—through which the spoils of ten thousand systems will someday flow into the Core, to replenish exhausted resources. One day there will be a second great empire amongst the stars."

That much, Vailetta did not doubt, but still the question remained: whose?

"All created in his name!" The vice proctor spread his arms wide and rose, as though to embrace the whole room in his broad vision. He then looked directly at Vailetta, dark eyes demanding her complete attention. He spoke softly this time, "All in his Name, the Unspoken One, the Dragon," he smiled beneficently, lips stained dark with fresh wine.

"I doubt the Emperor has much to do with it out here," she replied smoothly. "No, my Lord, you are free to treat Carinaena's Shell as though it were your very own..."

"Yes," agreed Momuso, his round face beaming deceptively.

General Shecut's bone cane creaked as he pushed himself back roughly from the table and stood. He paced to the giant space portal, limping slightly.

"Dangerous words, Vailetta Strom. Surely the Emperor would not take kindly to such views should he hear of them," objected the colonel, glancing nervously around the table.

"The Emperor is busy solidifying the galactic Core. To all purposes he is content to let the Shell struggle on its own," Saikenall grumbled in a raspy tone.

"He should be careful," Momuso spoke quietly, requiring the others to lean in to hear his words. "Or one day he'll turn his eye this way and find he no longer controls it."

Silence greeted this statement. A single current of tension flashed through the room, like a brush fire; everyone present seemed momentarily frozen in their movements—tumblers paused on the lips, forks hung motionless in midair. Vailetta felt a chill run down her back. The men at the banquet table were held riveted in their places—they exchanged glances across the table, and then slowly each resumed his meal.

The fine hairs at the back of Torg's neck stood straight on end, and all his nerves endings tingled with the electricity and anticipation in the room. His fingers brushed against the cool steel of his blade as he carefully watched the diplomats from his position directly behind the vice proctor's chair, having silently and subconsciously flowed from the shadows—alerted by the tension that had coursed through the hall. It was as if a ghost had passed through the room; Torg reluctantly sheathed his dagger—the prelude of an assassination attempt triggered the same queasy-but-exhilarating sensation in his gut. He wished he could see Barrett's face, but the man's silence offered no clues to his expression.

A crackling pop sounded as Barrett singed the edges of an errant feather, twirling the stem between his fingers.

"In the meantime," Tholsen interjected, breaking the silence, "the trade restrictions are whipping the keiretsu into a frenzy. With free trade nearly impossible they're on the verge of open warfare."

In the background, Torg masked his sudden appearance at Barrett's side by stepping in front of a server. He sampled a new dish then replaced the cover and returned it to the frightened man who departed with it immediately, the dish held before him as though tainted. Colonel Riikesarh leaned over, enthralled.

"Poisoned?" he whispered loudly. "Arsenic again?"

"Not fresh," the assassin replied, flexing a glove with apparent disinterest.

"You mustn't forget," Vailetta warned, "that all of this is made possible by a larger threat."

"The empire?" Solia asked.

"You could hardly call this an empire," Moiren quipped. "Not in Carinaena's Shell at least. There are millions of systems throughout this galactic arm that have never even seen an Imperial ship. At best there are limited proctorialships in some of the better-known sectors, but an empire? I don't think so."

"Indeed." Vailetta sipped at her wine. She licked her upper lip, considering the men at the table. "Have you all really fallen so far? Do you really believe that the base of our power does not in fact lie in the galactic Core?"

"We are all well aware of the power that rests within the heart of the galaxy," Barrett interceded. "And we are all grateful for the chance to serve the interests of that power. It is merely that out here…" Barrett waved his hand casually over the table is if trying to conjure the proper words. "Out here we must rely on different means of achieving the same results. We do not have the resources available to the centralized Core, nor do we have the expansive military base. Without the direct threat of the full Imperial fleet, more subtle pressures must be brought to bear."

"Subtle pressures?" Qui-son nearly choked on the phrase. "The subtle pressure of nineteen dreadnaughts in low orbit over Khelhan is what swayed our High Council."

"Yes, Lord Barrett," Solia enjoined eagerly. "I am most impressed with your naval forces. If the rest of your fleet is as impressive as this task force, I do not see the need for modesty."

"You've never been to the Core," muttered Saikenall.

Barrett raised his hand to silence them. "What Master Qui-son neglects to mention is the Foresallen mining trade upon which Khelhan's economy is dependent. Four centuries of poorly regulated thruck mining without proper seeding of Foresall crystals in the magma had stripped the planet's crust of all but the very last of its Foresallen ore and left the planet at the brink of economic collapse. Without Imperial subsidization of both the planet's mining industry and the entire system's mineral co-dependence, there would have been riots, revolution and massacre on a worldwide scale. The whole planet would have crumbled under its own misery within a few scant years."

The Khelhan representative remained impassive, starring at his dessert plate.

"The empire committed to stabilizing the economy by supplying ore from the Tylals to all the mining guilds at a price only slightly more than it would have cost them to rip it from the crust themselves. And we began a recrystalization plan unheralded in breadth or scope. In a few hundred years, the Khelhalls will be able to mine their crust once more."

"As an Imperial fief."

"You made your choice willingly," Barrett reminded the man. "There's no need for bitterness. I invited you to my diplomatic table so that you might see the broader picture, so that Khelhan would be properly represented in the coming order."

"We had no choice," Qui-son persisted stubbornly. "What could we have done?"

"Oh, please," Barrett chuckled. "The lesser of two evils? How the drink does ply your maudlin side, Qui-son."

"Hardly," the Khelhan slurred as he fingered his tumbler. "Face self-destruction from a starving populace or survive... at a price."

"What price?" Riikesarh asked.

"Submit to Imperial rule. A new charter was drafted. Elections were held."

"Merely a reorganization of a highly inefficient decentralized regime."

"Ahhh... a reorganization," Qui-son mumbled, the wine clearly getting the better of him. "That's what all those ships were for."

"A high profile was necessary to ensure a smooth transition. Rival factions were mounting resistance in the outer belts, the new elections were in jeopardy. I sent the dreadnaughts to assist the Council enforce—"

"—Nineteen?" Qui-son protested. "You really expect us to believe that it was necessary to send nineteen Noee Bend Dreadnaughts? You had enough firepower there to—"

"A precaution," Barrett said, dismissing him. "Our needs are sometimes best served by a direct approach." The Vice Proctor glanced at Commander Arnas. "In any case, as the strength of this proctorialship grows, the empire's presence is strengthened in the Shell, and the fear and respect for the dragon grows."

"As does the size of your fleet," Vailetta remarked. "The Khelhan turned over several thousand vessels. Refit and refurbished, they'll prove a worthy addition to your arsenal."

Barrett looked at the captain of his Guard stolidly, one hand absently twirling his unused dessert fork.

Vailetta matched his gaze with a rebellious stare of her own. "But of course," she announced to the table as her eyes bore into his, "it is all in the name of the Emperor."

A subdued silence held the room for an awkward moment as all the diners looked to Barrett for a response. The Vice Proctor stopped twirling his fork. "Yes, of course," he said flatly. A single current of anger coursed through his jaw as he watched the woman who seemed undaunted by his stare or her lofty surroundings. But the anger gave way to a smile of satisfaction and pride. Was it not exactly this rebellious spirit that had drawn him to this young woman? Should he expect any less from her on her first visit to the diplomatic table?

Barrett stood abruptly, pushing his encrusted chair back with a high-pitched grate. He raised his tumbler high over his diplomatic corps. "Well spoken!" he bellowed. "To the Emperor!"

A bone-chilling screech echoed through the banquet hall as the diners rose as one. Two-dozen platinum tumblers sparkled in the soft, amber light thrown discreetly across the table. Barrett surveyed the proud, confident faces of the men who would someday rule the galaxy at his side. All the men looked to him, a giddy expectance in their eyes.

"To the Emperor!" Momuso cried.

"The Emperor," the table echoed.

Vailetta watched Tholsen as he tilted back his tumbler. As the wine touched his lips, he glanced furtively at the vice proctor. Barrett returned the look, some unspoken message passing between the two men in that brief flash. When the vice proctor lowered his drink, the faintest knowing smirk passed his lips, and then he returned his attention to the rest of the table.

To the Emperor indeed, Vailetta murmured silently.

8

REVELATIONS

THE BIG PANDA, SID, SAT BEHIND GARRAND ON THE
bridge as he studied the navi. His presence was now a daily
ritual. Garrand wished he could keep the creature from grinding his teeth on the thick green stalks that now littered every
deck on the ship. It was unnerving to have the animal so close,
docile or not. Helen had said they were peaceful which meant
nothing coming from her. It was possible he could rouse them
to aggression with even a wrong glance. This one looked strong
enough to kill him, with its massive arms and rows of teeth
that ground away thick, hardened stalks. Sharpening for the
kill. And those claws! Why did the animal want to sit on the

bridge anyway? Maybe Helen was right and the creature just wanted human company.

How had the panda gained access to the bridge in the first place? For such a notorious hypochondriac, *Destiny* certainly wasn't putting up much of a protest over having a foreign visitor in her command nexus. As a matter of fact, she didn't seem to mind at all. Haven only knew who had programmed the ship to recognize the big panda's clicks and grumbles—it didn't seem like any other panda ever got inside. Plus, why did *Destiny* dutifully roll a command pod up to the entrance every time Sid entered? He was almost afraid to ask.

Hovering behind and slightly above him, Sid sat patiently on the navigation pod's acceleration couch. Garrand didn't notice how closely the panda took everything in, eying his fingers moving over the controls. Watching closely enough to learn, memorizing the sequence of motion. Close enough to repeat. The panda grunted some as he shifted on his haunches, his movement causing the captain's hands to freeze for a moment over the board.

Sid scratched himself behind an ear with the half-eaten stalk until the captain's shoulders relaxed again. He didn't want to alarm the human, but he felt a certain sense of pleasure at the way his bulk allowed him access to the most interesting compartment. Let the others play in the holo room or with the library datacore. Here he could sit in the midst of a thousand futures, all spread out before him like the stars beyond.

A star winked past the ship, half-seen out of the corner of his eye. A potential future, like a pleasant daydream, tickled his consciousness. He felt a tingle at the back of his neck and then a jolt surged through his body, causing him to shiver involuntarily. The beginning was always electric and he had to work to control the adrenaline that rushed through his veins. He closed his eyes and took a deep breath, centering himself. Blue halos of possibility began to gather in his mind's eye. Sid tried to prepare himself for the vision, slowing his heartbeat and allowing his conscious mind to slip into a gentle trance-state. His breathing slowed and his conscious brain activity relaxed — he could sense the tingling beginning of the *tromaveint*, the waking dream, hovering just past consciousness like a drowsy recollection.

Sid closed his eyes and could see sizzling halos of energy dancing before him. The bluish rings were like the purple splotches one saw after staring at a primary for too long. The arcs of energy wavered as his mind was freed from its conscious ties and he slipped easily and readily into the *tromaveint*. Crackling rings of energy spun lazily in his mind and began to rise. The halos turned golden as their frequency intensified, accelerating upward with fervor. As he concentrated, his vision began to take shape, the golden rings of energy flowing together to form a tunnel through time. The white-hot glow of the future burned at the other end, hazy and irresolute.

Sid swallowed with anticipation. He focused his concentration and willed himself forward. In his mind, he imagined himself racing through the golden rings, yearning to bring the future into focus. At first he rose slowly through the rings. Soon he left the present behind and found himself rushing toward the blinding energy. He hit the luminous end of the tunneled rings with a shower of sparks that tickled the soft pads on all his paws. His mind entered the future with a flash of brilliance.

He blinked softly and tried to sit up straight. His environment had not changed dramatically. To his surprise he was still seated within the great glass hall aboard the world-ship. He was in fact still seated at the navigation station, but the ship was no longer within the soft glowing iridescence of what the captain had called the Krestyaninov Cluster. With some degree of bemusement, he watched his claws skimming the nav board, tapping the slick display which responded by displaying beautiful multi-colored projections of a dozen or so glowing worlds which rotated mysteriously above him.

He experienced the future, his future, as a hazy dream-like experience over which he had little control. Even now, his body was performing functions that he had not yet learned in the present. His claws continued their sure, steady manipulation of the console until a small greenish-grey planet crowded out the rest of the worlds and appeared solo, shimmering over the projector.

Words formed beneath the rotating world:

ARCHIVA, ALSO KNOWN AS MARDELL'S WORLD—GGS FORTEN, RIGHTS CLAIM ZR664786 IN 29,302 (COLLISTAS CALENDAR, UNCORRECTED). RIGHTS TO REVERT TO AIKE VHO DUCALITY (EXTERMINATED 29,879 LC) AFTER MILLENNIAL FIEFDOM—OCCUPATION RIGHTS UNSECURED.

LOCATION: UNKNOWN

SYSTEM: UNKNOWN

EXISTENCE: DISPUTED; HISTORICAL REFERENCES ABOUND, BUT NO PHYSICAL TRACE OF THE PLANET'S EXISTENCE CAN BE FOUND IN ANY OF FOUR HUNDRED PLUS CARTOGRAPHIC SURVEYS COMMISSIONED SINCE THE BEGINNING OF THE SHELL'S DIASPORA.

LAST KNOWN CONTACT: BUCCELATI MIGONTUS, THREE YEARS AFTER THE ONSET OF THE BI'JANTA JIHAD (SEE GREAT DARDACIT VOLUME IX/ERROR: FILE NOT FOUND). POSSIBLE CAUSE FOR DISAPPEARANCE: BUCCELATI ANNIHILATION.

DARDACIT RECORDS INCOMPLETE; MIGONTUS AND ALL
SUBSPECIES ALSO BELIEVED EXTINCT (SEE DARDACIT, "THE
COHAIM PURGE", VOLUME XII/ERROR: FILE NOT FOUND).
MIGONTUS HISTORICAL ARCHIVES INCOMPLETE.
SPECULATION: IMPOSSIBLE/ERROR: INCOMPLETE DATA.

"We'll never find it this way," the captain said from behind him.

Sid turned to see the human standing on the navigational pod, hands on his hips, a stern look creasing his face.

Sid looked back to his controls. His claws tapped out a new series of commands. A star chart materialized, filling the interior of the glass hall. Sid scraped the slick surface of the nav board and a bright line arced through the miniature stars, showing their course through the volume. With a feverish intensity, his claws conjured up a dozen such charts and then hundreds, the images flashing one atop another, illuminating the hall with a sparkling dance of color. The captain watched in silence, his eyes reflecting the shimmering display, but his mouth a thin, firm line, his jaw set rigidly.

Suddenly the displays stopped coming, and one lone chart hovered before them, green and still. It was nearly barren save for one minor solar system. Sid touched a control and the display zoomed in on a volume of space between the orbital paths of the sixth and seventh planets.

"What?" the captain demanded. He squinted at the descriptive coordinates. "That? Nothing there—hasn't been for centuries at least."

But Sid knew. He tapped the board and a string of coordinates flashed into existence along with orbital data, inclination and orbital position relative to the sixth planet's period. Data scrolled beneath the sartographic display which rotated

lazily before him: atmospheric projections, gravitic and magnetic core readings, and below it all, a single word—*Archiva*.
Sid turned triumphantly to see the captain's reaction, but as he
shifted the human's form narrowed and began receding from
him at an alarming rate until it was a tiny dot amidst the yawning darkness of the rest of time.

Sid opened his eyes and blinked. Purple splotches clouded
his vision. The bridge spun before him in the present, making him grasp at the railings. Nausea filled his stomach and he
groaned audibly. Narrowing his eyes, he tried to focus on his
immediate surroundings. He found the bamboo stalk lying in
his paws, half-eaten.

The great glass hall slowly stopped spinning and Sid regained his bearings. Captain Garrand still sat hunched over the
command board below him. After a moment, the disorient-
ing effects of time displacement began to fade and his sight
returned to normal. His view of the future had been brief, but
poignant. The abrupt focus of the vision and the degree of clarity seemed to point to a relatively high degree of probability.
He nodded his head to himself. He felt certain that he had seen
a future that he would someday experience.

The solitary nature of the dream disturbed him though. He
wondered if the rest of the tribe would also experience that future. Best to recount it at the session this evening and see if any
of the Elders had dreamt this future as well.

The hatch to the bridge trundled open, servos whining as it
stuck at quarter open. Helen kicked at the door in frustration
but it refused to budge. She sighed deeply and crawled underneath.

"You're a lot of help," she growled at Sid. The panda gave a
snort and his pod creaked back to the gantry atop the bridge.
The panda lumbered over to the hatch, forcing his bulk be-

neath it. The portal's hydraulics screeched under the strain and finally gave way as the hatch slid partially open.

"Be a little quicker next time," Helen muttered, getting to her feet. Puffs of silvery dust clouded off her hands as she clapped them together. She turned toward Garrand and began to chide him. "You need to look at that atmo recycler again. I think the atmospheric processors need an overhaul."

"Don't bother," Garrand muttered. "It's full of panda hair. The system's fine ordinarily. It wasn't designed with a bunch of fur balls in mind."

Sid shuffled back to his pod, which rotated dutifully back into its former position. Sid picked up a long, new stalk of bamboo, his leafy meal accidentally smacking the back of Garrand's head. Helen giggled.

"And keep your smelly bears off my bridge! I can't concentrate like this."

"Oh, you're doing just fine," she said. "Besides, as a mere passenger I would never *dare* go above your head by ordering the crew about." She gave him a warm smile. "Captain if you want him off your bridge just tell him so."

Garrand glanced over his shoulder. The panda was carefully examining the stalk for any missed shoots, his long claws remarkably dexterous as he twirled the plant back and forth.

"No thanks. I'd rather get to know him better first. Maybe I'll make him co-pilot." The panda snorted behind him and once again Garrand had the strange feeling in his stomach that the creature understood his words.

"Finish programming these new coordinates," he said to Helen. "I've got to get down below to help Bailey. Repulsor modules aren't going to repair themselves," he complained. The command pod did a slow orbit of the bridge and arrived at the entrance where Helen awaited.

"I can't wait to get to the end of this job." He stood up to allow Helen access to the station and gave the chewing panda a last look before he ducked through the partially open hatch.

"Open it all the way next time," he growled, but Sid didn't even turn around.

❖ ❖ ❖

"SOMETHING'S BEEN BOTHERING ME CAPTAIN."

"What is it, Bailey?" Garrand sank deeper into the morass of wires and conduits pulled out of the wall for repair.

"It's the lack of bodies, sir."

Garrand pulled back slowly, his eyes appearing over the open wall plate. "Bodies?"

"Corpses. Rat corpses, to be precise. There should be a daily count, but for the last three cycles, there's been nothing."

"Maybe Bernadine eats them. She is getting pretty hefty for such an active little thing."

Bailey sniffed with offense. "Little Bit informs me that she never eats her kill. In fact, the first week of hunting she presented me with no less than twenty-six bodies."

"Perhaps she's gotten them all, then." He ducked behind the plate again.

"Unlikely, sir. By my calculations even Bernadine would have to work full-time for two cycles in conjunction with your own weekly hunts in order to eradicate our nonpaying passengers and their progeny."

Garrand's head reappeared. "You're saying she's put them somewhere? Twenty-six bodies a week since we started? And it's been — how long has it been? Three weeks! There's close to a hundred corpses hidden on my ship? How is that possible?"

"You're bellowing, sir."

"A hundred bodies are decomposing and breeding bacteria!"

"Those veins are beginning to stand out in your head. Do you need a shot of demexus?"

"Bailey," he was shaking his finger at the artificial, "you find them, understand me? You find them and space them. Now. And I mean all of them. The pathogenic infuser has been offline for close to two months now. Human immune systems need constant challenges to keep them healthy and strong."

"Yes, Captain, I know."

"With nothing but recycled air, all the bacteria and mutagens Helen and I might have been carrying should have gone extinct long ago. I haven't had so much as a sniffle for the last three weeks. Our immune systems will be weak and vulnerable by now. You get those rats off the ship before they breed something so nasty that none of us will make it off."

"With the infuser down, your immune systems should be in need of a fresh challenge," Bailey said quietly.

"This wasn't exactly what I had in mind."

"Of course not, sir. I'll see to it immediately."

"Start in the cargo holds, that's the most obvious place. Zag seems to operate from there. Work your way fore to aft, then sweep through the reactor chambers."

"But, sir, all the pandas are sleeping."

"I don't care. You roust them all out if you have to."

Bailey looked downtrodden. "As you wish."

Garrand tore off his diagnostic headgear and extricated himself from the tangle of wires and relays.

"Are you going to go to sleep yourself, sir?"

"No," Garrand growled flatly. He stalked out of the corridor.

"I really think you should get some rest, sir."

Garrand ignored his friend and headed for the one place where he knew he could lose his frustration and anger.

Bailey watched the captain disappear around the curving serviceway and stood silently for some moments, contemplating their last exchange. On a theoretical level, he knew that he should be devoting his access time to determining the most efficient course of action, planning the search for the expired rats. Yet he could not tear his core away from the nagging concern for his dearest companion. Too much had passed between them—seventeen years of blood, sweat, lubricant, a thousand composed subroutines, the death and destruction of a hundred men and artificials, souls and matrices dear to them both.

The sensation of loss had never been programmed into Bailey, yet years of deprivation from stimuli he had come to know and love had taught him what that sad, empty feeling was. He had observed the captain standing alone on many a blustery night, staring off into a stiff wind, into nothingness. Such nights reminded him of times spent in the service of the Emperor a century earlier, bleeding off energy from field reactors during downtime, wondering what his existence meant, why he bothered fighting day after day. Feeding off soulless reactors left an art copious time to examine his subroutines. He found that the dark forces of the past could be all consuming. The captain was no different—an entity forced to fight to survive, yet sensitive to the subtler affects of his actions, and completely defenseless against his own past, events he could not control and people he could not bring back.

He could see it eating away at his friend. And the destructive forces of those past losses were never so strong as when Captain Médeville was growing close to someone who could be taken from him once more.

❖ ❖ ❖

SLEEP DID NOT COME EASILY FOR ALEXANDER. GROWING UP IN A
colony of self-aware pandas had been complicated by constant
uncertainty and fear. Dr. Tchelakov had moved them no less
than nine times in Alexander's short life. Each move was preceded by a flurry of hasty preparations and anxious late night
council sessions. His mother would come home from the
Elder's Council eyes red and mind exhausted from extended
dream-trance. Alexander knew better than to ask what the future held, instead he would watch over his mother as she fell
into an uneasy sleep. Then he would practice the breathing and
centering techniques that his mother had taught him and try
to emulate the work of the council: he would try to search his
dreams while conscious.

He had never been successful, though his mother promised that with time and patience, he, too, would see the future
whenever he chose. "Patience," she said. "Enjoy this time of
not-knowing, go out and play, for innocence will be all too
brief."

Yet Alexander yearned to know the futures of his choosing,
he desperately wanted to help the tribe search out its fate in the
galaxy of possible futures and be an Elder who helped choose
the Path of Fate, the once course of action where all in his tribe
would survive.

All he had now was the night, and the uncertain and frightening futures that his unconscious dreams held for him. He
had no control over where his innate precognition would lead
his unconscious mind, and thus he was ill equipped to prepare his mind and senses for the experiences he faced in his
dreams. He had learned to avoid sleep, preferring instead to

study that night sky of whatever moon or planet the tribe was calling home.

He often would trek through the forest to Dr. Tchelakov's laboratory and gently scratch at his back door. Grandfather kept late hours and seemed to welcome Alexander's little visits, sometimes giving him a few cubes of sugar for his persistence. He would let him sit on his lap and practice his reading. The warmth of the man's smooth skin and the sound of his voice were always reassuring to Alex, and he never had to ask for a scratch behind the ears.

Tonight, however, he was particularly restless. The Elders did not have their normal look of calm confidence. Even his mother looked troubled. And there was also their hasty departure from El-Bouteran to consider. And worst of all Dr. Tchelakov, the tribe's collective creator, his "Grandfather," did not accompany them aboard the world-ship for this, their latest journey. Alexander stirred uneasily on his makeshift bed of bamboo and shredded insulation.

Sleep finally overcame his exhausted body, and with sleep came the release of the powerful precognitive abilities his young, unschooled mind. He could not yet consciously summon or manipulate his dreams, but while asleep they came unbidden. Though his body rested, his mind still struggled with the events of the past several days, racing through hopes, fears and expectations. His emotions ran the gamut between worst fears and deepest desires. As the electrical activity in his brain increased dramatically, expectations and energy coalesced into shimmering arcs of vibrant possibility, the golden rings of concentration rising through the murky fog of his subconscious. Deep blue rings of energy swam into view, slowly hovering above the golden rings, gathering strength and circling gently upwards as they gained momentum. The rings began to grow in hue and intensity, the higher energy shortening the wavelength of the released light-energy, giving the halos a crimson glow. The now rapidly ascending rings began to form a turbulent vortex that twisted in Alexander's mind. He was aware of an incredibly bright beacon at the pinnacle of the energy vortex, and as his subconscious mind focused its fears he found himself rushing towards the blinding whiteness.

He was back in Grandfather's forest. Water dripped off every visible form. Steam rose from the ground, glutting his sense of smell with death. He dropped to all fours and began to run towards the compound. Trees along the path were charred black and splintered from blaster and cannon fire. Ozone hung heavily in the air along with the suffocating death-smell. He rushed towards the low grey building just visible through the deciduous pines and undergrowth, wishing under his breath that the worst had not happened.

He leapt across the small stream that cut through the forest and bounded up the smooth stone pavers. The massive wooden doors that served as entrance to Grandfather's compound were torn from their hinges and hung limply open. Alexander reared back to his full height and sniffed cautiously. The stench hit him hard. He dropped to all fours and stepped slowly inside, his eyes narrowing in the relative darkness. Furniture and equipment lay strewn everywhere, monitors smashed, datacores blackened and smoldering. Everything that was once so familiar and inviting now lay sickeningly twisted.

Dreading what he would find, he stepped quickly into the bedchamber. He found that he was too late. In the center of the sparse room lay Grandfather, the man who had brought them all into existence, arms and legs splayed unnaturally as if he had just fallen and did not have the willpower to rise. His eyes were closed and across his upper chest a huge blackened wound smoldered. Alexander rushed to his side and pressed his ear to Grandfather's chest, searching for breath and the sound of a heartbeat. Silence. Nothing but char and silence. Alexander picked up the Doctor's lifeless form, hugged him tightly to his chest and howled the Cry of Bereavement.

The pain of the vision was acute. Alexander slammed his paw onto the floor of the sleeping deck, tears still welling up in his eyes. Of all the futures he had dreamt, this one he could not allow to happen. He glanced at the pandas nearby, wondering if his Cry of Bereavement had been real or imagined. Around him the other pandas shifted slightly in their sleep but none woke up. Afraid to sleep-dream again Alex sniffed deeply of the panda nearest him, her warm, sweet smell reassuring. He watched the slow steady rhythm of breath rise and fall in her chest and gently smoothed out a ruffled section of fur with his paw as his own breath slowly returned to normal. With a sigh he rose to all fours and ambled out, heading for the holo chamber.

The room was occupied when Alex looked inside. The captain was working, shirtless and sweaty. He had his hands inside one black box while concentrating on another. The lean muscles of his upper arms and shoulders were taut from exertion. Alex softly padded into the room to get a closer look. The captain's hands were wrapped around a hard slippery substance within the blackened display and twisting the glowing material violently. His attention was focused on a display two meters away. He wasn't watching what his hands were doing at all.

"Alice you're not touching point five," he complained.

A low female voice countered, "That's not possible at the moment."

"Like K'ye it isn't. You've been holding this pose for two hours and now you say it's not possible? Reset and reconfigure."

"Specify program and parameters," the voice returned.

"Same program. Haven's end, I swear you do this just to be difficult. Alice program. Inverted contrapposto pose fifty-nine."

Alexander squinted at the display in the center of the room. The image of a humanoid woman flickered and then reappeared within a pale cone of purplish light. The figure inside was naked and twisted in a dynamic position, with two slender legs arching upwards while balancing on a pair of hands. Hair tumbled down the woman's back as she strained to touch an elbow to the flashing point the captain had indicated.

"Program, raise left elbow three-point-five to mark seven-two off the torso's midpoint."

The figure sucked in its imaginary breath and strained its hips.

"Good! Perfect Alice." The captain's hands worked feverishly within the mercurial box. He reached down and withdrew a huge glob of the slick glowing material from a container on the deck and slapped it inside the dark display.

Across from the captain and the model, a dark substance grew and changed forms as if by magic. Bathed in a deep amber glow, the black burnished material began to resemble a life-size rendering of a female form. Alex watched the sculpture take shape in wonder as the captain wrestled the glowing material before him. It was as if huge invisible hands were molding the dark material before his very eyes.

Alexander watched a moment longer and then shuffled back to the sleeping room, his mind quieted. For the rest of the sleep period he dreamt of nothing but furless humanoid figures rotating slowly in starlight.

❖ ❖ ❖

BREAKFAST WAS A QUIET AFFAIR THE NEXT MORNING. GARRAND was surprised to find the mess unoccupied. Jean-Wa wheeled in with fresh biscuits and a pot of steaming janda.

"What, no guests today?"

"I sent them away, Capítän—as much for me as for you. They were in such a state for so early in the morning—troublemakers, the lot of them."

Garrand smiled as he sipped the gently spiced contents of his mug.

"No, today we have not the flying meals. Today you dine alone—normal like."

"But Jean-Wa, I thought you were excited about having so many guests aboard," he needled the poor chef.

"Bah—don't vex me Capítän. I have much research to do before I can adequately feed the giant beasts."

"So it's 'giant beasts' now is it?" Helen sauntered into the mess looking relaxed and confident. She was dressed for the cool temperature of the ship's corridors: woolen leggings and a double-breasted tharka shooting jacket, tight about the torso with loose arms for ease of movement. She did not wear a blouse beneath the soft, tan jacket and the long swath of exposed skin beneath her neck revealed a sprinkle of brown freckles. She snatched a biscuit off Jean-Wa's tray and sat down on the edge of Garrand's table.

"Seen Bailey this morning?"

"Try the amidships hold," Garrand said without looking up from his clipscanner reports. "Jean-Wa's got him working out in the fields." If someone on Letugia had told him that he'd be growing waves of giant grass in his hold someday he'd have laughed in their face—or worse.

"Thanks." She lingered over a crumbly bite of biscuit, eyeing the captain. He was wearing his usual heavy-threaded trousers. The dark lengths were tucked into his boots. Today he wore a coarse green pullover instead of his customary shift. *Sort of rugged-looking,* she thought and pushed away from the table.

Garrand stole a sideways glance at her as she left. At the same time, across the mess, a lone panda turned his nose inside a separate entrance for preliminary reconnaissance. With a pleased snort, he discovered the presence of food, and... ah, yes, the captain. How fortuitous! With a happy half-skip, the panda bounded around the corner and trotted up to the center of the chamber.

Garrand shifted his eyes to the panda for a moment, noted that it was the little one again, Alexai. He resumed studying the clipscanner.

Alexander hovered at the end of Garrand's mess table, peering uncertainly over the edge. He sniffed, looked away shyly then focused his huge round eyes once more on the captain. Garrand could feel the panda's eyes on him and tried to ignore him as he chewed. The cub would not relent. Finally he couldn't stand it anymore.

"What?" he demanded. "What do you want?" Pieces of biscuit sputtered from his lips as he slammed his fist down on the table.

The little panda's nose retreated from the edge of the table as he backed away. Garrand regretted his outburst immediately. He closed his eyes and let his anger ease from his chest, the accompanying breath hissing out between his clenched teeth.

He opened his eyes as the panda turned away.

"No, wait—I'm sorry." He broke off a piece of biscuit and held it out for the panda. "Here, try this."

Alexander hesitated, but only for a moment. The image-memory of Grandfather Tchelakov offering him a sweet lump of sugar was all the reassurance he needed. He eagerly took the proffered tidbit and gobbled it down.

"Like that, do you? Want some more?" Garrand pushed his plate to the edge of the table. Alexander didn't need any encouragement; he sat back on his haunches and extended forward, putting two front paws up on the edge of the mess table. Turning his jaw sideways, he snagged a full biscuit and quickly dropped down to a seated position to examine his find. Twisting the biscuit between his forepaws, he determined the proper angle of attack and bit into the flaky concoction sending crumbs scattering.

"You're going to eat me out of my profits, the lot of you," Garrand grumbled, though he was actually enjoying watching the messy destruction of the biscuit. He reached down and tentatively scratched the panda behind his ear like he had seen Helen do. The cub's fur was warm and incredibly soft, not coarse at all. Alexander rotated his head around so that he could scratch the other as well.

"Ah, both ears need it, eh?" He let his chest relax and looked around the mess. "Where are all your brothers today?" It actually seemed empty without the pandas.

Alexander finished his biscuit and grumbled up at the captain. Garrand broke the remaining biscuit in two and handed half down to the cub. Having company for breakfast wasn't so bad, after all.

❖ ❖ ❖

HELEN PUSHED THROUGH THE THICKENING GROVE OF BAMBOO
for several minutes before locating Bailey. The tight branches
put up quite a struggle and her boots sank some inches in the
soft dirt with each step, making the going more difficult than
she anticipated.

"Good morning, Miss Tchelakov," Bailey greeted her.

"What are you up to?" she asked, wiping sweat from her
brow.

"Kitchen duty," he replied sheepishly, running his hand
down a thick stalk in assessment.

"Out here? There's nothing but bamboo," she frowned.

"Exactly." Bailey's face glowed with elegant distaste.

Helen smiled, "Oh, that again."

"Yes, that. Jean-Wa is determined to sway our guests from
raw to cooked bamboo. His latest exercise is pickled bamboo
shoots. But he has such trouble getting about he'd never traverse these uneven fields, hence my presence here."

"He's really devoted to this cause, isn't he?"

"If I had a stomach I'd been in trouble for sure. He'd be ever
forcing me to endure one experiment after another. And I do
not think I would like what a panda tastes."

"You're kind to help. May I assist?"

"It would be delightful, Miss Tchelakov."

"Helen," she corrected, repositioning his hand further along
the stalk towards the tender shoots at the top.

"Helen," he sighed beneath her hearing, savoring the light-
ness of her guiding touch. His battle-honed senses could pick
out her warm, slow pulse, the slightly sweet smell of her breath,

and the shimmer of pollen along her exposed skin, collecting in the hollow of her throat. There was an abrasion on her wrist. Absently he thought of a salve he would make for it. She looked up at him and smiled, then lopped the head off the bamboo shoot and handed it to him.

Helen moved on ahead and he followed close behind, his eyes riveted on the gentle undulation of her body as she maneuvered through the giant grass. She was so lithe and natural that if he had a heart it would ache.

Something in his wiring was disturbed, out of place. He would do a full diagnostic check later. But now, now he would... What was it he would do? This was ridiculous, simply ridiculous. It was silly to be moved by these innocent, natural things. But there it was, the impulse to lean over and press those moist lips to his, to feel that dewy heat warming his oral processors. Absurd. It was absolutely absurd how he found himself doing just that, how naturally he reached for the nape of her neck and swung her towards him, how innately he whispered a kiss into her lips, drinking the sweetness, her startled gasp that deepened to another sound entirely. He straightened and removed his hand, blinking down at her. It was impossible to tell who was more surprised: Bailey with his look of revelation or Helen with her flushed cheeks.

"Was that your first kiss?" she murmured.

Bailey cocked his head to one side and gazed with a fond expression, just a hint of a smile playing about his lips. He nodded.

"Oh." She looked away, dazed. She'd never been kissed tenderly. Darstin had never swiped his mouth against hers long enough for it to be considered a kiss. She had never known a gentle lovemaking. All encounters had been as brutal as hand-to-hand combat, which this art excelled at. But he offered so much more. She touched two fingers to her lips, trying to match his cadence. Unable to, she whirled and reached for him. As they kissed again an emotion she'd never felt flooded her belly and she broke away, fleeing through the bamboo.

Bailey watched her go, twirling a new shoot between his fingers, humming the Tolsata battle hymn.

9

THE GRIFFIN

GARRAND WALKED INTO THE HOLO ROOM AND WAS HAP-
pily surprised to find it transformed into an armory and shooting range complete with an armorer's table. Two long counters
were stacked with equipment and weapons and a target simula-
crum rotated down a long narrow aisle.

"Hope you don't mind," Helen said, looking up from loading explosive darts into a rack. "I found an old subroutine in
memory."

"No, not at all," Garrand said brightly, surveying the impressive array of firepower at her disposal. "I used to use this before
I had a dedicated armory within the ship."

"Yeah, well I needed a break—get away from all that bamboo and dirt and panda hair. So much organics."

Garrand nodded, "I know what you mean. There's something simple and reassuring about steel and, well…"

"It's okay, you can say it. Weapons." Helen looked up at him and smiled.

"Yeah," he shrugged sheepishly.

"Nothing to be ashamed of. Humans have always had an affinity for instruments of destruction. Complements our ruinous nature, don't you agree?"

"I don't know about that, but weapons do seem to have always held a certain fascination for humans. I just sort of feel like we might outgrow them."

"Doubtful. They've gotten us this far."

"I'm not sure that's what's gotten us this far. Ingenuity, courage, determination—the drive to expand, explore—"

"—Conquer."

"Survive," he countered.

"All right, well then they've *kept* us this far. Kept us from slipping back, or giving up. We constantly have to keep moving forward to meet the new challenges. Before someone else gets ahead of us. Can't be complacent in an ever-lasting arms race."

"Your metaphor for survival in Carinaena's Shell?"

"Why not? Humans certainly aren't the only species with a fascination with all things destructive. And we're certainly not the only expansionistic creatures around. Look at the Trogands, the Larken, and the Geihan of Fors-tanêsse."

"Hmm," he picked up a Rimoda hip cannon. "Or the T'chell for that matter."

"All aggressive species use weapon technologies for springboards to other advances," Helen argued. "You can't forget the mythic warrior codes of the Osakk and the Gambor."

"I suppose," he murmured. "Can this be adapted for a two-stage plasma pulse charge?"

"Yes, could you hand me that phase emitter?"

He searched through the pile of coils on the counter and handed her the long wand.

"Humans are just good at it," she glanced up at him slyly. But he had hardly heard her, lost in the array of weapons. She grinned.

Garrand picked up a blunt, silver blaster from a soft case. He held it up to the light and examined it carefully.

Helen looked up and wiped back a strand of loose hair. "You have a good eye—that's one of my personal favorites."

Garrand flipped the weapon over and sighted along the barrel. "Chen-Vespor Snub-nosed special, igrelum spec casing, eleven millimeter, smooth bore, rhythmic pulse feedback, dual optical sights, bio-tag sight, electro-chemical signature protection. Very impressive." He thumbed the catch and popped the coil out, turning it over in his palm, examining the make and model. "Phorensus. Nice. Thirteen kilojoules?"

"Fourteen and a quarter. Four point two max discharge."

Garrand whistled, "Not bad. No problem with the pulse buffer? Some of those old Kasey's tend to overload when you jack in a high grade charge—"

"Chen designed the eleven millimeter with the Phorensus pulse pack specifically in mind; I haven't even notched a burner yet."

"Hmm…" He replaced the coil, smacking the charge back into the base of the pistol with the palm of his hand and gently placed the well-oiled weapon back onto the surface of the armorer's table. He sniffed politely as he surveyed the rest of the hardware neatly arranged upon the surface—Naisus hand cannon, Dy'lal multi-clip three-stage AP missile rack with full

Ki Zentor sensor package and opticals, shoulder-mount WERT charges, a slick looking full-bore bio-accelerator with Hold-Tite living cartridges, five millimeter custom-order Thol dart sling, bio-elective finger tabs, Perseus Limited *Ghost Net*. All the equipment was factory-new, in mint condition.

He rubbed his thumb and forefinger together roughly behind his back. Too bad Bailey wasn't around to see this. Maybe he should think of some excuse to call him up here… He gingerly lifted a Thykol finger gun and slipped it onto his hand.

Helen set down her phase emitter. "I feel much better." She stepped back, hands on her hips, surveying her work. "Ready for lunch?"

Garrand looked up, checked to see that the offer was genuine and was half-surprised to find that it was. He put down the Thykol and shrugged, "I guess."

"Jean-Wa promised me a picnic in the bamboo grove, care to join me?"

THEY WERE WALKING side by side down the corridor when Bernadine scampered between their legs and rushed ahead of them down the hall. Garrand gave a brief thought to chasing after her, but knew it would be futile.

A moment later, the hollow sound of metal rolling against metal preceded Little Bit's arrival. Garrand stepped back against the wall, gently pushing Helen back as well as the artificial rolled past at full speed, moving quite a bit faster than was safe for the narrow corridor. The art was bleeping furiously at the departing exel. He swiveled a receptor node toward Garrand as he whizzed past and paid him a cursory hello.

"Go get her kid," Garrand encouraged the art.

"He'll never catch that tube of fur," Helen commented.

"Yeah, at least he's trying." He watched the art roll around a corner. "If *I* ever get my hands on that fat little rodent..." he let his threat trail off.

Helen smiled and almost reached up to pat him on the back as they turned into the amidships hold, but stopped as she thought of Bailey. She hesitated at the entrance. Was he still in here? She peered inside the hold, but could see only a dozen or so pandas happily grinding down the stalks with their thick teeth.

Jean-Wa greeted them immediately.

"I must say, Capítän, that despite my disappointment at not tempting these colorful guests, I am quite delighted by them."

"Now this is a surprise, Jean-Wa."

"Look at this ballet before us — so graceful, so poised as they eat. Nothing edible is wasted; and they in turn waste no energy in reaching it. And the way their sixth claw aids them in their task, why it is as if they were created in tandem, the panda and the bamboo."

The artificial spied one panda who was gnawing at one of his legs. He wheeled quickly over to the young cub.

"They're not going to go vanish away if you worry at them," Jean-Wa admonished the panda. Helen glanced at them with curiosity.

"What are you telling him?"

"He is biting at those warts again. They not go anywhere like that. I make a poultice. Then we'll see."

"Jean-Wa, you're right about the biting but I really don't think that's necessary."

"That's all right, miss. You don't need to think with Jean-Wa around. I make the poultice. Then we see." He trundled away from her on his cart, passing Garrand.

"Your chef is infuriating."

"What offense have you committed now?"

"It's not me. *He* insists on making a wart poultice!"

"I didn't realize you needed one."

Helen punched him on the back rather sharply. "Not for me, you slort, for Shakra."

"A panda, I take it?"

"Yes. I can't have him administering to them like some backwater medica."

"What's the harm in a wart remedy? The most it could do is wet their fur down and I hate to say it but they could use a bath."

"And what refugee couldn't?" she snapped. "Since you mentioned it, I think it's time we did something about bathing them. The cubs got loose in the bamboo during the irrigation sprinkling and then ran through the dirt in hold two."

"The Kess dirt? The aromatic Kess dirt?"

He wasn't laughing now. She began to speak faster.

"Yes, so you can imagine the importance of freshening them as soon as possible. All of them could use it, really."

"Where exactly did you *imagine* this happening?"

"Don't you have a rather large fresher in your quarters?"

"Are you serious? You think I'd let thirty-seven pandas covered with manure into my fresher?"

"They're not *all* covered, just the cubs, like I said." She said casually.

"I don't care *what* they have on, I'm not letting any pandas in my quarters. I ought to space you for suggesting it."

"Well, I didn't realize you'd be so objectionable. Why, when I told Bailey to go ahead — "

"What?" He started for the door.

"There's no need to shout, I can hear you just fine. Bailey was reluctant at first, but I said I'd take care of it. Well, I hope you don't yell at him," she shouted down the hallway at his retreating form. She crossed her arms, leaned against the doorjamb, and smiled serenely.

IN HIS QUARTERS, Garrand's heart rammed against his ribs. His fresher dripped with dark manure that had nowhere to exit since the drains were clogged with black and white fur. A lone cub remained, his mouth yawning wide to catch a latent spray of water. He spit the liquid out and bit at the spray again. Garrand hit the switch to turn the fresher off. The cub stood on his hind legs and grasped the spray head with both paws, looking with disappointment into the empty pipe. Finally, he dropped to all fours, braced himself, and began to shake dry starting with his head and working the motion down through his tail until three sections of his body moved in opposite directions, spraying water. Garrand shouted and the cub jumped in fright. He yowled and scrambled out the door, his paws leaving wet streaks on the deck plates. Garrand, turning to watch his flight, caught sight of Bailey, arms laden with makeshift towels, hoping to make his escape.

"Not so fast, partner. Since when do you turn my quarters over to guests? And not even guests, but cargo bay occupants, by K'ye?"

"Sir, I had no idea the plumbing would malfunction."

"I notice Helen didn't offer up her fresher for sacrifice."

"Well, it was a bit small, sir, for so many."

"Bailey what possessed you to take orders from her?"

"They weren't orders, exactly. She just... suggests things, and they sound so reasonable you just follow through with them."

"Without thinking."

"Yes, sir."

Garrand surveyed the damage again, wrinkling his nose against the lingering stench.

"Can you fix it?"

"I hope so."

"Yeah, well do so. And no more surprises, understood?"

"Quite, sir. I'm very sorry."

"Not as much as Helen's going to be. I can't have her running my ship. When I'm through, a wart poultice is going to be the least of her worries."

"Wart poultice?"

"Don't trouble yourself." He pointed to his clogged fresher. "Plumbing."

Bailey lowered his head and placed the towels on the floor before making his way into the wet compartment.

"*Destiny*, where is Miss Tchelakov at the moment?" Garrand asked.

"I'm afraid I do not have an exact location for her at the moment. There are quite a few large lifeforms rummaging around this morning."

"What's your best guess?"

"Well, Captain, there are quite a few life signs in the aft cargo hold…"

GARRAND FELT HIS pace quicken and his muscles tighten as he maneuvered through the tight passageways on the lower deck, making his way toward the aft hold. He was going to have a word with that woman about her allocation of ship's resources, in particular, his fresher. The thought of her leading muddy panda after muddy panda through the ship and into his quarters sent needles of anger pulsing through his very being.

He stopped before the massive aft hold's door, sealed tight and locked—*from the inside*, he noted with derision. *She didn't actually think she could keep him out of his own hold, did she?* Not bothering to disturb the ship aurally, he simply flipped up the access panel and keyed in his override. The first two he tried didn't work, but the third was accepted and the steel doors split open and trundled apart.

Garrand stood silently outside the hold as the scene was slowly revealed. Along the near wall, pandas seated atop six-meter-tall packing shells directed two sets of workers who, heads down, shoulders pressed to the task, were maneuvering two large Geggin shells across the deck plates. A guttural bark echoed through the bulkheads and the first group stopped pushing and began lashing the shell to stanchions in the deck. The second group deftly slipped their Geggin up tight against the secured shell and without a sound, set to fastening the webbed cables.

Eyebrows knitted at the strange sight, Garrand let his gaze flick to another set of pandas who were adroitly unpacking equipment from an open shipping pallet. The equipment appeared vaguely familiar. One piece looked to be part of a water reclamation unit, a second resembled a mid-sized Larkson field generator, but the controls and surface articulation were all wrong. He squinted at the equipment as it was lifted out. Curving slots and strange holes filled places where standard handholds should have been. Perhaps it was all custom-built. Then it dawned on him, and he chided himself for his own thick-headedness. *It was all custom-built for creatures with claws, not hands.*

It was fascinating watching the pandas work. They were smooth and agile, not at all like the cumbersome creatures they appeared to be. A sixth claw located near their wrist acted as an opposable digit, deftly operating much as a human thumb.

Against the opposite wall, a group of younger pandas were carousing in an open space. They did look cleaner, he thought to himself, pleased to find his sense of humor returning.

Garrand wondered if Helen had staged this activity as an impressive show for his benefit, but the frantic scrambling seemed more chaotic than choreographed—any pretense of a pre-planned effort quickly disappeared.

CABEUS LOOKED UP from an articulated water condenser that he was unpacking and fixed a worried gaze on the captain who stood in the entrance scanning the interior. He barked a warning and punctuated it with a long, low growl.

Sid ambled over to the truly giant-looking panda and flicked a whisker sideways.

Cabeus rolled his neck toward the entrance, "Should we be working with the captain standing there watching?" The swift delivery of rhythmic clicks betrayed his obvious concern, almost fear.

Sid placated the worker, "It's all right, the restrictions have eased a bit."

The adult panda growled back, "So soon?"

"The last Council session debated the issue. Captain Garrand is no longer considered any kind of a threat. And he was actually upgraded to *vo'halahn.*"

"*Vo'halahn?*" The big, strapping panda clucked to himself. "Friend of the tribe? This *is* interesting. Your dreams of the *Griffin* are intensifying then?"

"Yes, they are," Sid clicked. "The Elders have been forced to pay them serious heed."

"What of Leusta's objections?"

"They are not carrying the same weight they once were. More are coming to believe that he is the one."

Cabeus scratched behind one ear. "Tcht-grrr ek'ckahl," he rumbled.

"Very interesting, indeed," Sid agreed. "Now finish what you started there. We'll discuss this further tonight."

The giant panda slid a long claw up under the restraining strap and snapped the release. Sid watched him for a moment, and then, satisfied with the progress, ambled back to his position observing the captain.

GARRAND FROWNED. THERE was more than just the off-putting sight of seeing the pandas working together so fluidly. He paused, trying to place a finger on it. It was not a visual difference, though. He sniffed tentatively at the stale air. The hold had a spicy smell to it, he decided, almost exotic. He inhaled deeply, trying to remember why the scent seemed so familiar. Something from his childhood, he thought. Perhaps in the old ship's galley, on inspection with his father. He remembered the antiquated cooking pots that Lieutenant Vars insisted made food taste better. The burnished metal tables dusted with alien off-world flours. Hanging nets of pears from Hothhor and apples from Merudo. Lieutenant always made special treats for his rare visits. That was it. The spice cookies.

He smiled, a last eye-closing whiff of childhood searing his nostrils, disarming his anger. Garrand let his eyes drift across the rest of the hold.

He watched some of the younger pandas playing. They staged mock attacks, their powerful jaws snapping air. He began watching more carefully and a slow shiver ran the length of his spine. On the surface, the cubs were simply playing, twisting and groping for better position during the close quarter bites. But as he watched, the pandas made the same precise and startlingly complex movements time after time. The cubs were not making random, playful attacks. Instead they were performing carefully choreographed moves over and over again under the watchful eyes of four larger adults.

Garrand eyes grew wide as the realization dawned on him. The pandas were being trained to defend themselves, being trained by their own parents with sophisticated moves. He swept his eyes over the interior, searching Helen out. It was one thing to have trained the pandas to unpack delicate equipment; even the lowliest of tech arts could be programed for that. But it was quite another for the pandas to be training themselves.

His eyes found her. She stood before three pandas thirty meters away. The implications of what he had just witnessed sealed it for him. He strode quickly across the hold, emotions running high. He opened his mouth to get her attention but caught himself and slowed his pace as he neared her from behind.

Glancing at the young pandas who had stopped their practice to watch him, Garrand felt a moment's uncertainty. He reached a finger up to his collar and considered whether or not to call Bailey. These creatures could be quite formidable. Helen acted as though the pandas had a sense of right and wrong, a free will. Maybe they had been trained to obey certain commands. Or perhaps it was much more than that.

He decided that he would face the truth alone.

The largest panda stood up on its hind legs and gestured toward the unsecured Geggin shells with a low bass reverberation that seemed to emanate from deep inside his chest.

"No," Helen said firmly. "We cannot do that."

The second panda growl-clicked in response.

"No, you'll have to be patient," she told the creature.

"They don't actually *understand* Strahlinvek, do they?" Garrand asked as he watched the curious exchange, referring to the language spoken by most of the trading cultures in Carinaena's Shell. Some variation of the dialect was spoken by almost every race that had spacefaring ties, facilitating the exploration and colonization of most of the galaxy. It was taught like a second language, in addition to the native tongues. For the life of him, it looked like Helen and the pandas were carrying on a conversation.

Helen spun on her heel. If she was surprised to see him, she hid it well. "Oh, no," she said airily, "of course not. They just understand the tone of my voice, a couple of simple commands, that's all."

"But you understand them," Garrand said, his face growing stern. He pointed at her bracer. "With that thing."

"Oh, just bits and pieces really, it's not all that complicated."

"So," he interrupted her, "they have their own language."

"Well, I'm not sure I would call it a *language*."

"Miss Tchelakov," he spoke sharply, closing the distance between them. "There are serious intercultural statutes prohibiting the transportation of intelligent, sentient species without their approval, not to mention the moral and ethical issues of which I'm sure you're well aware."

"But Captain—"

He stepped forward with the speed of a bladesman and grabbed her left arm, twisting it so that the bracer was in full view. "This acts as a language interpreter, does it not? Modified to whatever they speak. These are not dumb animals—they act beyond their basic instincts, they have intelligence, they have *language!*" He shook the bracer at her.

"Captain Médeville, if you'd just let me explain."

"By Haven, they're out there training their young," he pointed at the group of cubs who had been sparring. "In basic combat techniques." His eyes blazed with anger.

"They're just a few things I taught them, it's nothing to get upset about."

"Not exactly standard fare for 'exotics'," he said venomously.

All the pandas had stopped working and were staring intently at the two humans. More were entering through the open doorway, edging closer. All were paying rapt attention to the captain's tirade, almost as if they were drawn in by the sound of his voice. Even the cubs were strangely silent, held in check by the firm paw of a parent.

Garrand swept his gaze around the cargo hold. "No. These are intelligent creatures—*sentient* creatures if my guess is correct. Not some 'exotic bios' as you've led me to believe." He dropped her arm and further invaded her personal space, extending a forefinger up to her chin. "I am not a *t'hulkein*," he used the ancient term, spitting out the word with obvious distaste, "and I do not abide slavers. I'd sooner space your hide and deliver these pandas to wherever *they* want to go than give them up to the Imperials or to *you!*"

"Captain, I am not taking these creatures anywhere against their will!"

"Prove it!" Garrand glowered at her.

The pandas had surrounded the two humans, pressed in shoulder-to-shoulder, bearing silent witness to the standoff.

Helen fought hard to keep her composure with Médeville hovering so close to her, his eyes filled with the conviction of his words. She swallowed back a lump and straightened her shoulders.

"Think about it," she challenged him. "If they can speak and I can understand them, then I can take them where they want to go, right? And does it look to you like I am doing anything to them against their will? Do you think I'm capable of over-powering thirty-seven of them — kidnaping them and taking them somewhere against their will?"

"You could have them fooled."

"Captain, please…" she stepped back and crossed her arms.

Garrand frowned and gave the pandas a hard look, glancing from face to face. Their dark eyes held his gaze unblinkingly. She was not going to slip out of this so easily.

"Well then, what do you intend to do with thirty-seven giant pandas? They're a little large for pets, don't you think?"

"What?" Helen seemed startled.

"The pandas — they're a little big for pets, aren't they?" His question almost seemed like a hazy accusation.

"They're not pets, Captain," she snapped.

Finally I strike a nerve, he thought. "So?"

She changed gears immediately. "What, a sudden interest in your *cargo*?" her words dripped with undisguised sarcasm.

Garrand shook his head, "You and I both know this is no ordinary 'cargo.'"

"You'd never know it, the way *you* talk."

"Hey — you learn to create a little distance between yourself and your clients after awhile. It's called being professional."

"It's called being an insensitive, self-centered lout."

Garrand rolled his eyes and continued, "That was before — "

" — Before what?" she demanded.

"Before I risked my life saving one of their fat, furry behinds. Before I had one check on my sleep in the middle of the night. Before they covered the mess with wheat cakes." His voice continued to rise. "Before Sid over there began following me every-where I went."

It was Helen's turn to frown. *He can recognize individual pandas now?*

"Before I got to know them," he finished with a quieter em-phasis.

Helen rolled her eyes, masking her own surprise at this sud-den passionate outburst, and tried to divert him. "Oh, please! You're telling me that *you* had a change of heart?" Her disbelief was palpable.

"Yeah, believe it or not. It's called Captain's prerogative. Now don't change the subject! They're obviously too big and too much trouble to be pets. What do you plan to do with them!"

Helen stood stock still, green eyes staring up at him. The tight circle of pandas leaned in closer. It was so silent that the atmo processors could be heard droning overhead. Garrand couldn't decide if she was shocked by his bluntness and was stalling to concoct a believable story, or if she was sizing him up for the truth.

"Is that a demand?" she finally asked, her voice soft and pliant.

"No," he growled. He straightened up and tried to muster some diplomacy. "It's a question."

"Well, I'm afraid that's something I can't tell you, Captain."

Garrand felt the knot of anger returning to his throat. "Why not?"

"Because," she stammered, "it's not your need to know."

"My *need to know*," he wrinkled his forehead in consterna-tion and utter disbelief. "What in Haven's name does *that* mean?"

"It means, Captain, that there is nothing in our contract that binds me to tell you what I intend to do with my cargo."

"Oh, so now it's *your* cargo, is it?"

Helen stood her ground defiantly.

"What if I told you that I will refuse to transport you one jump further until you tell me what you're doing with thirty-seven beautiful, intelligent, warm sentient creatures!"

Helen paused, shocked by the genuine passion behind his words. She bit her tongue and plowed on. "I would say," she intoned, adopting as frumpy a tone as she could manage, "that you were in violation of contract and through such grievous breach must forfeit all funds made in payment as well as return me and my cargo back to our port of embarkation."

Garrand turned abruptly and waved his hands in dismissal. "Oh, cheplus. We both know that going back to El-Bouteran, or Letugia for that matter, is out of the question. At best we'd be at the bottom of a Trelt dungeon scow by the end of the week, being eaten by harvester rats. More likely, though, we wouldn't live to see planetfall."

He stepped directly in front of her. "Those Imperials didn't just happen to drop in on El-Bouteran. Those were Shock Troops—the Emperor's planet smashers. And they don't pull front line capital ships to round up wayward keiretsu operatives."

Helen bristled at the implication. "What makes you think I work for a keiretsu?"

Garrand ignored her, "If they were after you—they could have picked you up *anytime*. No," he wagged his finger at her, "they waited until you were on El-Bouteran." He gave a trenchant snort. "No, they were waiting for you to *lead* them to El-Bouteran. They're after those pandas and I want to know why!"

"I am not working for any keiretsu," she protested.

Garrand shook his head. "It's all over you, honey. Your equipment is state of the art. Not even a scratch. So new, they don't even have serial numbers etched in yet. Prototypes even I haven't even seen. Your movements tag you the second you walk in a room. You were immersed in combat at birth: survival, geinsha, thoraultso, small arms, guerrilla tactics, and deception. Not exactly standard Imperial protocol. You handle *Destiny's* encryption like it's shorthand." He paused to look at her. "Need I go on?"

She gave him an icy stare.

"You were trained from a very young age to serve as a deep cover agent for a keiretsu — hand-picked if not part of their selective breeding. Probably Gordon, Black Hand, or Nralda by your tics. Believe me, I've seen enough to know."

"You don't know what you're talking about," she spat out. "What makes you think I had a choice in any of this? You think I *chose* to work for the Nralda?" the hatred was thick in her voice.

"So it is Nralda."

"You should be careful what you say," she adopted a combative stance, legs spread for balance, and her hand dropped to her belt. "The past is a dangerous area to tread."

Garrand noted her subtle shift in demeanor. "But that's beside the point. My life is in as much danger as yours now."

"Ah, we come to the heart of the matter."

"That's not what I'm getting at, Tchelakov," he glared at her. "The fact that my life's in danger merely means that in order to operate as efficiently as possible, I have to know what's going on. The insinuations behind the words, the orchestrations behind the actions, the details behind the facts. Otherwise, we're all lost. And these overstuffed fur balls — who obviously understand every word we're saying — will be gone. And they're important, aren't they? Not just to you. Not just to the Imperials."

Helen silence confirmed his suspicions.

"I'm not the heartless bastard you like to pretend. Why has Vice Proctor Barrett taken such a keen interest in our friends?"

Helen looked up in surprise. "What makes you think Barrett's involved?"

"That was his flagship we slipped past back there, the *Shiva*."

Helen turned away and frowned — eyes growing wide with frustration. She was going to *have* to stop underestimating Médeville. He had an unbelievably shrewd eye for detail. He was certainly not the man she had bargained for. With a calming breath, she regained her cool composure and turned back. "What makes you so sure that was Barrett's flagship?"

"Give me a break. I'd recognize it in my sleep. What do you think I did for eight years?"

"Peel onions?" she offered.

"That was the *Shiva* heading up that fleet," he yelled, moving even closer. Helen took an involuntary step backward brushing up against a panda, but Garrand pressed closer. "Those were top of the line troops pulled just to secure your pandas, and Barrett doesn't pull troops on a whim. The man is *serious* about conquest. He wouldn't divert resources from his precious rise to power unless he had a good reason. Now what in Haven's name is going on? Are you smuggling information within one of the pandas? Did you *steal* them? Are they some research project? What is so important that has an entire Imperial task force trying to track us down?"

Helen tried to turn away, but Garrand held her shoulder with one hand and brought her chin back to bear with his other. Helen's eyes flitted briefly past Garrand, and for one awful instant he feared that a massive claw would tear into his spine. But the hairs did not stand up on the back of his neck, not a single panda moved — there was no danger here. Helen squirmed in his grasp, but he would not let her free. Unable to look him in the eye, she stared off glassily at the far bulkhead.

"The pandas—" she faltered. "The pandas are not what they seem…" her voice trailed off.

Garrand waited impatiently.

Helen sighed. "They are—" she stopped and frowned, then restarted. "They are precognizant."

"Pre-what?"

"Precognizant—prescient. They can see into the future."

Garrand released her and stepped back into the middle of the circle.

"Self-determining intelligence was developed around a sar-tokian model for future speculation. The pandas were geneti-cally engineered to accept the Sartok chip as part of their ascent to sentience. The probability ratios and percentages of sarto-graphs have evolved into consciousness and future visions."

Garrand looked around the circle of pandas uneasily. He ad-opted a cautious smile and shook his head.

"Why is that so hard for you to believe?"

He continued to shake his head. "Sentience is one thing— that I can believe. They can understand Strahlinvek? Okay. They speak their own language? Fine. But seeing into the fu-ture?"

"My father has spent his whole life bridging the gap between the future and the present."

"And he decided to put his life work into a bunch of furry herbivores?" Garrand almost chuckled.

"Pandas do eat *meat*," she said ominously. "There's just usu-ally not enough around to feed a full-sized adult."

"Why pandas?"

"No one would suspect a panda of having a keen intellect, much less the capacity for envisioning the future. It was for their safety—for the safety of the project. They're innocuous and innocent. Plus they live long lives. Their hearts are strong and they have an iron constitution. They adapt to foreign environments—" Sid growled thickly. Helen glanced over at him, "—despite their objections to the contrary. They nurtured their young long before man ever learned to walk! They existed in peaceful tribes for millennia before anyone ever contemplated elevating them to sentience. Their minds were large and complex. They were perfect."

Garrand felt a pang of doubt, but remained unconvinced. "I've heard a lot of crazy stories in my day, but 'visionary panda bears,'" he waggled his hands over his head in a mock mystic gesture. "That tops them all!"

"How do you think I knew that Imperial forces were on the way?" Helen challenged him. "Figured that one out yet? Think I just waved my magic wand and said, 'Oh, yes—by the way, we're going to be attacked here any minute.' What—you think my female intuition is just really on track?"

That one pricked Garrand's attention. He had indeed wondered how Helen had known with such absolute certainty that Shock Troops were on the way. She hadn't faked her concern for Alexander. The fear and dread in her eyes had been real. How *had* she known?

"If you weren't so close-minded and biased to what fits into your perception of what's real and what's not you'd see it. It's sitting right in front of your nose. Sid *foresaw* the attack. It was presented to him in a dream, and he warned me, and I warned you."

The mention of a dream struck Garrand cold. The dream. The wind demon. The mysterious pounding on his door. He felt the color drain from his face. The panda could have come to *warn* him about the dream.

Garrand stared at her hard, disbelief in his face and eyes, but curiosity in his heart. Like a flower blooming, each piece of the mystery began to fall into place. Alexander had *chosen* the correct path on El-Bouteran. The little panda had *known* which path to take. The pandas did not attack him here because they *knew* he would do her no harm.

He turned away from Helen, a stunned look on his face. The circle parted for him and he walked silently out of the hold.

GARRAND'S DEPARTURE LEFT the hold crackling with energy. The Elders drifted off to one corner while the rest of the tribe eagerly discussed the confrontation in expressive voices.

Sid looked to Ell'han and nodded toward the captain. "I told you he was one to watch."

The older panda smacked his lips contemplatively and watched the human depart with a whimsical expression of interest and doubt creasing his whiskered face. A low guttural growl of contemplation echoed out of his chest. "We shall see, Elder Sid. We shall see…"

Archimedes glanced at Sid, a bemused sparkle in his eye. "The old boy still has a lot of life left in him, eh?"

"Quite a bit for a human," Tulli interjected.

Ell'han grumbled, "He defends that which he doesn't understand."

"Just like the prophecy."

"It's not a prophecy," the old panda argued, "it's just a dream."

"A dream that all of us have had," Sid countered.

"Yes," Archimedes chuckled, "that sounds rather *prophetic* to me."

"Did you see how the whole tribe watched him? They were transfixed."

Ell'han remained obstinate. "They merely gathered to gawk at a curiosity."

"Ell'han, he was defending us from a stance based on pure ideology — that we were worth something because we were sentient. Living, breathing, thinking creatures worthy of equal treatment."

"Maybe there's something to this one after all," Archimedes reflected. "Perhaps those dreams Sid's been telling us about mean something."

"It could just be a coincidence."

"You could make an argument that all of life is a coincidence. What we are here to determine is will this man's future continue to *coincide* with ours."

"It will," whispered Leusta, a worried growl creeping into her voice. It was a simple statement, remarkable in its brevity from one so prone to didactic aphorisms.

Sid tried to weigh the significance of each of the Elder's half-hidden mannerisms, looking for clues that might help him decipher the captain's role in the tribe's fate. With so many dreams of the future to cull through, determining the true path was difficult.

Each of the pandas had visions, any one of which might hold something of significance to the fate of the tribe — learning to focus the dreams and envision a specific time or place or possible event took years and years of trial and error, much of it devoted to trying to accurately interpret what the dreams actually meant. There was so much about the universe they did not understand, had never seen, or could just not fathom. Each day held something new.

It was important to find the significance in everything—in even the most minuscule clue.

Leusta's brevity was a tribute to her genuine concern that Circle of Elders might actually be on to something. It was scary to think that the dream of the *Griffin*—a man who would risk everything to lead them to salvation—was actually unfolding before them.

"He defends what he perceives to be innocent, defenseless," Sid said.

"I must admit, it is curiously honorable… for a human." Ell'han allowed. Sid looked up hopefully at the cantankerous Elder. Begrudging respect for the captain's impassioned tirade from him was a good sign.

"'Curiously honorable?' Nonsense! It is as I foresaw," Farley exclaimed. "Exactly as the dream said."

The senior Elder rumbled back, "It does appear that the captain walks the same Path of Fate." He looked around the circle. "Are we at least agreed that his destiny and ours are intertwined?"

"Unfortunately," grumbled Leusta.

"Perhaps he is the one."

"Perhaps, but the path branches in many directions."

"But my dreams have proven true…"

"Yes, Elder, they have. So far. We must see if they continue to trickle up into the present—like bubbles rising from the bottom of a clear mountain spring, sometimes a single rivulet rises true to the top. We must wait and see if *our* present continues to meet *your* future."

10

HELEN

HELEN WALKED INTO THE DARKENED INTERIOR OF THE central mess, pausing cautiously in the shadows. Garrand sat hunched over a table, head resting on a propped-up hand, fingers splayed through his hair. A single beam of light cut the darkness, spotlighting the table. She walked up slowly and slid onto a bench opposite the man.

"I stopped by the kitchen on my way in." She hefted a bottle up onto the table. "Thought you might could use a drink."

Garrand lifted his eye from its deliberate stare at the burnished surface of the table and found hers. "I'm a step ahead of you," he said, hefting a bottle of his own onto the surface. "For a change," he added in a wry tone.

She wasn't sure where to begin. "I think maybe I owe you an explanation."

Garrand poured himself a measure into one of Jean-Wa's treasured *shai* teacups. He tossed the contents down his throat and set the cup back down, pushed it gently across the table. Helen pulled the stopper out of the golden bottle, noted the label read 'Taken's Root BBVDA' and poured a shot into the porcelain cup.

She sniffed at the liquor once and then swallowed the contents in one mouthful, cringing slightly as the liquid burned the back of her throat. Setting the cup back down she fixed Garrand with a long, hard look.

"He murdered my mother."

Garrand kept her gaze.

"The Nralda's Director of Acquisitions, Carrelle Darstin, butchered her to keep my father in line." She poured another measure and splashed that one back as well. The cup was pushed across the table to Garrand. "And he kept me at his side so that my father would continue his research—he held my life over his head. The threat was implicit: produce results or the daughter suffers the same fate."

Garrand poured another double measure into the cup and pushed it to the center of the table.

"My father's work was virtually taken over by the Nralda. For months after her death, he could barely function. It was only after a particularly sickening display that he was able to pull himself together." She paused and looked away. "The bastard dragged me in by my arm, held me up in front of my father and said, 'This is what will happen if you remain so reticent.' He dropped my arm down to his knee and snapped it cleanly."

Garrand watched her rub her right forearm as she spoke.

"Apparently it was effective. I'm still alive and my father became productive once more."

"So you became a pawn in the Director's game?"

"Yes," she answered softly. "Ever since I was a little girl, I was lead to believe that if I didn't follow Darstin's instructions, father would be killed."

"A living hostage," Garrand said softly.

"Over the years, I developed a cold, dark core deep within my heart where I stored my hatred for Darstin and the Nralda. I realized at a very young age, that consent was less painful than struggle. I kept my humiliation, fear, and loathing inside me, and appeared willing on the surface. I sought out Darstin's trust and confidence. Trust so that one day I might have the opportunity for revenge.

"My father's research progressed—brilliantly in fact. The first pandas were reaching maturity. I was a teenager then, and was finding other ways to gain Darstin's confidence. Later, I became a personal courier, trained by the Nralda and sent on special missions where a delicate touch was needed. He tested me often, giving me opportunities for freedom—allowing me access to damaging secrets. But I never took the bait."

Garrand looked at her stolidly.

"I wasn't looking for small victories anymore. And simply escaping would leave my father unprotected. No, there was nothing that would satisfy my dark hidden places—the black heart that *he* created—other than devastation utter and complete."

A single tear flowed down her cheek. She was sure Garrand would mistake it for a tear of remembrance. In actuality it was only in recognition of the vast differences between her life then and now, between the unyielding cruelties she had grown up with at the hands of Director Darstin compared to the gentle kindness afforded by the captain and his crew.

The memory itself wasn't what saddened her; she had learned to repress the painful scars long ago. It was realizing how large the gap was between what she'd endured under Darstin's tutelage compared with what she might have experienced had she been with someone like Garrand Médeville. The sweet, sad disposition below his gruff exterior was not lost upon her.

Garrand reached forward and gently touched her hand, first with a fingertip, then with his whole hand encompassing hers. He studied her silently, her beautiful green eyes moist with memory, her lips slightly parted, vulnerable—much more fetching when they weren't spouting an acerbic remark, he decided.

Helen gazed back at him with unblinking resolve. The simple brush of his hand over the top of her fingertips was the tenderest gesture she could imagine. Nowhere in the hard, strictly-regimented society of the Nralda was there room for such a gentle expression—nor had she ever felt even a flicker of such genuine affection or empathy from Darstin in all the years spent in his clutches.

"So it's to be devastation, is it?"

Helen swallowed hard and nodded. "Yes."

"And how do you plan to bring about the fall of the Director?"

Helen gave a half-snort and continued. "I did not suffer years of humiliation for nothing. I became his trusted agent and confidante, utterly loyal and submissive, so that one day I could betray him completely. And that day has arrived."

"So instead of simply moving the pandas, you are taking them away from him?"

"Exactly. He will be accountable for trillions of credits and a quarter century of research with absolutely nothing to show for it."

Garrand chewed this over silently for a moment. *It wasn't enough, she wasn't telling him everything.* He fished a little deeper. "And what about the empire—what part do our Imperial pursuers play in this?"

Helen flashed him a swift look. "An added difficulty—not completely unexpected, they've been after the tribe for years—"

"On this scale?"

"No. Barrett only recently grew so desperate. The task force was assembled perhaps a year ago… maybe less."

"And why me?" he demanded finally.

Helen wrinkled her nose and bit nervously at her lip. She decided to tell him. "You weren't my choice. Director Darstin chose you."

Garrand grimaced. "Darstin?"

"I would rather have flown the mission myself," she explained. "Would have made things much simpler from my point of view. Fewer variables to deal with. Easier to get the dirt." *Less lies to tell*, she added silently. "But Darstin was adamant. Wouldn't let me use any of the Nralda's gunrunners— didn't want anything traced directly back to the Nralda."

"Why would Darstin select me?" Garrand was concerned. He didn't like being on the top of anybody's list, particularly a keiretsu lord's.

"He said you would prove invaluable to the mission." *And he was right*, Helen thought to herself. Darstin always seemed to know things before she recognized them herself. Could he have guessed then about her betrayal? Had he already have planned for just such a contingency? She shook her head free of such fears. "He said your background in the Imperial Guard would help us evade the empire. 'Who better to elude Imperial capture of our cargo than one of their own?'" she quoted.

Garrand sighed. His name was resurfacing in high places again. His decade of anonymity was apparently over. He pressed on. "What about your father?"

"I arranged for him to be taken to a safe place for now."

"How did Darstin agree to all this?"

"Moving the pandas is not something all that unusual. My specialty of late has been geared toward supervising such movements personally. Whenever Imperial agents or other keiretsu were getting too close it's time to pack up and find new dirtside facilities."

"Why not something discrete and orbital? Harder to find, easier to defend."

"I don't know about that 'easier to defend' part, but the main reason was the pandas themselves. They have special needs that can't be met in a small, confined vacuum-oriented environment."

"The bamboo?"

"For one thing. There are others."

"I see," he said, wondering how much she was leaving out, how many deals and alliances she was skirting over.

"Anyway, the research had become too valuable to remain in my father's isolated care. The empire had nearly captured them on several frightening occasions. Rumors of super-intelligence genetic engineering experiments have swirled about the Shell for too long, and there are too many agents now that know the truth. Marshaling the Nralda's resources to plan for new hidden research facilities, arrange secret transportation, provide complex local cover stories, bribe officials, kill those who learned too much, and stem the inevitable flow of information to Imperial agents has become too expensive, too risky."

"I can imagine," Garrand mused. "So Darstin decided to pull the plug, huh?"

"Not before seeing the pandas for himself. Darstin came to witness the progress before he made his final decision." Helen nodded as she recalled the experience. "The pandas were impressive. Their abilities were not yet complete, as my father was constantly reminding him—he said he was stymied in the development of their prescient abilities. They could only *dream* the future, or see it in limited visions of uncertain accuracy—not much better than the sartographic simulators he said. But Darstin suspected otherwise—as I did myself. Darstin decided it was time to act."

"And you decided to act as well?"

"I had to, before Darstin hid them where no one could find them."

"Where would that be?"

"Who knows," she shrugged. "I'm only supposed to deliver them to a specific point in space at a specific time." She took another long pull from the bottle. "Your ship is to be sacrificed, and the pandas are to be never seen or heard of again…"

"My ship?" he asked incredulously. "My ship is to be sacrificed?"

"Well that's Darstin's plan, not mine," Helen slurred defensively. "We'll never be there to see it—we'll be long gone by then."

"With the keiretsu on our trail as well."

Helen shrugged. "Maybe." A little sparkle shone in her eye. "Maybe they can slug it out with the empire—" she started to say, but abruptly shut up.

"Yeah, that would solve all our problems."

Helen swallowed another measure of Taken's root and examined the bottle. "You know, you were right, this stuff's good."

Garrand scowled at her. "And how do you plan on avoiding the keiretsu?"

"You know," she said, ignoring him. "How did you know that was Sid back there—I mean, how did you know his name was Sid?"

"I heard you call him that when we first landed on El-Bouteran and later in the mess, you let his name slip again."

"Oh," she sighed.

"How come he's been following me around everywhere?"

"Why don't you ask him yourself," she said cryptically.

"Ask him?"

"You might as well find out for yourself. You don't need me for an interpreter."

Garrand's comtab chimed twice.

"What is it?" he snapped into the air.

Bailey politely responded: "Captain, I am preparing to re-move the housing of the actual trace itself. All self-destruct mechanisms appear to be disarmed."

"You sure it's not rigged with any tamper charges?"

"Captain I have done the most thorough possible series of magnetic resonance, infrared, electro-chemical, and pathogenic scans and found no sign that there were any further triggers."

"Okay, okay, I trust you. Go ahead I'll be there soon."

He looked to Helen and gave her a rueful look. "I better get down there."

"Go, go," she said kindly. "I wouldn't want you to miss any-thing."

"But wait, how are we going to elude the keiretsu?"

She stood up to leave, stopping to pat him on the shoulder as she went by.

"First things first, my Capítän," she drawled, mimicking Jean-Wa's pronunciation. "You just get us to P'tymor, and you let me worry about the keiretsu."

"And the Imperials!" he called after her.

"Yeah, and them too," she hollered from the serviceway.

❖ ❖ ❖

THE LOW GENTLE THRUM OF *Destiny's* REACTOR CORE CREATED A reassuring harmonic that pulsed through all the ship's bulkheads. Garrand placed a palm against the cold surface of the secondary hull and felt the ship's pulse vibrating through the cerasteel, his fingers tingling. The surface quickly imparted the absolute zero of cold vacuum and he paused for a moment, feeling his body warmth bleed away.

Bluish-green waves of energy rippled across the surface of the reactor, arcing upwards and disappearing into the array of power coils above. Static discharges burst white-hot across the electrically charged chamber, creating loud pops and crackles that echoed back and forth within.

The central engineering station was suspended midway in the reactor space encased in a steel cage to protect occupants from the discharges. The setup looked like a giant birdcage, but was quite effective for providing an onsite datastation.

Garrand watched Bailey as he carefully extricated the trace from within the primary coolant nozzle inside the quantum drive's housing. A devious and effective hiding place. He vowed to upgrade the ship's security systems when this mission was over. There was a great satisfaction in finally locating the trace—it was like removing a cancerous leech that had betrayed the ship's invisible passage through the ethos.

From the engineering station he could not hear Bailey as he extracted the foreign device. The usual hum that permeated all the ship's surfaces was a dull roar here, punctuated by loud pops from the crackling static discharges that escaped from the magnetic housing protecting the ship's dual reactors. The buzz only accentuated his light-headedness.

Bailey stepped into the engineering cage and presented him with a small, irregular box fit with four small cylinders and trailing a number of severed cables.

"We are clean, sir."

Garrand closed his eyes and nodded thankfully. He grasped the railing and stared down into the crackling cauldron of energy that pulsated below.

"What is it Captain?"

Garrand smiled ruefully, a flicker of recognition passing his lips as he remembered the discipline his father instilled aboard the *Toulenbe*. The man would never have allowed such behavior on his ship. The thought of one spare coil out of place aboard the cruiser was unthinkable.

The thought of *discipline* aboard *Destiny's Needle* with its current roster of colorful passengers struck him as quite comical. He wondered if he was finally breaking free from the genetic bond that seemed to inexorably lead him down the path of strict and unyielding discipline. Almost without thought he had always insisted upon order on his vessels. Despite himself, he was much more like his father than he would ever wish to believe.

Bailey's eyes gazed at him with deep concern. Garrand grasped his friend's shoulder warmly and sighed.

So much was happening aboard the ship, and Helen Tchelakov was a greater mystery now than she had been the first time he laid eyes upon her in the Oak Room. Elements of deception, innocence and chaos seemed to color her every move, following her like a cloud of disruption, a fugue. He tried to pinpoint the strange, dangerously intoxicating state of flux that held him, his ship, and his crew in rapt attention. After years of hard work, and deadly, sometimes numbing routine, they had become an easy target for upheaval, for the promise of a new adventure.

Such promises danced behind her every word, like the flames that burned behind her eyes when she spoke of her family. Helen Tchelakov was a dangerous woman. But the pandas were magnificent, and far more gifted than he had ever dreamed. And, of course, far more dangerous.

The line had been crossed once more, and his lot had been cast. He wished he could say he had less to lose this time, but he could not.

11

GEUTVOHN MADORA

DESPITE ITS HUMBLE ORIGINS, GEUTVOHN MADORA HAD become something of a major center on the Imperial reclamation world of Galzeki. The base was located twenty kilometers from the first Imperial hard-site port facility at Pelling's Point—way station for the hundreds of heavy lifters and scores of smaller scows that ferried scrap from low orbit to be redistributed across the planet's scarred plains. High altitude dumps were routinely performed over the southern hemisphere, but anything valuable enough to carry down to the surface intact came through Pelling's Point. As a result, nearly two hundred reclamation engines had been erected at Geutvohn Madora to handle the overflow.

What had started as an engineering camp and muddy hovel for the criminal diggers hauled in from out-system had grown over the decades into a full-fledged city. Much like the engines that defined it, Madora had been burned to the ground fourteen times in the first hundred years of its existence, torched by the Gambor, the Breyer, and the other resident sentients who fought to reclaim their planet. Time after time, Madora rose from the ashes, rebuilt with grim determination by the men who serviced the machines and culled the mounds. After decades of brutal attacks, the city had slowly turned its efforts to subterranean growth.

The Imperial garrison was not the first structure to be built beneath the surface. For years the workers had lived out of primitive tunnels carved into the mud and rock for protection from the frequent raids by the Gambor, Jic Jics, and Breyer. Soon the whole city was burrowing into the mud. The garrison's small cluster of armor-drip bunkers had grown into a sprawling complex of underground tunnels that linked every significant facility for fifty kilometers.

Almost every soldier unfortunate enough to be assigned to Galzeki spent their first few months in Geutvohn Madora's moist, filth-ridden hollows carved out beneath the mounds. Most of the steady stream of indentured laborers necessary to work the mounds were funneled through Madora for processing and assignment. Thanks to the combined efforts of the native populations, there was an unending need for replacements.

Lieutenant Jorge Scullata stepped out of the underground garrison bunker and started down the dimly-lit tunnel toward the surface. He was tagged to relieve the officer of the watch in the Com Relay station. Already he was drenched. Not fifteen minutes ago he had scrubbed himself raw with sand and dry detergent—a once a week luxury. He put on a freshly recycled uniform, but the oppressive heat and constant seepage of tainted groundwater had already rendered him foul. How he longed for the cold, pristine spaces of interstellar ships. Five more months within this planet was going to kill him.

Not that life above ground was any better. Between the fanatically hostile hardbacks that constantly plagued topside operations and the choking atmosphere filled with ash and the toxic byproducts of the reclamators, rotations topside were extremely dangerous.

Scullata acknowledged the salute of the guard at the outer lock and motioned the sentry to open the gate. The guard checked his external scope and then unlocked the steel doors, swinging the rusted metal inward on old-fashioned pin hinges.

The heat hit him before the stench. Scullata stepped up the last steps into daylight and squinted into the reddish glare. The sentries guarding the subterranean lock barely glanced at him. They were at the end of a long, tedious shift. Agitated from the heat, sweating beneath their body armor, they nervously kept their eyes focused outward—toward Sark's Pile. Geutvohn Madora's 'grubbers' named the mounds for the soldiers who died defending them.

Scullata gave the horizon a quick glance and felt that his sidearm was still in place. He unhooked the safety strap before he left the relative protection of the sentry post. He trotted across the muddy avenue cut between the mounds and ducked under a plascrete archway into a hardened bunker dug beneath Sark's Pile.

In a similar stop and go fashion he cut across the avenues until he had made it to the base of the relay station at Taston's Heap. A cave-in had cut off the underground access to this mound.

He flashed his ident-link, keyed in the security code and twin doors sluiced open granting him access to the repulsor lift. At the top of the shaft, a pair of eyes scrutinized him through a narrow slot before he was allowed into the elevated relay station. The officer of the watch signed over the codes, introduced him to Private Lopps, and apprised him of current com traffic before gratefully leaving the station.

Lieutenant Scullata sighed and stared out the tinted glazings. He saw nothing but row after row of endless mounds stretching from one end of the horizon to the other. *A lonely place to spend a year,* he thought.

❖ ❖ ❖

A LONE BEETLE STOOD SHIMMERING IN THE HEAT, PERCHED atop the belly of a flipped destroyer. The vessel had been cut into neat forty-meter chunks and stacked up before a defunct reclamator. The beetle's smooth-shelled body segments shone glossy black save for the dark, pitted scars that crisscrossed his exoskeleton. A crimson sash was tied across his shoulder. Ka'vaelus, Cha'halen first grade of the Vaelus burrow, wore his burrow's banner proudly. The tiny saplings in his satchel bore the physical and metaphorical hope of his planet: that someday Galzeki's forests would be returned to their former splendor and the Imperials would be driven back into the cold of space.

Ka'vaelus scanned the tetrahedral abominations that lay festering in the late afternoon sun. The vile mounds filled the flat burnt-out plains where a mighty forest had once stood, where thousands of species had once coexisted in peace and prosperity.

A small hiccup squeaked out from beneath his sash and he could feel tiny feet scraping against his shell. With a single claw, he delicately lifted the edge of his sash and Thurligan poked his head out. The white mouse sniffed up at the Gambor before he scurried up the giant beetle's shoulder.

"Ready for battle?" Ka'vaelus asked. Thurligan stepped over the ridged dorsal plates and disappeared back under the decorative bandolier.

Stretching his stiff elytra out across his back, Ka'vaelus lifted his thin, translucent inner wings upward and beat them rapidly against the humid air. His body arced into the air and he lifted his three horns to the sky. Starting deep in his thorax, he began a long, high-pitched call that reverberated throughout his body segments and out to the very tips of his wings.

The trumpeting cry echoed through the pyramidal mounds of rusting equipment and scrap that was piled in hundred meter stacks. The native cry drowned out the rattle and roar of the mechanized diggers who paddled through the mounds, turning the heap so that the scavenger corps could find recyclable materials in the scrap. The Imperial soldiers guarding mound 472B-West at Colah's intersection bristled at the ominous call. Blast rifles that had been shouldered were uneasily lowered, the muzzles carving silent arcs over the shadowy slope of the mound directly opposite their exposed bunker. But there were no targets to bring to bear, just the omnipresent rumble of reclamation engines that forever shook the ground, unearthing new treasures for the Imperial war machine and pouring putrescent smog and toxins into the darkening skies.

As the call faded away, dozens of Gambor erupted out of the hillsides, springing forth from the garbage itself. The Imperial foot soldiers stationed at the northern edge of Taston's Heap dove for cover as the insects materialized out of the scrap. A barrage of low-velocity projectiles pinged against the decaying cerasteel around the soldiers, making 'pock' noises as their explosive heads detonated on impact.

Pinned-down against the face of the mound, the soldiers fired a volley of AP mortar rounds. The pill-shaped steel shells fanned out over the heap, plunking down in the path of the advancing beetles. In quick succession, the anti-personnel rounds popped up three meters in the air and erupted in spherical blasts. The hail of steel barbs ripped through everything in their path. Three Gambor fell.

The soldiers defending Steven's Stack directly across from the besieged mound quickly popped the hood off their Tortian cannon and swung it around to face the marauding Gambor. The Tort spit forth white-hot arcs of energy, the blistering particles lancing across the muddy avenue, forcing the beetles back into crevices in the mountain of scrap. Shards of molten steel blistered and popped beneath the cannon's steady onslaught.

Ka'vaelus landed smoothly on the pinnacle of the opposing mound and surveyed the opposition. A vicious firefight had erupted amid the rubble and the attack had bogged down. He soon spotted the difficulty. Spreading his vulnerable wings, he launched himself off the face of the mound and glided down the steep slope angling toward the cannon emplacement. With a brief flurry of beats he pulled up short of the men that had his forces pinned down. He slowed his efforts and dropped down directly in their midst.

Before the Imperials could even turn, he plunged a sharpened claw from each arm into the sides of two men and lifted them overhead. A soldier turned in horror to see his mates rising in agony and swung his blast rifle to bear, but Ka'vaelus kicked him savagely away.

The fourth man was behind him. Ka'vaelus felt his presence as a bolt of energy seared through his wing, cutting through the cartilage and nerve. With a moan he felt a searing pain as the severed wing fluttered to the ground. He quickly retracted the nub and the good wing beneath the protective elytra, but it was too late. With a sad thought he realized he would never fly again.

He dropped the two gutted soldiers from his pincers and whirled to face the last man. He felt a sick sensation in his thorax and looked down to see a blade plunged into his midsection. The soldier grimaced, placed his free hand against Ka'vaelus' shoulder plate for leverage and wrenched his arm sideways as he tried to disembowel the massive insect. Ka'vaelus could feel his internal soup of organs resisting the man's blade. The soldier thrust deeper into his abdominal cavity, but Ka'vaelus cut him short, clipping off the man's arm at the elbow with a pincer. The human fell away screaming.

Ka'vaelus reached down and slowly extracted the severed forearm with the fist still clutching the blade. White liquid goo poured out of the hole that had been punched in his thorax. With haste he pressed a mossy clump of mud from his satchel into the wound and patted it tight. The field dressing felt cool and strange against his hot insides but he had little time to ponder the sensation. He gingerly climbed atop the bunker and watched the attack unfold.

Without overlapping fields of fire to keep them at bay, the Gambor closed in on the Imperials in seconds. Vell'lairn and Su'lairn were upon the soldiers first, their claws dripping with blood by the time Ka'vaelus negotiated the heap of rusted rubble.

The guard post sentry station fell and Ka'vaelus watched with satisfaction as four neat holes were quickly dug in the muddy soil. Four fresh saplings were planted in the humans' stead. He said a word of thanks and dipped his hide cistern forward, dripping two milliliters of water on each of the saplings before they pressed on.

He climbed atop the stripped down hull of a Halvanute air skimmer and flicked his antennae to the southwest. Subsonic waves signaled him that all three sentry stations at the base of the mound had fallen. The Relay station lay vulnerable and exposed—like a Ferg's freshly laid eggs.

With precise movements, he rubbed a pair of hind legs together, signaling the Gambor to move forward with the attack. He clicked to his team and they set off by threes across the dark canyon floor.

THE IMPERIAL RELAY station was perched just above the peak of mound 470-East, its antennae and com booster cables angling up from its roof like wispy filaments of a gigantic web.

Private Lopps looked up from his station. "Sir, getting reports of coordinated attacks on sentry posts three, five and six on mound 472B—all compass points—the slag pile at Colah's intersection and sentry post nine."

Lieutenant Scullata looked up from his digger allocation Sartoks. "Post nine? That's not half a kilometer away." He cursed. *How had the hardbacks gotten through the picket without tripping the early warning systems?*

"Better get the 119th up. Activate the inner penetration beacon." He consulted his mound chart. "We need containment across Lolan avenue—mounds 470 through 474. Get Major Starne on the tightbeam."

"We've lost contact with post eight and twelve."

"If they get to that new reclamator, Teak's going to have a fit. They just got it up to spin last week."

The private looked up with concern. "Sir, it doesn't look like they're headed for the engines."

"I told you to roust the grubbers!" The lieutenant strode angrily over to the flashing relay board and repeatedly stabbed the alarm for the 119th infantry division stationed below the elevated Relay Headquarters.

"Who we got patrolling this watch?" he asked, scanning the hazy sky through the slanted windows glazings. With the constant belching smog from the reclamation combines as well as the smoke from burning forests, Galzeki's sun was hardly ever visible anymore. There was only the dull, reddened glow of fire reflected against the grey pollution.

"Tippsey's down—engine problems—Moro's scheduled to be up but I've got no blink on the board for him. Flight two got pulled this morning—" he looked anxiously at the lieutenant.

"No air cover? Great." He'd warned Teak for months that without adequate air support, the outlying Relay stations were vulnerable to commando raids. The hardbacks certainly didn't lack courage—or audacity. He was afraid, however, that it was going to take a disaster before Teak would act.

The sound of blaster fire echoed just below the floor. He looked to the private. "Better pull the encryption disc," he said, drawing his sidearm. Standard procedure was to not merely lock up the codes in case of attack, but to destroy them outright.

Without warning, two Gambor burst through the glazings and dropped neatly to the floor. The first Gambor gouged a claw deep into Private Lopps' stomach and dropped him quivering to the deck. Both beetles turned to Scullata.

In a screechy rasp, the larger Gambor pointed a claw at the human's chest and said, "I'll take that if you please."

Scullata swallowed hard and lowered his sidearm partially, reaching forward as if to hand over the disc. Instead, he spun on his heel and fired point blank into the small beetle's nearest eye socket, smearing his brains across the glazing. He wheeled back to Ka'vaelus and fired three bolts in quick succession, aiming for the softer-shelled abdomen beneath the Gambor's exoskeleton hoping to hit one of the vital protected organs. The blaster bolts seared into Ka'vaelus' shell, just above his left breastplate. The armor cracked and the final bolt seared into his flesh, rupturing a lung, but missing his heart.

Ka'vaelus leapt over the table with a gasp as the human fired and lunged for the soldier's head. Scullata fired again, but the bolt glanced off Ka'vaelus' armored dome. He took the officer's neck in between his giant pincer and, with a snap of his wrist, decapitated him. The man's spine made a pop-cracking noise as the claw sliced through.

Ka'vaelus flicked the disembodied head away and gently picked the disc out of the human's fingers. The golden disc glittered in his claw. Within it lay the cryptographic data relay codes that would translate all Imperial transmissions throughout the Shell for several days—perhaps even a week if the Imperials stayed true to form. The disc would give them access to all com traffic—turning Imperial communicades from static gibberish into decipherable Vort Magellan, cryptic shorthand between datacores and easily translated into any language.

Ka'vaelus clicked his mandibles together with grim pleasure. There was no need to find the rogue bios himself. He could now count on the ruthlessly efficient servants of the empire to do the work for him. *Destiny's Needle* could not escape detection forever. Vast resources and interwoven allegiances would eventually turn up the ship and her priceless cargo. The Imperials would lead him to Tchelakov, the Director would have his prize, and he in return would have the weapons he needed to drive the empire off Galzeki forever.

He searched in his satchel for a Folgantu Oak, finding the sapling carefully wrapped in a moist cloth. A very special tree would be planted in this human's stead. He turned a sad eye to the Gambor lying sprawled out on the floor. Ka'vaelus knelt over Dell'lairn's lifeless form, carefully removing his sash and satchel. He was bound by honor and duty to sing of the young Gambor's valiant death and to plant each of his remaining saplings—carrying on his fight even unto death.

12

PREPARATIONS

THE ASSASSIN TORG HEEDED THE CALL THAT SUMMONED him to Vice Proctor Barrett's inner chambers aboard the *Shiva*. He paused briefly in the outer antechamber, beneath the gently rocking cages, and hung an object from a gut cord on the nearest rung of the ladder.

"Make some music of your own, boy," he rumbled to the sticky darkness above. He could hear Drazon Vorge's shallow, uneven breathing echoing in the rafters.

Gripped by curiosity, Drazon strained in the ensuing silence, trying to hear beyond the flutter-scrapes of the restless birds as they prepared for their nightly concert. To all his senses, the assassin had truly left. Finally he scrambled down the ladder, stopping one rung short of the gift and dropped over it to the floor. He grunted at the impact and felt for his loose tooth, hoping it had been jarred free. But no, the root still held stubbornly despite the glacial push of the adult tooth crowding in above it.

He stood and craned his head at the object hanging from the ladder. It looked like an oblong of dried mud crudely turned in the shape of a frog, just like those the assassin was becoming known for. Its back was riddled with black spots that upon closer inspection turned out to be openings. He gingerly plucked it from its mooring and examined it, trying in vain to see into the tiny holes. They had circular indents over them that perfectly fit his tiny fingers: eight above and two below the belly. When all fingers were occupied by these openings, he experimentally pursed his lips and applied them to what appeared to be the mouthpiece, an outcropping of mud before the stumpy tail. He blew hard, but no sound came. He tried again, straining his neck muscles as he poured his breath into the tiny aperture. The hinged jaw of the frog lowered open and then closed, mutely. In frustration he huffed; finally giving leave to a sigh. In echo, a mournful sigh issued forth, a sound as lonely and broken as the song the imprisoned creatures prepared to sing. At this he looped the cord around his neck and leapt to the ladder. He climbed into the rafters and awaited the concert — excitement replacing dread for the first time since they had begun.

Tonight he followed the discordant rhythms of the song carefully, waiting for a quiet passage. He whispered his breath into the belly of the frog, as lightly as his faith. As Drazon's sorrow entered the mix, the mournful concert above him slowed and became silent. For a long moment only the sound of his wind rose and fell through the chamber. Then the main song resumed, softer with a subtle change in the motif.

Drazon continued to play, aware that the melody around him had altered, turning into a song only the wind itself could tell. It brought the outdoors in, spoke of wrapping around century trees and caressing mountaintops, of making waves on tiny brooks, of wandering, always restless, seeking, touching everything along the way. It murmured of the intensity and thrill of the journey, and it whispered of power, the power to be free. A note trilled in accompaniment, to be joined by others as the symphony altered. A new emotion had entered the mix: hope.

The boy finally laid the whistle down, rolling the warmed ceramic against his chest. He started in on the loose tooth again, turning it from side to side aggressively until it turned three hundred sixty degrees and hung only from a thin nerve. His tongue scooted into the narrow cavity created by his industry and he worked the tooth convulsively for several minutes. Finally it popped free with a firm twist. The boy held it out and studied it in the bluish light. It was a fine specimen of a front tooth, with three tiny holes bored into it from zalva parasites on Galipsus Minoirte. He toggled the bit of nerve still clinging to the tooth and furrowed his brow. It was too good, really, to give away—but barter had to be made. Minoirte's dictate. He might be a thousand worlds away, but he remembered the rules of exchange.

❖ ❖ ❖

HELLIUS BARRETT LOOKED ELEGANT IN HIS LONG FLOWING robes as he stood grasping the observation handrail. He stared back over the irregular shapes of his fleet and watched as the two fastest picket cutters in his command pulled up alongside the *Shiva*. The knife-edge forms of the *Ilyovahtna* and the *Jjaeyg* were a mute black against the dazzling stars. It was time to send forth the best and the brightest. He sighed unhappily—part of him wished he could go along with young Captain Strom, but he would only get in her way. She must know that she was in total command of this mission. There was but one last thing he could do for her.

Star glow sketched a whisper of a silhouette around Barrett's body, interrupted by the creases in his robe when he turned to face the assassin entering his chambers. The large man dropped briefly to one knee before the platform. Barrett waved him up.

"I have a task for you, my friend."

Torg bristled minutely; Barrett's invocation of closeness in relations, something beyond the dictates of professional behavior, always put him on his guard. There was nothing but cool detachment in his voice as he answered: "Yes, my Lord?"

"You have served me admirably these past three years."

Torg bowed his head, acknowledging the compliment.

"My stature has risen considerably and your reputation has grown in accordance. More to the point, my heart still beats and my lungs still draw sweet breath. In the Shell that is no small feat. You have done your job well."

The Vice Proctor paused, fidgeting uncharacteristically with the hem of his robe. Torg waited silently, watching.

"Captain Strom departs in three hours. I'm sending Arnas as an added measure..." He looked to Torg for a reaction, frowned, and continued. "He will accompany her team with a platoon of the 41st marines. The frigate *Ulusi* is almost as swift as the pickets. It will trail only slightly behind with men and matériel for support."

"Yet you're still concerned," Torg murmured following the creases around Barrett's temples. "But not with the success of the mission..."

"No. I am confident that Captain Strom can capture them. She is a remarkable young soldier."

"You fear Nralda intervention. You fear something unexpected."

"Yes," Barrett grated. "Always the unexpected. Plans within plans and all contingencies considered, the probabilities worked out beyond all doubt and *still* something goes wrong..."

Torg picked up on the direction of the subtle insult. "Arnas has done a soldier's duty," he retorted. "Without him you would never be this close."

"He has made mistakes."

Torg shook his head. "He's made *decisions*."

"Mistakes," Barrett said flatly. "Mistakes that cost precious lives, gobbled up hard-won resources, swallowed the time spent as well as the time now needed to make it right. It is all a matter of time. I only have so much of it I'm afraid. My life is finite and I have so much to accomplish."

Torg's eyes narrowed at these words.

"These creatures are the solution," Barrett said. "They will change the art of warfare forever. Imagine being able to travel in time without ever having to leave the present. Now we must rely on intuition and assumption, but with the Tchelakov creatures there will no longer be any guesses. The Shell will fall one system at a time."

The perfection of the sartokian model, Torg thought quietly. *The science of future probabilities raised to one hundred percent.* Torg tried to imagine the consequences of not merely guessing the future, but knowing its every twist and turn. "Captain Strom will bring them back."

"Yes, I'm sure she will…" Barrett said distantly. An awkward silence filled the chamber.

Torg sighed quietly. "You wish for me to join the *Ilyovahtna.* You wish for me to go on this mission to protect Captain Strom."

Barrett nodded and looked back to his assassin. "Very astute."

"She won't like it."

"She doesn't have to *like* it, she's a soldier."

"What is to be my position?"

"You are now *her* personal assassin. Follow her, watch her, keep her alive. She must not come to any harm." Barrett gave him a hard, careful look. "Just bring her back to me."

Torg returned the gaze. "As you will, my Lord." He turned to leave.

"Have your things ready for transfer to the *Ilyovahtna* in one hour. The last Geggins are being ferried across then."

The assassin took his leave and walked back through the antechamber. As he swept beneath the cages, the boy scampered down the ladder and shoved a token into his hand. The assassin examined it carefully in the low light, his eyes gleaming as the tooth rolled down the crease of his glove. Torg smiled down at him before moving on, a real smile, not the conciliatory one Drazon was accustomed to from adults. No, the assassin knew and appreciated the value of the tooth. He exhaled slowly after he had gained the ladder again. He had chosen well.

❖ ❖ ❖

ACHIEVING THE RANK OF CAPTAIN OF THE IMPERIAL GUARD RE-quired a great many skills but foremost among them was the ability to lead. Least necessary was a proficiency in datacore programming. Most officers relied on pod-techs rather than master the skills themselves. Vailetta was not an exception in that regard. Although as a child she had realized a great agility in scampering around the virtual playground that datacores offered, she had not developed that ability along with her others. Therefore, she felt barely adequate to tackle the labor of plotting intercept points in overlapping, shifting volumes of space. Not to mention trying to tackle the advanced sartokian models or the achingly-complex mathematics of time decay and probability, all of which was necessary to track *Destiny's Needle* on a theoretical level. Haven only knew what she'd do if she had to rely only on herself, however, Lord Barrett had instructed her to cull her crew from any among Arnas' ranks, including his bridge team. It had been some time since she had dealt directly with the strange caste of pod-techs, what the navy referred to rather nastily as 'poddies.'

There had been attempts to keep the pod-techs continuously in the pods with adaptive liquid oxygen mix, but the failure rate had been prohibitive. Until science found an answer, pod-techs were cycled by a special corps of arts who acted in many ways as exoskeletons. Inside the datacores the pod-techs could float, spin, race, their programming graceful and sure. But once removed they seemed spineless and lackluster.

Throughout, they were so remotely human that Vailetta expected to find they had taken a new shape, one better suited to their environment. Strange that they were manufactured in a land-based form for immersion work. Why had the scientists conformed their function to the limits of such an inadequate shell? Was it to give them a link, however distant, to other humans? Was it hubris? The creation of a new man? Or was it merely a human variation on arts? Using a 'safe' organic rather than the unacceptable artificial that had spawned galactic outrage and wars.

She spent several crew rotations on the bridge, seated at an observation datacore niche that overlooked the row of communications pods before she located the pod-tech she needed. He utilized rather unorthodox paths through virtual space. His programming had real character: shortcuts that seemed to lead only to dead-ends eventually resulted in breakthrough bursts of brilliance.

She read the tattooed cyberhandle on his neck and approached him as his shift ended. An art was removing him from the pod, detaching various cables that snaked through hooped earrings along his neck. Delicately, the artificial lifted away the heavy reality blinkers. He seemed to retain some use of his sight despite what must assuredly be partial optic nerve damage from the blinding shield. He blinked away the gauze of jell over his eyes and squinted up at her. Like all of his caste, he was small. She towered over him by several centimeters.

"Yarvek-EZ?"

"Yes?" The raised pinpoints of tattooed caste markings covering his face bunched together. He looked startled, maybe a bit frightened. She didn't blame him; in the ensign's position, she, too, would have assumed the worst. Officers did not seek out pod-techs except to demand an accounting for mistakes.

"Is it your sleep cycle now?"

"Eating, ma'am-sir." Despite the support of the art, his spine sagged. His unformed muscles dribbled globules of pod jelly onto the deck plates that gobbled them up and drained them to recycling vats. The art enveloped the man's nakedness with a simple hooded wrap inset with cloth carrier handles so that he could easily maneuver the ensign.

"Shall I join you?"

"As you will, ma'am-sir. But I just plug in at my quarters. You know." He tapped an orange-tipped catheter port among those dotting his collarbone that would receive nutrients intravenously. She had forgotten. The pod-tech caste did not have a social space for eating or for anything else. They only met in virtual space. Otherwise, they were on their own, stuffed into gravity booths for muscle massage and strengthening of their rubbery bones while they slept. Vailetta found the idea as strange and distasteful as the others did. Poddies were necessary but avoidable. To face them meant to question what humanity was shaping itself into in order to win the stars.

She needed to take this ensign out of his cycle, to challenge his fears, find out if he was up to the task ahead.

"Why don't we try the mess today? Can you handle that?"

"Why wouldn't I?"

His easy answer surprised her.

"Good." As they exited the bridge, she signaled to a waiting exo-cart and hopped aboard. The art lifted the ensign next to her, where he slumped against the restraints built in for just such use. She turned toward the art, who snapped to attention.

"Send ahead for the appropriate meal bag."

"Nutrient and plasma, Mistress," the art corrected softly, head bowed.

"Mess three. Have it waiting."

"By your will, miss."

According to ship's chronometer, Mess Three was undergoing transition as shifts changed. Vailetta glanced nervously at the crested dragon that guarded the entrance to the mess. Its talons curved around an ornate timepiece that seemed out of place amid the streamlined, minimal design of the ensign's mess. The Coryl-Tuluyt Picket *Ilyovahtna* was being fueled and prepped—her team was to depart in hours and she still had decisions to make. In the back of her mind she could see the sartographic blip representing *Destiny's Needle* rushing further and further away.

Three mechanics brushed past the pair on their way out of the mess. The nearest turned to look over his shoulder.

"Bunch o' bloody poddies. Telling us where to go. Like to see 'em come fight in null gravity, I would."

Vailetta stopped to reprimand the ensign but Yarvek-EZ tugged on her cape, shook his pale head, and urged her on. She hesitated for a moment, but followed; she was unaccustomed to turning the other cheek.

She had wanted to remove him from the familiar, to see how he could adapt when habit was broken. And she had wanted to demonstrate the respect she could command for him until he earned it himself. Small crews could be very intense, and she had no intention of allowing any member to separate himself, not even a pod-tech.

"You like the E2?"

"Truly, ma'am-sir, but it's a bit crowded in there for me. I like to ride it alone, you know?"

"I can offer you that."

"It's not polite to joke, ma'am-sir."

"Not at all. I am offering you a temporal commission aboard my ship, the *Ilyovahtna*. It's equipped with the old E1 — smaller but nearly as fast. You'd be solitary."

"To begin when?"

"Immediately. We have much to plan."

"The commander flush with this?" He looked as though Arnas would pop up from beneath the table to snatch him from this opportunity.

"Lord Barrett assumes all responsibility for your removal and return."

"Lord Barrett," he murmured, patting his knees spasmodically. "Well, all right then."

Vailetta smiled; Yarvek was going to do just fine.

"Good. Have your things packed and ready to go by — "

" — I have no *things*."

Vailetta furrowed her brow. "Nothing?"

Yarvek glanced briefly past her, swallowed and met her gaze. "What you get is what you see."

"Even better," Vailetta said firmly. She stood to leave, squeezing his shoulder gently as she rose. "No need for all the clutter anyway."

It was Yarvek's turn to smile. His cheek twitched upward, unaccustomed to using his facial features in that manner.

❖ ❖ ❖

DR. GARDNER WAS DEAD. HIS BODY, BY ALL ACCOUNTS, STILL LAY twisted unnaturally in his medical laboratory. Yet he still had his thoughts and worse, he still had his memories. With chilling clarity, he remembered the awful shimmering silhouette of the assassin as his hands reached out to wrench his neck. He was screaming, and he could hear the pop. It was as if he still faced the agony of those final moments, the sheer terror of being stalked by a master assassin, the terrible frustration of knowing no way to forestall the inevitable coming of one's own murder. In his shadowy wraith shape he twisted in torment.

Observing the ghost, Torg fingered the silver shells of the bandolier slung over his shoulder and waited patiently for Dr. Gardner to break from the past and enter the moment. The wispy translucent form of the doctor stood before Torg, the faint beams of holo emanating from his shell just visible as they projected his image three-dimensionally into the room. His body was still twisted in a sickening position, neck snapped, head nearly facing backward. The ghost finally caught sight of the assassin and coiled in on himself, quivering.

"Oh by Kal'hela, the devil is here," he groaned.

"I made a promise to meet you," Torg murmured.

"I remember. But you said in K'ye." The ghost inspected his surroundings with suspicion. "K'ye looks very much like an Imperial vessel."

"What did you expect?"

The ghost untangled his image and gaped in horror at his rear end. His head was on backwards.

"Did you have to save me with my head all twisted around like that? This perspective is going to give me a headache. I look straight down and see my own ass."

"I'm surprised you can see it. There isn't much to it."

"Easy for you to say. Your ass probably isn't even your original. A transpecial nightmare, you are."

"If you continue to be testy I'll put you back down." The assassin tapped Garner's shell on his bandolier, his other hand hovering near the controls on his belt.

"Shut me off again?" He snapped to attention, though his head still lolled to one side. "No, thank you. Really, I've had time to think, quite a bit actually, and I don't see that I deserve such a fate. I understand why you might hate augmenters, considering your past, but I never operated against anyone's will. In fact, I was quite sought out for my exclusive services."

"Oh, I'm certain of that doctor. How do you think I came across you?"

"I'm sure I wouldn't know. But I'll tell you, a flat state is an awful way to live."

"No one said death would be easy."

"Technically I'm dead. Specifically I'm still me. I've worked on enough bodies to know there's nothing special about flesh. It's just meat and bones and some nerves. No, the essence is up here," the ghost tried to tap his head but his finger dipped into his own skull creating a distorted sparkle.

"Some would argue the essence is in here," Torg tapped his chest.

Gardner's ghost sniffed: "The heart? Just another muscle, easily interchangeable, *as you well know!*"

Torg allowed the ghost a thin smile. He found the man imminently more enjoyable now that he was dead.

Gardner continued: "No, I'm still me — just an electrical essence, recorded and transcribable, a 'personality shadow' lacking only a corporeal body, a proper forum to act from. You might consider the benefits of dumping me in an art. I could be useful. Very useful."

Torg seemed to consider this.

"There's no need to keep me flattened out in that sensory-deprived matrix."

"A link-up might be arranged. You'll not like the cost, though."

"I don't care about the price. It can't be worse than flatland."

"So you believe. Very well. I happen to have some plans for you."

"The honest assassin."

"Careful, doctor, you're not a god any longer. I am your new deity, and your existence depends on my generosity."

Gardner's mouth dropped open.

"That's very pompous. Who ever heard of a god being paid?"

"Naive. They always demand payment. As for your first comment, I'll forgive you that due to the strain of your transition. But have no doubt I will not hesitate to dispatch you as quickly as I did the first time if you do you not heed me."

"Yes, sire."

"No sarcasm," Torg commanded, carefully unhooking his bandolier of silvery shells. He laid the long strand across a table slab and began flicking switches. New images began to coalesce within the room.

"What's this?" Garner asked in surprise.

Torg said nothing, his eyes briefly flashing to red before he turned his back. The assassin left the chamber, the portal sluicing closed behind him.

Garner glanced with apprehension around the circle of ghosts that glowed in the semi-darkness. Each glanced at him in its own peculiar way, eyes sparkling.

"Who might you be?" he asked no one in particular.

"We're the good assassin's *Inner Circle*," said one apparition in mock seriousness.

"Doctors one and all," croaked another. "Each of us has his or her own specialty, but we're bound by a common thread: we're victims all…"

Garner shifted his focus to the closed portal. "He left us 'on?'"

"Our shells are still activated, yes," the ghost of Becca Voornay said patiently.

"To what end?" Garner demanded.

"How else shall we fulfill our role?" spoke the ghost of Dr. Taylor.

"Our *role?*" Garner asked, incredulity getting the better of his disdain.

"As advisors," Becca Voornay answered.

"Medical advisors?"

"In part."

"You'll find assassins don't have many friends," Orveytka murmured absently.

Garner snorted. "Imagine that."

A ghost, silent to this point, spoke up. "You're taking too narrow a perspective on this, old boy."

"Too narrow! Might I remind the 'distinguished members' of this circle that each of us was murdered by this abomination. We've been robbed of our mortal coils by this dark specter. I think I'm allowed a little leeway here. My cynical reflection is not only called for," he twisted his torso in indignation and was surprised to find he was no longer staring over his ass. He straightened up with pride. "But it's also part of who I am. This is my essence, is it not?" His holo fingers carved through the equally insubstantial air. He watched his hand twist back and forth, observing the details of the far wall through his transparent digits.

"Yes, you'll remain the same insufferable prig you were when you still drew breath," the brooding ghost said.

"He's gotten himself facing privates first," observed Taylor. "That's a start."

"At least we don't have to stare at his rear end any more," Becca sighed with relief.

Garner was finding renewed strength in being able to control his physical manifestation. Anger seemed to work best.

The more his righteous fervor grew, the easier it was to move his limbs. He ventured a step out into the circle of apparitions.

"So, for 'lack of friends' we're being kept in this state—" he waggled his arms and then crossed them. His forearms passed through one another in an unnerving sparkle of light. "For how long?"

"In perpetuity."

"Prisoners? Slaves?"

"Advisors."

"Trapped here forever?"

"As long as he wishes. Would you rather be completely dead, without thought or wish or hope?"

Garner considered this. "What of the next plane of existence?"

The ghost of Dr. Lorgin guffawed. "Your bones are dust, your mind and essence gone as well. You, a man of science, seek a hereafter?"

"Perhaps this is the hereafter," Dr. Voornay said softly. "We still have room to think and scheme."

"And hope," Taylor said, staring at his feet.

"But how can you behave with such decorum, dare I say respect, when *he* is around?" Garner spat. "The man who dispatched us all, who stood and watched our blood cool, our bodies atrophy."

"The passions of the past cool with time, fading like memory. Our fate now rests with Assassin Torg. As go his fortunes, so go the fortunes of us all," Becca said. "If the man ever finds peace, so might we."

"Man!" Garner harrumphed, finding his vaporous body much more controllable. "He's hardly a man at that."

"His heart is human."

"I've seen that heart," Garner retorted, "and it is definitely not human."

"What's past is past, Garner. You're stuck with us and you might as well get used to it."

"You'll find there're benefits to not having a corporeal body," Lorgin added.

"Oh, please," Garner protested.

"This is a new phase in your 'life,'" Becca said. "A chance to reflect and redirect with no consequences."

"Yes, we're already dead," Taylor piped in.

"Someday we'll all have bodies again."

"What? Artificial bodies?" Garner bristled at the thought.

"Better and stronger than mere flesh."

"Hmm," Garner remained unconvinced.

"But all our hopes for the future rest on Torg's forbearance… and survival."

"From what I've observed, he should have no problem there."

"There's much you do not know," Dr. Voornay stated plainly. "If you're to be of help, you must be briefed."

All eyes rested on Garner's shimmering image.

"Death does not have to be the final word."

"Think of it, Garner. Your own practice again…"

As an artificial, he thought. He looked at his colleagues, his curiosity piqued. As much as he wanted to see Torg die a gruesome death, he would love to feel the cold steel of a scalpel in his hand again.

After a long pause, he relented. "Tell me what you know."

Becca smiled. "What do you remember about the Gambor?"

13

THE EMPEROR'S BUTCHER

VAILETTA WATCHED THE STERILE WHITE RADIANCE OF THE nearest star erupt into a long spectral tail of color as the *Ilyovahtna,* the *Jjaeyg* and the *Ulusi* broke from the rest of the fleet and made the leap into quantum space. They were on their way: a dozen Gokazoku Kaigi, two pickets and their complement of crew, one master assassin, and a fast attack frigate, the *Ulusi,* for support. The half-squadron of Torrellian fighters in the frigate's belly were an invaluable asset. She had been given only one ship capable of hauling fighters, leaving the 74th squadron's sister ship, the *Acklivedo,* behind; it was probably for the best—she wanted speed not brawn.

The inclusion of Commander Arnas and his first platoon bothered her though. She didn't need Shock Troops—the failure of their heavy-fisted, blunt approach had made this mission necessary in the first place. Lord Barrett, however, thought otherwise; apparently he foresaw some use for them, or else he liked to hedge his bets. At least they were stationed aboard the *Ulusi* and she would not have to deal with them personally.

Listeners were spreading out all over the systems that fringed the Krestyaninov Cluster. The *Ilyovahtna* and her strike team would be on the far side of the cluster in eleven days and the hunt would be on.

She dimmed the lights in her cabin and slipped back against the berth, unbelting her robe. What troubled her the most was the mysterious presence of the assassin Torg on her ship's roster. The mission's dynamics did not call for an assassin, and yet here he was. The haunting familiarity the slender man invoked coiled its way into her exhausted mind, summoning childhood memories. She relinquished her desire to divine the truth and fell asleep.

She dreamt of being back in the Emperor's court. She saw the baby dragons, the games of go, and the white tiger rugs. She remembered a man like Torg—the Emperor's personal assassin, the Butcher of Yuzbek—a man of shadows with no clearly delineated features.

The bomb threat aboard the *Shiva* replayed itself in her head. Torg's calm confidence overshadowed the tense moments before the bomb was defused with the game's go dragon winking out the threat. Her dream twisted to her past, her beginnings, and she could see it all again, feel the curling of another decade's incense wrinkle past her nose. She had picked up the game of go in the Emperor's court. Back then He had simply called her His Myshka. His Firebird.

Somewhere out of sight a tabouli played a plaintive tune that wound its way through the stout pillars holding up the Emperor's Great Hall. Normally stuffed with the bustle of court pageantry, the cavernous room appeared empty except for the raised dais at its core where a man and a child were seated opposite each other over a gaming table.

Sinking into the white tiger rugs on their knees with homage, crimson-robed state councilors hovered imploringly, bobbing level with the man's shoulder. Leading the phalanx was the State Speaker, who gave voice to their telepathically confirmed requests. He skated in practiced movements upon his knees, careful to stay out of talon-reach of their ruler's sullen but beloved chained dragons. Their miniature stature in no way lessened their lethalness, of that the State Speaker was well aware.

"But Your Most Glorious, surely you could see to some Core matters today!"

The Emperor frowned with concentration and remained hunched over the tiny table. "Not until I beat Myshka at go."

"Oh, Brightness Itself, the matter requires your exalted attention."

The child giggled, cupped her hand and whispered: "You don't want to lose your empire, father."

"Insolent brat," he growled, pinching the ticklish part of her knee. She laughed and squirmed away, hiding in the nearest councilor's voluminous robes. Its occupant, the jilted speaker, twisted to look down at her and whispered peevishly, "Couldn't you let Him win one?"

"I did—yesterday."

"Oh, no, that one was legitimate," the Emperor insisted, narrowing his eyes and waiting for her agreement. When the child shook her head vigorously, grinning, he sighed and shrugged to his councilor.

"Well, now I shall have to win two games to redeem myself. It is not a good thing for a child to overreach her parent… so soon. Who knew that the greatest strategist in my kingdom would be my tiny daughter?"

"Will I be a general, father?" she clamored, eyes shining.

"You will be what will be. But always my Myshka, my *firebird*."

Normally this stage of the game nearly emptied the Great Hall save for a few servants and fewer guards. But today the Emperor had snarled at those minor retainers.

"Bah! Take those guards away! They spoil my concentration with such sour looks!"

Most of the petitioners had left in despair of ever gaining audience over the Emperor's newest obsession. It was demeaning for him to spend so much time over a child. But he would not budge.

It had always been this way to some extent: the Emperor tutoring one child after another, checking their progress, teasing them, before turning his attention to Imperial matters. One advisor had been dismissed after objecting.

"These children are my matters of state," the Emperor had snapped. "Loyalty begins in the blood, at home. Why build an empire only to lose it when I tire of life and move to my immortal plain? In them my work lives on as I do, forever." But the Emperor spent the most time of all with Myshka.

She was not numbered among his official heirs, that the Empress saw to, making a mark against each new mistress her husband favored. But Myshka, born to a concubine allowed to conceive, was the heir of his heart. The Emperor frequented a number of concubines, and favored ones were sometimes allowed to bring a child to term, as Vailetta's mother had. The Emperor could certainly afford the children, and, when he tired of the women he married them off to officers, further securing alliances. Children from such births were not considered legitimate, but the Emperor considered them his 'special children' and treated them to His attentions despite Her displeasure.

Now He took it too far and, as though infected with madness, had neglected everything else for days, remaining to replay His daughter, who often napped during His lengthy moves. Even His stiff golden robes had not been changed. For the first few days the Court had been full of novelty seekers, but those had grown bored and, not commanded to remain, had moved off their knees on to more ready entertainment, leading the mute, neon carnival of vendors and hawkers with them. But while the pageantry of the court had left, pretenders to power had gathered among the mute gargoyles in the whispering gallery above. Watching. Waiting.

Besides the State Speaker, only a lone soldier, ragged and nondescript, remained at attention on the exotic pelts that lined the stone floors in careless layers of wealth. Something about him made one's gaze not want to linger on him, something about the way his features blurred if one looked more than a moment. He had waited patiently the last four hours, saying nothing, standing at a respectful distance, knees slightly bent, hands crossed before him, eyes on the game. Only Myshka seemed curious about him; the fact that viewing him was difficult only made her more determined to see and hold him in her vision. With the obstinacy of childish intent, and instilled with the challenge, she turned around every so often after she had finished a move, as if to see what this statuesque supplicant thought or if he had truly turned to stone. She was disappointed at last to see that he had gone.

Only the State Speaker remained, as still and silent in his obstinacy and frustration as a stone statue. He hovered at the edge of the table, staring blankly at the playing table.

"Glorious One, I most humbly insist," the Speaker tried once more, his moustaches quivering with indignation as the Emperor waved him away yet again. The child would never forget the moments that followed. As she turned back to the game, time slowed to show her the scimitars that leapt from the Speaker's sleeves as he swept the blades in unison towards her beloved father. She watched how the lead scimitar deflected away from the Emperor's head before completing its blow and turned against the straining hand guiding it to cleave through its holder's neck. The severed head toppled, hit the floor and rolled straight to the roaring dragons. The Emperor never shifted from his pose. Around Him alarms sounded, voices shouted as He calmly laid a final stone.

"Aha! The eye! I think this time, my dear, you will find when we have counted the stones that I am victor." He looked down into her stricken eyes and pushed aside the table with a careless gesture that spilled the stones from the board. He gathered the child into his arms and strode from the Great Hall, oblivious to the shouts of servants and guards running in. Already word spread of the Emperor's miraculous escape, witnessed from the gargoyles' gallery above. Careers were falling and rising determined on who had been where when the attempt had been made.

In a darkened alcove off the Great Hall, where sound barrier fields muffled the clamor, the Emperor set her gently down and took her hand.

"I must thank you, my friend," the Emperor spoke into the shadows. "You were right; my perceived madness brought the quisling out of hiding."

A figured shimmered out of the shadow and the ragged soldier stepped forward. His features were no longer disguised. Myshka gasped at the rough scars that riddled the man's neck and wrists and disappeared into his clothing. The man looked down at her kindly.

"My special child," the Emperor stated, drawing her in front of him for display.

"She honors you."

"Yes, this one always will. I want you to consider her the same as myself."

He knelt before them and laid his hands formally at her slippers. "I will safeguard you until my blood cools with death."

"Are those your pets?" she asked shyly, seeing for the first time that tiny red frogs clung to his clothing, mouthing silently as their cheeks puffed in rhythmic fashion.

"No, friends," smiled the man, though the smile frightened her for his eyes shifted color with the emotion from dull silver to red. "But they cannot be yours," he warned as she crouched down to look closer. "They carry poison in their skin."

She sat back on her heels and cocked her head at him. "But they don't hurt you. You touch them."

The man chuckled with a scratchy laugh that sounded rarely used. "Yes, but I belong to them; I am one of them."

"I shall have to ask professor about your species," she said politely. "Your planet must be wondrous indeed."

"No, Myshka," admonished her father, stroking her head. "There is no creature in the universe crafted as this one, his kin are many species from many worlds, and not all of them are known even to me. He will go as the Emperor's Butcher, but you will never forget that within the man, as within every creature, beats a heart. You must always listen for that heartbeat, Myshka."

"Yes, father, I promise," she agreed solemnly.

"Always listen..." his words rang again. Then she awoke.

"Professor," she called drowsily to the datacore, "I want the files on Class One Master Assassin Torg."

"Certainly, Captain Strom. That would be in Commander Arnas' private files," answered a mellifluous feminine voice. A moment later, the datacore apologized. "Sorry, Captain, that file is locked."

"Well unlock it—my authority."

"I'm afraid I can't. It's tagged with a five claw dragon seal. Beyond my clearance—and yours as well. Commander Arnas has no knowledge."

Vailetta folded her arms behind her head. "Try code breaker subroutine *firebird*—you'll find it encrypted in my files. I authorize its release to you—vocal confirmation, Vailetta Strom, Captain of the Imperial Guard."

The datacore whirred with intent then broke in again.

"Still locked, Captain."

Vailetta sat up abruptly. Her secret entry into restricted virtual space had never been refused before. Something was terribly wrong.

"Try again."

"Captain, I did not *err*," the datacore reported tartly.

Vailetta leaned back, worry creasing her face. She thought of her father. That she had strayed from the courtly life and gone into the military had impressed the Dragon, but that she had done so without ever linking herself to her former station proved her loyalty. She had taken a new name, Vailetta Strom, and the Emperor's Minister of Intelligence had personally created an identity and a background for her. She would be known as the daughter of an obscure, but respected diplomat, and it was under this guise that she was accepted into the Bordëgian Academé. In her heart of hearts, she would always honor her true father.

She remembered the fateful day when He had called her to the attention of His personal assassin to safeguard the same as Himself. Even now, under the guise of training and age, the Butcher would know her. Though she had met the Butcher, seen him save her father's life, she'd only seen him fully that one time in the alcove. After that his image had always been blurry—his outline ragged and difficult to look at. His color and texture shifted as often as the mode of court dress around him, like a cuttle fish caught in a confusing parade of colors. None heard him speak, but a croaking always surrounded him: the toxic red toads of his home world that were his trademark, copied now by virtually all Imperial assassins. A few had even died from their eagerness to emulate him, but some species had found they could tolerate such companions without self-harm and the prestige of it grew. No, toads alone could not peg the Butcher.

True, she'd heard his voice, but it was soon after his operation and he obviously hadn't much the use of it then. He'd had years to work on his speech, and she'd had years to forget the hearing of it. She could not place him by his speaking either.

It seemed like an impulse that took her to Torg's cabin, but all along Vailetta knew she'd end up there, asking questions. A map check revealed that the assassin had sequestered a space near the storage holds, a quiet place. This area of the ship was left under the chill breath of space, warmed only to a tolerable level. Even then, Vailetta found herself wracked with shivers before she halfway arrived. She announced herself to the nondescript door. When the portal opened, eclipsed by the bulk of the assassin, Vailetta took a step back even though he held only a small, innocuous-looking bottle, not a weapon. A pungent fog curled out around his legs as the steamy air inside clashed with the frigid vapors of the hallway.

"Visiting, Captain Strom?" Torg asked as pleasantly as his gravelly voice allowed.

"Are you occupied?" She tried peering around his considerable bulk blocking the way.

"Only taking care of my creatures." He stepped aside to give her a clear view. "Why don't you come in?"

Inside she spotted his assassin's lamp. The convoluted evader coils laid out a shadow like a distracted scribble of brains stretched up to hold an optic candle's light. It was a strange, archaic device that did not belong even here in these unnatural quarters.

"You're a peculiar man, Assassin Torg," she said. "There's something about you that doesn't fit."

"What about me puzzles you, Captain?" His voice slid over her.

Vailetta looked around the room, at the wall-to-wall glass pens of dangerous reptiles and plants, all either camouflaged or colored brightly as a warning. *That's what Torg needed, a bright warning to stay away. Avoid him, he's poison!*

"It's all so cozy here, isn't it?"

"Some might not think so," he chuckled, indicating a tangle of deadly snakes in the case below.

She turned to face him, tearing her gaze from a gaggle of Ganglian snails smearing their way across a stairway of glass. "I meant your position on this ship."

"What concern is that of yours?" he returned softly, flexing his hand around the bottle.

She continued on, stubbornly, blindly. "Assassins are ranked but not profiled. I've often wondered *who* ranks you and *how* if your pasts are erased? Do you belong to some neutral guild that guarantees you? As assassins you sell a binding loyalty, so the past is no concern, and it's censored. Wiped. Untraceable. Or restricted to commanders and their superiors. Or, at times, only the Emperor knows."

"The visible presence of an assassin is a deterrent."

"Yes…" she said carefully. "But such a deterrent is usually most effective for someone in a visible position of power. Heads of state, praetors, proctors and the like. But on a specific mission such as this…"

"You think of me only as a *weapon*," Torg spoke the word as if it were an affront. "Lord Barrett does you honor by sending me to stand in your shadows."

"Hmm, yes — the man does seem to favor your services."

"After Proctor Nesbitt's unfortunate demise, the vice proctor has been understandably cautious."

"So, Barrett thinks I'm in need of protection now?" she splayed her fingers against the glass.

"He merely wishes for you to succeed *and* survive."

"So you are here to watch over me?" She in turn watched the slow progression of the snails.

"Does that disturb you?"

She turned back. "Are you under my command or not?"

"Officially I'm here as Lord Barrett's observer."

"I see…"

When she said nothing more, Torg turned away and positioned the bottle nozzle over the custom Trioxin screens that topped the tanks. A muscle along his neck seemed to work involuntarily.

She watched the mist settle as Torg continued to disperse moisture into the air over the tanks. She had played her hand too soon, said too much. Perhaps she could recover the advantage, though. "They look well-cared for."

"Part of my profession."

"Hmm, somehow I don't think that's everything." She pushed off from the glass to face him. "I came here to discuss a matter with you."

"So it seems."

"Your files are locked, even to Commander Arnas. That isn't right. I want to know why. Oh!" She winced with sudden pain and put her hand up to her head, swaying.

"Captain, is anything wrong?" He smiled politely at her, continuing to pump the spray into the air.

"Your files—" She took an uncertain step towards him, holding her head.

"Do you need assistance?" Torg reached out, his hand stopping just short.

"I've met you before—I *know* you. Not this you. Different. But the Emperor—" Her eyes rolled back and she collapsed into his arms.

"Oh, Myshka," he sighed regretfully into her hair. He depressed a switch on his belt and spoke into his collar. "It's done. Get here." He carried her to a sleep slot recess in the wall where a pallet slid out. He laid her down carefully, her long hair draping to the floor.

The cabin door swished open and an ormedica wheeled in a black box with cables running out.

"Well, well, some repair job here," he said cheerfully, moving to the bed. "Let's see what can be done." The man wore the gold-emblazoned black of an Imperial organic medic, those

rare human overseers of the swelling ranks of medicas. On the
back a large red circle proclaimed his office: ormedica.

He tossed the garment aside then briskly adjusted the light
overhead to a blinding intensity and flipped enyohanse glasses
in place over his eyes, which loomed large and unreal under
the thick lenses. He set a switch on the box he'd brought, and
a high-pitched whine rose as it charged. Pulling a pair of self-
adhering wires from a recess the ormedica touched them together briefly. A long spark arced between them. He twisted his
lips in a grimace.

"Turn her over."

The ormedica finished his business quickly.

"You were careful?" Torg commented tonelessly.

The ormedica paused as he wiped the bloodied wires and
coiled them back into the case. "She won't detect anything," he
promised.

"She already does," Torg murmured, looking down at Vailetta so peacefully unconscious on his bed.

"The chip, assassin?" asked the ormedica, squinting against
the light as he faced Torg.

"Certainly. You've earned it. And you know what disclosure
will earn you," he warned quietly, motioning the ormedica to a
chair and pulling another one up beside him.

"You'll need these," said the ormedica, pulling off the enyo-
hanses.

"They get in the way," Torg waved his offer aside and his usually silver eyes glowed red, the pupils wide as a mercat's in sunlight. He parted the ormedica's military collar and dug his nails
into the man's skin. He peeled back a bloody flap of synthetic
skin. Hidden just below the collarbone lay a standard hexagonal dataport, a permanent fixture on artificials. The ormedica
was not human but an organic artificial whose continued exis-

tence had been banned universally after the Gai'han Jihad. He had been masquerading as human, but Torg had detected his true essence. Knowing a creature's greatest secret was a powerful lever for negotiations.

"You're lucky they didn't retrograde you and have it built into the internals as this would be impossible," the assassin commented while performing a quick assessment of the wiring.

"Yes, the new safeguard against this sort of deceit — tagging organic arts as if they were mere machines. To think of that leash hooked into my central wiring," he shuddered visibly and quite convincingly. "Removing or altering it destroys the data-core..." he trailed off, lips twisted back in a grimace.

"I agree, it's highly unpleasant. Of course, what they did to you at inception is not much better, having explosives attached. But you're about to have your freedom granted."

"Her freedom for mine — a good trade."

The assassin worked quickly with a set of Imperial override code keys in the grooves on each end of the chip. Removing it set off a tremulous beeping that a well-placed key easily silenced. A bead of sweat hung at the end of the ormedica's nose. The nervous response did not escape Torg's attention. The danger was not over yet for either of them.

"You're an earlier model. The XO series?"

"Yes. From before the Lashback," he said, jutting his chin out.

A sly smile escaped him at the art's daring to use the renegades' name for the Art Wars. "Ah, yes, the Gai'han Jihad."

"Depends on what side you were on."

"It always does."

"Very astute. I've been wondering, how exactly did you find me out? I've been able to disguise my true nature for years. When you contacted me I was in a terror!"

"I could smell the difference in you."

The artificial looked aghast. "What?" he tried to stand. Torg's hand forced him back into the seat.

"I'm still working," he growled. "You have an armed bomb at your neck. Do you want to kill us both?" *Wouldn't it be just if all doctors had an armed bomb at their neck that the patients had control over,* he thought.

"Sorry. It's just——"

"Quiet and I will explain."

The art sucked in his lower lip and remained silent.

"Part of my heightened olfactory senses includes discerning between natural and manufactured blood. Most organics mix when they can, but you've grown slack, let your ratio fall. Hooked on the real thing?"

"I'm trying to quit."

Torg laughed, a discomforting sound like metal plates scraping together. "Obviously. I must say no one else is likely to figure it out. Sensor scans aren't usually tuned to my level. Besides, they've grown lax themselves, those damned Eyes."

"Yes, it will be good to be free of them."

"For a time. Have no doubt the empire is spreading as fast as she can conquer. In the meantime, work on that mix. Too much natural blood inhibits your filters, and like an overwhelming aroma, intensifies your plastica scent. Any Gai'han bounty hunter worth the price could peg you in an instant. With or without the dubious protection of human certification. The Sullusts always kill first anyway," he said referring to the fanatics who had lead the holy crusade against the artificials. Organic arts were forced to live secret lives as they were still hunted by the zealots.

He grunted with disparagement at the lack of finesse in his gloved fingers. He hesitated, then pulled off the Trioxin mesh and flexed his hand. The pale white fingers didn't seem real, particularly when compared with the artificial's perfect skin. He hoped his caustic touch would not damage the art's organics too much, but the bomb was his first concern. Torg glanced at the ring of holo ghosts encircling his chest. He would have liked to bring one of the doctors out to watch the proceedings and check for mistakes, but he couldn't count on any more beings knowing about this, dead or alive.

"I have lasted well these years without certification. Indeed there were dark times directly following the Lashback, but the need for trained and experienced human medical officers was so great that many petty officers didn't think twice about letting a qualified ormedica aboard. Once I was accepted as 'human' there was really nothing to it. I've never given any reason to doubt me. My performance is excellent in and out of the operating field. Plus it helps to look the part."

"I've always admired your design. Absolutely lifelike. But then, I never trust what I see in the empire."

"Well, I never trust what I don't," the art responded coyly.

"Now, the exchange." He whistled and then waited for a red frog wearing a glass-fiber pouch to hop near. The creature held still and croaked as the assassin pulled a new chip from its package. The ormedica wisely flinched his synth-skin away from the toxic messenger and watched Torg's fingers work the replacement in.

"You have such style," sighed the art happily, and looked on eagerly as Torg implanted his new ID. To be certified human created a problem that plagued administrators for years following the Art Wars. Against the perfection of the organic artificials produced in the final days before the conflagration, any criteria seemed ineffectual. Testing of blood, mixed or not, and tissue samples was not enough to ferret out imposters. An Imperial cipher committee finally decided on visual data recordings proving infancy and childhood, visual verification possible with the use of sartographic technology. The sophisticated chip in the ident-link could easily hold several lifetimes of such proof. Torg, however, always suspected that a tribunal of organics had infiltrated the committee to influence the decision to their benefit. After all, visual data could still be manufactured, at a price, including the requisite calendrical watermark.

The organic artificial—outlawed by the Gelicus Art Convention, and hunted by the Gai'han Sullusts to near eradication had all the outward appearances of a human. Internally he was a mixture of living organs and dedicated machinery with the added inclusion of a self-destruct device—the failsafe control of his makers. To be certified "human" he needed the proper memories implanted into his ident-link—proof that he grew like a human through adolescence and was not created intact as an adult.

Suddenly there popped up on holo projection the grainy image of a memory implant from the ident-link. In the picture the art's features were reduced and softened to the round innocence of a four-year old boy. The child was rocking away happily on a stuffed taro beast and making pleasant, gurgling noises. The digital pixels flickered and abruptly shut off. Torg tapped around the edges of the new ident-link and, satisfied, surveyed the hard look of longing on the ormedica's face as he stared blankly to the space where the holo had played.

"Congratulations," Torg stepped back, his eyes flaring from the red to a bright blue of some intense emotion as he said, "You're certified human, now, with all the prerequisite childhood dramas and ID file moments. You'll find the visuals are unimpeachable. Any Sartok will declare ninety-five percent probability that these images were you as a child."

"It's amazing—I almost believe it myself."

"You can serve any client you wish, at any price. Now you have the best of both species: artificial precision and human freedom. Just don't become *too* human…"

"Not to worry," chuckled the ormedica with a tinny laugh that echoed mechanically in the cramped room and hung in the air as he left, again a mechanic pushing a diagnostic case.

Torg shut the door and returned to sit beside Vailetta. Under the harsh light she looked very pale, her skin almost translucent. Without replacing his glove, he lowered his hand to her face. His thumb, with its nail ragged and stained, traced a blue, spidery vein down the side of her neck. Bruises bloomed under his touch, purpling out like enlarged fingerprints.

"Now here's a map I remember," he murmured, softening the light. He removed his poisonous touch reluctantly. Vailetta sniffled and began to stir. The assassin stood, straightening his tunic.

"Captain? Captain?" he asked gently, shrugging off the irrational urge to curl a loose strand of her hair around his thumb as he had long ago. She blinked up at him and groaned, reaching around to rub the back of her neck.

"Have I embarrassed myself?"

"Not at all Captain, though perhaps I should call a medica." He turned to the com by the door.

"Medica? No," Vailetta hastily swung her legs off the bed. "I don't feel up to dealing with that now. It's just—oww."

"I think the fumes got to you. I forget sometimes how dangerous they can be. I'm not accustomed to visitors."

"Fumes?" Vailetta tried to focus on him, grabbing the wall to stand.

Torg smiled patiently. "From my wards… the creatures. It won't do you worse than a headache, though."

"Oh. They don't—they don't affect you then?"

"I grew up around them; I'm tolerant."

"Making me intolerant, I guess." Vailetta worked her way to the door.

"Only untouched, innocent," Torg replied, moving only his head to follow her.

What an odd thing to say. "That reminds me, I came here to tell you something, didn't I? But now I can't remember what it was."

"The contest on New Haivello, wasn't it? You were talking about it before you fainted."

"Oh," she paused, trying to remember. That was the story going around regarding her mission. An excellent cover. Apparently the assassin had believed it. Perhaps he wasn't the man she remembered. *Yet there was one more thing...* "Yes. You'll come, then?"

"I'd never miss your victory, Captain Strom," he replied solemnly.

"Very well," she smiled brightly. "But now I must take leave of you, my strange man. Here, this one got out." From behind her she brought a handful of red frog, chirping faintly in her palm, eyes blinking calmly.

Torg's jaw dropped for a moment, and then he snatched the frog from her, expecting to see the flesh curling back from a bloody abscess. Instead he realized she held a small square of glass against her skin: protection from the toxin. But he had not thought to hide his resistance; in his haste he had used his bare hands. The Trioxin gloves were by the door. He studied her expression, discerning nothing.

She held the glass up, flipped it in the air and snapped the fingers on her other hand. The square was gone. She stepped out of the cabin with a forced smile on her face and turned away, sweat dripping. Wasn't it interesting how Torg had tolerated the toxins?

The door hissed shut behind her. Torg frowned and clenched his hands before him, staring at them in frustration.

14

JHEI PŌLOC

A TRANSLUCENT, SHIMMERING SARTOGRAPHIC DISPLAY
glittered in the center of *Destiny's* crystal bridge. Upon first
glance, the depiction of the Krestyaninov Cluster's amorphous
outer fringes appeared to be nothing more than a vivid abstrac-
tion of color—the daydream doodles of a creative child. But
upon closer inspection, details of the complex gravitational
vortices that contended for the ship's mass began to emerge.
Purple spherical shells mapped out each white dwarf's influence. The violet bubbles overlapped in complex patterns, like
toys tossed randomly in an enormous box, leaving narrow tunnels of negative space snaking through in places. Each bubble
was shown as a bright burst of violet at its core, its hue suf-

fusing as it expanded. A jagged red line curved through the bubbles, representing Bailey's intended course out of the maze.

Garrand slumped back in his acceleration couch, his pod situated deep in the sphere behind the sartographic display. He chewed absently on the back of a chomped-off stem of bamboo, observing Bailey's progress, eyes glassy from staring at the ripples of color. The outer edge of the cluster was finally within sight, after twelve days of painstaking navigation at achingly slow sub-light speeds. He hid a thin smile of satisfaction behind the stem as the ship wended between the last of the bubbles. A sparkle of pride for Bailey shone behind his weary expression.

The door hissed open above him, and Garrand glanced up to see Helen standing at the edge of the gantry, her hands on the railing. Strangely she remained silent.

Bailey's hands passed smoothly over the controls and the colorful display melted away. He rotated his pod next to the captain's. Outside the bridge, the plumes of ionized gas faded into the velvety darkness of vacuum. "The ship is free and clear, sir."

Garrand took a deep, relaxing breath. "Nicely done."

"Thank you, Captain."

"Set a course for Eemon Nores."

"Random pattern of jumps?"

"No, better lay in a straight shot. After twelve days in the soup, there's no telling what the Imperials are up to. We'd better not risk bumping into any Imperial listeners by trying to be too fancy. Set a course with the shortest number of jumps. We don't have the time or fuel to waste on anything else." Garrand looked up at Helen. "Nothing to say, Miss Tchelakov?"

She peered down at him and shrugged. "I don't know whether to be relieved that we're no longer in, or worried that we're out."

Garrand laughed and rubbed his eyes. "I know what you mean. Was kinda cozy in there." He ordered his pod up to the entrance. "Care to join me for a hunt—you never know, you might enjoy it."

"Don't you think sleep might be more relaxing?"

"No, thank you. I'm not going anywhere near that cabin."

Helen folded her arms. Was he referring to the mess the cubs had left behind, she wondered, or something else? "It looks like you could use some rest, Captain."

"Do you want to come or not?"

She studied him for a long moment. "I think I'll have to pass—I have a date with your chef."

Bailey's head jerked up rather suddenly from his navi board.

Garrand looked at her curiously; she almost sounded concerned for him. "You sure? That Thol dart sling looked like it could bear some use." "Not this time. But feel free to use it yourself."

Garrand grinned, a glitter in his eye. "That's awfully kind of you." He ducked under the door and spoke into his comtab. "Little Bit, gather up the gear, I'm on my way."

HELEN MET THE spindly artificial outside the amidships cargo bay. This space was now filled with bamboo saplings planted to ensure their survival during the long journey. Jean-Wa carried a long bundle under one of his many arms. He was no longer attached to his cart. Helen raised her eyebrows as she spied his ungainly new appendages.

"I see you brought your legs. I wondered how we'd navigate the bamboo with your cart."

"The right tools for the job as I say."

"Shall we?" asked Helen, keying open the doors and eyeing his bundle with mild curiosity.

"Indeed." Jean-Wa gallantly allowed her entrance first and then followed, smoothly popping open the package and angling it over her head.

"What's this?" she looked up at the bright, opaque stretch of silk.

"A parasol. Can't have your delicate skin toasting in such bright grow lamps."

"It's not necessary."

"I will not hear of protest. Since you will not do so yourself, please allow Jean-Wa to look out for you."

Suddenly a mottled blur shot between them and disappeared in a crash of dry leaves in the thicket before them.

"And who invited her, I wonder?" Jean-Wa followed Helen unsteadily. Despite his precarious gait, he still held the parasol over her. He wished he had the exel's agility in such rough ground. His legs were not very effective. The lack of subtlety was offensive to his sensibilities.

Helen had not spent much time in here other than analyzing samples and checking growth rates, but she realized it felt very much like a real field of bamboo out here under the grow lamps. The air was chill, but the exertion made her sweat before long. She wondered why she had indulged the chef's wish to come here. Could it be that already she would do anything to appease such an artist? That nothing could be too much to keep the culinary delights coming?

Jean-Wa was several paces behind her, the attempt at covering her with the beauty-saving parasol discarded before the more urgent problem of walking. A small shadow crashed through the bamboo, upsetting Jean-Wa's already precarious balance. She struggled to help him up, swallowing a smile at the severe threats he issued to the smug exel, who sat nearby licking a paw with no small satisfaction at the art's dilemma.

"No exel cookies for you, you bad girl! Scaring Jean-Wa like that."

Soon they were up and on their way again. The exel raced ahead once more, and Jean-Wa seemed to steel himself against another surprise attack by grabbing thick handfuls of bamboo stems with six arms.

"It's very hard to see in here," Jean-Wa complained.

"Visibility is poor; bamboo provides both food and safety for pandas. They're in here now. Do you see them?"

"I can't see anything. But the smell! It's distinctly theirs."

"Yes, the spice scent. It's their signature."

"My dear you have a strange nose indeed if you detect 'spice' in *that*."

"What do you mean? I don't smell anything else."

"The markers they leave?" Jean-Wa prompted, two appendages resting on his hips. "It's sprayed all over the ship."

"Oh. You must mean the notes; your sense of smell is more finely attuned than mine. They have a gland for that and spread it with their tails. It's how they tell each other their whereabouts. Another panda will pick up the scent of such a note and know who left it and how long ago. In the wild they might sample over three thousand stems. You cover a lot of ground like that, perhaps never crossing another panda's path. Besides, as you say, it's very hard to see. How else would they ever meet up?"

"That's all very well, miss, but I'm not a panda designed for passing through thickets. I wish I was back in my bright little kitchen whipping up a batch of something filling."

"I thought you were determined to assess their diet."

"Yes, yes. Forgive my complaints. It is just I had no idea that a mere garden would be this difficult to traverse. And, you know, I am not designed for walking. Cooking, yes, but walking is another

matter…" He shook his head sadly.

"Nothing to forgive, Jean-Wa." She skillfully parted another thatch of leaves and stopped. "Here is what you were seeking."

"Droppings? You found them?" His enthusiasm returned immediately. "Ah, yes, it looks as though the digestion is not all it could be, just as I thought. After all, how can one possibly live off what is ninety percent water? Even fishes need more to survive." He studied the large, neat pile of droppings so full of partially-digested bamboo parts that it looked like a mulching attempt.

"I tried to explain to you before—"

"Yes, but they are not on their own now. Jean-Wa myself is here to cater to their needs, and I must insist again that this is not the evidence of an efficient herbivore. I think that anatomically they are designed like carnivores, with a simple stomach and short intestines, not like the ever-efficient taro beast with its eight stomachs and mile of intestines. Why the taro beast can and will eat an entire tree and leave no such evidence of its meal behind."

"Jean-Wa, meat is not plentiful for pandas."

"Ah, a seasonal delicacy. I understand. The greens, they are fresh and available no matter the seasons. Miss, I begin to realize."

"It's a real problem for them. A taro beast might be able to eat a tree, but it has the volume of all those stomachs and time to digest it. A panda only has one and he must keep it full of calories to stay alive. They spend two thirds of their day eating, and sleep in shifts of two to four hours."

"What a horrible prison then. One is only free when foraging is no longer necessary. When there is a surplus of ready food and time."

"What do you suppose they would do with a surplus of time?" Helen was fascinated. Was it possible that the chef could suspect their potential?

"Why, what all thinking creatures do: they would build things, create."

"It's such an odd notion. What makes you believe they are sentient?"

"Why, miss, my head is not all of it in the kitchen. I watch carefully to know the needs of my gourmands before even they know of their desires. And sometimes I see other things as well." He waved her interest away and began the arduous task of retracing their steps. "This is intolerable. From now on, Bailey does all my garden walking."

❖ ❖ ❖

HELEN FOUND GARRAND IN THE HOLO ROOM. HE WAS COVERED in a sticky, brown material. "Finished sculpting?"

"For now." Garrand walked to the equipment locker where he proceeded to strip. Helen did not look away as he peeled away his sweaty clothes and stepped into a narrow tube-like receptacle set in the wall. Twin beams of energy leapt into existence on opposite sides of his head. The green radiance twisted slowly around his torso, traversing his body from head to toe. Hot streams of water began firing from all sides. The tube filled with steam.

"Those pandas are special to you, aren't they? You've been with them since the beginning?"

Helen nodded.

"Why program time decay physics into a sentient anyway? Why not an artificial for that matter?"

"Arts rely on logic exclusively. Logic derived from subroutines, programs, experience. Humans and other organic species do not. Intuition and conjecture play as large a part as logic in our decision making. My father's theory was that an organic mind would be better able to bring context and meaning to predictions, that the very nature of the Sartok chip—dealing with uncertain possibilities and probabilities—was more the province of less structured minds. Datacores and artificials operate under much more rigorous mental 'rules' than we do. We can skip over flaws in our thinking, errors in logic, in order to grasp a larger whole, a greater truth. Dad felt that the pandas would learn what to skip over and what to pay attention to through experience. That they might develop an intuitive sense of the future, and that passed on from generation to generation they would learn to see through the vagaries of time with greater and greater clarity."

Garrand emerged from the 'fresher and dried himself with a warm towel left by Jean-Wa. "No need to design better and better versions of the chip if it develops itself." He retrieved a clean shift and pulled it over his head.

"Exactly."

"Sentient Sartoks, able to learn from their mistakes, develop intuition, and not bound by rules of logic. Quite a theory."

"It's not a theory, Captain," Helen said softly.

"So he created living, breathing crystal balls, eh?"

"In a manner of speaking, yes."

"But why pandas?" Garrand asked, opening the storage locker and stuffing protective gear inside.

"He needed a species that he could give a fresh start to, with no preconceived notions of the greater universe. The giant pandas of Solvaeigh Do-böen were already viable candidates to be lifted to sentience. They were healthy and strong—easily able to handle the strains that would be put on them—adaptable to new climes and relocation. Their brains were large and complex. They formed broad tribal families and nurtured their young—who knows, in a million years or so if they continued on the same path they might have evolved into sentients naturally. As it was, there was a certain degree of safety in choosing an obscure species—no one would suspect a panda of being a great intellectual, much less a conduit into the future."

"So what are the differences between these biological sartographs and, say, the one in my ship?"

Helen smiled serenely. "That, Captain, you will just have to find out for yourself."

Garrand face turned sour. "If they're so smart, then why do they need us around?" he growled, slamming the locker shut and wheeling back to face her. "Why don't they just read the future and figure a way out of their mess?"

"They don't read the future. They see it in dreams."

"Oh…" he rolled his eyes sarcastically. "What? They're not intelligent enough to interpret their dreams?" He snapped the dirty, crumpled shift open and pulled it back over his head.

"It has nothing to do with raw intelligence, Captain. They simply have no context on which to base their interpretations! They have no experiences to fall back on. They have nothing to compare their visions against. They are ingénues in a galaxy they do not fully understand—with dreams of places they have never been, visions of people they have never seen, full of machines they do not understand. Their dreams are filled with creatures they've never met who wish to do them harm — enslave them — use them to their own ends. They place mystical significance on everything, for they have no shared experience to rely on. They are prodigal innocents learning things for the first time."

Garrand slumped back against the bulkhead and sighed, considering this. "If they don't understand their own dreams, then what can I do?"

"That's just it; they hope to look to you for guidance. They're in need of a *Jhei Pôloc* — someone to interpret their visions for them. Your insights could be invaluable to them. You've traveled the galaxy, lived in the very social order that threatens to envelop them, experienced what they have only dreamed. You could be their link between dreams they don't understand and a reality which is very harrowing."

Garrand looked skeptical. "Cheplus, there's got to be a better-qualified soothsayers around than me."

"I wouldn't argue with you on that point, but my opinion doesn't matter. They believe otherwise."

Garrand sighed. "What exactly am I supposed to do?"

Helen fidgeted with a lock of hair, shifting her weight from one foot to the other. "Well, specifically, they want you to lead them to a place they call the forgotten land."

"The forgotten land?'" Garrand guffawed.

Helen grew immediately defensive, and the feeling was intensified by guilt because she knew that these pandas were never going to see anything resembling a promised land, forgotten or otherwise.

"They've never had a true home, a place they could call their very own. They've been moved from one place to the next since their inception."

"What does that have to do with me?"

"They've had tribal-wide dreams of a planet that will be theirs alone—a place of safety and sanctuary. All of them have had the dream. They call it Archiva."

"Archiva? That old myth?" He ran his hand through his hair and stared at the floor. "Why can't they just dream up its location—or foresee it—or whatever it is they do, and get themselves there?"

"They have dreamt of it," she said impatiently. "They've had thousands upon thousands of dreams of it. They can tell you exactly what it looks like from the surface—down to the finest details of the bark on the trees, what the ruins look like—"

"—Ruins?"

"—Where bamboo can be planted, even where they will build their first nests, places that will be revered for generations."

"I don't understand."

"You still don't get it! They have information without context. Visions so precise that it boggles the imagination. But there is no great map of the cosmic future for them to use as reference. They have a common vision of a wonderful planet, truly a paradise by all description. They can tell you exactly what it looks like, feels like, even how it smells at certain times of the year. But they do not know where it is! There's no map with a giant arrow pointing to it with a caption saying, 'Paradise here.'"

Garrand sighed and shuffled to a grimy settee set by the locker. He dropped onto the cushions with a whoosh and lay his head back against the rest to stare up into the ship's superstructure. "There must be clues within the visions."

"That's what they want you to help them with."

Garrand was not overly optimistic. "History is strewn with the sad tales of disenfranchised souls searching for a better life. There must be a thousand races in the Shell who seek sanctuary. And every one of them believe there is a 'promised land' where there are marvels to behold and wonders that defy the imagination."

"What's your point?"

Garrand shrugged. "I make it a point not to be misled by such promises," he glanced at Helen, "Especially those told by wandering beauties."

"Well this isn't being told by me," Helen reminded him, her lips twisting into a wry frown. *Does he really think I'm beautiful?*

"Then who?"

"This is straight from Sid's mouth."

"Then I'd like to speak to him."

"Be my guest," she said. "He's in the holo room I believe." She gestured toward the serviceway with one arm.

"You're serious?"

"Absolutely."

Garrand chewed this over. It was probably time he found out for himself. "Fine," he stood up and walked down the hall. Helen watched him disappear, an uncertain but playful smile creeping across her face.

GARRAND PAUSED JUST inside the entrance to the holo room. The scene inside the chamber gave him a frightful start. The chamber was configured into an eerie replica of the ship's crystal bridge. Seated at what would have to be the navigation pod was the giant panda. He watched with amazement as the panda summoned up starcharts and detailed sartographs. Garrand stepped out cautiously into the room. The deck was still solid despite the visual illusion otherwise. He gestured toward the corner of the room where the giant panda sat with his back to the two humans and raised his brows questioningly.

"His name is Sid," Helen said pointedly.

Garrand heaved a nervous sigh and glanced over at the back of the panda's furry head, clearing his throat. "Excuse me," he edged closer, hand reaching out as if to tap the creature on its massive shoulder. "Sid?"

With a low grumble, the giant panda lifted his head and shifted to peer at the captain. Dark, hypnotic eyes peered out from beneath the heavy black fur that framed the panda's visage. The panda looked at him inscrutably; whatever emotion he felt was hidden beneath all that fur. Garrand wondered if Helen could tell what they were thinking, if there were visual markers or ticks that he was missing, or if they always appeared so stoic. The panda wrinkled his nose and gave a polite sniff. Garrand stood silently looking at the creature.

The panda tilted his head to one side, eyes narrowing a bit, and said, "Yes?" His voice was deep and resonant with the barest trace of an accent. Probably a remnant of their tutor. The panda still looked at him inquisitively, creases of concern fanning out around his eyes, the corner of his mouth edging down in a semblance of a frown. It wasn't difficult to read their emotions after all; had he been so self-absorbed that he hadn't noticed?

This time it was the panda that cleared his throat, a wonderful rolling noise like snore of a dragon. "Pardon me Captain, but was there something that you'd like to say?"

Garrand snapped out of his thoughts. "Miss Tchelakov here neglected to inform me about your capacity for speech. I didn't know you could talk."

"Yes, of course Captain. How else would one communicate?" The creature spoke with great finesse and refinement as if he had been brought up in one of the Noble Houses. There was even a subtle nuance of irony in his tone, as if he were gently teasing Garrand at the same time.

"Well, I knew—or at least I *assumed* that you had some means of communicating amongst yourselves; I mean you're obviously intelligent."

Sid smacked his lips together and used his tongue to try to dislodge an errant sliver of bamboo from between his teeth.

Garrand continued, frowning only slightly, "I just didn't know that you could speak—well, not Strahlinvek at least."

"Yes, well," Sid mumbled as if growing bored with the captain, "there's much you have to learn."

Not knowing quite how to take that, Garrand shrugged and looked back to Helen. She giggled between pursed lips. "You're right; they can talk."

"Mmm, hmmm. Any other questions, Captain?"

"No," he snapped. He turned back to Sid. "I, uh, understand that you have a propensity for dreams." The giant panda regarded him silently. "Actually, I'm told that you can predict the future, sort of. Like a Sartok."

"Indeed," the panda rumbled, as if this was all plain as day. "The sartokian model was a starting point for Dr. Tchelakov's genetic re-engineering. The *tromaveint* is as intrinsic to our self-awareness as daydreams are to you."

"Excuse me, the what?"

"*Tromaveint*—the waking dream. We have the ability to force ourselves into a trance state where our energies are focused toward unraveling the future."

"Interesting," Garrand's fascination was growing. "And you can do this whenever you wish?"

"Within reason," Sid allowed. "The dreams are not always conclusive."

"But you foresaw the attack on El-Bouteran."

"Yes."

Garrand thought of something that had been bothering him. "If you knew it was coming, why didn't you warn Miss Tchelakov sooner?"

Sid twitched his whiskers back and blinked slowly, patiently. "The attack was believed to be an event that would occur three months further in the future. The last visions, when young Alexander was deemed to be in peril, showed subtle differences from previous versions. The sequence of events leading to the attack was accelerated by occurrences that we cannot yet explain. Unfortunately, the future is in a constant state of flux. Certainly, not all dreams come to pass, and events do not always transpire exactly as they were foreseen."

"But some do."

"Yes, surprisingly enough, there are some things that seem to be fated to occur, that unfold just as if they were part of the vision itself."

"Helen tells me that I might be of some assistance to you. Perhaps help you with some navigation, correlate some of your 'dreams' with real stars and real systems."

Sid's face transformed subtly: his whiskers straightened out and his ears perked forward. His tongue licked the tip of his nose self-consciously. "That would be quite nice…" he was trying not to let emotion get the better of him. "Quite nice indeed, Captain. The tribe will be happy to hear tell of this. There's been considerable call for a new interpreter—well, specifically, for your interpretation."

"Interpretation?"

"Yes, yes: dream interpretation. That is to be part of your destiny with the tribe, I believe. The beginning of it, at least. You're to be our *Jhei Pôloc.*"

Garrand hesitated, taken aback. "Then maybe we can help one another."

"By all means, Captain. How may I be of service?"

"Why don't you meet me on the bridge in half an hour…"

Sid waited impatiently for Helen and Alexander to follow him up the corridor to the bridge. The anticipation of exchanging thoughts and perceptions with the captain had curtailed his normal staid stoicism. Captain Médeville had agreed to help them! His claws clicked against the cerasteel deck as he paced in front of the door.

"What's with you?" Helen asked, observing his restless motion.

Sid just looked at her, ears back, whiskers flicking upward briefly, like a snort.

"All right, all right, you didn't have to wait for me." She held the cub Alexander firmly by one ear as she neared the door. The panda was protesting loudly and trying to squirm free of her grip, but she had a handful of fur and knew better than to loosen her grip. "Little one here seems to want to follow you everywhere. Won't take 'no' for an answer."

Sid grunted noncommittally, but cast an eye toward the cub. Alexander started squealing again, trying to prise himself free. Sid growled sharply. Alexander lowered his head to the floor immediately and held still.

The door to the bridge cracked open and rose with a wheezing sigh of released pressure. Sid ducked his head under the door and rose up on two feet to examine the bridge properly. It did not matter how often he visited this magical, darkened place with its curving panorama of a million world-stars, suspended platforms, and girded depths. Each time was like the very first. He stood in awe of the futures that stretched out in all directions, limitless possibilities twinkling beyond the crystal panes; he, an acolyte, bearing witness to the yawning majesty of time itself.

Garrand's head appeared at the foot of the gantry as he ordered his platform to the entrance. The captain smiled and beckoned him onto his personal rostrum, a first. Sid dropped back to the deck gently and eased onto the platform. Speaking softly to his ship, Garrand ushered him forward as the railing extended behind him. Sid braced himself with all four legs as the platform rolled in somersault fashion around the inner circumference of the spherical edge of the bridge and ended up at the base of the chamber looking back up into the empty volume above.

"Sit down," he indicated a long, black shelf that curved behind the displays covered in a soft, shiny material. "I have a lot to show you." Sid climbed up onto the shelf and settled back comfortably.

With a word from the captain, thousands of brilliant dots of colored light materialized in the center of the sphere. A whole miniature galaxy came alive in the darkness.

"This is a sartographic display. With this I can visually represent stars, planets, whole systems in great detail. And depending upon the nature and volume of information at my disposal, I can show these things at various stages in their development: past, present, and even the future with varying degrees of reliability. For a ship her size, *Destiny's Needle* has a pretty impressive sartographic array. Her powers of prediction allow me and two artificials to operate a vessel that normally would demand a crew of eight or more. She foresees problems before they occur, allowing us to do preventative maintenance instead of having to wait for things to break down before we fix them. Navigation, security, targ and scan—all that can be handled by a good sentient ship."

Sid murmured appreciatively. "This allows you to concentrate on higher, intuitive functions?"

"Well," Garrand scratched his chin, "I don't think she'd put it that way—but, yeah, it leaves us free to make decisions on a broader scale."

"The details of which are handled by your world-ship. The sartographic array can calculate the consequences of your actions, filter through the fluctuations in its new future and arrive at its probable fate much more quickly than you could compute it yourself."

Garrand laughed—the panda had an amazing grasp on the vagaries of 4th dimension physics time decay. "Exactly. Problem is, she generally doesn't like her new probable fate. She worries too much. Always complaining about the consequences of my decisions."

"So the combination of your intuitive decisions and the ship's logical projections are what have allowed us to escape the Imperial fleet."

Helen smiled in the darkness above.

Garrand rubbed his hand slowly over the outer shell of the display board. "Yeah, she's a good ship." He turned back to the sartographic display and narrowed the field until a single star dominated the interior. Planets could be seen revolving around the fringes of the bridge. He pointed upward: "This is El-Bouteran, where we first met." The display shrunk by some degree, the star still visible, but smaller now. "And this is the Pakken system, home to El-Bouteran."

The display shifted once more and this time erupted in a shower of swirling gases that bathed the bridge in a surreal glow. Plumes of energy spiraled toward dark splotches devoid of any ambient starlight. "This is the Krestyaninov Cluster, which we have just departed."

"Quite beautiful," Sid murmured.

"Yes, and as dangerous as it is pretty." He paused and looked at the big panda. "I can teach you how to use this, how you can use it to help you find things."

"But Captain, we already have use of sartographs, in a manner of speaking. We're the next evolution of the technology."

"Yes, but the difference is, the ship's sartograph has access to hundreds of years of navigational data in its memory. You've been started off raw; the ship has you beat by way of experience. You can add to its knowledge. Things you remember, little details, things you dream — anything can be valuable. The ship will help you narrow your search. We can come up with a list of viable planets that most closely match your dreams."

A deep appreciative sigh rumbled out of Sid's chest: "Marvelous."

"And I can tell you what I know, share with you what I've seen, help you narrow things down further."

Sid's whiskers turned down. "But how can I help you?"

Garrand nodded once and turned back to his display. A new series of stars lit up the sphere. "This is where we are headed." He pointed into the darkness. "This is the path we've chosen, and this is the planet which I have decided to land on — Eemon Nores."

"It's bright," Sid observed.

"Highly reflective surface: it's covered in ice. I want you to tell me if it's safe."

The big panda shifted in the acceleration couch. "What do you mean, *safe?*"

"Safe to land on. Specifically, are the Imperials there waiting for us?"

Sid licked his lips and rolled his shoulders upward one at a time; he understood now, the captain wanted a vision, to back up his decision. "Very well, Captain." He closed his eyes.

Garrand looked up at Helen who still stood on the gantry, arms on the railing, listening—then back at Sid. "You mean you can do it now? Right here?"

Sid opened one eye. "Yes. If you can leave me in peace for just a few minutes, that is."

The big panda began to take deep, slow breaths. Garrand pursed his lips, leaned back against the display and watched respectfully. He wondered if there would be any indication of what was happening. After several minutes he gave up trying to detect anything unusual: to all appearances the panda had fallen asleep.

Sid blinked rapidly, looked uncertainly at his surroundings and snorted once. The captain stood up straight and leaned forward. "You okay?"

The panda yawned and stretched, the vertebrae making an audible noise as they popped. "Yes, thank you Captain. The Ice-world—the place you call 'Eemon Nores'—is quiet and safe. Our world-ship falls and rises unimpeded. All the tribe survives."

Garrand breathed a sigh of relief. He wasn't sure how much stock to place in this dream business, but good news was good news—better not to have the whole thing cursed to begin with by some ominous prediction. Maybe these pandas were going to earn their keep after all.

"But there was a watcher," Sid rumbled.

Garrand faltered. "A watcher?"

"In the distance, standing on the plains."

"An ice wrangler? Someone from the farm?"

"No, someone who did not belong."

"An Imperial someone?"

"I cannot say, Captain."

"Are you sure?"

Sid licked his nose with a brief upward swipe of his pink tongue. He blinked once. "There are always slight discrepancies between dreams. You have asked me to examine a future that lies on the cusp of our Path. There are still many things that could happen differently between now and then. The mere knowledge of your own possible future may in fact influence your behavior to the extent that my dream becomes meaningless — merely a vision of a *possible* future, something that never comes to pass."

"I'm confused," Garrand said with exasperation creeping into his voice. "How do you ever *know?*"

"Through practice and experience. One never knows with absolute certainty — but if enough of the tribe agrees…"

"The future through consensus?" Garrand asked.

"I could try to foresee this future a thousand times — still I would see this Ice-world, still I would see our safe departure, and still I would see this watcher. Through clarity and what you call 'instinct' I am certain that this is a future that lies on our collective Path — we are fated to land on Eemon Nores. Believe me, Captain, there are far worse fates to dream. Horrors lying just on the edge of this vision."

Garrand grunted: "Horrors, huh?" He did not doubt that for an instant. "All right, we proceed as planned to Eemon — no deviations from our set approach. We make it short and sweet. We'll tightbeam my friend C'tereino when we're in system and Eemon's rotation gives us a clear shot at the farm. We won't stay on the surface any longer than we have to."

15

EEMON NORES

GARRAND WAS ENJOYING AN IMPROMPTU SNACK IN THE
ship's mess when Helen walked in, trailed by a fat panda. "We
should be entering the system in a couple of hours," he spoke
in her general direction. "Planetfall a few minutes after that."

"There's just no excuse for this, Miss Helen," the panda said,
following Helen doggedly.

She turned to confront the panda. "Lander, I'm sorry, but
there's nothing else I can do."

"What's the problem?" Garrand asked.

"Dinner," she said with exasperation.

"Aw, that's no problem. There's lots of food."

The panda shook his head and rolled his eyes. "That depends on what you desire—"

"We're talking about bamboo," Helen explained.

Garrand chuckled heartily. "There's plenty of that too—you see the amidships hold? Looks like we're a giant flying terrarium."

"It's not as simple as that," Helen said, casting a sidelong glance at Lander who tapped a claw impatiently. "Bamboo is the king of grasses. Some planets have over fifty different genera, which contain well over a thousand species. That opens up the possibilities considerably. There are probably hundreds of thousands—even millions—of strains of bamboo available on worlds throughout the Shell."

"So?" Garrand asked as he munched on a spice cookie, crumbs cascading down his chest.

"Well," Helen began, wondering exactly how to put it without hurting Lander's feelings. "This tribe has become accustomed to a certain genera of bamboo."

"*Basilica formentus,*" Lander intoned, annunciating the words very precisely.

Helen sighed audibly and bit down on her lower jaw. After a beat, she rejoined, "Yes, basilica formentus—whose strains are common on many worlds, but unfortunately nonexistent here."

"Mmm," Garrand grunted, his mouth full. "I see." He leaned over to the persnickety panda. "I know exactly what you mean. I like what I like, and there's just no getting around it. A guy can't help if he knows what he wants… We're creatures of habit."

"Quite." Lander said, adopting his most grumpy tone.

Helen was getting flustered. "Why don't you at least try it, Lander. I'm told it has a rather delicious honey aftertaste. You shouldn't turn up your nose so quickly, you don't know what you're missing out on." Helen nodded at the three young cubs hungrily devouring the blonde shoots. "Look at Lin over there. She likes it."

Lander snorted and said, "Lin will eat anything that's put in front of her. She's by no means a reliable barometer of good taste."

Helen threw up her hands. "Suit yourself. I did the best I could."

"I think I will go investigate what emergency stores Ban Rutheua has kept of *real* bamboo!" And with that, Lander turned up his nose and wobbled out of the mess.

Jean-Wa waited in the serviceway for the panda to pass, his eyes glowing red in the darkness, and then made his move. Garrand saw him coming, no tray of delicacies in his arms, and grimaced.

"Jean-Wa, please, don't start…"

"But Capítän—Toulon is the perfect stopping place. There's no market quite like it in the universe. It's Old Galaxy-style."

"Jean-Wa, it's out of the question," he said, rubbing his eyes. "There's something to be said for staying alive until the next meal."

"Well, yes," Jean-Wa shrugged. "For you humans that is a concern. But if the meal is not up to the living—what can one do? Capítän, please reconsider."

"No. I'm afraid we go to Eemon Nores."

"Perhaps Corgone then? It's on our route," he wheedled, rolling a marble-sized ball of dough between the fingers of one hand.

"Sneaking into the navi again, little chef? Then you know there is no timetable for such an excursion."

"Bah!" Jean-Wa threw up two sets of arms in consternation. "All Eemon Nores will have are vegetable hustlers selling reconstituted molecular goop as flesh."

"I'll bet *you* of all master chefs could make something tasty out of goop."

"Capítän, this time flattery will get you nowhere. Goop dressed up is still goop underneath. Nothing hides that taint."

"Hmm. I guess I'd tend to agree with you—that could be said about a great many things."

"Then you'll go to Toulon?"

"I'm sorry, Jean-Wa."

"Then I will try to make nothing of something."

"That's something of nothing."

"Either way, they are equal. Good eve, Capítän. I go now to prepare this night's repast."

Bailey wondered why the chef had summoned him. Certainly it wasn't to sample the delicate aromas developing for dinner, though they pleased him and he had said so.

"You have a lovely sense of smell," Jean-Wa commented as he tied a pile of violet asparagus up in a ribbon of white bell pepper. "Why to be able to detect that the roast is only three quarter's done! Even I must open the door to look and see that the blood it is running down."

"It's necessary for tracking quarry."

"The heat of the blood, yes? The pungent stench. One can never tire of it. It means the quarry is still fresh." He sighed eloquently and looked down at the shriveled vegetables he had culled earlier. "Not like these. Their time has passed. Too quickly." He scooped them into the hungry maw of a mulching shoot. They could still feed other plants, if no one else.

"How I miss those early days aboard the master chef's cart when I apprenticed him. The excitement of the market. Such sights! Such danger!"

"Danger?" Bailey asked dubiously.

"But of course. One can be quite taken in by the monger's chant, his promise of better quality for lower prices when he cannot deliver other than a substandard product at moderate price."

"I still don't see the danger—"

"Ah, but think. You who have been to market for me. Many a time you have brought something other than the order."

"Only when your request could not be filled."

"Nonsense. They took you. Without insistence they will never yield up their best."

"Ridiculous. I am obviously a soldier. I could kill them."

"But would you, for food? You, who have never known hunger?"

"No," he admitted. "Not for cuisine. Although the captain might for yours."

Jean-Wa leaned his head back in remembrance, his red eyes glowing. "For me they conjured up the tenderest medlars, most succulent giant sweet peppers, rondulas with the roots still grasping rich soil. At the southern end of the markets always the seafood was gathered. Perma-racks of fish, mouths still moving. Crustaceans breaking from their crates and scuttling sideways in great arcs. They had runners to catch them, mobs of small boys who risked the pinchers for a few bits of coin or day-old fish for the pot."

"And where was this origin of such happy memories?"

"Toulon," he said wistfully. He then snapped upright. "But Capítän will not even consider it."

"Our mission takes us to Eemon Nores, surely they will have adequate provisions."

"Leviathans, great chewy fish good only for stews. Hardly worthy of my talents. But at times in the alleyways between the huts, more precious items are offered to those able to afford them."

"You've been?"

"No, thank Senii Vilne, ancient chef."

"How do you know this?" Bailey pressed.

"Why my chef's galaxy sourcebook tells me so." Jean-Wa returned his full attention to four hands braiding dough into baskets.

"What am I to look for?"

Jean-Wa concentrated on his braids, slipping tiny speckled eggs into the weave. "It will be obvious, so out of place in a tundra market."

"Obvious," Bailey sighed. When it came to food, it was never obvious to him.

❖ ❖ ❖

FROM ORBIT, THE GREAT NORTHERN CITIES OF EEMON NORES lit up patches of the planet's surface like fires burning beneath the clouds. Towns and villages scattered between the vast metropolises winked through the obscuring veil of atmosphere like fireflies dancing in the night.

Garrand nudged *Destiny's Needle* into a steeper descent and Helen watched the steady brilliance of the stars fade overhead, resuming their coquettish winks. The ship bumped through the upper atmosphere, rattling through turbulence and the planet's jetstream.

Beneath her feet, one of the larger city glows spread and grew as they approached, the orange hue changing to an artificial green radiance as they cut through the last billowing clouds. The lights of the city burned at the low frequency green end of the spectrum, wavelengths no longer lengthened to the red end of the scale by vast stretches of atmosphere.

Helen imagined herself approaching a great palace, fancying herself a long-lost princess returning to her domain. The city appeared to be fashioned exclusively of jade. Emerald towers stretched upwards as far as the eye could see. She imagined it as a place where no one could reach her, no one would chase her, where all the pain and all the memories would melt away. She found herself disappointed when the ship roared by twin stacks belching smoke, spinning down past huge storehouses festooned with keiretsu trade markers. The illusion was shattered, and she was left with nothing but the present reality.

"That's low enough," Garrand said. Bailey increased the repulsor spread and the ship leveled off. Prodding the sub-light engines, Bailey sent the ship roaring southward, streaking along between the city's industrial structures. "Keep an eye out for local traffic."

Soon the ship was past the outskirts of the industrial district and a greyish blur whipped beneath the crystal bridge.

"This is an awfully big ship to be this low," Helen muttered.

"Maybe you'd like us to show up on every orbital tracking scope on this side of the planet? We filed a false flight plan for the largest port. Be a shame to let them see that we're actually destined for a small ice-farming agro south of the equator."

Helen grated at Garrand's insouciance. "Why not just make planetfall at the farm?"

"Oh, I don't know," Garrand mused aloud turning in his acceleration couch to look at her. "Maybe 'cause I'm just the sneaky sort."

Helen bristled from his reprobation, but recovered quickly. "Ah, yes, the smuggler's sensibilities."

Garrand glowered at her but turned back to watch his scopes. "Reading a big heat sig 250 kilometers south. We should be coming up on the village that skirts the edge of the ice farm."

"What does this C'tereino owe you anyway?" Helen asked dubiously.

Garrand did not look up. "His life."

❖ ❖ ❖

THE NO-ENTRY LIGHT OUTSIDE THE WAR ROOM ON *Ilyovahtna* had been on for more than eight hours. Inside, a side buffet table was littered with used dishes. The supple anti-fatigue couches had only one occupant, the warder Mr. Wicek. Everyone else stood around a rotating holo display of the surrounding systems, blinking red dots indicating the positions of Vailetta's teams of Gokazoku dropped in air skimmers into the atmospheres of planets high on Yarvek-EZ's probability table. A blue blip marked the *Ilyovahtna's* current path and a yellow swirl issuing out delineated the possible courses they might take. Underneath the projection Yarvek rotated in a sunken makeshift pod chamber, his observations emitting from a speaker in the base, as Vailetta, Torg and aide Huis Clos looked on.

"He's from the list we recommend, names culled from Médeville's life, persons loyal to him, help he could count on," explained Huis Clos, standing at ease before Vailetta. Despite his recent transfer from General Shecut's contingent, he still wore the grey-blue uniform of the diplomatic corps with its cluster of oak leaves on the collar rather than the comfortable field uniform Vailetta had adopted for this mission. Even the flamboyant warder had donned the plain, non-Imperial outfit, only accenting it with a gaudy striped pin on one lapel.

"This C'tereino, what's his connection?" asked Vailetta tersely. Most of her men were in place. The Gokazoku Kaigi were co-ordinating the vast web of listeners and informants loyal to the empire. But there was still a chance *Destiny's Needle* could slip through unnoticed.

"He was one of Proctor Birmaldon's Guardsmen during that time period of Médeville's life that I am sure you are familiar with."

Vailetta sucked her breath in. The *Stanzer* rescue, of course. The event that lead Médeville to become a *Freetrader*. Everyone associated with the incident had been disbanded and widely dispersed.

"And what does C'tereino do now?" She tried to quell her rising excitement at this first real lead.

"After the disgrace he returned to the family ice farm on Eemon Nores, here," he indicated a glowing spot on the holo display. "There would be fuel there."

"And enough big cities that Médeville could slip in, avoid detection. Fine work. Progress reports?"

"Lieutenant Dasko has made contact with the High Consulate on Tebbs. Sygne-YB reports full cooperation on seven fronts. Still listening for Boulez, Losworth, and Hueneker. Which team shall we drop on Eemon Nores?"

Vailetta studied the display. The ice planet showed up as a green globe to their far right. "What's the probability of success on Eemon?"

"Looking good," Yarvek said. "Thirteen point two percent— highest of the lot."

"Then we'll take that chance ourselves. The rest of the teams will continue as planned. The past might not be as convenient an indicator as we think."

"Assassin?"

"Yes, Captain."

"Why don't you and Mr. Wicek put those fine, scheming minds together and see if you can't come up with a plan for breaching ship's security. Doubtless he's found the original trace by now. The disabler unit will be difficult to get aboard, and I wouldn't count on Tchelakov being any help. In fact I think we shouldn't alert her at all as to our presence."

"Her loyalty is much in doubt," rumbled Torg, flexing his Trioxin gloves.

"Huis Clos, have you anything to add?"

"Proctor Birmaldon kept a detailed account on Médeville after he left the Guard. He was one of his favorites. There are several notations concerning a rather talented art chef aboard."

"A chef?" Vailetta frowned. "I don't see the significance."

"Traditionally chefs take every opportunity to stock up the larder, to sample the regional offerings dirtside. To lend credence to the Proctor's stories we might believe that Médeville's chef, due to a mobility problem, sends out the former Imperial Varsis to do his shopping."

"I've never heard of such a thing. It doesn't sound very workable."

"Exactly, and Eemon doesn't have much to choose from in the way of culinary delights. There's fish, a bit of low-grade mutton, and more fish."

"Doesn't sound very tempting."

"Which brings us to two possibilities. One, that with the only other formidable member of Médeville's crew away shopping we have a better chance of boarding the disabler undetected. The other is to set up a decoy stand and get the art to take the disabler in himself."

"Those are pretty slim chances, but do the legwork. I'd still prefer to send Assassin Torg in, that is if we even catch up to them. Are the percentages narrowing any, Yarvek? I could call the teams in, concentrate on Eemon, take them right there, even."

Yarvek input the new variables and worked the mathematics. "No, Captain. Just holding. Neither idea increases our margin by much. Not enough to mention."

"Then we'll have to stick to schedule."

❖ ❖ ❖

Destiny's Needle SLOWED AS SHE APPROACHED THE VILLAGE COMplex. To Garrand's surprise, Bailey was forced to maneuver around crude ore smelting centers, belching fire from exhaust ports. The smog and soot cast an eerie glow across the village rooftops. As the ship banked steeply, Helen could make out narrow muddy tracks cut through all the icy avenues. The roads were filled with fat, furry pack beasts that pulled archaic carts on wooden runners. Frozen repulsor sleds lay abandoned in every avenue, covered with snow and trash, victims of the extreme cold.

"Looks bigger than any village to me," Helen said, leaning over the captain's shoulder.

"It's grown," Garrand said uneasily. "I can't believe how big it's gotten. The ice lichen market must really be taking off. Bailey, how long has it been?"

"Just shy of five years, sir."

Garrand whistled. "C'tereino must be doing all right."

Broad flat expanses of glacial ice spread out in all compass directions from the burgeoning city, dotted along regular intervals with tall, blackened towers. Bailey banked the ship steeply over a rectangular pad of ceracrete raised up some meters from the surrounding plains. With a subtle precision that Garrand himself might be unable to duplicate, the artificial set the ship down stern-first, distributing her mass across the landing struts one at a time, clockwise—like a spinning plate coming to rest.

The whine of the repulsors and thrusters died down and for the first time in weeks, the interior of the ship was strangely silent.

"Welcome to Eemon Nores." Garrand said, ordering his command pod up to the gangway. "Bailey, unlock the outer fuel nacelles."

The ship spoke up immediately: "Captain, I am perfectly capable of handling the refueling protocol."

"No, I want you to concentrate on security. I want a 100-meter perimeter set up around the ship. Anything enters within that zone, you lock down all functions, seal the airlocks and wait for my command. Nothing's getting inside this time!"

TWO TECH ARTS loped into view as a gantry arm swung into place over the ship. They were tall, fantastic-looking affairs with long triple-jointed leg fit with enormous snow-pad feet. Their long, dark legs with outsized joints were stained with oil and lubricant. Corrosion was eating away at their steel outer skin, revealing the gears and hydraulics within their limbs. Garrand stepped out into the bitterly cold air and took a cautious breath of the planet's atmosphere. The air was achingly cold — the first lungful hurt, but was palatable. He watched as the two tech arts expertly maneuvered the gantry arm into place.

His comtab crackled as Helen called him from her vantage place on the bridge. "Where's C'tereino?"

"Nowhere near this place," Garrand chuckled. "He agreed to let us refuel — for a price. But he's not about to risk his thin neck by being here personally in case we're caught."

"Noble of him."

"Hey, no one else would touch us. He's risking a lot just by letting us land."

The com stayed quiet. Garrand climbed atop the ship and watched as the tech arts locked the fuel nozzles into the nacelles. He leaned in to check that the coupling gear was properly seated. Satisfied, he twirled his gloved hand overhead and the tech art engaged the pump. He rubbed the ice off the display welded onto the gantry, inspected the rate of flow and confirmed it with Bailey before climbing back down.

A cadre of stalwart tech arts stood at the foot of the ship's ramp, awaiting permission to board. Garrand spent five minutes convincing the stubborn machines that their services were not required. He then set about the task of offloading the ship's refuse himself. Dumping in space was preferable, of course — unless one was being pursued and leaving a trail of organic material was undesirable. He spent the better part of an hour shuttling repulsor sleds in and out of *Destiny*.

Garrand paused to wipe his brow with the back of a gloved hand and felt self-conscious, suddenly experiencing the feeling of approbation that made his jaw ache and set the hairs on his arms standing up. He let the repulsor sled settle into the snow and straightened up. He slowly pivoted on his heel, scanning the horizon, until he saw her.

A native girl, taller than normal, head bent against the strain of lugging a gas-powered ice saw, its long blade dragging a furrow in the ice. Despite the heavy parka, Garrand could tell she was thin. She halted before an incline and looked up in his direction, as if to see whether to bother the climb. She seemed content in that spot and cranked up the saw, angling it down into the blue flow. A cloud of ice shot up around her, obscuring his view. Her hood fell back. When the cloud dispersed he saw that she had telescoped a long rod into the hole and had her eyes pressed against the periscope piece, a fish probe most likely. The antennae at the top would radio the results back to base camp. He felt some relief: this watcher only hunted for fish. The panda had been certain only about the presence of a watcher, not the intent.

He fished an optic triode out of his vest pocket. The small, clear lens fit over his right eye. Garrand squinted, the muscles around his eye controlling the triode's focus. After a moment his eye was accustomed to the enhanced image and the woman's form filled his vision. Startled by what he saw, his cheek twitched, sending the focus awry. Garrand fought to regain the image.

The face came back into focus as the woman looked up and squinted in his direction. She was beautiful. Dark hair tied up in a curly tangle at the top of her head, some tendrils falling down around her lips. If he were closer he could reach up and straighten it. If... no, that was Kate. He shook his head; the girl in the distance was only some local, probably already married to a fishmonger.

Yet, for a moment, his mind played tricks on him. The woman was the embodiment of Kate Rea Ellison. Dark flinty eyes, the crease of a smile hinted at the corner of her mouth. The image wavered. If could only see her closer. He exhaled sharply and removed the triode. *It's been too long,* he thought, *even beautiful ice girls look like you now.* He let his natural vision drift back across the snow to the woman. His chest tightened. Even from the distance, she looked so much like her...

Vailetta mashed her feet in the snow, trying to keep her toes warm. She thought of her men spread out across a dozen planets, teaming up with Imperial agents, sympathetic praetors, adjucates, magistrates and the like to string together a network of 'listeners' waiting for their web of informants to spot a ship fitting *Destiny's* description. What were the odds that she had picked the right planet in the right system?

Thirteen point two according to the final projection Yarvek had given her—the highest on a list of forty some odd planets, moons, orbital platforms and asteroids. Report of an unscheduled landing in a remote caritu deep in the southern hemisphere had sent her blazing across the ice plains. The *Ilyovahtna* and the *Jjaeyg* were on their way to retrieve the rest of the Gokazoku and would rendezvous outside Eemon Nores in nine hours.

She had donned this native garb that Mr. Wicek had procured, and slowly made her way on foot through the surprising bustle of the village to the outskirts of the farming compound that was harboring *Destiny's Needle*. Pausing at a harvesting pylon just over a hundred meters from the edge of the blast pad, Vailetta flipped the lens cap off the monocular fitted to her shoulder epaulet. The thin tube-like apparatus snaked down her back and up her sleeve where it was jacked into the ice-flow rod. Vailetta decided she was close enough and drilled the hole to provide her ruse of ice fishing, a conspicuous setup that allowed her to appear to be looking under the ice while she studied her subject discretely and in detail.

She jacked up the magnification until she had a clear view of the man walking down the ship's boarding ramp, intent on her first magnified glimpse of Garrand Médeville. He had stalwartly refused to let any tech arts onto his ship, and was ferrying repulsor sleds down the ramp himself. As she feared, the captain had become security conscious after the discovery of the Imperial trace. Nearly invisible or not, Torg would be unable to slip inside the ship — he could mask his visible presence, but not all his bio signs. They would have to proceed with Wicek's ploy because the refueling would certainly not take more than several hours.

Vailetta watched with amusement as Captain Médeville offloaded pallet after pallet of discarded bamboo shoots. Leaning heavily against a landing strut, he rubbed his eyes and yawned. He looked terribly fatigued. It must be emotionally taxing to always be on the run, it occurred to her, constantly looking over your shoulder, wondering who, if anyone, you can trust. She felt a small twinge of guilt for her role here.

As if he had somehow read her thoughts and sensed her presence, Médeville abruptly stopped what he was doing and turned to face her. Without thinking, Vailetta looked up from her periscope and looked at him with her own eyes. He studied her for a few moments, turned away, and then looked back once more.

Then a large furry face poked its head around the edge of the landing ramp's threshold. The creature's huge eyes peered at the tarmac and the pallets and its nose sniffed at the alien smells. Vailetta watched transfixed as the creature emerged completely, lumbering down the incline ramp on four huge feet, body swaying back and forth slowly in an almost ridiculous swagger.

The creature was much smaller than she expected—its fur rustling in the stiff wind. Garrand, too, caught sight of the creature and hurried quickly over. Vailetta could not hear what he was saying, but she gathered from his stance that he was not happy. He pointed back up the ramp and barked a command. The furry creature promptly sat down and shook its head back and forth. Garrand put his hands on his hips defiantly and continued talking to the creature, as if it could understand what he was saying. Were Lord Barrett's stories true, then?

She popped the lens cap back onto her monocular, and used the distraction to slip away.

GARRAND WAS GROWING flustered. The little panda, Alexander, would not budge. He tried to usher him back to safety but the panda just seemed to think he was playing. He suffered long, repeated licks across his face as he tried to reach around the panda to pick him up. Alex scampered down the ramp.

"Get back up here!" Garrand yelled. "You want to be seen?" He looked back to where the woman had stood, but she was gone.

"Mrrrahhh," Alexander cried. Another panda appeared at the airlock, then two more.

"Cheplus," Garrand muttered, and the exodus began.

The two rust-red tech arts looked up uncertainly from their refueling gantry. The sight of the creatures spilling out onto the blast pad had distracted them from their duties.

Garrand began to shout in anger, but stopped, realizing the futility of his efforts. It was ridiculous, of course—pandas everywhere, snow flying, loopy grunts and roars drifting across the tarmac. It looked more like he was running a nursery than a star-worthy vessel.

He watched as the pandas continued to romp out of the airlock and cascade down the ramp. The guttural cries of pleasure sang out into the cold air as dozens of pandas emerged from the ship and sledded down the hills on the edge of the blast pad. They were all having a perfectly marvelous time.

He began to see the sly, sublime side of the situation. Planetfall always tended to be a time to let off steam. Why, then, should playful pandas be a problem? Why should he have to be the bad guy, spoiling everyone's fun? He tried to put aside his concerns for security and stealth; if the woman in the distance was a 'watcher' then she already knew. He hoped that Sid's prognostication was accurate, that they would all lift safely.

"*Destiny?*"

"Yes Captain?"

"Expand your security perimeter to 150 meters. Anything moves inside that distance, I want to know about it."

"As you wish."

Garrand tried to relax. From a different perspective, the pandas were actually quite entertaining to watch. So much carefree energy and camaraderie. He remembered times when he had gone sledding down the wooded slopes on his home world. Why did he have to be the one that demanded discipline? He had hated when his father had made him come inside and take a warm bath.

It was too late to start insisting on rigorous order now. *Discipline...* he shook his head sadly, *too much rigorous order in his life.* The invisible ties of years of service and the bonds of his genetic past followed him even now.

The pandas were completely oblivious to the human's concerns. They tumbled across the snow escarpments lashed by the winds into curious formations at the edge of the landing platform. Garrand walked to the edge of the blast pad, a thick slab of ceracrete poured atop the icy knoll to accept the weight of freighters. The slab protected the delicate ices that sprawled across the limitless flat expanses of permafrost that extended as far as the eye could see. To the south, escaping thermal gasses rising out of twin pipes marked the entrance to C'tereino's underground compound. The gasses fogged immediately in the frigid air and swirled back down over the three low bumps that were the only outwardly visible elements of the vast living complex that spread out beneath the farm.

Garrand let his eyes drift out across the barren plains to the west and north. The sun was at a low slant and the characteristic blue color of Eemon Nores' ice could be readily seen. The thin, overlapping layers shielded the blue ice lichen from the harsh winds that normally whipped across the tundra. Today it was strangely still, almost pleasant. Garrand dragged his toe through a small puddle of water at the edge of the ceracrete. Ice and snow on the pad steamed away by the hot exhaust gasses from *Destiny's* thrusters were already recrystallizing into a layer of slick, blue ice.

Garrand gave a thought to firing some pitons into the ice clips around the landing pads that bore the ship's weight, but dismissed it. No wind, level slab—she wasn't going to slide anywhere. He walked over to the ship and leaned back against a strut, arms crossed casually over his chest. The clouds were magnificent. A super-cell towered over the flat icy expanse, rising 20,000 meters into the air, crowned by an enormous anvil head. The weather front stretched hundreds of kilometers across the horizon, the tops of the clouds a brilliant white in the setting sun. Tiny droplets of moisture reflected the sunlight that sank directly behind his back, casting an amazing spectrum of brilliance along the leading edge of the storm. Silent thunderstorms roiled in the darkening mass of clouds below — lightning strikes crackled in the distance, mute fingers of light illuminating the icy plain. Garrand breathed deeply, his shoulders relaxing.

Barren plains of ice fell away on all sides of the blast pad's knoll, the faint symmetrical bulge of farm equipment visible beneath the snow cover. Blackened harvesting pylons rose up at regularly spaced intervals like burnt-out tails of aged rockets that had nose-dived into the permafrost. Eemon's southern reaches were sparse, desolate and strikingly beautiful.

The sun shone brightly here, the storm still some hours off, but little warmth fell upon his face. He wasn't particular to the cold, but he almost didn't mind it here — sky a radiant blue-green, the air sharp and clean, not too ripe with conflicting smells like their last port of call, El-Bouteran. *And no Shock Troops*, he thought grimly; just cold air tinged with the smell of fresh ice.

His breath fogged before him, a vaporous swirl of crystals that bent back inward and compressed strangely in the still air before sending new tendrils tapering off into the twilight. He couldn't help but think of the Byrethylen Wraith as he watched his own exhalation dance into existence. He wondered what fate awaited the lush rainforests of El-Bouteran. How many men had the beast taken? What about the animals on the planet? Were the native beasts intelligent enough to attract the wraith's attention? Would they have enough neurological activity to allow the wraith to sustain itself? Or would it lie dormant upon the planet's surface, waiting… *What a cruel legacy to leave behind,* he thought. *And for what?*

The wind began licking at his face, heralding the coming storm. He could feel his muscles tighten as the gusts picked up. *And thus it begins,* he thought. He scanned the tribe of pandas as they romped across the tarmac. The price of survival did not seem to trouble them—or else they masked it well.

Death always accompanied survival he reminded himself, feeling along the rough edge of his blaster—particularly in these times. Self-perpetuation was genetically encoded in most species—at least most that he was aware of—there was no getting around it. The drive to endure, persist, outlast was unavoidable—moral justifications came later, if they came at all.

Yet he recalled facing a Byrethylen Wraith three times before—the first in the service of the Emperor. He had born witness to the million-acre swath of devastation the creature had left behind. Whole ecosystems left in ruin, set back thousands of years. He had heard the screams before—had seen the terror of his worst fears summoned up inside his own mind. Shuddering suddenly, he turned away from the tarmac, cheek up against the hull, hand against her steel. The sight of the wind demon was all too real in his memory. The wraith had conjured up that horror, and it plagued him to this day. The demon was the embodiment of all those terrified screams, a manifestation of death and loss that ate subconsciously away at him just as the winds tore through his mind and body on a hundred worlds now.

Garrand shook his head. *The wind was inescapable, just like the past.*

He remembered the power he had felt as a Captain of the Imperial Guard. The resources at his command: men, matériel, weapons, expertise, intelligence—the raw brainpower of thousands of arts and organics. The tools to shape life and forge worlds. And the power to destroy that which we created along with that which we did not, he mused sardonically. The grisly memory of fallen soldiers rushed back at him from a decade earlier. Lifeless husks consumed by the wraith lying strewn across the scarred battleground and blackened fields.

Yet still we march onward, across the stars... And in his own hubris, he still decided what creatures were fit to survive and which were not.

Garrand turned back to the pandas, a burning sensation forming in his chest and fingertips. He would not become a slave to second-guessing. There was more here than running a load of sentient bios out from under Vice Proctor Barrett's nose, more than releasing a long-held foe upon a hapless world. He mustn't succumb to his own doubts, there was too much at stake. If the pandas were to have any chance to survive and flourish as a species—despite being hounded across the great reaches—he would have to set aside his own demons to help them.

He sniffed at the cold breeze, surprised that he could now recognize the scent of the pandas. He looked down at the slushy mess that had been hastily plowed aside in anticipation of *Destiny's* arrival. He reached down and scooped up a glove-full, mashing the crystals into the rough approximation of a sphere, unaware that he was being carefully watched.

Sid eyed the captain from an advantageous position, directly behind him and downwind. Lowering his head and scrunching his rear paws into he snow for traction he coiled himself for the pounce. His substantial rear end wiggled back and forth just before he leapt. Oblivious to his impending doom, Garrand carefully shaped the snowball in his hands.

With a final jittery shake, Sid charged across the icy blast pad, long claws shaving skid marks behind him, and tackled the captain at the knees. Garrand grunted in pain and surprise, his knees buckling under the impact. He didn't have time to get his arms up to break his fall. Panda and human tumbled over the edge and slid down the snow-covered slope.

Garrand came to a rest on his back in a pile of mush with the giant panda straddling his waist. Sid reared up over him and roared ferociously, shaking his head from side to side, gleefully announcing his kill. Garrand hesitated under the toothy cry for only a moment, then sat up and smashed his snowball into the panda's face. He shoved the ice and slush directly into Sid's open jaw and rammed his shoulder into the panda's gut.

Sid grunted and looked down in surprise as Garrand wiggled free and began scrambling across the snowy plain, scooping up snow in his hands as he ran. Sid spluttered the slush out of his mouth and cantered off after him, roaring. He quickly closed the distance to the captain, his big jaws snapping at the human's heels.

"Oh no you don't, not this time!" Garrand hollered over his shoulder.

Sid roared again, but suddenly the captain stopped, dropped down on one knee and twisted backward to face his attacker. He grabbed the panda's loose neck fur and heaved the massive creature over. Sid tripped over Garrand's outstretched leg and felt the man using his momentum to flip him over his hip. He landed with a grunt on his back and Garrand quickly scrambled onto his chest, pinning his shoulders to the snow with his knees.

Still holding the folds of fur around the panda's neck, he tilted back his head and let loose a great scream of his own. He shook his head back and forth in mocking tribute.

Sid frowned for a second and growled up at the captain. Being at the top of the carnivorous food chain, he wasn't accustomed to such an obstinate meal, particularly one that could so easily handle his size and bulk.

"Little taste of your own medicine," Garrand replied.

Helen appeared at the edge of the blast pad. She surveyed the intertwined panda and human and marched frumpily down the slope, boots scrunching in the snow.

"What are you doing!" she demanded as she pulled off a glove with her teeth.

Garrand raised his eyebrows at her as if he didn't know what she could possibly be referring to. He got up off of Sid who made a hasty exit, scrambling with all four paws across the snow. Apparently the big panda knew this tone.

"Oh, fine—you big traitor. Run away when the going gets tough..." He made a show of brushing himself off.

Helen ripped into him. "Any ship in orbit over this hemisphere is going to pick this up—giant red flashing heat sigs on all this miserable ice. You might as well put out a galactic bulletin: pandas right here!"

Garrand rolled his eyes, "C'mon Helen. You really expect me to keep all those fur balls locked up the whole journey?"

"Oh, so it's 'Helen' now, is it?"

"Yes," Garrand growled sarcastically, "it's *Helen* now. I've had just about all I can take of all this polite, gentlemanly behavior. Mistress Tchelakov this, Miss Helen that; while all the while you're hacking security, subverting ship protocols, dumping invaluable fuel, and generally leading me and my crew on a merry farce."

Helen looked pale and chagrinned. "But—"

"—No 'buts!' You haven't been straight with me since you helped yourself to my table in the Oak Room. Este used to warn me about girls like you."

"Girls like me? I caution you to watch your tone Captain Médeville!"

"Oh, so now it's 'Captain Médeville,' is it?" he mocked her. "Why so formal *Helen*? You've been cozying up to me for weeks."

"Cozying up to you?" her face was beginning to grow flushed.

"Yeah, your demure facade may fool Bailey, but I know what coy is," he enjoyed watching her anger grow. He liked getting the upper hand for a change.

"Coy! You've been in space too long Médeville! The mere sight of a pretty girl has sent your imagination into fantasy overdrive."

"See, you said girl, too."

"What!"

"You called yourself a 'pretty girl.'"

"Girl, woman; what's the difference?"

"You're the one making the distinction. Which is it? Delicate girl full of demure glances and wistful looks," he carefully reached up and straightened an errant lock of her hair, folding it back behind her ear. She watched him carefully, but did not flinch. "Or deadly, Nralda-trained deep-cover agent, a woman who doesn't know a soft touch?"

Helen's voice softened. "What do you think?"

Garrand smiled and leaned forward. Helen looked at him, lips slightly parted. He was so close that her eyes had to dart back and forth between his left and right eye, not sure which one to focus on. A warm beneficence seemed to wash across his face. His eyes sparkled in the crisp, cold air. She leaned into his warm arms and their lips touched, gently at first, then hungrily. Her arms slid back over his shoulders and she rocked forward on the ball of one foot. Garrand's arms wrapped around her, squeezing warmth into her midsection. Even beneath the thick tickarac he could feel the gentle curve of her waist rising from her hips, could sense her back arching up as she pressed into him.

The kiss left a chill running down her back as they parted. Garrand glanced over her shoulder. All the pandas had stopped playing and were watching the two humans merged as one.

Helen followed his gaze and looked back over her shoulder. "Oh, great."

Garrand smiled as he watched the silent, seated pandas. All eyes were locked upon them. "Voyeuristic lot."

Helen crinkled her nose. "I don't think they've ever seen this before."

"Mmm."

Sid watched the pair, wrinkled his nose and turned back to the glorious, cold, wet snow. The pandas resumed playing.

"How much time do you think it'll take to finish refueling?" he asked.

Helen looked up at him eagerly. "Enough."

Garrand thumbed his comtab. "Uh, Bailey? Could you come out here? We, umm—need you to ride herd on these pandas for a few minutes."

"*We*, Captain?"

"*Me*—I need you to come out here."

"Captain, I'm still coordinating the nav tables."

"That's all right. Let *Destiny* finish. I just need you to watch them for awhile—it's cold out here," he added, looking over at Helen with a smile.

"Cold?" she bit her lip and narrowed her gaze. "I'll show you *cold!*" She reached down and scooped up a handful of slush.

"As you wish, Captain."

Garrand sprinted back toward the boarding ramp before Helen could get off a good shot.

"Thanks Bailey," Garrand said as he rushed by the art on his way up the ramp. Bailey stopped and turned his head to follow the captain's progression up the ramp, a concerned expression growing across his face.

Helen misfired in mid-stride, smacking the bulkhead over Garrand's head with a slush ball.

"Miss Tchelakov?" Bailey queried, confused.

"Hi Bailey," she rasped breezily as she hustled after Garrand.

The artificial turned to watch the two dash inside the ship, considered the meaning of the strange behavior for a moment, but could reach no logical conclusion. He turned back to observe the pandas who were scattered across the snowy glade, engaged in various forms of exuberant behavior. Such a display; he had not seen the creatures engage in such frenetic activity since their original embarkation. Perhaps the aerobic activity had somehow influenced the captain and Miss Tchelakov. He quickly verified the physical presence and assessed the relative safety of the thirty-seven pandas and locked their individual positions into memory before reconsidering the matter. He replayed the scene of the captain and Miss Tchelakov rushing up the ramp.

After several million calculations he sighed and gave up; humans were so complicated.

16

C'TEREINO

ICE CREPT EVERYWHERE ON THE SOUTHERN REACHES OF
Eemon Nores, a reflective glaze that covered every surface of
the village. It dripped from ships docked only for hours along
the heated grids of landing slabs on the outskirts of the trading bazaar. Nothing grew here in the great southern reaches
but the microscopic creatures that flowed over the ice, lending
it a blue phosphorescence. Everything was imported from the
northern equatorial straights where the village's principle trading partners lay, and off-planet from inter-system scows. But
what Eemon Nores did have was the blue ice lichen. Used in
everything from petroleum products to food supplements, the
lichen was a prized commodity.

Frost permeated his processors. Bailey flinched as he slipped on the ice and sent a cold jolt along his leg. His annoyance toggled an internal switch and ice prongs extended from the soles of his feet. He looked back at the ship, steam rising from its outports. A bundle of silver fur sashayed down the gangplank. Wind puffs ruffled back the hood revealing Helen. He waited as she came over. She blew circles of condensed air out of her mouth.

"It tastes so crisp here, the air is so fresh." She sighed and took deep breaths, her footing sure over the slippery ground. She looked different to Bailey somehow, something in her face, her manner, had changed.

"You're glowing, do you have fever?" he queried.

"Oh, Bailey," she smiled and put her hand on the crook of his elbow. "Where are we going? I'm ready for adventure."

"I've secured most of the items on Jean-Wa's port-call inventory," he said, leading the way across the slab. "There's only an hour remaining until refueling is complete; Captain said ramp-up and locks-sealed at oh-one-hundred ship's chronometer — that leaves us scant time. I intended to purvey the duty-free for Jean-Wa, though I doubt I'll ever shop to his standards."

"Then away."

They shuffled along the snow to the iceplast huts along the edge of the village. The white plasticine domes with their open rectangles of orange light looked very inviting in the greyness of the cloudy white night, the quiet broken only by the sound of their feet breaking through a crusty layer of snow to the ice beneath. Even the beggar playing a tabouli could not ease the weight of the silence around them. It swallowed all human sound. Only the distant machinery endlessly drilling through the permafrost, and the great plumes of fire that shot up, could breach the stillness.

As they approached the duty free, the odd pair, so striking in their difference, he shining and fluid, she a soft blur of fur that moved with every breath of wind, both silver against the blue ice, drew admiring looks in their direction and venders' cries rose in anticipation.

"Chahk-san, got your chahk-san here."

"Tusks. Native carved tusks. Beautiful carved tusks."

"Dailyern green, just the nip to ward the cold. Dailyern green."

"Wolven eyes. Prime wolven eyes. Charms for lovers. Antidotes for enemies."

A throng of duaro woolies being shepherded through the main street blocked their way, but Bailey easily stepped over the placid beasts and lifted Helen over as well. She wrinkled her nose at the ripe smell of the woolies. They skirted under a skin being stretched across an alley, where village elder-women stood by with their stone scrapers to finish the tanning. A steamed leviathan, already split to be stuffed with smoke-dried eel, was carried by four men down the lane to the pack house, followed by a gaggle of whooping boys. A row of packing crates served as ready tables for card players willing to ignore the cold and inhale the janda fumes from the nearby bakehouse, where children and old persons alike pressed their cold noses to the glazing and dreamed. But cutting through it all came the venders' cries, beckoning the art and the lady in silver.

Bailey gently ushered Helen past it all, to the far end where fishmongers in rubber suits laid leviathans out on the ice, dragging them awkwardly with long hooks. One fishmonger wiped a scaly trail along his rubber apron and lifted his goggles. A long mustachio popped into view, uncurling and quickly freezing. His yellow misshapen eyes regarded Helen keenly and then deferred to Bailey.

"What shall mistress have today, servant?"

"Companion," Helen snapped, turning away with embarrassment. Bailey held fast to her arm. The fishmonger grinned, revealing double rows of filed teeth much like the yawning mouths of the leviathans as they gasped the air for water. He shrugged and clapped his thick rubber gloves together, spraying fish scales.

"What shall it be, eh?"

"Eels," came the low call behind them. Helen spun, her fur hood falling back to see an eel skinner sitting nearby, his back propped against a portaburner topped by a steaming kettle. A plank with a nail held a squirming eel before him. His knife flew down the length and back up the other side.

Helen felt a rush of recognition. In Letugia there had been an eel skinner, after the prophecy. *"It honors the memory of the father,"* the crone had proclaimed, offering her a candle. *"He's still alive,"* she had insisted. "Oh, Father," she whispered, tears frosting in her eyes. She could stomach all that had happened to this point, could even justify in some remote part of her mind the risks she was taking, but the thought of what lay ahead flattened her brisk mood. Risking the tribe's fate to avenge the past could only be seen as a betrayal by her father. There was that word, that awful, biting word: betrayal. Darstin, Barrett, her father, the tribe—she was betraying them all. And now Garrand Médeville, too.

She stared at the skinner, gripped in a shiver, her eagerness for adventure shed instantly. Bailey pulled her hood back up and led her away, rubbing her arms. They slipped past the skinner and proceeded into the alley.

"The past often reaches for us, Helen, when we least wish it. But look, now, at the summer laid before us."

She cleared her eyes and managed a smile. Indeed the ice-plast hut he had chosen looked like a crazy mirage of vines and flowers. A wizened little man in a checkerboard shaven fur suit spread a span of pastel blooms before her.

"Flowers for the lady, sir?" he asked, his rainbow tipped hair floating in a frosty cloud around his face. Bailey held out a credit chit.

"But naturally," the little man smiled, extending the delicate blooms up towards Helen's hands.

"*Coriantha arletis,* on this planet…" she shook her head, fingering the petals. "Not your typical hothouse flower." She turned to Bailey. "They don't like to be forced."

"Ah," sighed the vender. "A true connoisseur. Then come inside. Come inside. I have much for you to see. All the glories as we wend our way among the stars." He moved back in an undulating gait, his fine hands beckoning.

As they passed through the portal, Bailey felt a warm draft from behind and caught a glimmer of movement to his right. He spun, instinctively shielding Helen with one arm and drawing a Naisus hand cannon with his other, but the alley appeared to be empty. The lines of the nearest iceplast hut seemed wrong, convoluted. Ripples of energy lingered on the infrared spectrum of his sight, but he couldn't keep his eyes focused on it. His sensors detected nothing, not even the draft from before. Still wary, he entered the hut.

Across the street, the assassin Torg shimmered into view for a moment and then coalesced back into his surroundings. He should have been more careful about his body temperature. The art had well-honed battle senses and would prove a formidable adversary. Most interesting was his obvious concern with the Tchelakov woman, more that of a prospective lover than a crewmember. He strode away in the direction of *Destiny's Needle*. The warder Mr. Wicek in his ridiculous fur suit would take care of those inside.

Helen paused before a bin of bright orange fruit, obviously hothouse and quickly perishable, some already beginning to frost over despite the heat strips that lined the case.

"Tannerelos." The little man scooped a few into a handful of ice chips and offered them to her. Smelling of hot, lazy days, they beamed orange against the blue ice chips.

"Bailey, these might please Jean-Wa. Bailey?"

"Just what I was thinking," he replied absentmindedly, his mind still on the ripple against the iceplast hut. Perhaps the strain was getting to him, but he could not shrug away the feeling of some watcher being present. Gone now, but nearby. They should get back to the ship.

"Please, take your fill," urged the little man with a sly grin. He filled a small bag.

"That's enough," Bailey said sternly, remembering Jean-Wa's earlier admonishment. The man placed the bag on a scale and adjusted the weights. "We should not linger," he said to Helen.

The little man handed the bag over the counter. "Have a pleasant voyage."

❖ ❖ ❖

GARRAND DIDN'T REALIZE HOW MUCH HE HAD BEEN LOOKING forward to seeing C'tereino until he started down the slab in a slippery descent toward the compound as *Destiny* had directed. He hadn't warned Helen of his visit; better not to risk his old friend's neck. C'tereino had been a dominating presence in the

Officers' Mess, his booming voice echoing off the walls during the telling of some elaborate joke. His pranks were just as boisterous. Once he and his fellows had duca-welded a pompous diplomatic art to the rails outside the bridge. The big man had been skipped over for promotion after that episode, but he claimed it had been worth it. Besides, C'tereino never intended to rise above active duty. He loved striding in the thick of things. Being promoted would have interfered with his fun.

"Generals must shave," he'd laugh, plucking his thick, curling beard that he wore despite regulations. A giant of a man, able and willing to best a dozen others, he'd commanded a complement of gender-specific Honor Watch within the Guard.

"Can't beat females for cunning," he'd say, cocking his head to one side in a quick jerk of irony. "Never met a man I couldn't beat, or a woman who couldn't beat me." Then he'd belch out a laugh. Truly, though, his Honor Watch had held one of the finest records in any system. They had even been requested to serve on Daulinbêres itself. That is, until the incident. A sudden chill crept down his spine as he remembered the rescue at Sardis. Water rushing into the bridge, the crushing pressure, the thought of his men trapped helplessly below. He shook his head and returned to the present; C'tereino was here. That thought alone was uplifting; it had been so many years. He missed the spirit and adventure of his friend.

The footing improved as he walked. The ice had been scored and was pockmarked where salt pellets had been scattered. The ring of three interconnected iceplast huts seemed strangely quiet to belong to his friend. Could it be that C'tereino would not meet him after all? Did he fear Imperial reprisal that much? Garrand shook his head. Not the giant he had known. He scanned the ring and headed towards the largest hut. Its dome glistened with promise in the grey light. He pinged a fur-covered mallet against the dark iron bell hanging by the entrance and then shoved aside the oily fur to enter.

Smoke stung his eyes. He blinked rapidly, crouching to escape embers floating in a dangerous haze. He coughed and shuffled closer to the interior where the air might be clearer. He paused, gaining his vision, aghast at the surroundings. Enormous skewers impaled stacks of insulation wadding, apparently to be used for fuel. An open fire licked towards a sooty hole in the ceiling. Glass bottles hung in murky cascades down the walls. Rotting cloth draped a tier of cots to one side. A broken doll lay on the floor.

He had the wrong hut, obviously.

"*Destiny,*" he called into the comtab. "This isn't it." With a sense of relief he turned to exit and froze. A dragon shield hung over the doorway. The beast's golden claws held the three staffs of diplomatic glory, indicating a proctorial contingent. The furs below parted and a stooped man entered. His head hung to one side, as though perpetually supplicant, so that though he was a good deal taller than Garrand, the man had to look up at him. His beefy shoulders hung at his sides, as though useless. Garrand stepped back and tried to think of a way to apologize for being there, but a hollow voice interrupted him, whistling out of a hole in the man's throat.

"I never meant for you to see this. I was late getting to your ship."

"C'tereino?" Garrand could hardly believe that the former hulking soldier had been reduced to this husk. Deprivation. Hardship. Imperial wrath. Garrand knew them all. But he had assumed that his friend would have survived as well as he. Anger turned his stomach.

"My friend."

"You know not what to say. As should be. Better the memories, yes?"

"No, I came to you for help, but I see that you are in need of mine."

The big man shook his head sadly. "There is nothing you can do for me." C'tereino laughed, if the thin wheezing could be called that. "It is enough that I can still be of service to the Brotherhood. My time has come and gone—you know it is true. We are the same, you and I—Griffin to the core." He made a fist as if to thump his chest above his heart, but instead merely rubbed the edge of his thumb down his ragged tunic. "One of us must show them." He seemed to tire. "I have my memories. For me it is enough."

"But there is so much more."

"For you, my friend. Look at me," he said quietly. "But you..." The big man's eyes softened as he took in Garrand's form head to toe. He looked strong, vigorous. There was still fight left in him—perhaps more now than he could ever recall. The years were there, creased in his face, his boyish looks hardened into the strong, angular features of a man. C'tereino paused: Garrand was no longer the volatile charmer, endless energy bubbling just below the surface, emotions held barely in check. This man was stolid and watchful, ennobled of a quiet strength. Yet his eyes were still filled with a familiar passion. Bright and bold, they carried a light that C'tereino would never forget. Garrand was the epitome of the Princes of Blood. It was sad that it had all come to an end. Yet still, his eyes foretold adventures to come. Much more lay ahead of him: it was obvious he still had hope left in his heart. C'tereino sighed deeply and looked at his crusted fur boots. It was almost too much to see him again.

Garrand took a half step forward but hesitated. C'tereino held up his hand and his gaze rose back to his friend. "For me, memories are living." He kept up his hand, as if to ward off Garrand's rebuttal, but then wavered and let the hand drop. He held Garrand's hazel eyes. "You could create a few more. Enough to fill a good long tale." A smile crept over his blistered lips. "Come back with a bottle and give me an evening. We will drink like young men and you can tell me your tale and I will have new memories to keep me warm."

Garrand reached forward and grasped his friend's shoulder. C'tereino lifted a big hand to Garrand's shoulder and nodded. "That will be enough." He stared into the big man's eyes and realized that they were all that he found familiar. Beneath the veneer of decrepitude, C'tereino was still the same person. He shut his eyes tightly and felt the big man draw him into a huge bear hug. Garrand found that he had no words to speak, but in his heart he swore it would be so.

❖ ❖ ❖

DUSTY WHITE CLOUDS OF ICE AND SNOW SPEWED INTO THE night sky, swirling outside the crystal bridge as *Destiny's Needle* thundered off her landing slab. The glow of her collision lanterns cut a brilliant swath through the tumble of frozen debris whipped by the wind and repulsors into a low fury. Sid wrinkled his nose as he observed the storm from his quiet, dim perch within the hollow globe. The reflected light from the lanterns cast a murky translucence through the bridge's truncated superstructure, touching the edges of the captain's face. Sid had been granted the privilege of sitting on the captain's command pod, offered without a word as the railing had slid open. Having gained the captain's acceptance, Sid was trying to remain respectfully quiet as the man piloted the ship low across the frozen rooftops, despite his many questions.

The village slipped beneath them and the captain accelerated the ship, though Sid could still see the silhouettes of icy escarpments mere meters below. Sid looked questioningly at the captain's profile; apparently he was aware of the look.

"We're down on the deck until we hit the pole," he said without looking over. "We'll make an ascent straight off the polar axis." The bright lantern beams winked off and Sid suffered a minor fright at the sudden lack of visual impetus—the ship had been perilously low to begin with. But the captain's attention had turned to a small sartographic display and Sid relaxed. Once more darkness prevailed within the globe.

Garrand smiled, full of energy. It was like a fresh beginning, cutting across the surface in the dead of night, hugging the surface like an old two-man air skimmer. His ship full of fuel, his cargo of precious lives safe and secure, he felt like he had been granted a new beginning. And best of all, there had been no sign of Imperials, merely a fisher girl and Bailey's account of the strange ripple against the iceplast hut. But true to Sid's vision, they had made it off the surface without a hitch. He was feeling positively buoyant.

Vailetta stood on the steep ramp of her personal sloop, the *Lolovanti*, and watched as Torg escorted Wicek across the icy pad. The two men paused before her, their breaths creating a misty fog between them.

"Well done, Mr. Wicek," she congratulated her warder. The little man bowed his head, deferring to her compliment. Vailetta glanced briefly at the assassin, who managed a bemused expression without actually smiling. "You even have our assassin's begrudging respect." Wicek looked up at the pale man, made even more so by the bitter cold.

"Not begrudging at all," Torg murmured. "I quite admire a soft touch."

"Well, come aboard," Vailetta urged. "*Destiny's Needle* has just lifted."

"What is the status?" Torg asked.

"We are to rendezvous with the *Ilyovahtna* in under an hour. The *Ulusi* and the *Jjaeyg* are collecting the remaining Gokazoku Kaigi, and should join us soon thereafter. In the meantime, we follow the prey."

❖ ❖ ❖

A SMALL BOWL OF FRESH FRUIT LAY ON A SPOTLESSLY CLEAN table inside the ship's kitchen. The small tannerelos were lovingly placed on a pristine linen cloth, the edges of which draped just over the edge of the silver bowl. Jean-Wa had been quite pleased with the unexpected gift; Bailey had outdone himself this time, and without instruction. Perhaps the art was learning after all, he mused. Jean-Wa left the fruit to ripen fully; they would be a surprise addition to the morrow's breakfast. He left to deliver a pot of janda to the bridge.

Inside the ripened tannerelo the nanite waited. It existed for one driving need that had required thirty-five hundred art hours to program and fabricate. A compound machine miniature, it's tiny shell held a mass of fine-tuned sensors, and a gel-based neural matrix. An eight-legged driving mechanism rendered it the look of some bizarre crecklin bug.

Leaving the iceplast hut had awakened the nanite. Sensors detailed its journey to *Destiny's Needle* and the short trip inside to the kitchen. It noted the absence of activity, human or otherwise. Using an elongated claw, the nanite sliced through the pulpy strands inside the fruit and burst out of the skin. It skittered across the table and tumbled quickly to the deck. Extending its antennae, it put forth a number of sharp-edged legs and scrambled confidently to the door. Sighting the distance to the door's sensor window, it shot a pellet of light, activating Humhal's involuntary open program. *In case of fire, release all forms before sealing in the flames.* Unknowingly, though, the nanite also activated the personality within.

"Fire!" shouted Humhal, opening his sensors wide. "Fire?" His sensors just caught a glimpse of a tiny artificial skittering down the serviceway. "Oh, someone new. I wonder if it sews?" Then he powered down again, grumbling about prankish newcomers.

The nanite finished its odyssey uninterrupted, making a methodical scramble through the ship seeking out the greatest energy source, arriving finally in the engine room. It located the quantum coupler and quickly clawed its way inside the fibrous insulation. Once touching the smooth cylindrical surface of the coupler itself, the nanite latched all eight legs to the power regulator coil and went dormant. One lone sensor remained active, awaiting the pulse of energy that would herald the quantum drive's activation just before a leap to quantum space. There it waited, and with it the fate of *Destiny's Needle*.

17

CONVERGENCE

DESTINY'S NEEDLE SHOT OUT OF EEMON NORES' MAGNETO-sphere, the blue ice of the southern pole spread out beneath her like the splayed fingers of a giant fist. The ship's hull glowed from the rapid ascent. Helen stood at the back edge of Bailey's navigation pod, watching nervously as the art prepared the ship for the quantum jump.

Garrand quickly worked his way through the pre-jump checklist. The coordinates had been laid in for hours, the ship merely needed to put some distance between itself and Eemon Nores. His hand passed gently over the quantum activation board and the reactor slowly warmed to life. Almost immediately a warning flashed. His hand froze over the display, eyes scanning the sartographs. "No, no, no," he whispered.

The ship continued to feed energy to the quantum drive, the reactor that would take them through the light speed barrier and allow the light engines to take them well beyond into quantum space. Precious seconds passed as Garrand tried to locate the source of the warning. It was a minor circuit failure according to the flashing display, but anything concerning the quantum reactor got his full attention. At first he thought there must be a drain sapping energy away from the reactor, but the allocation feeds showed a standard flow. A second warning lit up and Garrand reached forward to shut the whole thing down, but it was too late.

Deep inside the engine room, attached to the quantum drive's power regulator coil, the nanite awakened and performed its final and definitive function: it self-destructed in a shower of sparks, taking the regulator coil with it. Without the PR coil there was no way to govern the vast fluctuations in the quantum drive's efficiency. If the reactor operated in too efficient a manner, the PR coil bled off regenerated dryexcellon ions, keeping the reactor from going supercritical. Without it, *Destiny's Needle* might easily breach the reactor in a quantum jump, terminating all life aboard.

Garrand watched the newest warning wink and felt his whole body sag back into the acceleration couch. Without understanding the details of what had happened, he knew immediately that *Destiny* had been effectively crippled.

His voice was barely a whisper as he spoke into his comtab: "Little Bit, get down to the engine room and have a look at the quantum PR coil." The ship was still rocketing away from Eemon Nores, no longer shielded by her mass or magneto-sphere. He sighed and turned to Bailey. "What've you got on the scope?"

The art performed a cursory sweep and glanced up. "Nothing, Captain."

"Check again."

"My apology, sir. There is a ship hovering at the edge of our sensor range."

"Identity?"

"Unknown."

"What can you make out?"

"Small ship — thirty meters prow to stern."

"The vultures circle fast around here," Garrand muttered.

"Vultures?" Helen asked skeptically.

"It's an Imperial follower. Haven's End! How in K'ye's name did they sabotage us this time?"

"We're sabotaged?" Helen asked.

"We can't make the jump to light speed. And now there's a ship at the edge of scan, watching us. There's gonna be more soon."

"More vultures?"

"Call them what you will — that ship hasn't closed in 'cause she's waiting for something."

Helen felt a knot tighten in her gut. "Waiting for us to realize we're trapped?"

"More than likely, she's waiting for her big brothers to show up. I guarantee you there's more on their way."

Helen turned away, frightened and nauseous. It was too soon — much too soon. Barrett had jumped the gun once again. Her breeding pair was not safely stashed away yet. All she had left to protect her bargaining position was the viral parasites inside the pandas, kept at bay by her weekly 'serum' injections. But if he called her bluff — there would be none who would survive to carry on the line. She was beginning to feel sick.

"What can we do?"

"For now, nothing. Change out the coil if we had a spare…"

"Why don't we have one?" Helen asked, accusation and desperation creeping into her voice.

"Can't carry a replacement for every part on the ship," Garrand snapped. "We're built for speed—military redundancy just isn't part of our design."

Helen growled, "What are we going to do?"

"Sir," Bailey interrupted. "Picking up three new targets." He bent over his scope. "Two Coryl-Tuluyt Pickets and what looks to be like a variation on the standard Imperial attack frigate."

Sid slowly closed his eyes, his shoulders slumping.

Garrand's fingers slid across the board and a new sartograph leapt into existence overhead, filled with sensor details on the three new ships. He quickly assessed the burgeoning display of information.

"I'll tell you what we're going to do," Garrand said, his voice cracking slightly with determination. "Attack."

"Oh Haven—not again," Helen sighed.

Garrand spun his command pod to the forefront of the bridge and began rerouting energy to the sub-light reactors.

"Shall I bleed energy to the forward deflectors?" Bailey asked.

"No. I doubt we'll meet with much resistance this go around—they want us in one piece."

"Pulse cannon?"

"No, give me everything you've got to the B'varts. I've got something else in mind."

The slender forms of the Imperial pickets slowly emerged from the gloom. Garrand barked into his comtab. "Little Bit, you find the problem?"

A shrill whistle sounded, followed by a garble of Vort Magellan.

"*Destiny?*"

"The PR coil has been disabled," the ship filled in smoothly. "There seems to be some evidence of foul play."

"No kidding," Garrand muttered darkly.

"The remains of a destructive device are lodged inside."

Garrand cut the ship short. "Little Bit, I want you to rip out the defective coil, clean up all the relays, make sure there's no other collateral damage from shrapnel, and be ready to slap a new one in."

"I thought you said we didn't have a new one," Helen said.

"We don't." Garrand eyes raced across his command board while the ship closed distance to the nearest picket.

"But—" Helen started to argue, but stopped, eyes growing wide.

"We may not have a spare power regulator coil," Garrand said, his eyes narrowing as he tried to pick out the ships with the naked eye, "but that frigate will."

Helen felt the last of her resolve melt away. The pandas were doomed. "The frigate?" she asked meekly.

"It's not as fast as those Coryl-Tuluyts — it's gotta be there for support. Advance troops always have supporting units trailing behind for resupply and reinforcements to fuel their efforts."

Helen wondered whether she dared harbor a hope.

"Better lock those pandas down," Garrand said.

"If the Imperials get aboard there's not going to be much to stop them," she replied.

"So the trick is to not let them aboard. If we're attached to the hull of that frigate—"

"Wait a second! Did you say *attached?*"

"Yeah, how else are we going to get inside? There's two main quantum supply store holds on that frigate, and in one of them there's going to be a power regulator coil that'll fit our B'vart reactors."

Helen rolled her eyes and nestled her head into her hands.

"As I was saying, if we're locked on magnetically to that frigate, they're going to have a hard time maneuvering close enough to latch onto us."

"If we're attached to the hull, couldn't they board us through breach in the frigate?"

"We'll have that covered. Bailey's been defending entrenched positions for 200 years."

"And a vacuum approach?"

Garrand looked at her with a dour expression. "Would you order men into the void to board this ship? It'd be suicide. *Destiny's Needle* would cut them to pieces before they got close enough to cut their way in."

"Not if they used heavy assault cannon and fire support from those pickets."

"They wouldn't dare. Remember, they're after the pandas. What if they accidentally ruptured a compartment with the pandas inside?"

Helen frowned, but her confidence was growing bit by bit. A glimmer of hope surfaced.

Destiny's Needle sluiced in toward the triumvirate of Imperial vessels, cutting below their angle of attack. Garrand imagined the surprise and consternation the Imperial commander must be experiencing. There was no way the ship could outrun the pickets, his quantum drive was disabled, he was outgunned and outnumbered. Yet here he was, lancing under their bellies for attack. He grinned with satisfaction as he cut beneath them with no resistance: for the moment it was sweet not to have them firing at his ship. In the back of his mind though, he knew it meant that they would soon be trying to board him.

"Captain, I'm reading seven new vessels mark eight one starboard aft."

"More vultures?" he frowned.

"I'm afraid these are birds of a different feather."

Helen squinted down into her targeting scope, slaved to Bailey's master on the navigation pod. A surge of fear raced through her bloodstream, as if things could get any worse.

"Bailey, can you make out any ship registry?"

"They're older vessels. Energy signature is full of heavy isotopes; the reactors are older, less efficient. Tvultàk Skullers from the look of it. No registry; ship ID's have been deleted."

"Not too worried about appearances I guess," Garrand muttered.

"Mercenaries would be my guess, Captain."

"Or pirates. Veekpot raiders?"

Helen studied the readout with a grim expression of abject disbelief. Bailey was right; they were Tvultàk war vessels, left over from the Galncy Campaigns twenty years ago. There was only one place they could have come from, but they were too soon, much too soon. That rendezvous was not scheduled for another three and a half weeks in a system far removed from this desolate volume and well after her first bit of treachery. Something was wrong—terribly wrong. Panic wrapped around her throat; she was finding it hard to breathe. Darstin knew, and he had found her. Followed her, found her, tracked her down. But how?

"I can tell you who they are," she rasped, her voice abandoning her.

Garrand spun around to stare at her. "What, more visions from our friends?"

"No, not this time. I recognize the design. Those are Gamborian Jave O'Wars."

"The Gambor?"

"Director Darstin's mercenary army of choice when he wants to work outside Nralda channels."

"How'd they find us? What'd you do, publish an itinerary for the entire Shell?"

"Hey, it's your ship. Apparently its as stealthy as a supernova."

"They didn't follow us," he muttered. That the Imperials had tracked them to the far side of the Krestyaninov Cluster was bad enough, but now this… "They must have followed the Imperial picket or picked up a stray communication."

"Unlikely."

"*Destiny*, have there been any transmissions from anywhere on the ship apart from our tightbeam to C'tereino before planetfall on Eemon?"

"I'm hurt," the ship replied.

"Don't be—it's not you I'm thinking of."

Helen looked confused. "What, me? You don't think *I* had something to do with this?"

"Maybe not directly. But, what if Darstin implanted some sort of low frequency homing device inside one of the giant pandas?"

Helen shook her head. "Wouldn't penetrate far enough beyond the hull to make a difference."

"Yeah I don't think so either, but you never know. Keiretsu proprietary technology can be pretty frightening sometimes."

"I haven't heard of anything that could pull it off."

"There have been no transmissions of any sort from the ship Captain," *Destiny* said.

"Another mystery," Garrand sighed. "Bailey, get us out of their line of attack. Put those Imperial pickets between us and the Gambor."

"Yes sir." Bailey's hands danced across his display before he gently gripped the control spike. Outside the crystal bridge, the stars pivoted and spun to a new position.

"Let's hope the Imperials value the pandas enough to protect us from the Gambor." Garrand studied the sartographic display. The Gambor would have to fight past the Imperial pickets to get to them.

"Coming up on the frigate. She's a heavy."

The form of the Imperial vessel grew rapidly and roared past in a blur.

"Tight flip."

Destiny's Needle wheeled over, sub-light engines pouring thrust against the ship's inertia.

"Zero velocity in 25 seconds. Match target's delta vee in 47 seconds. Overtake in two minutes 14 seconds. Deceleration to match target: 12 seconds."

"Very well."

Bailey aligned *Destiny's Needle* with the stern of the Imperial frigate and let the ship's superior thrust close the gap between them.

"Bailey, get us attached along that ventral spine." He pointed up at the frigate's belly as it loomed perilously close. "Right about there."

"Yes sir." Bailey's hands danced along the display before he gently gripped the control spike. The ship rotated to seat herself against the gigantic ship and, with the briefest whisper of thrusters, touched hull-to-hull. The magnetic claws engaged and Garrand shut down the sub-light reactors. The odd metallic clank that reverberated eerily throughout the ship signaled their physical attachment to the Imperial vessel. Garrand watched his scopes and nodded with relief and satisfaction as the two pickets jumped ahead to intercept the Gamborian Jave O'Wars.

"This is a lot closer than I ever wanted to be," Helen murmured, squinting up through the crystal bridge at the carbon-scored hull of the much larger Imperial frigate.

Garrand rubbed his temple. "It's not my first choice either." He looked up at Bailey. A tough decision faced him. Did he take the art with him or did he leave Bailey to protect the pandas, Helen, and the ship? He looked at Helen and the decision became simple. It was going to take two to make it through the frigate and back, and Helen was more than capable of defending the ship.

Garrand pointed at Helen. "You're in charge of security."

"Her!" *Destiny* cut in, obviously distressed.

"You set up some of that arsenal you've got and don't let anyone board this ship from inside that frigate."

Helen nodded.

"Captain, I must protest this obviously ill-thought selection," the ship cried.

"Stow it. I need Bailey with me and you've got to keep our exposed flank protected. That leaves Helen. She won't let anyone get to those pandas, believe me."

LITTLE BIT EXTENDED the airlock's temporary seal until it settled against the Imperial frigate's hull. Air hissed into the aperture. The lock cycled open. Wielding huge, bulbous fusion welders, Garrand and Bailey stepped up to the frigate's exposed hull and began cutting through the thick cerasteel.

"We've only got a few seconds before they pinpoint exactly where we're coming through. We need to get inside before there's a welcoming committee waiting on the other side."

The glowing steel circle of the outer hull plate fell inward and Garrand stepped hastily aside. Sparks of molten cerasteel danced across the deck as the plate hit. As smooth as a choreographed Liyten dance, the captain and the art stepped into the opening and set their torches back to work on the inner hull, separated by ten centimeters from the outer plate by bulwark bracing.

Thirty seconds later the twin arcs of energy met at the top of the circle and Garrand kicked the plate forward into the frigate's interior, blaster drawn. Bailey stood at the mouth of the airlock, long-bore Brute cannon cradled in his arms, muzzle sweeping the opening. In a moment, the smoke cleared and Garrand poked his head inside. The chamber was empty.

The captain glanced at Helen who watched from behind the airlock. "Don't let anything happen to her," he whispered. The woman stared back at him, an icy expression on her face.

Garrand looked at his mate and swallowed back the lump in his throat. Bailey nodded to him. In tandem, the man and artificial ducked through the glowing circle and disappeared into the smoke.

18

SCAVENGING

THE *ILYOVAHTNA'S* BRIDGE, A SCANT FIVE AND A HALF ME-
ters wide, tapered from the slender ship's port bow like a long,
thin thiretsen reed. Captain Vailetta Strom paced down the
central aisle with calm, assured strides. In single-file stations
hung above and below the gangway, her bridge crew focused
on their various tasks. Vailetta looked down through the transparent serviceway at the top of each man's head as she passed.
With the whole bridge encased in crystal glazings her men
looked to be hanging by thin strands over the stars.

She reached the forwardmost point, an observation star-
bubble, and paused, her weight resting on one heel. *Destiny's
Needle* was out there — invisible to her unaided eye — but there

nevertheless, racing along a parallel course directly off their starboard bow. Soon the *Jjaeyg* and the *Ulusi* would return, flush with their contingent of Gokazoku and Shock Troops, and she could close the noose once and for all. She glanced ahead to her personal ship, the *Lolovanti,* a bright speck fifty kilometers ahead. She was the task force's eyes and ears as the picket remained just beyond *Destiny's* sensors.

Vailetta turned and walked back up the line, this time staring up at the feet of the men stationed above the aisle. She stopped beneath Yarvek-EZ's pod and gazed up through the murky goo. Drumming her fingertips against the glazing she soon caught the ensign's ire. He shifted in agitation, cable guides swaying behind him.

"It's coming," he said impatiently, his voice distant through the crackling speaker at the pod's base.

"No rush," she said with a convincing air of distraction. "*Destiny's Needle* isn't going anywhere." Still, her fingers drummed the pod. *It was too simple.* The apparent ease with which the mission was unfolding had to be an illusion, a voice inside her head kept saying. Captain Médeville was a Captain of the Imperial Guard just like herself—a member of that vaunted sect within the Guard, the Brotherhood of the Princes of Blood, founded three centuries before the Gokazoku convened. That alone made him dangerous. She had seen his encrypted dossier, courtesy of Lord Barrett. Psych analysis pegged him as bold, intelligent, loyal—to a fault, she reminded herself—with a huge streak of pride, tempered only by dedication to those he trusted. He had successfully led his complement of Guardsmen through six tours through some of the Shell's finest campaigns. This was not a man who would simply sit back and allow her to board his ship and take his cargo, no matter what the circumstance.

Yarvek's enthusiastic voice interrupted her thoughts. "Picking up the *Jjaeyg*. Two million kilometers and closing." He rotated skillfully through the goo to face her. "Right on the tick, too." He beamed proudly, his strange, toothless grin obscured by the translucent jelly.

"Not bad, Yarvek," she acknowledged. She continued to drum on his pod. "Any sign of the *Ulusi*?"

Yarvek concentrated for a moment. "She's right behind her."

The com officer turned to face her. "Sub-lieutenant Dasko reports all Gokazoku present and accounted for."

Vailetta clenched her fist with excitement. "Very good. Apprise Mr. Dasko of the current situation and tell him to ready the men for battle." She strode back to the front of the bridge, anticipation tingling throughout her body. With two pickets and an attack frigate at her disposal, *Destiny's Needle* would have no chance of escaping without her quantum drive. With his options dwindling fast, there were few tricks that Captain Médeville could conjure to save his cargo now. She smiled with grim satisfaction; her father would be proud. The Tchelakov creatures would soon be in hand.

"Helm, close position on the target."

"Aye, ma'am."

Vailetta felt a small jolt and caught herself on the railing as the ship's internal gravity compensated for the new thrust.

"Captain, we are within sensor range—she's aware of our presence."

"Very well, ensign, proceed. She's tried to make a jump by now. She'll recognize the futility of escape soon enough."

With quiet satisfaction, Vailetta watched the *Jjaeyg* take up formation off her port bow. The ship glistened in the starlight, lean and beautiful. Coryl-Tuluyt pickets were the fastest capital ships in the Imperial Navy. Smaller and stealthier than destroyers, they were used as extremely effective interdictors and blockade busters. The pickets were slender, jagged affairs, with wicked-looking weapon and sensor arrays arcing far beyond the narrow superstructures. Lacking the multi-tiered support of onboard Shock Troops, planet assault vehicles, and marines, the Coryl-Tuluyts relied on speed and a small contingent of tactical support fighters for defense.

"Captain!" the startled targ ensign cried out. "*Destiny's Needle* is assuming an aggressive posture."

Vailetta frowned. "Aggressive posture?"

"She's attacking." He looked up at her with surprise.

Vailetta ran her fingers through her hair. "We've seen this maneuver before. All power to the forward deflectors." She pointed a finger down at one man. "Helm, hold your course." Pacing back to weapons and targ she reiterated the standing order: "Repeat to all gunners — do not return fire!" Both nodded, subvocalizing the captain's order.

Vailetta watched the sartographic display as the ship angled in toward her formation. He was spiraling into a prime firing position. Part of her watched his strategy with admiration. Yet she still gritted her teeth, awaiting a kinetic burst of energy from the ship's pulse cannon. She suspected he would not fire — his weapon could not have had time to charge — but she could not be sure.

"Captain, I'm picking up new targets."

Vailetta turned in surprise. "Where?"

"Mark two point one off the port quarter. Multiple vessels."

Vailetta spun back to the sartograph. There, beyond *Destiny's Needle*, appeared several new yellow blips. "Yarvek?" she asked quietly, fear pounding in her throat.

"Tvultàk Skullers," he said studying his virtual displays. He shifted with discomfort. "It's not good," he said in a gravelly tone. "They're Gamborian Jave O'Wars — and there's seven of them."

"Caught you napping, eh?" The ensign looked at her through the goo, wounded. "Not to worry Yarvek, they caught me too." Vailetta turned and watched the glowing sparkle of reflected light that was *Destiny's Needle*. Like a flower's petals opening to catch the sunlight, the ship rolled lazily onto its back, exposing the twin V-shaped prows that lanced asymmetrically ahead of the ship's hull. The ship grew rapidly, closing the gap at a frightening rate. She flashed by the starboard superstructure, cutting between the two Imperial pickets without firing a shot.

"She's changing course," scan reported.

"Getting himself out of the Gambor's direct line of attack," Vailetta watched the changing numbers on the tactical display.

"What's he doing?"

"The frigate," Vailetta murmured. "He's going to raid the frigate."

"What?"

"He needs a new quantum coil."

She straightened back up and took a moment to collect her thoughts. And then in a staccato burst of energy, she rattled off her orders. "Scramble the phantoms — both *Jjaeyg* and *Ilyovahtna's*. Helm, bring us about. Plot an intercept course for the frigate. That's where Médeville is heading: that's where the action will be. Com, open a link to Mr. Dasko."

Static echoed through the bridge and then Sub-lieutenant Dasko's voice rang clear. "Yes, Captain?"

"The fighters are launching. We're going to swing back around to intercept *Destiny's Needle*. Get the Gokazoku on a shuttle and ferry them over to the *Ilyovahtna*. I want the *Jjaeyg* to run point. Order Captain Locke to engage those Skullers point blank. Concentrate fire on the lead vessel. If we can knock down the first Jave 'O War then their formation might break. After that, inform Miss Locke that she may pick whatever targets of opportunity she wishes."

"Yes, Captain."

"On the bounce, Dasko. I need the men back here."

"Consider it done."

"Captain," targ interrupted. "The ship appears to be lining up with the *Ulusi* for a—" he hesitated.

"Out with it, lieutenant."

"Well, he's matched course and speed and has closed to within a hundred meters. It looks as if he plans to board her." The lieutenant looked up with doubt.

"Get me Commander Arnas."

Arnas responded almost immediately from the bridge of the frigate *Ulusi*. "Your orders, Captain Strom?" he asked coarsely.

"Ready the Shock Troops. Prepare to be boarded."

"Boarded?" Arnas choked over the word. "By whom? The Gambor? What brings those wretched creatures this far from their unholy fight for Galzeki?"

"On an errand for Director Darstin of the Nralda, no doubt," Vailetta responded. "They're here for the same thing we are. But in answer, no, they're not in any position to board you just yet."

"Not the Gambor? Then who?"

"Captain Médeville."

"Ai'Gonet?" Arnas snarled. "What's that madman doing? Boarding us, you say?" There was a long silence over the com. Vailetta could imagine the thoughts of revenge floating behind his words. "I thought we were trying to board *his* ship!"

"We are, but he's decided to make it more difficult." *Imagine that,* she thought. "We're going to have a tougher time getting aboard with him latched onto your hull."

"No matter," Arnas replied smoothly. "I'll repel his assault and pick up the creatures for you."

"Negative," Vailetta snapped. "I must deal with Tchelakov myself. The Gokazoku will take the pandas, and you and your men will keep Médeville engaged upon the frigate. And ready your men for a search and destroy, not a ship defense—light body armor, I should think. Suiting up for a hull-breach style offensive is unnecessary—he's not out to inflict damage."

"If Médeville is not *attacking*, then what's he up to?" Arnas asked incredulously.

"He's *scavenging*," Vailetta shot back, "and you'd best be ready for him. While he's busy looking for spare parts I'm going to take the Tchelakov creatures. I advise you to keep him occupied."

"Don't worry, he won't escape a second time" Arnas said with a coldness that sent a shiver down her spine. The crease of a frown marred her brow. Was she empathizing too much with her fellow Guardsman? She shook her head; there was no time for such thoughts.

Energy licked across the picket's hull as the fat-bellied Skullers rumbled beneath her. Vailetta watched the enhanced image of the Gambor vessels on the sartograph. The ships angled up and away from the *Ilyovahtna*.

"They're not going to come around again," Yarvek declared as he gauged the Gambors' tactics. It was a cursory pass, with an obligatory raking of the hull. The Gambor were here for the Tchelakov creatures, same as she. The Jave 'O Wars headed full bore for *Destiny's Needle*, now wedged up under the *Ulusi* like a remora.

The Gambor would board the *Ulusi* as well, and this would be fought hand-to-hand in the cramped spaces of the Imperial frigate. It would be a nasty affair. *Like the old days*, she thought. For the first time since she'd left, she was glad to have the Shock Troops along.

"Shuttle is docking, Captain."

"Match course and speed with the *Ulusi*. Prepare to make a physical link with *Destiny's Needle*. Shut down all weapon systems."

"Captain?"

"I want all available power rerouted to forward shields and deflectors. *Destiny's* not going to just let us slip right in without putting up a fight."

"What about the Gambor?"

"They won't fire at us once we get in close—they can't risk hitting *Destiny's Needle* anymore than we can."

"As you say, Captain."

Dasko swept onto the bridge with an energetic step. "Reporting as ordered," he smiled.

Vailetta turned and looked at her lieutenant with relief. She had felt detached and vulnerable with her men spread out across the stars, away from her protective care. Is that how Médeville had felt when he'd been forced to leave the Guard? "It's good to see you, Dasko. Let's get to the armory. Lieutenant Vek, you have the bridge."

INSIDE THE CRAMPED armory, her men were suiting up for battle. "I want a four man detail when I confront the Tchelakov woman. The rest of the Gokazoku are to help the Shock Troops," she informed Dasko.

"Help? The Shock Troops?" He chuckled.

"We all serve one cause. They're going to need all the help they can get once the Gambor board the frigate—and there's no doubt they will. One picket and a squadron of fighters won't hold them off for long."

"How do you plan on boarding *Destiny's Needle?*" Dasko asked in a worried tone as he struggled into his body armor.

"I imagine we'll be invited aboard," Vailetta said with a devilish smile.

"Invited! By whom?"

"You'll find out soon enough Dasko," she said, her commanding tone returning. "We play this right and we'll take the Tchelakov creatures without firing a shot." She relished the thought of upstaging Arnas and his egregious shows of force.

Dasko shrugged and wiggled into his body armor.

❖ ❖ ❖

JUST INSIDE *Destiny's* AIRLOCK, HELEN PACED NERVOUSLY, UNable to resist looking up every few seconds to glance through the small tempered glazings into the frigate's interior. Each time she half expected a grizzled face to be staring back at her, one of Barrett's minions come to fetch his prize.

The little panda, Alexander, sat just in front of the airlock's sealed doors, his nose millimeters away from the cold, oilysmelling steel, trying to ignore Helen's distracting movements. It took all his concentration to remain stoically patient, but each moment stretched out forever. The captain — his rescuer and perhaps the tribe's long-sought *Jhei Pōloc* — was out there with his loyal *thola*, trying to save them all. With each second that passed, he felt that he could not wait one moment longer. The captain needed his help. It was time for him to return the favor. Alexander glanced awkwardly back at the hall and sighed.

Sid was still there, watching and waiting for the captain to return as well.

The ship's voice halted Helen's pacing.

"Miss Tchelakov, are your defenses in place?" The ship
sounded nervous.

Helen looked at the unopened racks of equipment sitting on
the lighter in the serviceway. The antipersonnel cannon still sat
in its casings — sensor packs, dart slings, armor drips were all
stacked neatly on the hovering lighter. Helen reached up to the
comtab at her collar. "I'm ready," she said staring at Sid. If the
panda was concerned, he did not show it.

"Well, I hope so. The lead Imperial picket has aligned herself
for a physical link. We're going to be boarded."

"Where?"

"Bottomside, port airlock three near the engine compartment, by the looks of it."

Helen glanced at Sid. "Come on." The ship's voice followed
her, clicking through the nearest speakers as she trotted.

"What should I do?" the ship asked. "We cannot overwhelm
the picket's defenses, they have found a way to boost their
shields. Our pulse cannon is in a fixed position and cannot be
brought to bear as long as the physical linkup with the frigate
is maintained."

"We can't break the link," Helen said as she trotted through
the ship.

"I concur. What, then, shall we do?"

"Don't worry, I'll deal with them myself," Helen muttered,
wondering if the ship would protest. She listened expectantly
for a sharp retort, but *Destiny* remained silent. There was not
much the ship could do, she reasoned. Without a corporeal
body, it could do little to stop her now. It could lock her inside,
but the Imperials would just burn their way in.

Alexander watched as the woman ran down the hall. The nerves tingled in all his legs, the pads on the bottom of his feet itched and he felt his claws extending as his heart raced. Fur stood up along his spine, and he fixed his eyes on the round, red button that the captain had punched to open the airlock's outer doors. He dared not look behind to see if Sid had followed Helen, for he might never again muster the courage. With a deep breath he lunged up on his rear paws and stabbed his nose at the red knob. The doors opened with a scream of hydraulics. Alexander dashed through the opening and raced down the darkened hall, the scent of the captain strong in his nose.

Sid turned as he heard the hiss of the doors and stopped to listen, letting Helen continue without him. After a moment, the hiss-clank signaled that the doors had closed. Sid's heart pounded; *the little one would not have been so brash, would he?* With fear rising in his mind, Sid loped anxiously back down the serviceway. He rounded the corner, opened the inner doors and found the airlock chamber empty. He shut his eyes and growled angrily through clenched jaws, the roar echoing back and forth through the hollow lock. How had he missed this? A thousand dreams of every side of the Betrayal, agonized nightly for month after month by the Council, and not one of the Elders had foreseen this? The Betrayal, the Griffin, Archiva, the Thief of Ships, the Veil of Tholas, the Silver Beasts — it was a harrowing Path, but it was the only way that *all* the tribe could survive. The Elders' mantra echoed in his head: *All must live so that they may someday sing within the Elder Circle.* Leave it to one unschooled mind to choose a course of action that might undermine that one basic tenet.

Sid sighed and stretched his legs, cracking the vertebrae along his spine. Then he depressed the control knob with one claw. He wished he had five minutes for concentration as he waited for the doors to screech open, but there was no time for visions now. Alexander had gone missing, and he must follow.

❖ ❖ ❖

THE DOORS JAWED OPEN AND COLD AIR HISSED INTO THE SER-viceway. Garrand watched his breath fog before him, and glanced at his mate. Heat was not wasted on the lower machine levels of Imperial frigates and condensation was forming on the art's surface. Bailey checked his weapon and nodded in the frigid silence. Garrand and Bailey had cut through the *Ulusi's* belly and had found themselves in a waste reclamation and disposal lock. The acrid stench was thankfully muted by the cold. Garrand flashed a hand signal to Bailey, who responded with three wiggling fingers that quickly knotted into a fist. Comtabs were off-limits aboard the Imperial ship—sensors would quickly pinpoint the transmissions. Garrand wore his bio-regulator, masking his vital life signs. As an artificial, Bailey had no signs to mask, his inner workings lost amidst the jumble of machinery in the ship's bowels.

The door opened noiselessly before his face. Garrand dove out the opening, rolling across the hall to draw fire from any lurking soldiers and flattened himself against the far wall. The mussel of Bailey's cannon swept a 180-degree arc outside the doorway, but no targets had taken the captain's bait. Garrand waited a moment then nodded to the artificial. His silvery form emerged from the darkness, arms cradling the enormous Borûlte—a weapon too massive for a human to carry. Seeing Bailey saddled with the cannon once more, coil package slung across his back, Ki Zentor sensor package and opticals partially obscuring one eye, Garrand felt very much like he was back in the Guard. It had been quite some time since he had seen his art as a warrior. He almost didn't recognize him behind all the devastation. The Borûlte was really too much for shipside combat, but then, this wasn't his ship.

Garrand swallowed back his past and nodded to his mate. There were two primary holds for maintenance crews, one fore and one aft. Imperial naval vessels were prepared for every foreseeable disaster, no matter how major or minor, the redundancy in vital control systems trickling down to maintenance preparedness. Long tours in deep space, particularly in the ever-changing political environment of Carinaena's Shell, necessitated a high degree of foresight, and spare parts for any problem. No capital ship in the Emperor's Navy would be left derelict in space just because she was unable to make port for repairs. The Navy was a model of self-sufficiency, and Garrand was counting on just this fact for their survival.

They trotted down the narrow serviceway with cautious haste. Garrand hoped that they could make their way through the sparsely populated reactor chambers and sub-levels without meeting any resistance. He did not believe they would be so lucky up on the primary maintenance corridors that wound beneath the ship's living spaces.

He paused before a repulsor lift. "Think they'll be expecting us through a manual tube?"

"More than likely."

"So why bother, let's take the lift."

Bailey stepped into the repulsor field and rose before Garrand's eyes. Taking one last look at the quiet darkness behind him, Garrand stepped into the ticklish field and rose through the humming energy. He stepped out into blazing light. Serviceways spread in all directions. Directly ahead the floor dropped off, though access gantries continued on, suspended over the humming reactor chambers. Garrand walked briskly to the nearest blast door leading to a central corridor and tried the access panel. It was locked.

"Bypass this." Garrand's eyes swept back over the chamber as Bailey dropped his weapon and set to the panel. Within seconds the door irised open. The hall was long and wide, riddled with pipes and conduits, thick electrical hawsers and coolant tubes. Portals dotted each side of the serviceway at regular intervals, blue glow strips along the deck illuminating each circular entrance. The hall's details disappeared into the darkness some two hundred meters down the ship's spine.

Garrand trotted gingerly down the hall, his footsteps ringing hollowly off the cerasteel plates, expecting at any moment to smell the burnt ozone and see the green flash of a blast rifle from behind a girded support in his path. Bailey's footsteps perfectly matched his own, so that there was a moment's silence between each stride. Garrand counted the portals as they ran, and pulled up short at the ninth door. It was unmarked.

"If we seal off this access then there should only be two entries to this corridor from topside—the service tube we used and the far aft tube at the other end."

"Captain, this access leads to the central reactor core."

Garrand looked down the dim serviceway. "No, no, no. This is the main tech art gantry—leads back to the repulsor lift on gregson level five."

"I'm afraid it's been too long since you've set foot within an Imperial picket," Bailey said carefully.

"It hasn't been *that* long," Garrand said, looking uncertainly left and right down the hall. "Besides, most of these capital ships are laid out the same way. We just passed the entrance to the reactor two doors down."

"That was the atmo processor. Captain, please," the art urged him down the serviceway. "My memory is a little less *fluid* than yours."

Garrand followed the art with a scowl. "If you knew where we where, why didn't you just say so?"

Bailey stopped in front of an identical portal and looked at the captain.

"This it?"

The art nodded. "I don't think we should risk opening it."

"Agreed. Seal it." He began down the hall, toward the rear of the ship. Bailey followed him, turning after several paces to take aim at the door. The cannon licked flame around the portal's control pad, fusing the circuits within, but not before its intruder-tamper subroutine locked down all hydraulics.

The aft storeroom lay near the very end of the corridor. The huge double blast doors were directly opposite the aft service tube for easy access to the rest of the ship. Bailey quickly set to work, deactivating the security overrides.

"What's taking you so long?"

"The door is being difficult," Bailey said calmly. "Are you surprised?"

"It didn't take this long last time." Garrand groused.

"That door didn't have a mind of its own—you know how they can get when they're being stubborn."

Garrand pursed his lips, thinking of Humhal. "Yeah, well I suggest you be a little more persuasive. There's little time to spare."

A strange scraping rhythm caught Garrand's ear. He held up his hand and Bailey paused; something was coming. Garrand edged back against a support girder and leveled his blaster at the noise. As the sound drew closer, he recognized a familiar quality to the cadence. Garrand frowned, lowering his weapon. *It couldn't be.* Out of the darkness, the black and white form of Alexander appeared as he loped along the hall, unable to mask the click-clack of his claws along the deck plates. The little panda leapt up into his arms.

"Gher-ahn!"

"Haven's End," Garrand cursed. "What are you doing here?" He sighed and glanced at Bailey who had paused in uncharacteristic dismay.

"Don't stop!" Garrand cried. "Get us in, we've got to have that coil." A second panda appeared, more silently than the first. "Sid? What in K'ye is going on?"

"My apologies, Captain. Alexander is impetuous and headstrong. It is my fault that I did not watch him more carefully, but Helen was acting strangely."

"Strangely how? She's supposed to be defending the ship."

"I'm afraid that is not foremost in her mind at the present."

Garrand stared oddly at the panda for a moment. *Not foremost in her mind?* His heart dropped. Had he misjudged her again?

"Got it," Bailey said triumphantly. "We're in."

The blast doors scrolled slowly aside and Garrand quickly ushered them into the hold. "Find the regulator coil. There should be an inventory clipscanner lying around somewhere."

It only took Bailey three and a half minutes to return with the coil, factory-new, packed in grease in a clear, oblong tube. Garrand grinned with bemusement, his surprise at having made it this far turning to an uneasy confidence. *We're halfway home,* he thought. He jerked his head at the door and glanced at Bailey. "Think you can get that thing open one more time?"

"It's rigged for automatic release. Just punch the open command."

As Bailey said, the doors scrolled aside dutifully. Alexander hovered just behind his leg. Garrand glanced down at the panda. "You stay behind me, okay?" Alex clicked in affirmation. "Bailey, you watch after Sid."

Garrand swallowed and took a cautious peek around the corner. The dim hall was no longer empty. The forward end of the serviceway was filling rapidly with Imperial marines. The Shock Troops were advancing by two's, from support to support, checking each compartment as they made their way aft. He glanced the other way then jerked his head back to safety.

"What is it, Captain?" Bailey asked.

"Shock Troops—advancing from the fore."

"Trioxin?"

"No. Light body."

"Numbers?"

"Platoon strength."

"Ordinance?"

"Carrying close range plasma weapons, from what I could see. There are probably some heavier cannons bringing up the rear."

"Are we encircled?"

"Not yet. It's still clear to the aft—that's the way to go. Why don't you give them something to think about while the pandas and I get across to that lift.

Bailey's face tightened as the Ki Zentor opticals hummed to life. The art stepped out into the hall, legs comfortably spread. The Borûlte cannon was wedged against his hip. Green bolts of energy arced down the dim hall, the flashes of luminescence casting a spectral glow across the artificial's skin. With careful determination, Bailey walked the devastation from side to side. The Shock Troopers dove for cover, steel and ceramics splintering around them. After several seconds all the men were pinned down. Bailey released the fire control and scrutinized the smoky hall with the Ki Zentor optics. Energy surges and power coils glowed yellow in the optical scope. Unleashing the cannon's energy once more, Bailey pinpointed weapon supply coils and shield generators, firing quick bursts at specific targets. Orange fireballs erupted down the hall as the cannon found multiple marks.

Garrand made it to the service tube and looked up with dismay to find feet descending toward him. He yelped in dismay. "Can't go this way. We'll have to get to the next one." He reached his arm inside the shimmering field and fired several rounds up the tube. "That'll make 'em think about coming down for a minute."

"Captain, there's another repulsor lift on the other side of the reactors. We can take the gantry across."

"Good idea. Have any idea where the nearest gantry is?" he asked sheepishly.

Bailey smiled. "Two doors down. I'm proud of you, Captain. It takes courage to admit you're lost."

The party edged their way down the hall to the second portal. The door irised open, revealing a long narrow gantry suspended above a massive row of reactors that hummed and crackled with life twenty meters below. Bailey and the two pandas started across the abyss first with Garrand bringing up the rear.

Out of the corner of his eye, Garrand spied Shock Troops dashing along the next gantry across from him, racing them to the far side. Garrand stopped and took careful aim at the steel supports and suspension cables along the gantry's midsection. By his third shot he severed the first support. The beam and cable tumbled down onto the gantry itself, smashing through a railing and nearly dividing the serviceway in two. Garrand picked out another support and fired again.

This support, too, gave way, smashing in front of the Shock Troops with a deck-quivering thump. Flashes from the gantry's entrance cut short his next shot, and Garrand began sprinting along the suspended serviceway.

Sid followed Bailey and Garrand leaned down to pick Alexander up. At that moment the cerasteel deck plates ruptured in front of Garrand, white-hot blistered steel curling back around the edges. The entire gantry heaved up under the expansion of hot gases and shuddered back down. Bailey was able to bound over the weltered steel, but Garrand was thrown off his feet. He staggered against the bulkhead bracing, grasping the cold steel with his palms and leaning over to catch Alexander before the cub tumbled over the edge. Plasma bolts sizzled into the steel just over his hands. He looked down at the long green arcs of deadly static electricity that danced over the massive reactors below. The low shriek of the reactors sang in his ears, promising certain death if he dropped the cub.

Another burst of energy bolts ripped through the smoke, missed their mark, and panged against the distant bulkhead. This time Bailey returned fire, the green flash of his cannon momentarily blinding Garrand as he watched the art delivered a careful sweep of suppression fire at the foot of the gantry. Splintered chunks of steel scattered over the reactors, crackling in the static charges. Bailey released the trigger and looked expectantly at his captain.

"Hang on tight."

Garrand sucked in a quick breath of acrid smoke and pushed off the support. He took four long strides and clutched the panda to his chest with two arms. On his last step he launched himself across the breach cleaved in the gantry. They landed hard on the far side, upturned shards of steel gouging bloody chunks out of Garrand's knees. He rolled across the hot steel plates to safety.

Alexander licked his face as Bailey knelt to help him up. The door at the far end of the gantry irised open and they stepped breathlessly into the far hallway.

"Which way?"

Bailey motioned aft. Garrand grasped Alexander tightly to his chest and motioned Sid to follow. As Bailey covered their retreat, the human, the artificial and the two pandas ran down the hall toward the service tube. They made it safely to the lift and Garrand unceremoniously kicked Sid into the shimmering repulsor field, sending him down toward the reactor chambers, howling. "You're next," he shoved the moaning cub butt-first into the lift.

Garrand stepped into the field and motioned for Bailey to follow. Once they were all back to the frigate's lower levels, Garrand pulled Bailey aside. "Four's too many to handle all at once in these cramped corridors. You take Sid and get back to the ship as quickly as you can. Find out what's going on with Helen." The old scar along the back of his skull was acting up again. "I've got a bad feeling about this."

"But, Captain—"

"—Just do it," Garrand cut him off sharply. "One of us has to get back to the ship alive. The little one and I will take a different route. You just make sure nothing happens to Sid."

"You won't get lost without me?"

"I won't, now go."

Bailey and the giant panda started down the dim hallway. Alex moaned after them. "C'mon fuzz ball, we're going a different way."

Garrand stepped across the hall and opened a portal to a manual tube. "Grab onto my neck." The panda complied and Garrand began climbing down the oily ladder rungs.

He stepped to the deck and raised his blaster, checking both directions. "Hold tight." With awkward strides under the added weight, Garrand jogged down the hall, ducking under electrical conduits and thick pipes. After thirty meters, the serviceway opened up to a broad hall, studded with thin support columns. Red light glowed from fifteen meters above.

They were only ten meters from the end of the hall when fist-sized shards of molten steel splintered from corridor supports on each side of them as blaster bolts splashed against the columns. Garrand lost his grip on Alexander, and the panda tumbled to the deck. Two more volleys lanced over his shoulder. Garrand fired back blindly and took two long steps, diving around the corner. Alexander skittered to safety behind him. Garrand pressed his back tightly against the wall, blaster held ready, and inched back toward the corner. Holding his breath he risked a quick peek around the edge. He let the scene imprint upon his retina, then ducked his head back to cover. He closed his eyes and tried to relax, concentrating on what he had just seen. Smoke clearing. Chunks of wall blown away. Debris scattered across the floor. No sign of advancing Shock Troopers.

He brought his free hand up to his waist and released five concussion grenades from the autofeed on his belt into his cupped palm. The small spheres felt cool in his hand. Garrand crouched and smoothly reached around the corner, rolling the grenades down the hall. A minor diversion at best, but anything to slow down the attack and give them a chance to escape.

Alexander looked up at him expectantly, eyes wide with fear. The cub was holding up well, all things considered. He wondered if a human child would have made it this far.

Garrand held a finger up to his nose and pursed his lips, shaking his head gently from side to side. Alexander shook his head uncertainly. In a loud voice, Garrand called out, "Don't shoot, we give up. I repeat: we surrender—don't shoot!"

Clinching his teeth, he jerked his head the opposite direction. Alexander understood and began his funny four-footed canter down the hallway turning midway to check and see if the captain was following. Garrand motioned for him to go on, as he searched his satchel for a proximity detonator. Finding the oblong device, he activated its magnetic field, set the distance trigger to five meters and slapped it against the first hatch he came across. The voice of his Académe drill sergeant rang in his ears: "Diversions are key." And he could almost hear the gentle singsong of Bailey's mantra from thousands of hours of drill time in the holo chamber: "With nothing to lose, try to confuse!" He sprinted down the hall to catch up with Alexander.

UNCERTAIN AND READY for the worst, Arnas stepped away from the pillar that had shielded his body from the random blaster fire and stepped boldly into the center of the corridor. Crouching low, plasma rifle held ready, he scanned the length of the hall. Instead of seeing a man standing unarmed with hands over his head awaiting surrender, he found an empty, smoking hallway. He listened but heard nothing. For once he wished he was wearing his Trioxin suit so he could flip his bio-tracking sensors on. He kicked a chunk of debris across the floor, expecting a sudden flurry of blaster fire. Nothing. With a flick of his head and two fingers extended, he sent his men forward two by two in cover formation.

A blast shook the chamber as one trooper stepped on a concussion grenade sending he and his mate crashing into the far wall. Arnas quickly raised his hand ordering his men to halt where they were. With debris scattered across the deck it was nearly impossible to visually detect any further grenades in the red glow. This was becoming very tiresome, he thought. His fingers tightened around the plasma rifle in anger—his mind racing for a solution. All his men looked to him for an order.

Dropping one hand from his weapon he made a fist and flicked his thumb toward first one sidewall, then the other. He pointed forward. The Shock Troopers backed slowly to the sidewalls and proceeded cautiously forward. Chances were, all the grenades were scattered in the center of the corridor. Arnas stepped carefully to one wall and trotted forward quickly in the path his men had proven safe. Médeville would not escape a second time.

19

THE DEAL

HELEN STOOD AT THE INNER DOORS TO THE PORTSIDE airlock. Her fingers trembled as she deactivated *Destiny's* security overrides and ordered the outer doors to scroll open. Through the glazing she could see into the Imperial picket itself. A single man stood in the picket's airlock, awaiting entrance.

Helen swallowed back her anxiety as the inner door cycled open. The Imperial soldier stood calmly on the other side, weaponless save for a sheathed koummya at his belt. The only adornment on his black uniform was a five-clawed dragon stitched in crimson along his collar, the mark of the Imperial Guard. Two tiny daggers were stitched beneath the claw, encircled by a band of gold. Helen's eyes flicked back to the man's face; he was a member of the Gokazoku Kaigi. She felt her heartbeat quicken.

"Are you ready?" Dasko asked without preamble.

"You're early," she countered stubbornly.

"Would you prefer us to be late?" Dasko fired back. "Director Darstin would then have *your* head."

"This isn't much better," she snapped. "I'm sure the Gambor aren't here for *saplings*."

"You needn't concern yourself with the Gambor," Dasko spoke easily, as if the Jave O'Wars were as unimportant as a summer breeze.

"That's a relief," Helen said sarcastically.

"Miss Tchelakov," Dasko said with a polite, but firm, formality. "*Are you ready?*" Three more men clad in black appeared behind the Guardsman.

"Yes," she said flatly, emotion draining from her face. "Have your men come this way…"

LITTLE BIT WATCHED as the pandas were led through the central access corridor and out the airlock. Their heads were bowed and their feet seemed to shuffle to an even slower rhythmic cadence than usual. Yet none resisted. Armed guards paced slowly alongside the sad processional. Little Bit continued to send urgent messages to the captain in Vort Magellan, but apparently his com was deactivated. In impotent silence, the tech art watched as each panda disappeared through the airlock. At the end of the line, two men in black accompanied Miss Tchelakov. Little Bit expected to see her in shackles, but to his surprise she looked confident and relaxed, carrying two silver cases, one in each hand. Apparently, Miss Tchelakov was leaving.

Little Bit spit out a shrill screech of indignation and the last panda stopped and turned before entering the airlock. Little Bit whistled once more and the panda craned its head back to look at Helen. His large black eyes stared at her sadly. Helen frowned but ignored the heart-wrenching look. With a re-signed slowness, the panda glanced back at Little Bit, and then continued into the airlock.

Helen waited to board the *Ilyovahtna*, thinking that the worst was over. No more lying to Garrand and running from an enemy that would ultimately prove to be her savior. No more planning and scheming and waiting. Never again would she have to face Darstin—at least not all of him. Two weeks in transit to Wyx and then she could discuss the particulars of Darstin's demise with Lord Barrett himself.

As the last of the pandas boarded the Imperial ship, the air-lock sluiced close and Helen was left in the staging chamber. The two men at her side stepped to the far wall and stood at attention. Helen spun to see a light distortion screen obscuring one wall.

"Take off your clothes," a woman's voice barked from behind the rippling darkness.

"What?" Helen stiffened, wishing she could see the woman behind the screen. "Who are you?" she demanded.

"I am Captain of Lord Barrett's Imperial Guard, Vailetta Strom, and his personal envoy in this matter. You may call me Captain Strom. Now don't make me ask a second time."

Helen stood awkwardly in the center of the airlock. What new game was this?

"I wouldn't put it past Médeville to have an implant on you. I won't risk it. Take off your clothes, Tchelakov. There's a black-suit for you by the door. Afterwards throw them over."

"Yes, *sir*," Helen murmured sarcastically, moving to comply. She would have to accustom herself to receiving orders again, whether or not they made any sense. Such was the Imperial way. A feeling of loss flooded through her, but she swallowed it. Her sense of freedom on *Destiny's Needle* had been temporary. She pulled on the Imperial blacksuit, off-duty uniform of the Guard, and yanked the cloth belt into a punishing knot before tossing her clothing over the screen.

"Boots as well."

Helen sighed but followed the command, and, in umbrage, dropped them over the top without warning. The woman behind the screen grunted as one of the boots thumped against her.

Helen waited uneasily, her bare feet growing cold. What was the mystery? Why was Captain Strom concealed? Had she been injured in the firefight?

"Now what?" she asked hesitantly.

A rustle answered her, and then a woman appeared, the exact copy of herself down to the freckles. She was even wearing her clothing.

"*Shantikhi!*" Helen swore breathlessly. A wrenching pain gripped her stomach. Her double scrutinized her with a pleased expression, walking slowly around her.

"A very good likeness, don't you agree? It was capricious. We only had a sight-certified image of the left profile. But your face is free of scars. Symmetrical. Perfect fit. And the scent of you," she lifted one sleeve of the sequestered garment and inhaled. "All spice and musk. That replicated quite nicely. Yes, on the whole this is working out nicely."

Barrett's words, Helen thought. *Only he could be so insidious and cruel in his punishment. He had no intention of fulfilling their contract—he had betrayed her.*

"How?" she swallowed with difficulty. Her double continued to circle her leisurely, a predator confident that its prey had no escape.

"They call it the lifemask, a keiretsu innovation. Lord Barrett does love to turn an enemy's weapon. The idea of facial distortion is nothing new of course, but in this case the skin-sim uses living tissue." Helen shook her head, edging away.

"*They'll know.* It doesn't matter if you steal my face and my clothing. They'll know. You don't even sound like me."

"Ah, yes. Thanks for the reminder. It's only semantics, after all." She fiddled with something at the side of her neck, hidden under the wigged tangle of auburn curls. "*Commence.*" The captain's throat constricted over the tympanic command and she had to exhale forcefully.

"I never get used to vocal switch," she confided hoarsely. She repeated the words until the tone and timbre matched Helen's voice.

"No. This isn't possible." She backed away in horror as Vailetta advanced on her, working her duplicate face through a series of grim stretches, kneading the new skin with her fingers as though working out muscles.

"I'd love to explain the whole thing to you, but I have a schedule to keep and," she paused. "Two of us would only confuse our newly arrived guests. I need to dispose of you."

Helen lunged for the door, a shriek rising through her windpipe, her flight canceled as Vailetta yanked her back by her hair. They struggled for a moment, but despite her training, Helen was no match for a Captain of the Imperial Guard in close combat. Vailetta had her immobilized in seconds, trapped in a headlock.

"*Listen,*" Vailetta spit out. "You're not part of this mission. You're getting off here. Now whether that's death or back to that derelict is none of my concern. So make up your mind. Right now. It will be taxing to be you, but I have my duty." Vailetta relaxed her hold minutely. Helen gasped for air.

"There's something you should know. The pandas won't live without me. They—" The arm squeezed the breath out of her.

"Ego, Ms. Tchelakov," she chided, her voice heavy with warning. "But we have no need of melodrama here. If you next speak anything but an answer, I swear I'll drop you right here. It only requires a bit more pressure." She constricted her arm, demonstrating, and then loosened it. "What is it to be?"

Helen choked on the words, her face blue. "I'll go. By K'ye, I'll go."

Vailetta shoved her away and Helen stumbled to her knees.

"You must take me with you—that was part of the deal," Helen protested.

"It will not look convincing if you were to suddenly disappear with the creatures," Vailetta countered. "For your own safety, Lord Barrett has ordered that you are to be left behind. You will be a less likely suspect to Director Darstin and the keiretsu."

Exploding with anger and frustration, Helen stepped closer to the Captain of the Guard, eyes flicking momentarily to the officer at her side who dropped his hand almost imperceptibly to his sheathed blade. "The keiretsu is no longer my concern, or at least it shouldn't be! Lord Barrett has vowed to eradicate all traces of the Nralda's project in return for this delivery. Once I have relinquished custody of the tribe, my end of the bargain is complete. If it's my safety he's concerned with, he has only but to fulfill his end. I'll feel much safer when he delivers Darstin's head to me."

"The deal in not yet complete," Vailetta said firmly. "And of course, Lord Barrett's end will take some time. Until then, your safety *is* still in question."

"Then take me *with* you—and what do you mean 'not complete'?"

"There are only thirty-five creatures. I've been ordered to secure thirty-seven."

Sid and Alexander, Helen breathed to herself. *They must be with the captain.* For a moment she felt a tinge of relief—clinging to the hope in one corner of her mind that they might be safe with Garrand. An awful knot rolled through her stomach as the reality of the exchange began to crystallize in this one awful moment. The price of avenging her mother's murder, her father's enslavement, and her childhood suffering was not an easy one to bear—not anymore, at least. In the process, something had changed. But it was too late for second thoughts now. "They are not well," Helen stammered, swallowing back the tears.

Vailetta raised an eyebrow, "Not well?"

"Yes—you stepped in before the appointed rendezvous—you're two weeks early. I was not prepared to turn them over this morning."

Precisely, Vailetta thought as she measured the woman's words. She wondered what measures the keiretsu agent had taken to protect her investment and ensure her bargaining position. "Turn them over to me and I will see that they get the proper attention."

"I'm afraid that's not possible. They are *very* ill," Helen said, regaining her confidence as she saw a possibility. "Without my care, they don't have a chance," she said flatly. "In all likelihood they will perish…" she strung the phrase out, letting it hang in the captain's mind. "The sickness, I'm afraid, has been infectious," she continued ominously. "They weren't quarantined in time. The rest of the tribe may soon become ill as well."

Vailetta studied the woman silently. *Here it comes,* she thought, *the trump is being played.*

"You tell Lord Barrett that without me, all the pandas could conceivably die."

So that was it, Vailetta mused. A symbolic, but probably all-too-real pox upon the prize—and a pair held in reserve. More than likely a breeding pair. Well, then, Barrett's cadre of genetic specialists and bio surgeons would have their work cut out from them. And Mistress Tchelakov would have to be watched carefully—tracked, actually—in case the medicas were unsuccessful in ferreting out her failsafes.

The officer at the woman's side signaled her briefly. The tall man bent to her ear.

"Captain," Dasko intoned, "we have all but two of the thirty-seven—a king's bounty in comparison to all previous attempts. Dare we risk the safety of thirty-five in the pursuit of two more—two who may in fact carry an infectious disease?"

Vailetta nodded once, acknowledging her lieutenant's counsel. *Barrett wouldn't like this.* The officer straightened back to attention. Helen watched her anxiously. The captain reached a decision and acted quickly.

"I will relay your *message* to Lord Barrett," Vailetta spun to the two guards. "Miss Tchelakov is finished. Bridle her and return her to her ship. If she resists, kill her. No hesitation. And that," she indicated the bracer. "Stays with me."

"No!" Helen exclaimed, struggling from the two guardsmen. "The pandas won't survive without me!"

Vailetta had the remarkable sensation that she was making a mistake by leaving the Tchelakov woman behind. But Lord Barrett had been very precise with his orders. He hoped to follow Tchelakov and see what her contingency plans were. If he could interrupt her careful schemes then perhaps they *both* would have something to bargain with. He suspected that she might have medically tampered with the pandas. But if he had waited until Helen was ready to turn them over, then he would have had no recourse if they all died on him. Taking them before she was ready to release them, he could still bargain with Darstin's head for the survival of the creatures. "I'm sure they'll get along just fine," she said evenly.

"No, you don't understand. *They will die.*"

Vailetta studied her with concern. "I'm ordered to leave you behind."

"Barrett won't get out of his bargain so easily," she yelled as the two guards dragged her out of the chamber. "You tell him they will die if he does not accede to my wishes! You tell him that I alone can save them!"

20

BATTLE OVER EEMON

GARRAND DESPERATELY WANTED TO REACTIVATE HIS COM-
tab and find out what was happening aboard his ship, but he
dared not reveal his position to the pursuant Shock Troops. He
felt Alexander's claws tighten marginally around his shoulders
as the cub's arms began to tire. The little panda was gamely
hanging on through all the furor. The pair had nearly traversed
the entire length of the reactor chamber through a winding
auxiliary service corridor beneath the coolant housings. Ahead
of them, the faint blue glow of light strips marked the main
serviceway. They were close to the very bottom of the ship now,
within fifty meters or so of *Destiny's* airlock, and safety.

Garrand hazarded a look into the hall and then stepped back into the shadows, leaning against the bulkhead. Alexander grumbled softly.

"Almost home, fella." Garrand discharged the coil from the butt of his blaster, unclicked a fresh cylinder and slapped it into the weapon's base. He checked the power reading and temporarily holstered the weapon. He turned his personal shield on and flicked the power to standby. The panda wiggled uncomfortably against his chest.

"It's not time to get down yet," Garrand warned. "You hold on tight for a few more minutes."

"Yes, Gher-ahn."

The captain cocked his head to look at the panda. Alex looked at him with big dark eyes, innocent and unafraid. "You're just full of surprises today, aren't you?" The cub merely licked its nose. "Okay, we're going to get you home now."

Garrand stepped out into the corridor and was confronted by a three-meter giant beetle, its glossy shell nightmare black, one pair of arms clutching a plasma burner, another cradling what could only be described as a harpoon thrower, with a jagged, barbed tip jutting out of the housing. Garrand caught his breath as he looked up at the massive insect. *How had the Gambor gotten aboard so quickly? Had he lost track of time in his mad dash through the frigate?* The Gambor's smooth-domed head lowered to face him, three horns jutting ahead, and the harpoon tip dipped toward his chest.

"I'll take that," the beetle said with a gravelly rasp.

Garrand stepped carefully backward, Alexander still clinging to his chest. The cub was the only thing between him and impalement at the end of a harpoon. His shield would be useless against the projectile.

The Gambor gestured with its weapon. "Give me the bear."

"I don't think so," Garrand whispered. He glanced over his shoulder. There was an intersection of halls ten meters behind him where the corridor broadened. Through the open hatch, Garrand could see part of a battle taking place. The sounds of combat whispered into the corridor. He continued to slowly backpedal, raising his blaster to the Gambor's head. Instantly, a shimmering translucence obscured the beetle as its shield activated.

Garrand took the moment of confusion while the Gambor had to readjust its visual orientation and turned to run down the hall. He heard a click-spring and the harpoon whipped past his shoulder, clanging into the open hatchway with such force that the razor-barb stuck into the steel, its steel shaft quivering behind it. The attached cable drew taut immediately as the Gambor eagerly sought to reel in its fresh victim. The beetle had waited until the panda cub was no longer in his line of fire.

Without pausing to survey the situation, Garrand dashed into the broad hallway intersection and ran to the far hatch, dodging the combatants. He caught sight of three Shock Troopers engaged with half a dozen or so Gambor. Energy bolts rocketed back and forth within the hall, creating sizzling sparks as shields blunted their force and redirected their paths. Two silver darts plocked against the bulkhead by his right thigh. Garrand reached the hatch and kicked the manual release. Nothing happened. He looked at the creases of the opening and could see the signs of fresh welds: the hatch was fused in place.

Two Gambor turned to face him. His back against the curving wall, nowhere to run, he looked up at the tangle of pipes and conduits that snaked in a confusing jumble overhead. He made a quick decision.

He grabbed Alexander underneath his armpits and jerked his head upward. The panda glanced up and moaned. "You hang on up there and don't come down until I call you—understand?" The little panda cried with pitiful resignation. "Up you go!" Garrand bent his knees and threw the cub upwards as hard as he could. Alexander grabbed onto a pipe, and scurried upward, like he was climbing a tree. The cub wedged himself into the cramped overhead space.

Arms now free, Garrand lowered his head and glared at the approaching insects.

A blast rifle swung his way and immediately his hand dropped to his waist, activating the shield generator. The colors of the room shifted, and streaks of light washed across his field of vision as the energy field crackled to life around his body. He blinked rapidly, trying to pick out which of the forms was the Gambor with the blast rifle. A stuttered ripple of sound marked the impact of a fusillade of energy bolts.

Garrand focused on what he thought was the source of the fire, crouching low. He flicked the shield's power off and ripped off four shots, aiming for the Gambor's inverted knee joint—a fleshy spot between its armored segments. He found his mark and the creature listed to one side, blast rifle firing wildly into the upper bulkhead. Garrand blasted two more shots at the knee joint, splintering the cartilage and tendons.

As the Gambor completely lost its balance, screeching hideously, Garrand popped two concussion grenades from the autofeeder and rolled them across the deck. The giant beetle toppled over on its side, landing atop the grenades that detonated with a double-whump.

A dart thumped into Garrand's leg, imbedding deep in the side of his left thigh. Wincing with pain, he rolled across the deck and dove behind the imploded beetle's carcass. Fumbling with his belt, he found a silver-foil packet and ripped into its sterile interior. He popped the anti-viral save-all pill, having to swallow hard to make the thing go down. He'd puke his guts out for two days after this, but the million or so parasites in the pill would eat the poison in his bloodstream before it killed him — or his leg had to be amputated. Gritting his teeth and cursing back the tears, he pulled the dart out, the barbed edges ripping skin and tissue as it departed. He slapped a fuse-patch over the wound and felt the chemical burn as the skin was cauterized.

Peeking over the carcass, he surveyed his position. Three Troopers were backed against the near wall by three advancing Gambor. Garrand looked for an escape, and saw the Gambor who had nailed his leg standing in the open hatchway leading to the reclamation chamber and *Destiny's Needle.* Anyone who wanted to get to the ship was going to have to get past him. The beetle held a pair of dart throwers in each of his upper arms. The scabrous lower limbs cradled a thick-barreled plasma burner. The three weapons tracked slowly, almost lazily around the hall, picking off targets at will.

"Alexander, you be ready!" Garrand hollered up into the darkness.

The panda gave a long fearful cry in return.

"Hang on!" Garrand swung his arm over the carcass and took aim at the beetle's thorax. He depressed the fire stud and held it down until the coil was completely discharged. The Gambor staggered backward under the barrage, arms jutting out to the hatchway for balance, its plated shell cracked and smoking from the direct hits. Garrand rose to his feet and launched himself across the open space, heading back to the far wall. Not yet incapacitated, the Gambor swung its burner around, green fire erupting across the deck plates just behind Garrand's feet.

Garrand slid behind another fallen warrior even as the Gambor's burner painted its body with flame. He lay flat on the deck as crackling flames rose from the carcass. The burner relented and he rose to one knee. Smoke and ash rose from the vile-smelling victim, obscuring Garrand's position. He looked up through the haze for Alexander, clapping his hands and holding out his arms.

"C'mon, now's the time if you're coming with me."

The little cub, nearly petrified with fear, gave himself up to the complete faith he had in the captain, letting go of his clawholds. He dropped through the smoke, trusting the human not to drop him. Garrand caught him with a grunt, and swung the cub to his back.

"Hang on!" Alexander's arms wrapped around his neck.

He popped a fresh coil in his blaster, amped up the power setting, and fired three short bursts through the smoke The Gambor immediately activated its shield, its black shell now gilded with blue light. Garrand holstered his blaster, drew his blade and jumped over the charred torso that had provided his cover, twisting toward the Gambor that stood firmly within the circular hatchway. A long, silvery nimsha poked through the shield, its blade wavering.

Garrand skittered to a halt in front of the giant beetle. He looked down at his short blade, realizing that it just wasn't going to do. There was no way he could keep proper distance on the Gambor now, the nimsha sword was too long. Through the undulating wash of color, he could just make out the Gambor lowering an arm to a pouch slung between body segments. Garrand hitched up his shoulders, redistributing the panda's weight, and bent low to the ground.

The beetle withdrew a heavy hand cannon and thrust the mussel out through the shield. The weapon tracked back and forth as the Gambor fought the dizzying effects of his shield and tried to draw a bead on him. The cannon fired, shrill snap-hiss of energy stabbing blindly into the room, missing its mark. Alexander squawked as a second rivet of power tore over-head. Garrand reached instinctively for his shield housing, but stopped. His thumb wavered over the power stud; the buffer might not take another shot. It would be foolhardy to rely on it.

Garrand hopped forward and performed a balestra, kick-ing the blaster out of the Gambor's claw. The nimsha flashed down toward his neck, but he spun away. The Gambor closed distance with a surprisingly smooth shuffle step, and attacked with the nimsha's point. Garrand engaged the sword with his dagger, circling his arm to redirect the point past his shoul-der as the Gambor lunged. The razor edge of the nimsha cut smoothly through his jacket and into his shoulder as the point sliced past. Garrand felt the Gambor shift subtly, and he leapt backward. The giant beetle stalked sideways, a blur of blue iri-descence, and thrust forward again.

Garrand stepped into the attack, slapping the blade down with the flat edge of his dagger and kicked his foot forward, hoping to snap the blade between his boot and the deck. The nimsha flashed quickly away and slashed diagonally back down. Garrand rotated Alex away and thrust his blade overhead, par-rying the insect's secondary attack with the dagger's finial guard. This was not going to last long, Garrand realized, not while all he could do was defend. The insect coiled for another attack, only this time a dart thrower emerged from the shield as well.

"That's just a little bit too much," Garrand snarled, drawing his blaster. Roaring at the top of his lungs, he threw himself at the giant beetle, parrying the nimsha's blade with his forearm. He screwed his eyes closed and plunged into the shimmering bubble. His shoulder connected with something solid and he rammed his weight into the Gambor's thorax. The blow sent the surprised Gambor staggering backward and Garrand thrust his right arm into the shield's protective shell and fired off four rapid bolts. He could feel the creature go limp under his shoulder. He stood back hastily, shoulder burned from the shield. He looked at his right arm. The jacket and shift were nearly singed off his arm, parts of the fabric fused with the red, exposed flesh. The smoking arm felt like it was on fire. Garrand grit his teeth and stumbled awkwardly over the dead Gambor, the pain making him dizzy.

"Berr-ahvu grrrlvack!" Alexander growled.

"Yes indeed," Garrand muttered as they stumbled down the hall away from the battle.

❖ ❖ ❖

VAILETTA PRESSED HER FINGERTIPS GENTLY AGAINST HER CHEEKS and nose, checking the bone structure and facial tissue beneath the raw skin. Her own face felt alien and sensitive after the suffocating lifemask had burned away. The Tchelakov creatures had seemed to accept her. She had perfectly matched their handler in appearance. The timbre of her voice and the effectiveness of her scent might be something else entirely—particularly to creatures with heightened hearing and smell—but they had proved to be no trouble whatsoever, shuffling dutifully into the *Ilyovahtna's* specially prepared cargo hold.

Vailetta stepped off the shuttle onto the *Ulusi's* hangar deck. Flanked by Danelle and Lewg she quickly made her way through the chaotic chamber, echoing with the scream of repulsor drives winding down, reactors humming with energy, the cries of tech foremen directing the recovery of the Phantoms that survived the initial onslaught. She had no time to fully assess her losses, there were more pressing problems to deal with.

The Jave O'Wars had crippled the *Jjaeyg* and quickly moved on to the Imperial frigate, hoping to gain entrance to *Destiny's Needle* through her bowels. Even now, three Skullers were attached to the frigate's hull like taltus blood leeches, and there were reports of Gambor infiltration on six decks. If the Gambor overran the *Ulusi*, then the whole mission might be compromised—one third of her task force was already drifting through space. The *Ilyovahtna* herself would be threatened if the Gambor could not be driven off the frigate. Vailetta cursed under her breath; she would not allow her new wards to fall into the keiretsu's clutches.

The combined forces of Arnas' Shock Troops and the Gokazoku Kaigi were now battling the Gambor who were rampaging through the *Ulusi*. And Médeville was aboard somewhere, if he was even alive. The odds of that seemed to be decreasing rapidly.

A tall, thin man swung into view, face bleeding badly, dark shipsuit torn and reeking of smoke. The guardsman halted in front of Vailetta and drew himself up to attention. "Welcome aboard Captain Strom."

Vailetta observed her guardsman wryly. "Dasko, you're looking well."

"Still in one piece ma'am."

She gave him a once over. "Are you sure about that lieutenant?"

"All vital organs still present, arms and legs attached—I'm no worse for the wear."

"What's the situation?"

"Under control."

"Where's Commander Arnas?"

"The Commander is occupied at the moment, flushing out a pocket of marauders on gregson level two."

"And assassin Torg?"

Dasko shook his head. "Whereabouts unknown."

"Walk with me, Lieutenant," Vailetta said. Dasko fell into step at her side. "Have you broken down the intruder's strategy?"

"More or less," he sighed. "The Gambor adopted a twin-pronged attack: half of them went for the ship's command centers, the other headed for *Destiny's Needle*. Commander Arnas repelled the first wave before they made it to the bridge, but took heavy losses. The Gambor's last sustained push seems to be directed at the reclamation lock, deck twelve."

"Beneath the reactors?"

"That's where *Destiny's Needle* is attached," Dasko explained.

"Take me there."

Dasko hesitated a moment, catching Vailetta's ire.

"Now, Dasko."

The guardsman straightened up. "Yes, Captain."

If the Gambor were massed on deck twelve, then Vailetta wagered that Torg would be there as well, right in the thick of things. And Médeville would have to fight his way through them all to make it back to his ship.

Her comtab crackled: "Captain, we have found Médeville."

"Is he alive?"

"Quite."

"Delay him, I'm on my way."

❖ ❖ ❖

GARRAND EDGED ALONG A GREASY WALL, THE PANDA SQUEEZED against his chest, the only source of warmth in the frigid space. His clothes were drenched with sweat, and now hung limply from his body, growing cold. Reaching the edge of the wall, he took a deep breath and glanced around the corner. There was an open hatch fifteen meters away. Through it he could see the circular opening where he and Bailey had first entered the Imperial frigate. A temporary field had been raised between *Destiny's* lock and the inner hull to guard against catastrophic loss of atmosphere if the ship suddenly departed. He gently extracted himself from the panda's grasp and set the creature on the deck, listening for signs of life. The drone of the ship's internals drowned out all other sound. He looked down at the panda and swallowed. *They were so close.*

"It's now or never little one."

Alexander moaned up at him, eyes intent but still full of fear.

"When I tell you, run back to the ship as fast as you can. Don't stop for anything. Do you understand?"

The panda cub nodded at him.

"Sid will be waiting for you. You keep running until he has you in his arms, okay?"

Garrand flicked the power stud on his comtab. "Bailey, you there?"

"Yes, Captain. Thank goodness you're all right!"

"I'm sending Alexander ahead of me. You let him onboard, then seal the doors again. I'll be along presently."

"But Captain—"

"—Don't come out!" Garrand ordered. "I'm coming to you. Anyone lurking in the hall won't shoot the panda, and they might reveal themselves when he runs by. I'll be right behind him."

"Yes, sir."

Garrand knelt down on his injured knee and turned the little panda to face the open hatch. "Right through there. Ready?"

"Mrr-awww."

"Then go." He swatted Alex on his rump and sent the panda rushing down the hall. The cub careened through the open hatch and made a dash for the ship. Garrand could hear shouts go up in the hall. He drew his blaster and stepped around the corner.

To his surprise, two men stood silently by the far wall, like mercats waiting for a hapless prey. The two men separated, appraising him with their eyes. Garrand recognized the uniforms and the demeanor: Imperial Guard. His eyes flicked to the nearest man's collar. Five-clawed dragon, two daggers ringed by gold. Gokazoku Kaigi.

They were wearing mirror-sheen vests with electrostatic generators, and shield boxes on their hips. His blaster would be useless; one man would easily drop him before he could overwhelm the other's shield with blaster fire. Garrand holstered the weapon and drew his blade.

The two men circled in opposite directions, keeping a respectful distance, until Garrand was directly between them. The man standing before him was solid and humorless, carrying just the one blade that he held *teirendat*—high over his head, blade twisted back flush with his forearm. His free arm was held before him, elbow crooked so that his arm and hand formed a horizontal line across his chest. The man adopted a flat-footed stance, knees comfortably bent, feet shoulder-width apart, shoulders squared toward Garrand. With a quick stutter step to his left, Garrand switched his composite blade from his injured right to his left and hazarded a glance back over his shoulder.

The second Guardsman was twirling his black composite blade slowly and methodically between his thumb and forefinger. He casually stepped several small strides one direction and then reversed his course, pacing like an impatient caged animal. With relaxed posture and supple fluid movements the man smiled back at Garrand, a warm but thin expression. A gentle acknowledgment between predators.

They were performing the *olendasta*—or at least were opening their attack under its guise. One man would stolidly and methodically wear him down while the other waited for an opening to finish him off. It was a variation on several classic attrition approaches that could be taken when numerical superiority was already established. One man might even purposefully take a blade to his belly in order that his partner could deliver the coup de grâce while the target's blade was still withdrawing. Trading one casualty for one kill.

Garrand made a cursory feint toward the man facing him, shuffled sideways and whirled to engage the second man, arms swinging low, head bent to the task. The man kept a clean distance, stepping gracefully along the edge of the wall. Garrand lunged, a high probing attack. The Gokazoku parried smoothly with blade and opposing wrist, pushing him easily away with crossed arms. Garrand repeated the move, cutting beneath the parry. The feint lacked intensity and the soldier blocked the secondary attack, readily accepting that his foe was gauging his position.

Garrand lashed out with his foot, aiming a high kick. The boot connected with the side of the man's head. The soldier's ready acceptance that the attack had been a cursory move was his undoing. Without pause, Garrand sprang forward, feigning blade high, but spinning to the deck and slashing at the Guardsman's knees. The man tried to recover but was unable to get both legs out of the way in time.

Garrand's blade cut him just under the kneecap with ruthless speed. The Gokazoku hopped backward on his good leg. Without pause, Garrand clicked off his last six grenades into a cupped palm and pivoted back to the first Guardsman. The man had been steadily closing distance, but now drew up short, eyes locked on the burned and bloodied captain. Beneath the dirt and sweat on his brow, Médeville's eyes burned black. Assassin Torg was right—the dragon had not yet been extinguished in this one.

Garrand rolled his grenades smoothly and gently back toward the hobbled Guardsman, further incentive to keep him still—the man would have to hop over them on one leg to get to him. The *olendasta* had been neutralized. He could now concentrate on one man. Switching his blade back to his right, he drew himself up and turned his burned shoulder forward readying himself for a new assault.

The first man, however, straightened up, cocking his head to one side. One hand came up to his ear and he nodded as he received orders through his comtab. Garrand's body tensed, sensing a deceit. The Guardsman took a deep breath, relaxing his posture, and nodded to his compatriot. With a slow and graceful bow, the man saluted Garrand. Garrand's fist tightened on his blade, but he brought its edge cautiously to his eye, returning the salute.

The Gokazoku Kaigi nodded minutely, "Griffin."

"Dagger," Garrand murmured warily in return.

The Guardsman smiled and ducked out of the chamber. Garrand swiveled to face the other, but he, too, was gone.

Delay, Garrand realized. *They were merely slowing me down.* His heart began to pound as the realization dawned on him. If they did not want him, it could mean only one thing—the Imperials already had what they had come for. His fingers curled in anger around the blade's pommel. He slid the dagger back into its sheath and turned back to the hall leading to the reclamation airlock, bile welling up in his throat.

He only made it three paces before a woman stepped into his path, compact, sleek blast pistol in her hand, long cape swept back over one shoulder. Flinty dark eyes appraised him. She took a step toward him, weapon leveled at his chest. He resisted the urge to step backward and keep the distance even between them. He was already nearly up against the bulkhead, his personal shielding was off, his nearest weapon rested in his holster, and he was completely out in the open. He could duck and try to roll for cover, but he doubted she would miss from such close range. From the look of her shooter's stance and the icy intent behind her eyes, he doubted she would miss from forty paces, much less the five that separated them. She bore the mark of the Gokazoku Kaigi: two daggers encircled by a band of gold.

He kept his gaze locked upon hers, afraid that to glance left or right would incite an unfavorable reaction. With his hands at his sides he reasoned that he might be able to activate his shielding before she fired her first shot, but it would be a toss-up as to whether he could draw and get off a shot before her blaster fire overwhelmed its buffer at such close range. He didn't like the odds.

He decided he would not instigate a violent course of action as his silence and stillness had kept him alive ten seconds longer than he might ordinarily expect. Waiting for a distraction was his best bet. Perhaps someone would stumble in and give him opportunity to overwhelm her.

Watching her intently, he decided she faced some sort of dilemma here—her eyes conceded a certain sense of weighing possibilities. The fact that she hadn't immediately dispatched him seemed to indicate that she was unsure of how to proceed. He frowned, suddenly struck by her appearance. She possessed a quiet beauty, dark hair framing soft, understated features. And those eyes, even in the dim light, he recognized those eyes. It *was the fisher girl from Eemon Nores.* Sid had been right, they had been watched. And he was facing the watcher herself. Now that he could see her in person the differences between her and Kate became evident, though there was a marked resemblance.

Finally she spoke. "I don't have any orders for you."

"Excuse me?" Garrand asked. Vailetta squinted darkly at the sound of his voice. The man did not waver, however, under her scrutiny. "Orders for *me?*" he continued incredulously. "I don't recall being currently in the Emperor's employ."

Vailetta frowned. "Orders *concerning* you," she growled. "All I need is your cargo."

"Ahh…" Garrand said rocking his head back as if he suddenly understood everything that was transpiring. "So you're a pirate!"

The woman reddened visibly, fingers tightening around the cold steel of her blaster. "I am a Captain of the Imperial Guard—Brotherhood of the Silent Dagger—defender of the Emperor, bound and sworn to uphold the honor of the Dragon!" She snapped off the final word with venom, eyes ablaze. "I am not a pirate!"

Garrand pursed his lips and let his voice drop to a low growl. "Waylaying passing vessels and stealing their cargoes?" He shook his head, "Sounds like piracy to me."

The woman's face shifted subtly from anger and indignation to a smooth, conspirator's smile. "I was warned of you," she said in a low tone.

"Warned?" he affected a look of surprise. "Of me?"

"I offer you your life and you offer me an insult."

"An insult? No, no, no. That wasn't an insult. I was merely being cautious — prudent if you like. To tell you the truth, I wasn't quite sure what you were. But if you were a pirate and I called you an Imperial agent — now that's an insult. I'd have been shot for sure."

Vailetta stared at him for several long moments, her eyes absorbing his tense, coiled frame — the look of weary defiance permanently etched in the slender cracks that fanned out around his eyes. He had escaped the Shock Troops for the *second* time as well as thwarted the Gambor's attempts on his life. She did not have the heart to bring him in, and she doubted he would even let her. She would have to kill him first.

"I don't have specific orders to eliminate you, Captain. The Emperor, apparently, has no use for you."

Garrand tried to smother the sound of ironic amusement that billowed up into his throat. He savagely bit the inside of his lip to keep a straight face.

Vailetta paused, tightening her grip on the blaster still pointed at his chest. She took a half step closer, hesitating as she studied him. He almost looked like he was about to burst out laughing, but that couldn't be right. Then, in a brief flourish, she smoothly holstered the weapon and slung the cape back across her shoulder.

"Perhaps we shall meet again, Griffin, under different circumstances."

Garrand stood watching her, still caught in the strange shock of the moment. Being held dead to rights in someone else's sights was not something he was accustomed to. His blood pounded through his veins, throbbing against his temples — the roots of his teeth ached back in the deepest part of his jaw. And yet he felt a sudden elation, that moment of giddy realization that death had been escaped once more.

She strode toward the hatch, pausing to give him a fleeting, mysterious look. In later moments he could not recall if it was exactly a hint of a smile, or perhaps the briefest flash of desire that beguiled him. Perhaps it was just his imagination playing tricks on his frazzled nerves, but there was an unmistakable sparkle to her exit. He had the unnerving feeling that her words held some value, some hidden forbearance. And he felt certain that she had felt it as well. Some kinship that went beyond what was readily, or easily explained. She hadn't shot him because she dared not. There had been something in that brief moment, a recognition in that final glance — like turning on the lights and finding yourself looking into a mirror. He felt certain that it was not just his imagination. She had known it, too — somehow their destinies were intertwined, like the runes of a Darliven talisman, they were fated to meet again.

He paced quickly through the corridor, pausing just outside the reclamation lock. The sounds of fighting drifted with the putrescent stench out into the corridor. Peeking inside, Garrand saw a single human surrounded by three Gambor. The man was large and powerful, but still dwarfed by the immense shapes of the giant beetles that clicked and sang in a strange tongue as they coordinated their attack. Bodies were strewn across the deckplates, Gambor and human alike, so that all the combatants had to step over and around them as they performed their spectral dance of blood. *Destiny's* outer lock doors were closed, Garrand noted with some measure of relief, but there was still the matter of making it through the reclamation chamber.

Garrand edged into the room, back against the wall. The Gambor seemed to be giving the large man quite a bit of respect, clicking nervously back and forth, withholding their attack. The large man was dressed in black, with no discernable insignia. A long cloak hung off one shoulder and Trioxin mesh gloves protected his hands.

"We have a visitor," said a voice from the darkness just beside Garrand. A glistening form sparkled behind a fat bulkhead brace. The translucent image of a man sidled around the steel support. Garrand recoiled, a hideous jolt of fear and adrenaline raced to his head as he stumbled away from the sound, blade pointed at its source. One of the Gambor sensed the disturbance and turned to face him, blue veil of light erupting around its body as the shield powered to life. Without word the large man flew into action, kicking out with one leg at the nearest beetle and drawing a dart thrower from the recesses of his cloak. Darts whizzed toward the second Gambor, catching him expertly in the joints between body segments. As Garrand watched with disbelief the large man's body wavered and disappeared. The voice from the darkness cackled with laughter and the shimmer-form reemerged, wispy and pellucid. Garrand cursed; he'd been nearly frightened to death by the ghost.

"You will all join me in oblivion," the ghost tittered with delirious glee. "Master Torg will see to that."

Torg, Garrand thought. *Master Assassin Torg, the Emperor's Butcher. Here to board his ship? Or defend it? Or perhaps here just for the blood.* It did not matter; the distraction he needed to board his ship had just been provided.

"You will join me soon enough," the holo image sang.

"Bloody specter," Garrand snapped and walked through the glistening form. His eyes swept the darkness for the invisible assassin — he had not been a ghost, though he behaved like one. The Gambor, too, searched uneasily for the assassin.

Garrand angled toward *Destiny's* airlock, whispering into his comtab, "Bailey, I might need your help here after all."

"Acknowledged."

He was halfway across the room when the assassin's body coalesced once more, this time between Garrand and the shielded Gambor. The far Gambor shrieked in warning but it was too late; Torg's blade dipped into the blue field and twisted. The assassin had apparently struck a critical blow, for the beetle crumpled to the deck with an exaggerated slowness. Emitting a shrill cry, the far Gambor charged the assassin with a berserk fury. Torg backed toward Garrand, his cloak sweeping out as he reached for his shield.

The last Gambor stepped over two bodies and circled the assassin, cutting off Garrand's path to *Destiny's Needle*. Garrand had little choice but to turn his back on the assassin as the Gambor drew near, nimsha and dart thrower swaying in its arms. He took a reflexive step backward and felt something brush up against his back. Glancing over his shoulder, he realized that Torg and he were now back to back, each of them facing off a different adversary. A chill ran down his spine as the Gambor sized him up — an assassin at one's back wasn't exactly the kind of protection he was accustomed to.

With elaborate precision, the Gambor loaded a fresh clip of darts into his thrower with one pair of arms while the second held the nimsha sword at the ready. Garrand's right hand hovered just over his holster, fingers tingling with anticipation — if he drew too soon, the beetle would activate its shield. The Gambor snapped the spring-safety back into place and raised the dart thrower, aiming at Garrand's chest. In a single, fluid motion, Garrand drew, knelt and fired, hitting the dart thrower with one shot. The weapon spun out of the insect's claw and Garrand sprang to the attack, the blade already in his hand. He surged upward, aiming for the underside of the Gambor's chin, beneath the armor plate, but was a fraction too slow.

The Gambor caught the dagger in a claw and snapped the composite blade easily between its pincers. A set of arms wrapped tightly around Garrand's midsection and lifted him off the ground. His feet kicked helplessly in mid-air and he fought to bring his blaster's mussel to bear on the beetle. His shots panged harmlessly on the ceiling as he fought against the Gambor's grip. A claw reached up to his neck, the pincers sliding around his collar.

Tears rolled down Garrand's face as the claw tightened around his throat. He tried to cry out, but asphyxia had already choked the breath out of him. He saw a silver blur race out of *Destiny's* airlock and then he hit the deck hard. The Gambor toppled over on top of him, nearly crushing him, but the claw released it hold. Garrand gasped for breath, struggling to pull himself out from under the beetle. He rolled out and scrambled backward.

Bailey now knelt atop the floundering beetle, having knocked the creature clean off its legs. The Gambor had a claw around the artificial's silver neck. Garrand could see the tendons flex as the beetle tried to sever the steel and decapitate the art, but to no avail. Bailey drew back an arm and punched the Gambor's thorax with a fist, puncturing the shell. He pulled back and plunged his arm into the cavity wreaking destruction on the internal organs. Garrand rolled to his side and looked for the last two combatants.

The partially visible form of the assassin was pressed back against the far bulkhead in much the same position as he had just found himself in. The assassin's yellow eyes regarded him once, briefly—flashing to a silver translucence before resuming a more crimson hue. The large man parried a claw with one arm and swung his blade overhead, just missing the beetle's exposed eyes.

"Captain, are you all right?" Bailey asked with concern.

"Yeah, get back on the ship."

"Captain—"

He pointed at the lock. "Now!"

"Yes, sir." The artificial retreated.

The Gambor held the assassin pinned against the bulkhead, trying to engage the large man's neck with a claw while struggling to parry the lethal precision of the man's blade. Garrand reached down and picked a long nimsha from the deck, grasping the heavy weapon in two hands and charged. Held before him like a lance, the blade pierced the Gambor's hardened shell and slid home. He stepped back and watched the beetle collapse.

Assassin Torg looked down at the fallen Gambor and then up at the captain. The man looked hardly more than a ghost himself, clothes tattered, his face and arms covered in blood. Garrand stepped slowly and carefully backward until he was inside *Destiny's* airlock, never once breaking eye contact.

Doors hissed together and the ship broke contact immediately, curling underneath the frigate and rocketing away from the battle. Garrand watched the tangle of ships wheel beyond the glazing, the twin Imperial pickets, the frigate, the Gamborian Jave' O Wars, and a curious, slender chrysalis sloop. The shock and adrenaline began to wear off and he felt his knees buckling. Cool, steel hands caught him as he fell.

Torg watched the warrior disappear through the stuttering field that separated him from vacuum. He shut down the ghost shell and carefully wiped his blade dry. The Tchelakov creatures were in the *Ilyovahtna's* hold and the Gambor were vanquished; the mission was a success. Yet he could not erase the image of the warrior captain dispatching the final Gambor before the killing stroke could land and then disappearing into his ship. The dragon still lived within the man, of that there was no doubt. Such a man would know the value of what he had just lost. He would not allow such potential to slip away, not into the hands of a man like Barrett. Such a man would not rest until he had recovered what was lost.

He would one day be back to claim what was his. Torg sheathed his blade and wiped the blood pooling around his eye with the back of one hand. He continued to stare as *Destiny's Needle* disengaged from the frigate and disappeared from view. Médeville would one day find his way to Wyx, of that he was certain.

He looked forward to the day.

GRIFFIN TERMINOLOGY

Ackriveldt: lone planet of Galipsus, noted as birth world of Naius Sartok.

Adjucate: harbor judge; low level Imperial official.

Air Skimmer: agile low atmosphere pursuit vehicle. Single-seat design, though the D'arellak later commissioned some dual versions during the Vintson riots, 35,279. Simple rugged design and low cost made these the patrol craft of choice for most Free Will colonies.

Alexander: giant panda cub, third generation member or the Tchelakov Tribe.

Archiva: also known as Mardell's world. Location: unknown. After the destruction of twelve key data repositories during the War of the Three in 29,182 in which the entire ancestral records of deeds and fiefs for five thousand systems was lost, the network of information was deemed too important to lie 'scattered across the Shell like diamonds for the taking.' A central archival planet was deemed the solution, with a planet-wide system of data storage—a backup repository for the knowledge off an entire empire. The location was chosen in secret and the entire network was shunted through the planet's datacores where physical copies were recorded and stored in vast repositories. So vast was this archive that it became synonymous with the planet itself. The planet was discovered and later sacked (some say destroyed) in the time of Mardell III.

Armor Drip: versatile field armor developed by Pavelle Nest. Transported in liquid form and poured into a variety of molds on site, cerafiber bonds harden in under a minute after catalyst is added. Gives added mobility to light armor divisions.

Arnas, San Barrilito: battalion commander, 41st Imperial Marines; Shock Trooper.

Art Wars: a conflict that arose when the Sullust movement sought to curtail the rapid proliferation of Free Will artificials, specifically machines indistinguishable from humans. Fueled by fear and religious fervor, the push for curtailment quickly expanded into a genocidal Jihad that lasted from 35,110 until the Gelicus Art Convention in 35,307. Alternately known as the Gai'han Jihad, depending on one's point of view, the resulting conflagration plunged much of the galaxy into turmoil (see: Jihad, Gai'han, Free Will artificials, Sullust Movement)

Artificial: any of a wide class of mobile mechanical constructs possessing intelligence, self-awareness and the ability to learn through experience.

Atryx: race of large (1.3 meter tall, 6 meter wingspan) warm-blooded avians (sentient).

Bailey: Krellian Artificial, Varsis model VL1357-B8, incept date unrecorded. Master of Arms, Caius Minor, from 35,329 to 35,337. Assigned to Santos II as personal assistant to Captain of the Guard, Garrand Ai'Gonet Médeville in 35,337. Granted Free Will in 35,345.

Barrelian Corvette: Highly-maneuverable armed escort ship, smaller than a frigate, ranging in length from 100-150 meter; often used in conjunction with a larger fleet of vessels. Barrelian designs have been manufactured for over 700 years.

Barrett, Hellius: An ambitious Vecklorn who inherited his father's seat in the Royal Regincira and was later appointed High Magistrate in the Emperor's Court, he was a trusted confidante who lost favor after rumors of an illicit affair with the Empress surfaced. "Banished" to the political chaos of Carinaena's Shell, where his charms could not impress Chyrella, he labored in relative obscurity for some time. The assassination of ruling Proctor Lekkson Nesbit elevated Barrett into control of the Shell's third largest Proctorialship. Commonly referred to as Lord Barrett (whether it be in reference to Vecklornian nobility, or claimed in ancient Caluras rite is unknown), his title is officially Vice Proctor of Wyx.

Bordëgian Academé: ancient school of preparation for service in the Imperial Navy.

Brotherhood of the Princes of Blood: Order within the Imperial Guard. Founded 34,512 on Daulinbêres (see also: Griffin).

Byrethylen Wraith: race of large (4 meter tall), amorphous, multi-tendriled vaporous energy manifestations. Wraiths prey on the neurological fears of their victims, manifesting themselves as the delusional images found in their victims' minds. Wraiths feed on all energy sources, but prefer the cerebrum's neural energy. Wraiths were once the scourge of the Byrethyl System, wiping out whole planets and rendering them barren and lifeless.

By the Barthsa: Dalis colloquialism; mild curse.

Carinaena's Shell: (Car-in-ae-na) the massive outer ring of stars that forms a donut-shaped shell around the central Core of the Gli-Dawun Galaxy. Named for the Lallalopsle ship Carinaena's Hope whose quantum drive failed at the edge of the galactic Core, and thus became the first "seeder" ship of colonists (see Dolke's Historical tome "Carinaena's Fate: the Colonization of Chance").

Carrack Class Cruiser: large, fast, heavily armored and gunned warship; Imperial classification of Battle Cruiser, top of the line capital ship.

Cerafiber: synthetic material prized for its light weight and heat/energy absorption; crystalline threads formed from superheated dryexcellon powder and molecular ceramic are cast into an intercellular matrix of connective filaments. Bonded matrices are stored in liquid state and then poured into molds with catalysts creating solid fibers of great elasticity, flexibility and tensile strength.

Cerasteel: ceramic steel formed on site by combining polymer-bonded dryexcellon powder into molten steel. After cooling, the steel is superheated through conduction, bonding the dryexcellon and steel at a molecular level.

Cha'halen: rank in the military hierarchy of the Gambor; roughly equivalent to the Imperial rank of major.

Cheplus: Strahlinvek colloquialism; moderate curse.

Clipscanner: miniature (20 cm x 12 cm) personal datacore composed of digital reader, processing unit, fingertap board and display housed within a slim impact casing; noted for its versatility and interface capabilities.

Clipscan Visor: data relay that partially blinds user's real-time vision; primarily intended for use by artificials.

Coil: rechargeable storage field that uses magnetic coils to safely store massive amounts of charged ions. Capable of efficiently storing vast amounts of energy in a small physical space. Primary source of power for all energy dependent devices and engines.

Collistas Dynasty: (co-least-us) largest autonomous governing body in the Gli-Dawun Galaxy, ruled by a member of the Collistas family for 47 generations. The empire spawned from this stability now envelops much of the galaxy's core.

Consul: Imperial planetary governor, ranking below a vice proctor.

Core: (also: "Core worlds," "The Core") the densely populated center of the Gli-Dawun Galaxy; common designation for the vast volume of star systems currently under the domain of the Collistas Imperial Dynasty.

Coryl-Tuluyt Picket: escort warship of the fastest class; Imperial classification for its top of the line interdictors and blockade runners.

Cronix: a design line of datacores, a product of Si Bell Logiks, a proprietary arm of the Si Bell Keiretsu; Cronix datacores are commonly considered the industrial standard in Carinaena's Shell.

C'tereino: former lieutenant of the Imperial Guard, Griffin Order; operator of blue ice lichen farm on Eemon Nores.

Dailyern Green: bitter, slightly caustic alcoholic concoction formed from the lesser of the two saps from the Yourb trees on Dailyern (the other, red sap, is a fatal poison) and Kakin malt. A drink favored by the vegrauts who conquered Dailyern six centuries ago, their strong constitutions and thick abdominal lining able to handle the toxins. The two ingredients are unstable when combined, thus the drink is served in two equal portions and it is left to the patron to mix them.

Dalintus Commission: formed by the Gelicus Art Convention in 35,312, charged with the judgment of Free Will artificials—the Dalintus seal signifying the highest possible conditioning against taking a human life. Dalintus qualified artificials permitted to design and create Free Will artificials without human intervention.

Danelle: lieutenant in the Imperial Guard, Gokazoku Kaigi; currently assigned to Wyx, Carinaena's Shell, linguist.

Darcalyn: artificial construct, highly unstable isotope frequently used in the construction of tactical fusion devices; logarithmic scale for expressing the magnitude of energy contained within such explosive devices.

Darstin, Carrelle: Director of Research and Acquisitions, Nralda Keiretsu. Seat on the Nralda High Board, 4th Tier. Responsible for funding and perpetuation of Beh'In Tchelakov's research concerning the next evolution of the sartographic chip (see: Tchelakov Tribe).

Dasko, Lee: lieutenant in the Imperial Guard, Gokazoku Kaigi; currently assigned to Wyx, Carinaena's Shell, decryption specialist, 1st grade.

Datacore: programmable electromagnetic device that can store, retrieve, and process data; the heart of all mechanical thinking mechanisms.

Datapad: any of a wide variety of specialized technical data readers; poor cousin of the clipscanner.

Daulinbêres: sixth planet in the Wopäs System, situated in a prime strategic location near the heart of the Gli-Dawun Galaxy; seat of the Imperial throne for 137 centuries.

Daurrian Shipyards: the vast Pragen spaceworks in high orbit off Bingham; the close proximity of the Hames asteroid belt for raw materials and the industrial processing complex on Bingham itself has made this yard one of the most efficient operations in the Shell, capable of turning out a full destroyer in under eight years.

Destroyer: very large, fast, heavily armored and gunned warship; a classification usually reserved for a fleet's largest and most advanced capital ships.

Destiny's Needle: modified medium cruiser designed by Garrand Ai'Gonet Médeville and built by Le'hadn Vercks in 35,347 for the express purpose of breaking the Talen quarantine on El Phobadia. Presented to Médeville by the Sandhalles Grip, Bestriyx Dagen, soon thereafter as a token of his esteem, in return for the rescue of his daughter. Subsequently played a principle role in the Tchelakov Revolt circa 35,355.

Drazon Vorge: refugee youth from Galipsus Minoirte; currently under the tutelage of Vice Proctor Barrett.

Dreadnaught: large, moderately armored and gunned warship; an older classification generally reserved for blockade interdictors and fleet escorts. Upgrades in quantum drive technologies have rendered many of the dreadnaught designs obsolete. Properly refit, dreadnaughts play an important role in many developing navies.

Dryexcellon: mineral ore principally mined in the Restepheron system and refined on planets throughout the Shell into highgrade fuels, powders and industrial byproducts (see: cerafiber, cerasteel).

E2: the Empire's top of the line massive datacore processor, integrating the latest sartographic series II technology with group "e" Cronix mainframes; used aboard all Carrack class vessels (see: sartograph).

Eckreon: a design line of Cronix datacores, the product f Si Bell Logiks, a proprietary arm of Si Bell Keiretsu; Cronix datacores are commonly considered the industrial standard in Carinaena's Shell.

Eemon Nores: icy seventh planet of the Niyl System, situated near the Krestyaninov Cluster.

El-Bouteran: only planet in the Pakken System, far removed from all major shipping routes in Carinaena's Shell.

Elytra: the anterior wings of Gamborian beetles that serve to protect the posterior pair of functional wings.

Enyohanse Lenses: adjustable spectacles that fit over the surface of the eye with crystalline enzymes that adhere to the pupils' surface, stretching and bending the light as it enters the optic nerves. Once familiar with the enyohanse lenses, the user can adjust the level of magnification and clarity with the muscles of the eye and face.

Exel: wild echrine of Maltus adapted for Se-faillus hunters on Letugia; sometimes kept as pets.

Falto Earblocks: miniature counter-active dampers that absorb sound waves and project energy surges into the ear that flatten out the signature sine pattern of incoming noise, effectively negating the sounds as they enter the inner ear membrane.

Freetrader: colloquialism; broad term embracing what is in essence a wide variety of professions including (but not limited to) inter-system mercantile trading, freelance entrepreneurial merchandising, smuggling, and simple cargo hauling. Originally a term used to describe independent freelance entrepreneurs in early Colonial era, specifically the nine hundred year period that saw the Shell worlds successfully pioneered and settled (see: Great Diaspora). Working alone in single ships, Freetraders were an indispensable element of the colonization effort. The high risks and huge overhead involved in supplying hundreds of tiny colonies made it unprofitable to sustain and supply colonies on a corporate and/or commercial level. These entrepreneurs—private oneman operations flying single craft with low overhead—allowed colonies to flourish in their infant stages by bringing goods that could not be produced on fledgling worlds for decades. Private traders were colonists' lifeblood, shipping in needed commodities, spare parts, and resources in return for grains and foodstuffs for shipment offworld. Most Freetraders are thought of as colonial patriots of a sort. Without them, most colonies would have quickly failed and the Shell as we know it would not exist.

Free Will Artificial: a specialized class of mobile mechanical constructs possessing intelligence, self-awareness and the ability to learn through experience. Free Will arts are not designed with a specific underlying purpose. Without a rigorous code of conduct for higher functions, Free Will arts are left to choose their own course after inception. The Sullust movement sought to curtail the rapid proliferation of Free Will arts after the perfection of the indistinguishable-from-human designs. The resulting conflicts are alternately known as the Gai'han Jihad (see: The Purge) or the Art Wars (see: the Lashback). The 200-year upheaval plunged much of the galaxy into turmoil. Numerous commissions sprang up in the aftermath, attempting to regulate Free Will arts, and many prejudices still exist (see: Artificial).

Frigate: any of a broad variety of moderately armored and gunned warships, the classification of which differ widely from navy to navy. Historically: a moderate to large design; the workhorse of many a navy.

Gambor: race of large (3 meter tall) multi-limbed, smooth-shelled, winged beetles (sentient); home world of the Galzeki, tagged for garbage reclamation by Imperial Navy and site of 400-year-old civil war (see Po'tchantu's "Siege of Galzeki"). The Gambor have recently begun contracting their warrior services out to the Nralda Keiretsu in return for desperately needed munitions.

Gelicus Art Convention: contravened in 35,312, marking the official end of the Gai'han Jihad, its provisions forging an uneasy peace between the Gai'han Sullusts and the Free Will coalition lead by the Free Will artificial, Samuel. It's chief tenant: no machine was to be constructed indistinguishable from a human being. In compromise, the Sullusts lifted the death bounty placed on all Free Will artificials. Secondary precepts limited the creation of Free Will artificials: specifically, it was forbidden for artificials to create Free Will artificials (in essence procreate) without the Dalintus seal (see: Dalintus Commission).

Gokazoku Kaigi: Order within the Imperial Guard. Known as the "Brotherhood of the Silent Blade." Founded 34,819 on Daulinbêres.

Gravitic Repulsors: Fit beneath everything from cargo lighters to gunsleds to starships, Norgen generators project a harmonic field that negates the affects of gravity over a limited area focused in conical projections that dissipate over distance. The resulting gravitic null space creates buoyancy that is enhanced by standard field suspensors. The combined effect of the null space and the repulsor wave field is enough to allow most vessels, pallet, skimmers, and such to hover mid-air. In more elaborate configurations, they are enough to allow starships of massive tonnage to overcome the pull of planetary gravity wells and land and takeoff vertically.

Griffin: Collistas colloquialism; slang for Imperial Guardian, Griffin Order. Order within the Imperial Guard. Known as the "Brotherhood of the Princes of Blood." Founded 34,512 on Daulinbêres.

Gunsled: armored ground assault vehicles, fit with gravitic repulsors.

Gyropod: enclosed datastations typically found aboard military vessels, designed to insulate vital pod-tech ensigns from the dangers of battle and aid their interface with the ship's datacore (see: Pod-tech).

Haven's End: Imperial colloquialism; mild curse derived from the infamous travails of Giin Bly Haven, officer in the Royal Regincira, whose life was ironically taken by the very men he risked everything to save.

Holocube: miniature holographic display unit roughly the size of an Imperial quantis. Projects a small static image of subject that can be viewed from all angles.

Holo Ghost: the emotional and neurological essence of a creature captured by electronic means and stored in a digital matrix much like a datacore. The mortal subject's neural activity and the brain's electro-chemical signature is transferred (either during the death throes, or soon after death) by electronic conductivity and hard wired into circuitry chips, much like the creation of an artificial. The imprint is stored in a Tarkanian containment field and is manifested as a hologram. The resultant "ghost" is cognizant and self-aware, many times with full memories and recollections intact, though the manifestation exists with a painful echo of former emotions. A common theological belief is that the souls of ghosts are suspended in K'ye, awaiting judgment.

Ident-link: mathematical symbol(s) or icon used to represent a person or artificial; any of a wide range of identifying markers imbedded or cosmetic; standard Imperial identification system.

Imperial Guard: For over 3 millennia, the Imperial Guard has protected the interests of the Imperial throne, specifically the well being of the Emperor and his highest Ambassadors (see: Proctors). The Guardian caste is one of the most ancient and revered schooling bodies in the Empire. The noble warriors within have sworn to honor the Emperor and uphold the sanctity of the realm. Each faction within the caste has its own Order, full of timeworn tradition and a legacy to uphold. New members of the guard are sworn into a particular order, whose tenets they must obey and traditions they most honor.

Jean-Wa: Do-lât Artificial, Preparation model D430, incept date unrecorded; six-armed master chef with detachable legs and wheels. Purchased by Garrand Ai'Gonet Médeville from the Baron Senn van Basel of Daruma.

Jihad: (ji-häd) a religious holy war; fanatical crusade for a principle or belief.

Jihad, Gai'han: (see also: Art Wars) the doomed crusade against Free Will artificials, humaniform mechanical sentients, sentient machines, and conscious datacores begun in 35,110 and concluded in 35,307. It's chief result: the disappearance of all indistinguishable-from-human artificials.

Ka'vaelus: Gambor warrior; Cha'halen first grade of the Vaelus burrow, Galzeki. Rumored to have personal ties with 4th tier Nralda Director of Acquisitions, Carrelle Darstin.

Keiltraoma: a state of conscious dreaming; the keiltraoma requires a mastery of the body's physiological and physical states, allowing the conscious awareness of the brain's unbidden neurological activity, specifically, the subconscious creativity know as dreams.

Kess: fourth planet in the Dell Transim system; site of Gort's Agro Supply.

Keiretsu: corporate entities that have bonded together in Carinaena's Shell for protection and profit—combining trade routes and resources to form interplanetary cartels complete with defense fleets. Some keiretsu control whole systems, having subjugated the populace through economic monopolies and trade embargoes. While avoiding outright war with the Collistas Dynasty, many keiretsu are involved in an escalating cold war with the Imperial Proctorialships in the Shell.

Krestyaninov Cluster: a volume of space hundreds of light years across with complex and powerful gravitational forces due to the influence of a large number of stars in the white dwarf stage of collapse.

K'ye: the mythical "battleground of the gods," where the souls of the dead are said to be judged; purgatory.

Larkson Shield Generator: produces powerful resonating magnetic field capable of bending light around its focusing body. Used in conjunction with deflector arrays and an adequate system of null-dampers, the Larkson creates a viable protective field. Buffer coils store power bled from other ship systems and then feed pulses of energy to the shields' magnetic deflector fields. Energy that is not refracted or deflected is absorbed by null- dampers.

Letugia: fifth planet in the Nepestar system; site of the Il Touvé shipyards, largest in the system.

Lewg: lieutenant in the Imperial Guard, Gokazoku Kaigi; currently assigned to Wyx, Carinaena's Shell; master bladesman.

Lifter: huge obtuse transport shuttles, heavily shielded and fit with gigantic sublight reactors, but possessing no faster-than-light capability. Designed to safely and efficiently ferry cargo and men between planet surfaces and orbiting ships (see: Mules).

Lighter: mechanical construct of varying size fit with gravitic repulsors and possessing limited intelligence, designed to ferry cargo between vessels in docking bays.

Little Bit: Turkle Sphere II, model 339-74C, incept date 35,329; technical assist (modified) purchased by Garrand Ai'Gonet Médeville at the Syhan Fabrication Works on Tikus.

Lolovanti: light cruiser from the Daurrian Shipyards; Captain Vailetta Strom's personal vessel.

Lor Stanta Destroyer: warship of the largest and most heavily armed and armored class; Imperial classification of the largest capital ship currently in active service (700 meter).

Matrix: something within which something else originates or develops; material in which something is enclosed or embedded.

Médeville, Garrand Ai'Gonet: Freetrader, former Captain of the Imperial Guard, Griffin Order; purported leader of the Tchelakov Revolt.

Mules: Collistas colloquialism; slang for lifters.

Nesbit, Lekkson: Provost of Wyx and reigning Proctor of the Callus, Niramdi, and del'Trin system fiefs until his assassination in 35,347. Respected for his ability to create economic bridges between vastly different cultures. With the help of his ambitious vice proctor, Hellius Barrett, nurtured the Wyxian Proctorialship into one of the largest and richest Imperial fiefs in Carinaena's Shell.

Niramdi System: minor star system in the Outer Reaches (II Gallen Wei); hidden staging area for Free Will resistance during the Gai'han Jihad (see: Thrassin, battle of).

Nralda: Keiretsu; one of the largest and most powerful operating in the Shell.

Offloader: mechanical construct of limited intelligence designed to remove cargo from vessels quickly and efficiently.

Path of Fate: an expression unique to the Tchelakov Tribe; a series of events that are destined to transpire. The Path of Fate is a map of something that does not yet exist, but will inevitably come to pass (see: seitparen). To the Tchelakov Tribe, the future is fluid and ever-changing, with some paths more likely to occur than others, and some events almost impossible to avoid. The Path of Fate is the culmination of all dreams and all variables, the part of time that will come to be known as 'the past.' Seeing the Path before it becomes the past is the tribe's legacy, a blessing so coveted that it threatens to destroy them.

Phase Emitter: general diagnostic tool for setting correct power configurations on coil-based reactors and generators. Uses pulses of energy to calibrate null dampers.

Picket Cutter: small-to-medium sized, extremely fast and lightly armored warship; primarily used as lead escort ships, blockade runners, and strike interdictors.

Plascrete: a lightweight, strong building material formed by mixing industrial grade polymer plastic aggregates with cementing agents and catalysts that cause the plastics to set and bind the entire mass. Can be poured on-site making it useful in fortifications and mobile battle situations.

Pod-tech: Collistas colloquialism; tech ensigns who spend much of their time suspended in gyropods.

Praetor: Imperial magistrate, adjucatal overlord, ranking below a consul.

Proctor: the chief magistrate of an Imperial fiefdom.

Proctorialship: the principle sphere of influence or domain of specific Imperial fiefs created during the Great Shell Diaspora. Proctorialships are doled out to lords and barons within the Imperial Court as the Emperor sees fit. The relative domain of the fief may be expanded in the Emperor's name at the ruling proctor's discretion.

Provost: Imperial planetary governor.

Quantis: circular trebian alloy coin. Five Imperial credits. Accepted coin of the realm in most systems along with local currency. Although credit chits are more widely used, some small denomination coins are more efficient for limited purchases, such as food and beverage.

Quantum Drive: crucial middle element of all interstellar ships' three-tiered drive system; sub-light engines propel ships up to the brink of light speed (speeds and acceleration dependent upon design, size, efficiency, etc.), the quantum drive breaches the light barrier, lifting the ship into quantum space, and the light engines propel the ship through quantum space itself.

Reactor Core: chamber that powers all sub-light and quantum drives. The chamber is filled with cryxthlen gas at extremely high pressure. This gas, through which a series of directed neutron sparks pass, contains charged particles accelerated by the power field of the coils that wrap around the reactor core. As the field oscillates, it accelerates the charges back and forth, making them collide energetically with the cryxthlen atoms. Many of the gas atoms are actually torn apart by the collisions, yielding even more charged particles to collide with cryxthlen atoms, creating an exponentially expanding energy source. The cryxthlen acts as the fuel source that is slowly depleted as some atoms are not spilt by the collisions in the core, and thus are converted directly to energy without yielding any new charged particles.

Sartograph: highly specialized mathematical construct utilizing Dr. Sartok's revolutionary chip and representing a quantum breakthrough in 4th dimension physics decay. Used to create time-based models which accurately forecast the relative probability of any given circumstance; the visual output of such a projection.

Sartok: probability chip capable of assessing statistical future outcomes through rigorous analysis of past and present conditions (see: Sartograph); named after its creator, Naius Packden Sartok, theoretical mathematician and founder of the Seilhenn School of Advanced Logistics.

Seitparen: an expression unique to the Tchelakov Tribe; an event or series of events that are unavoidable; something that is destined to happen. The seitparen are a series of events seen ahead of time that will eventually become known as 'the past.' In terms of prophetic visions, it is the currently accurate map of the actual future as opposed to the myriad and chaotic possible futures that could occur. Determining and shaping events that will become part of the seitparen or "Path of Fate" are twin goals of the Tchelakov Elders, and part of the genetic legacy bestowed upon them by Dr. Beh'ln Tchelakov (see: Path of Fate, sartograph, tromaveint, Tchelakov Tribe).

Servo Limb: mechanical construct: any augmented lifting or reaching device.

Shecut: brigadier general (retired) of the Imperial Marines, 6th Army, special envoy to Carinaena's Shell.

Shields: (also: Larkson Shield Generator) shield combat was in vogue for almost 300 years until advances in optical targeting made the generators more hazardous than helpful. Still, some usefulness can be found, particularly in close arms combat (see Tolmer's "Optical Advances and other Technological Foibles" & Ku'bii's "Offensive Retreat—the Rise of the Projectile").

Shiva: Carrak class cruiser; flagship of the Imperial Third Fleet; currently assigned to the Wyxian Proctorialship.

Shock Troops: Imperial commandos, generally bred for cunning, viciousness, and absolute loyalty. Raised from birth as soldiers, completely immersed in the caste D'ai Mital, the cult of the warrior. The caste training emphasizes ruthlessness, survival and instills a near fanatical devotion to unit commanders; historically known as "the Emperor's elite."

Sid: giant panda, second generation member of the Tchelakov Tribe; youngest Elder in the Tchelakov Tribe, in charge of information retrieval.

Stanzer: Imperial picket crippled during the Battle of Sardis (35,345) by Ditraln Secessionists; sinking after atmospheric re-entry, the superstructure still rests in 2 kilometers of water off the shore of Callen High. Captain of the Imperial Guard, Garrand Ai'Gonet Médeville, rescued the Stanzer's crew and passengers against direct orders and sacrificed an Imperial battle frigate in the process. That ship, the Deil-Karo, became the first command frigate lost at sea in 10,000 years.

Strahlinvek: language spoken by most of the trading cultures in Carinaena's Shell; a simple trade language, its root forms easily derived from thousands of other dialects. Some variation of the language is spoken by almost every race that has spacefaring ties, facilitating exploration and colonization.

Strom, Vailetta: Captain of the Imperial Guard, Gokazoku Kaigi; currently assigned to Wyx, Carinaena's Shell. Illegitimate (and some say favored) daughter of Emperor Collistas. Nicknamed Myshka, or "Firebird," by the Emperor, the young Vailetta spurned courtly life and set out to make a name for herself independent of her royal lineage (and some argue, her father's stifling protective care) taking the name Strom as cover to her true identity and entering the Bordëgian Académe as an anonymous student. The Gokazoku Kaigi culled her from the top of her graduating class. She quickly rose to the prestigious position of Captain within the sect and accepted a post commanding Vice Proctor Hellius Barrett's Imperial Guard.

Su'lairn: Gambor warrior; Tginsahi of the Lairn burrow, Galzeki. Honor Guard to Cha'halen first grade, Ka'vaelus.

Sullust Movement: Religious order; Gai'han Sullusts believe in the genetic superiority of the Gai'han bloodline carefully cultivated for over seven millennia. After the capitulation of Gallen Wei in the War of the Three in 35,242, the Niramdi system became the focus of the Gai'han practice of 'holy sterilization.' This process of indiscriminate extermination of non-Sullust humans and artificials forced the Collistas Dynasty to re-evaluate their position of support for the movement. Some believed the Sullusts were becoming powerful enough to threaten the Emperor himself. After skirmishes along the edges of Carinaena's Shell, the Thrassin Campaign marked the Collistas Dynasty's first foray into the Gai'han Jihad in support of Free Will artificials.

TacOps: idiomatic for tactical operations; the neural nexus of Imperial battle command that analyses and processes all information, provides a link between human experience in the field and raw datacore projections, and coordinates the various arms of Imperial power. An integral part of the command structure of all Imperial warships.

Tai-wren: "the shadow of the maker"; anyone who has pledged their life to protecting another.

Tarkanian Containment Shell: Hardened cerafibrous shell that houses a strong electromagnetic field; capable of safely storing incorporeal lifeforms and manifestations.

Tchelakov 37: colloquial expression referring to the original giant pandas engineered by Dr. Beh'ln Tchelakov (see: Tchelakov Tribe).

Tchelakov, Beh'ln: visionary genetic engineer whose highly guarded research into the next evolution of sartographic technology resulted in the creation of a new species (see: Tchelakov Tribe). His fusion of sartographic technology with a sentient-level intuition resulted in a quantum leap forward in 4th dimension physics decay and the science of future probabilities.

Tchelakov, Helen: courier/agent of the Nralda Keiretsu; daughter of Beh'In Tchelakov.

Tchelakov Revolt: A blossoming conflict in the Wyxian Proctorialship the origins of which center around the pursuit, capture, and escape of the Tchelakov 37, circa 35,355.

Tchelakov Tribe: the giant pandas elevated to sentience and successfully fused with Dr. Naius Sartok's probability chips. The pandas' resulting mental matrix became viable probability engines, capable of using intuitive processes to make deductive leaps and accurately predict the future. Early iterations of the technology were only viable during dream state.

Tech Art: any of a wide class of mobile mechanical constructs designed to perform a broad range of technical tasks. Non-sentient, imbued with one (or several) highly technical skills, but possessing little overall intelligence due to high degree of specialization and desire for cost efficiency.

Tginsahi: rank of "Honor Guard" in the Gambor warrior caste.

Thiretsen Reed: any of a genus of tall, erect herbs of the nightshade family with little foliage and tubular flowers, cultivated for its stalks; the stems of cultivated thiretsen prepared for use in smoking.

Thrassin, Battle of: The Thrassin Campaign marked the Empire's first foray into the Gai'han Jihad in support of the Free Will artificials. Though technically a stalemate (the Gai'han drive was halted, but the Sullusts were not driven out of the system until 37 years later), most historians view the battle as a clear victory for the Free Will Coalition.

Thurligan: mythical demon; multiple cultural references to a demonic entity; a central figure in Gambor folklore.

Thurston Shields: proprietary design of defensive shield known for its massive buffers, ample null-dampers and wide field modulation. Generally considered the best.

Teirendat: literally "one with arm"; a style of handling a fighting blade with the pommel facing forward held between thumb and forefinger and the cutting edge held flush with the forearm. A wide range of variations of this grip are taught, though it is considered difficult to master.

Torg: class 1 master assassin, assigned to Vice Proctor Hellius Barrett, Wyxian Proctorialship. Much speculation exists concerning this soldier's original identity (see Vo Kamp's "The Emperor's Butcher"); it is said that Master Torg was charged as Vailetta Strom's personal Tai-wren by the Emperor himself.

Tortian: portable field assault cannon, tripod mounted.

Torvel Class Frigate: war vessel intermediate between a corvette and a ship of the line; Imperial classification of an escort defense ship between a corvette and destroyer in size.

Trioxin: short for Trioxin Battle Plate; armored drop suits vastly enhancing a soldier's strength, speed, sensory input, and firepower. In a fully operational Trioxin suit, it is said that just one Imperial Shock Trooper can easily outfight a dozen heavily-armed men. Unsuitable for some theaters of operation.

Trogand: race of large (2.7 meter tall) reptilian beasts with thick-plated hides, large dual-horned heads, and broad mouths full of 5 cm long teeth. The Trogands' gregarious disposition and meticulous attention to detail make them well suited for bureaucratic service.

Turkle Sphere: Syhan artificial design. All drive components and core matrixes housed within one-meter diameter sphere. Rugged and highly versatile. Primarily used as tech arts though some instances of sentient models can be found.

Tvultàk Skullers: small, highly-maneuverable cruiser used as interdictors and strike craft; aging but rugged and adaptable design favored by mercenaries and smugglers. A particularly dangerous configuration is the Gamborian Jave 'O War.

Varsis: Krellian artificial design, manufactured without interruption for nearly 160 years between 34,687 and 34,846. The inherent simplicity of the design along with the Varsis' unparalleled learning curve made the design one of the Krell's most successful to date.

Vegraut: race of large (2 meter tall) graceful quadrupeds that ruled most of the Outer Reaches for over a millennia. Their sympathies toward the Free Will artificials during the Gai'han Jihad nearly lead to their extinction as the Sullusts made no distinction between artificials and those who protected them. Today, their empire lies in ruin, and their numbers are estimated at less than 200 million.

Vell'lairn: Gambor warrior; Tginsahi of the Lairn burrow, Galzeki. Honor Guard to Cha'halen first grade, Ka'vaelus.

Wyx: 4th planet in the Bline system, seat of the Wyxian Imperial Proctorialship, one of the largest fiefdoms in Carinaena's Shell.

Yarvek-EZ: Virtruna caste, cybernetics specialist, 9th class, currently assigned to Imperial Battle Cruiser *Shiva* as pod ensign; bred in the Imperial Vats on Wyx for mathematical genius.

Yuzbek Sharlott School: medical research facility specializing in transgenics; radical medical sect destroyed in 35,324.

Yuzbekistin: 5th planet in the Core system of Wilkens Folly, site of the Biomaterial Implant Facility and Sharlott Research grounds; a level 8 quarantine is currently in place on the entire system, reason unknown.

TIME LINE

33,811 Last recorded contact with the seeder ship *Carinaena's Hope*.

34,290 Beginning of the Great Shell Diaspora. Major colonization efforts will continue for over a millennia.

35,110 Beginning of Gai'han Jihad.

35,307 Final battle of Gai'han Jihad. Gelicus Art Convention holds first open hearings.

35,312 Ratification of the Gelicus Art Proviso signals formal end of the Art Wars. Compromise includes ban on all indistinguishable-from-human artificials. Dalintus Commission formed to judge and regulate Free Will artificials.

35,337 Garrand Ai'Gonet Médeville graduates from Bordëgian Academé, receives commission in Imperial Navy. Selected for membership in the Brotherhood of the Princes of Blood, Griffin Order of the Imperial Guard. Varsis artificial Bailey VL1357-B8 is assigned as his personal combat assist.

35,341 Médeville is made Captain of the Imperial Guard.

35,342 Médeville accepts post on Santos II as Captain of Proctor Birmaldon's Imperial Guard.

35,343 At Battle of Sardis, Médeville distinguishes himself by rescuing Proctor Birmaldon from Ditraln Secessionists. In the course of battle, the Imperial picket *Stanzer* is disabled and left in a decaying orbit around Sardis. Médeville disobeys a direct order and commandeers a battle frigate to rescue seven of his men left aboard the *Stanzer*. Both ships are lost, but the Guardsmen are saved. Médeville is court-martialed and discharged from Imperial service.

35,345 Artificial Bailey is granted Free Will on lunar colony Fortrivance.

35,346 Proctor Lekkson Nesbit assassinated. Vice Proctor Hellius Barrett takes control of the Wyxian Proctorialship.

35,347 Médeville contracts with the Sandhalles Grip, Bestriyx Dagen, for the rescue of his daughter. Designs modified light cruiser for express purpose of breaking Talen quarantine on El Phobadia to reach the young Miss Dagen. Ship built by Lehadn Vercks in Lo Kamer-Daun Shipworks; christened *Destiny's Needle*. After completion of mission, Bestriyx Dagen presents Médeville with *Destiny's Needle* as a grateful token of his esteem.

35,355 Médeville contracts with Helen Tchelakov for transport of 37 "exotic bios."

About the Author

PHILIP WILLIAMS IS an author, artist and sculptor. A graduate of the University of North Carolina, Chapel Hill with a BFA in Studio Art, he has enjoyed a successful career creating powerful, gas-welded steel sculptures as well as designing and building unique furniture. Philip is a dedicated father of three and an avid soccer player.

Visit him online at *www.thegriffinseries.com*.

THE GRIFFIN SERIES

Ashes of Honor
The Dreams of Men and Pandas
The Dragon's Price
A Path of Majesty

Garrand Ai'Gonet Médeville's adventure
continues in Book 3, *The Dragon's Price*

THE GRIFFIN SERIES

THE GRIFFIN: ASHES OF HONOR
PHILIP WILLIAMS
CAT WILLIAMS

THE GRIFFIN: THE DREAMS OF MEN AND PANDAS
PHILIP WILLIAMS
CAT WILLIAMS

THE GRIFFIN: THE DRAGON'S PRICE
PHILIP WILLIAMS
CAT WILLIAMS

THE GRIFFIN: A PATH OF MAJESTY
PHILIP WILLIAMS
CAT WILLIAMS

www.ingramcontent.com/pod-product-compliance
Lightning Source LLC
Chambersburg PA
CBHW071149250626
47159CB00001B/35